"Are you concentrating, Dad?" Savannah asked, because he had stopped swirling the cards. He started again and thought about the only question he really wanted answered: How much more time would he have with Maggie?

Savannah took back the cards and laid them out. They looked all right to him. No Death card, no Devil.

"Look at this, Dad. Your future is the Knight of Wands. I've always loved that card. It's the card of journeys. Advancement into the unknown without fear. It's a card of risk."

Doug looked over at his wife. She turned suddenly and stared at him. "What's there to risk if you're already dying?"

He leaned back. Maggie was absolutely right. What did he have to risk except those few things that cancer could not devour and the bittersweet poetry of his soul?

If he was already dying, then the least he could do was go about it flying through thin air. He found himself thinking everything depended on whether or not Maggie thought him capable of poetry. All of a sudden, he had a million ways to say he loved her, and he had to get them all down on paper.

*Also by Christy Yorke*

MAGIC SPELLS

# The
# WISHING GARDEN

## Christy Yorke

**Bantam Books**

New York  Toronto  London  Sydney  Auckland

## THE WISHING GARDEN

A Bantam Book/August 2000

ISBN 0-553-58036-1

*Published simultaneously in the United States and Canada*

Bantam Books are published by Bantam Books, a division of Random
House, Inc. Its trademark, consisting of the words "Bantam Books"
and the portrayal of a rooster, is Registered in U.S. Patent and
Trademark Office and in other countries. Marca Registrada. Bantam
Books, 1540 Broadway, New York, New York 10036.

PRINTED IN THE UNITED STATES OF AMERICA

OPM  10  9  8  7  6  5  4  3  2  1

**Dear Reader:**

I'm thrilled to share *The Wishing Garden* with you. Its main character, Savannah Dawson, was inspired by my husband, Rob, who is nicknamed Mr. Positive. Like Savannah, Rob sees the good in everyone and finds the bright side to every disaster. Obviously he drives me crazy, but mostly because I wish I could be more like him.

While Rob breathed life into Savannah, my young children are the driving force behind all my novels. I began writing stories about the power of wishes and love's ability to transform us for one reason: I wanted my daughter and son to believe in a world of possibilities.

Like them, may you believe in magic. May you wish daily on stars.

**Sincerely,**

*Christy Yorke*

For Dean,
who makes me laugh

# The
# WISHING GARDEN

# ONE

## THE EIGHT OF SWORDS ✦ WARNING

When people first moved to San Francisco, they often cried through the whole month of June. They'd had no idea the rain would come in daily and sideways, that fog would accumulate to the consistency of puréed potato soup. Old-timers, however, knew the secret to living happily in the city. They didn't ask for too much. No more than a few days of sunshine in autumn, a decent parking space, a fifteen-hundred-a-month studio apartment. They certainly didn't ask for their hearts' desires, unless they were masochists to begin with and wanted to be hurt.

That was probably the reason Savannah Dawson had never made her living telling fortunes. No one trusted her ability to turn out one good fortune after another. Not only was she cheap—twenty dollars for half an hour and a ten-card tarot spread—she had never dealt the sorrow-filled Three of Swords. She promised anyone who walked through her door true love, yet only teenagers, the drunk, and the desperate took her up on it. They believed in little but destiny and grand passion, and Savannah assured them of both.

When the Devil came up, no one panicked. Savannah shrugged it off with a wave of ruby-red fingernails and told them they were going to lose something all right, but probably just those ten extra pounds or a tradition of lonely Saturday nights. By the time they put their twenty dollars in her tin, they were expecting greatness and no longer scared of a thing.

Savannah made her living working at San Francisco's Taylor Baines advertising agency. She headed up a creative team that had linked milk consumption with true love, but when it came to fortunes, she wasn't making things up. Take the case of the fifty-year-old spinster she'd told to look north for true love. The woman had gotten out a lawn chair, turned her back to the ineffective San Francisco sun, and refused to move. When the mailman she'd known forever came around the corner, carrying mace to ward off dogs, she wondered why she hadn't noticed before that his thinning hair turned gold in the sunlight. She started ordering from L. L. Bean, so he'd have to spend a few extra minutes lugging snowshoes and parkas she'd never use to her door, and every time he accepted her offer of fresh-squeezed lemonade, she got a little sick thinking of all the wasted time.

Even for a nonbeliever, like the gin-drinking man who only went to Savannah's house on a dare, there was no denying that when Savannah turned over the possibility-filled World card, his hair stood on end. He told everyone the fortune-teller was crazy. His wife had left him, his teenagers smoked pot and didn't listen to a word he said, and if some bejeweled psychic in a velvet-paneled room thought he was going to be happy, she was sadly mistaken. Still, the next night he didn't fix the gin and tonic the second he walked in the door. He stepped out on the back porch for a minute and was stunned by what he'd been missing during cocktail hour—an astonishing primary-colored sunset, shades of reds and yellows he had forgotten even existed. The wind scratched up clippings from his neighbor's freshly cut lawn, and his throat swelled. By the time he walked back in the house, he was a little bit taller, and that extra inch was pure hope.

Savannah had that kind of effect on people, so when she read her own fortune and the Three of Swords came up smack-dab in her own future, she could only sit back and stare at it.

Ramona Wendall, her best friend and a two-hundred-pound palm reader for fancy San Francisco parties, sat beside her on the leather couch in Savannah's house. Between them, they'd polished off a bottle and a half of Chianti, which hadn't made either of them the slightest bit drunk. Earlier, Savannah had let her fifteen-year-old daughter, Emma, have half a glass, and now Emma slept like the dead behind the bedroom door she had recently taken to locking.

"Lookie there," Ramona said.

"I was bound to draw it eventually."

"Well, sure."

"It could mean anything," Savannah went on.

"Absolutely. Probably just a bad case of indigestion."

Savannah nodded, but she couldn't steady her silver bracelets after she laid out the rest of the cards. Her crossing card was the Eight of Swords, the bearer of bad news, her final result the Nine of Pentacles, reversed, a card of storms. Her destiny was the Chariot, which always meant radical movement or change. One man had gotten it in his destiny and, the next morning, withdrew two hundred thousand dollars from his wife's savings account and disappeared off the face of the earth. Ramona had gotten it the night before her husband, Stan, proposed, and she'd driven four hundred miles before she turned around and decided to say yes. The Chariot meant to run, but where to was up for debate.

"Let's see," Savannah said, trying to find the thread of hope in the cards, the way she found it for everyone else. Even when a man came up with the Tower and the Five of Wands side by side, she didn't worry. The Tower might suggest ruin, and the Fives hard lessons to be learned, but often a good old-fashioned disaster was exactly what was needed to get a heart pumping right. Sometimes it took a hurricane to blow a woman out of a house she'd always hated anyway, or getting fired in the morning for a man to find his dream job by nightfall.

"So what does it say?" Ramona asked.

"Bad news leading to sorrow."

"And then?" Ramona laughed and poured more wine. "Don't tell me there's no good part. Savannah Dawson, you've always got a good part."

Savannah looked at her best friend and smiled. "And when I don't, I fake it."

It had been obvious, when she was growing up, that Savannah took after her father, Doug, a man who could not find a fault in anyone—much to the disgust of his wife, Maggie. "The two of you have no taste," Maggie had always told them. "It's absolutely essential to hate a few people. Otherwise, how will you know when you fall in love?"

But Savannah had not given in. All the girls on her block in Phoenix had considered her their best friend, because Savannah could do French braids and was absolutely certain they would all find their hearts' desires. At nine, when she had her first premonition—Dorsey Levins would meet a soap opera star and end up in a beach house in Malibu—no one could get the girls out of her house, they loved her so much.

"Idiots," Maggie Dawson had called them.

On Savannah's eighteenth birthday, her mother hadn't let a single one of them into the house. "They only want you to promise them a happy life," Maggie had said, "and believe me, they'll sue when they don't get it." Then she leaned over Savannah's double-chocolate cake and blew out all eighteen candles.

"That's not fair," Savannah said. "You stole my wish."

"I did you a favor. Unfair things happen every day. Just get used to it."

"Don't tell me you didn't wish when you were eighteen."

Her mother began slicing the cake that no one was going to eat. "I wished for a life of my own, and I didn't get it."

Savannah stood up slowly. She had imagined herself anywhere but there thousands of times, but now she thought she saw her shadow leaving. It picked up a suitcase and disappeared into deep fog. It would take another six months for her to actually pack that suitcase, but as far as she was concerned, from that moment on she was gone.

"I wish for true love," she said. "I wish for good health and constant happiness and a daughter I can teach about wishes. I'm going to wish until I'm sore."

Later that night, Savannah walked into the garden her father had escaped to every day for as long as she could remember. While he bent over his beloved flannel bush, she told him she had decided what she was going to be when she grew up. "I'm going to be not her," she declared.

Now, Savannah fingered the sorrow card. "I don't like the looks of this."

"Oh, honey," Ramona said. "You're taking this way too seriously. What's a little sorrow, after all?"

Savannah stared out the window at the smear of the Milky Way. May nights in the Bay area were so saturated, stars got blurry, dew dripped from the tip of the crescent moon. On such nights, when most people cursed the dampness and scrubbed ineffectually at mold devouring their windowsills, Savannah looked for watery red stars, which Ramona had always insisted were a sign of good fortune.

She picked at a thread on her silk blouse. She hadn't had any customers tonight, so she was still wearing her work clothes—white blouse, ankle-length taupe skirt, and a white beret. She'd bought the hat at Macy's after her ad agency won a Clio for her jeans commercials. She'd bought a bowler after she was promoted to assistant creative director, and a marvelous tricorn after receiving an Effie for most effective advertising—an award the other creatives loathed, but which she treasured. She loved hats, and she wasn't afraid to wear them, because a number of her colleagues wore dreadlocks, and her boss had been known to shave his head. The only people who got anywhere at Taylor Baines were the ones with style and a flair for the dramatic.

Some people were good at numbers; Savannah could make a vegetarian suddenly crave a steak dinner, and she had stopped apologizing for it. Some people just didn't know what happiness was until she pointed it out to them. To a stressed-out single mother, or a man who worked two jobs and never saw his kids, pleasure might seem like something they didn't have time for or deserve. Savannah's job was to talk them out of misery, to prove that sometimes they had to buy things simply for pleasure or go on a luxury vacation. They had to give themselves a break.

In advertising, there were no repercussions or side effects, and no one who worked at Taylor Baines wanted to hear otherwise. Savannah's coworkers bought funky clothes, smoked unfiltered cigarettes, and took trips to southeast Asia in duct-taped planes. They were generally young and out of control; they bowled in the hallways and couldn't believe they were getting paid for making things up. In the last year, when her daughter had grown more silent and huffy, and eventually lived almost exclusively in her room, Savannah had sometimes hated coming home.

But when she did, usually late, she turned on jazz music and cooked up fatty foods. She changed into ankle-length, loose-fitting dresses in shades of topaz, crimson, and royal blue, and wore silver bracelets all up one arm. She opened her door to whoever had the guts to knock.

"It's probably just a sign of an off night or two," Ramona said. "That card doesn't mean squat."

Savannah fingered the Three of Swords, its heart in the clouds, stabbed by three swords. Its sorrow was obvious. She had never had to pretty it up, and now she didn't know how.

"Then again," Savannah said, "it could be Harry. You think it's Harry? You think he's going to start in about Emma going to live with him again?"

"So what if he does? You know how Emma feels about that pretty suburb of his. That girl would either do some damage there or run away in two seconds flat. Harry can huff and puff all he wants. He knows Emma's a city girl."

Savannah nodded, but what she was thinking was that Harry had selective memory. He remembered the times she had let Emma roll off the couch as an infant, or slip into the deep end of the pool for a split second before she yanked her back to the surface. He remembered those years he'd worked such long hours at the auto dealership; he'd turned himself into a rare, precious celebrity, the one Emma couldn't help but love best.

Savannah had met her ex-husband sixteen years earlier, in Phoenix. She had been nearing the end of her sophomore year in college and discovered the tarots. Every time she read her fortune, she came up with the same thing—a lack of sound judgment in her future, which she immediately shrugged off. She was more interested in German beer and grand passion than common sense. She was drawn to the creative fields, majoring first in drama, then in writing, and finally in fine arts. "You're breaking my heart," her mother had told her. "You're killing me."

Savannah had ignored her. She was doing exactly what she'd set out to do—prove her mother wrong. She *could* enjoy every second. Every field of study held a certain appeal, every man she dated was worthy of loving. Joy was no more elusive than sorrow; she didn't see how her mother missed it.

Out of school, she read miraculous fortunes for her friends and the occasional daring customer who came into the small grocery store where she worked as a checker. Then Harry Shaw came into her line with the strangest assortment of items she'd ever seen. Brussels sprouts, buttermilk, canned red beets, Malt-O-Meal and amaretto coffee.

"You don't want to know," he said, when he caught Savannah ogling his cart.

"But I do. Whatever it is, it's wonderful."

He came back after her shift and took her to his tiny apartment, where he never ate the same thing twice. His refrigerator was stuffed with exotic mushrooms, smoked and whipped cheeses, and seven varieties of tofu. Fifty different boxes of cereal and a wall of plain, pickled and puréed vegetables lined the pantry.

"I don't cook," he said. "I sample. See, what I think is life's too short to eat bologna every day. I mean, bologna's good. I've got nothing against cured meats, but what if I died tomorrow and hadn't eaten egg salad? I mean, wouldn't that be a shame?"

Savannah fell in love on the spot. She closed the door to his pantry and kissed him until the air got thin. He tasted of exotic lime toothpaste. Three weeks later, over her mother's objections, they were married.

"My God, he's insane," Maggie said. "What kind of person eats beets for dinner? I'm telling you, Savannah, this is headed for disaster."

Her father never said a word against him, just went on tending his garden. The day of the wedding, he planted a lemon tree. When Savannah came out in her short-sleeved wedding dress, he covered the roots with his own mulch mixture, part puréed fish and sea kelp, part chipped bark. Every scent in his garden, coaxed out of the barren Phoenix soil, hit her at once—jasmine, hibiscus, the bite of lemons. For years after, the smell of citrus would make her cry.

"Daddy?" she said.

Doug Dawson stood up and shaded his eyes with his hand. Sweat dripped off the tip of his charbroiled nose. The thermometer had hit one hundred degrees on May eleventh and wouldn't recede again until October. All the birds, except the mean crows who might have even wanted it hotter, had gone north. All anyone ever thought about was leaving.

"Now don't you worry." He held her loosely, so he wouldn't sully her dress. "Love will carry you through."

Savannah buried her head in the crook of his neck

and loved her father more than anyone on earth because she knew he believed what he said. Yet it was her mother's words that had the ring of truth.

She dropped out of college to marry Harry and move to Danville, California. It seemed romantic, giving up so much for him, but as soon as they settled into the upscale suburb of San Francisco, she was disappointed. She'd expected more from California. She'd been hoping for hippies and psychics, possibly even prostitutes-turned-actresses, but all she found were the same square lawns and careful little lives she'd left in Arizona. They moved into a beige tract house and twice Savannah got lost in the subdivision, not realizing her mistake until she tried to fit her key into someone else's beige lock.

Harry loved Danville. He got a job as a salesman at a used-car lot and worked his way up to manager. He eventually bought out the place, and followed with eight other lots in the Bay area, and was seen on their block as a real go-getter.

Savannah, on the other hand, was more enamored with San Francisco, its wild colors and unnavigable hills and absolute optimism. Half the year, no one could see the sky, but they still built skyscrapers on fault lines and landfills; everyone just closed their eyes and hoped for the best. The heavens, on clear nights, were breathtaking, an endless expanse of pulsing, pleading red stars.

After Emma was born, Savannah enrolled at UC San Francisco and, on a whim, took a class in advertising. Right away, she was hooked. With Emma in her infant seat beside her, Savannah fell in love with make-believe. Her senior project was to devise a campaign for an unfiltered cigarette the government was trying to ban. She shot photos of hell-raisers and bruised hockey players, squinting through cigarette smoke. The caption read: Smoke Brigg's, if you *dare*.

She was hired as a junior writer at Taylor Baines the next week.

At first, she worked on obscure print ads, half-page, two-color art that would never see a national magazine, and slowly earned her stripes. Two years after she was hired, she assisted on her first television commercial for a new chocolate-coated cereal. A year after that, she was named assistant creative director.

She loved her job and worked long hours, because when she came home there was trouble. It was obvious she and Harry were toxic to each other. He was money hungry, he thought her new-age ideas garbage, he was unkind, she was not the type of woman he wanted to take out in public.

Not even a brilliant ad campaign could have convinced anyone they were going to last. Harry was embarrassed by her flashy style and shadowy premonitions. When Savannah took up the tarots again, he did not speak to her for a week. When she started practicing on a few neighbors, he put in a whole row of miniature roses, as if he was making something up to them. She ignored him and drew a card a day, leaving devils and wands on the windowsill. Harry told her she was turning into white trash, but she noticed he stuffed the sword cards down the disposal and left the optimistic Sun and Cups alone.

Emma was the reason they lasted as long as they did. They were stunned and often appalled by the things the other said, but with a silver-eyed baby lying between them at night, no one was going anywhere. Without Emma, they might have fought night and day about money and the right way to live, but instead they hushed themselves the way they hushed their daughter, with a finger over their lips, with pleas in their eyes.

Emma was colicky from the start and left little time for fighting anyway. She was a tight ball of fury, gulping formula then throwing it up, thumping her head against her crib bumper and wailing so hard she kept the mourning doves awake all night. The only peace came when Savannah took her daughter into her own bed or bundled her out into the cold. The instant wind struck Emma's face, her little fingers uncurled in sleep, as if she expected stars to fall right into the palm of her hand.

Harry started taking Emma camping when she was two. A few years later, Harry escaped to the mountains with Emma every weekend. They never asked Savannah along, yet at night, she saw stars instead of acoustic ceiling. Instead of traffic noises, she heard the rumble of the river and Harry's soft voice telling Emma he had never imagined he could love her so much and still be able to leave her.

On the petition for divorce, Savannah and Harry cited irreconcilable differences. On the day he left, she drew the Eight of Cups, the card of abandonment, and that night drew the Star, which meant she had never loved him right in the first place. She called up Ramona Wendall, a palm reader who had worked one of Taylor Baines's company parties, and asked her advice on going into business on the side, telling fortunes. There was only one clear thing, and that was that each person was born for something, and sometimes she didn't know what it was until she'd already made plans elsewhere. Sometimes, to do what was right, she just had to uproot everything.

She and Harry sold their picture-perfect house, which had a central vacuum system and his and her sinks, but never enough air. She couldn't count the times she'd stood at her Palladian kitchen window, taking tiny little breaths while she watched her neighbor Ken Sykes take scissors to his already flawless lawn.

Harry took his half of the money and moved up higher into the exclusive, manicured hills of Danville. Savannah took hers and leased a small Victorian near the ad agency in San Francisco. She still cooked up impressive marketing campaigns but late at night and on weekends, she told fortunes of love and riches beyond anyone's wildest dreams. She gathered a following of lovelorn teenage girls, but never the business she'd hoped for.

Then Harry found out about her sideline. He called in his lawyers and sued for custody of nine-year-old Emma before saying a single word.

Savannah didn't waste time either. She went straight to Harry's faux-Tudor monstrosity in Danville and plowed into his oak-paneled study, the one his new wife, curly-haired Melinda, had decorated in hunter green.

"You can't do this," she said.

Harry sat behind his desk, twisting his rings. He looked her up and down once, then let out his breath in a low, mean whistle. "You can't take my daughter down with you."

Savannah marched across the room and leaned over the desk. She had his collar between her fingers before he could even breathe.

"You're a cold-hearted snob, Harry Shaw."

"I can offer her a better life," he said, unblinking. "I don't want her in the city, hanging out with that crowd of yours. You've got her in that artsy school when she ought to be studying calculus. She needs to be around kids who are going to college. She needs to be around people with some class."

Savannah let go of him and stood up straight. She had a blinding headache, and she knew exactly why. She was having trouble remembering why she had ever loved this man. She was having trouble not hating him.

She walked over to the bookcases and took out one of his stiff, unread books. "I know you think I'm beneath you. But I don't know, Harry. You've searched half your life for something meaningful, and you've ended up in used-car sales."

"There's nothing wrong with what I do!" he said, bristling.

"Of course not. You're the only one who thinks there is."

"You know why I married Melinda?" He stood up and yanked down his sleeves. "So I wouldn't have to be psychoanalyzed by you."

Savannah put the book back and turned to him. "I'm not psychoanalyzing you. I'm telling you you're never going to be happy until you accept what you are, right at this moment. A used-car salesman making eighty thousand dollars a year. People would give their right arm for that."

"For the thousandth time, Savannah, it is not immoral to be ambitious."

"Absolutely not. But it'll kill your soul if you can't be grateful for what you've already got."

"As usual, you've got it all figured out."

"No." She paused. "But I do know one thing. I love reading fortunes. I was made to do it, and if that makes me common, I don't care. All that matters is giving Emma a full life, trying to be good to people, and sampling every food there is."

He hung his head, and Savannah dug down and found that last speck of love. She'd just have to make do with lukewarm devotion; in truth, it was surprising even that much was left. She went to his side and put an arm around his thin shoulders. His hair was the exact same shade of sandy blond it had been when she'd first met him, but aside from that, nothing was familiar. He ate Melinda's tuna salad every day for lunch and had given up his pantry in favor of a wet bar. He wore too many rings now and often spoke in a voice he must have stolen from some radio pitchman.

"It's not always about money, Harry."

He pulled away. "You know I would win if I pursued this."

Savannah dropped her hand from his shoulders. "Your lawyers would win," she said quietly. "You, Harry, would go straight to hell, if you're not already there."

Harry dropped the suit, but at the end of every summer visit, he asked Emma to stay in Danville. He asked even though she called every girl on his block a snob, and she came in at night smelling of spray paint and rotten eggs. Even a used-car salesman couldn't finagle a girl out of knowing where she belonged. Emma couldn't sleep in the suburbs for the awesome quiet. By age eleven, she had announced she'd stopped dreaming in sunlight. She'd fashioned her entire wardrobe in shades of gray.

All Harry could do was keep up the backpacking. He tried to instill in his daughter an appreciation for open spaces, he tried to make up for everything by taking Emma to every wilderness area in the western United States. Maybe he figured all that space would cover up the fact that he had left them. Maybe guilt dissipated a little in fresh air. Whatever the case, he was there when Emma met her first bear, and then he gave her the greatest gift a father could give: He taught her not to be afraid. To appreciate that running into a wild beast was something that didn't happen every day.

They had both done their best with Emma, taught her what they thought was important. Until Emma was ten, Savannah had shown her only the good cards—the Cups, the suit of happiness, and the best card in the deck, the Sun, which signified joy, love, and devotion. The elements that made up a good life.

Now, that good life seemed threatened somehow, though the sky had not altered; the only difference was an impaled heart on a 3×5-inch piece of plastic.

"Honey, just don't worry about it," Ramona said. "It's a fluke is all. Like that time you read me the Lovers and I started on Slim-Fast and wearing eye shadow again and then nothing."

"Ramona, you lost seventy-five pounds and met Stan three months after that reading. You can't expect split-second results. I'm telling you, I'm never wrong."

"Oh, I doubt that. You just haven't heard about it, that's all. When you're on, people come back and say, 'Oh my God. I can't believe it. I met that man just the way you said I would.' But when you're wrong, they just shrug it off and swear never to fork over twenty dollars again."

"*You're* never wrong," Savannah said.

Ramona threw back her head and laughed. "Are you kidding? You think all the answers are in a few squiggles on your palm? You think life is that easy?"

"I think it should be."

Savannah went to the kitchen and took out the army knife and sachet of mint she had stashed in a drawer. She walked to Emma's door and shimmied the lock. Her daughter might be fifteen and starting to use Savannah's name in curses, but Savannah was still going to make sure she was safe in bed each night. Emma might have taken up clove cigarettes and a ferocious coffee habit, but at night Savannah did what she could to counteract the damage; she sprinkled mint across her daughter's doorstep to guard against sorrow and bad dreams.

She turned the lock, then tiptoed into Emma's bedroom. Her daughter's hair was strewn over the pillow, the same color as her own, like pine logs when they were split open, but cut at the shoulders, with a curl. She still had on the eye shadow she'd taken to wearing. Blue, because some boy at her school, a boy who was well on his way to flunking algebra and pumping gas at Texaco, had said it would bring out the silver in her eyes.

Savannah tucked the blankets under Emma's chin and sprinkled the mint on the floor, but she still felt panicky. Terror zapped her all the time now, whenever she caught a glimpse of blue toenails or a tattoo sketched out in washable ink. When she saw where things were headed, with or without her consent.

She walked out and closed the door, relocking it with the knife. Ramona came up and put her arm around her. "Don't believe it," she said.

"How can I not believe it? You think I let people in here and then make up stories? You think I'm just scamming people?"

"I think you believe in yourself. I think people pick up on that and believe in you, too. But this . . . this is letting superstition rule your life instead of living it and seeing what happens. This is assuming the worst and, frankly, I'm ashamed of you."

Savannah breathed deeply. Outside, she could hear a neighbor trying to start up his 1970 Volkswagen van and the gay lovers two doors down serenading each other with old love songs. In the morning, if it was clear, the sky over the bay would turn red as desire. There would be nowhere else on earth she'd rather be.

"Go to sleep, Savannah," Ramona said. "In the morning, you'll wake up laughing like always. A bad thing has never happened to you your whole life."

Savannah did not sleep all night. She sat on the stoop of her narrow house, drinking gritty, black coffee. Just after dawn, when the sun struck the top of the pink-and-blue Victorian across the street, her own shadow walked right past her, holding a suitcase with one hand while the other stroked the fur of a wolf.

Emma slammed open the front door and trudged outside in her robe. The right side of her face bore the imprint of her pillow, the hollows beneath her eyes were caked with blue eye shadow. This was the girl who, a year ago, had gotten up every morning at dawn to practice penalty shots in the street, until her debatable best friend, Diana, told her soccer was for jocks, not for anybody's girlfriend.

Emma sat down on the stoop and took the coffee out of Savannah's hand. She drank the remainder in one gulp.

"Something wake you?" Savannah asked.

Emma said nothing, just squinted into the morning sun.

"They say when you're startled awake," Savannah went on, "it's from the kiss of your future lover. He's already out there looking for you."

"That's bullshit," Emma said, but nevertheless she looked down the street, where a couple of handsome college students had recently moved in.

"I woke up every morning at dawn the week before I met your dad. I swear to God."

Emma pulled back and stared at her. "I worry about you, Mom."

Savannah laughed. "Well, don't. I'm the happiest person on the planet."

"That's what I mean. You ought to be laying out those cards for yourself until you come up with some dark-haired hunk who'll buy you a place up in Pacific Heights. You ought to be trying for something *more*."

Savannah shivered, because everything she wanted was right here, and if she hadn't taught Emma that by now, it was unteachable. It was something you knew or not, it was the difference between feeling happy or lost.

"Don't worry about me," Savannah said.

Emma snorted. She noticed their legs were touching and quickly yanked hers away. "You're unmarried, and hanging out with crazies. You ought to be freaking out, having some kind of midlife crisis like Diana's parents."

"You can't judge the world by the Truffs. Things haven't always gone their way."

"You know what they talk about at dinner?" Emma went on. "She tells him it's his fault she got pregnant so young, and she never got to be an actress, then he tells her if she wasn't so goddamn fat, she could still try, then she says he's an asshole, then he says he never loved her, then Diana tells them both to shut the fuck up, then they yell at her for cussing, then they watch *Home Improvement*."

Savannah put an arm around Emma's tight shoulders, but Emma shrugged her off. Her daughter stood up and walked across the soggy grass, leaving imprints of tiny feet, her middle toes adorned with slim gold rings.

Savannah sighed. Emma had dieted herself down to nothing, wore hideous makeup and said 'Fuck' like an anthem, but anyone with eyes could see that her skin was smooth as water. Even when she cut her hair herself—which she'd done on a dare a week ago—it curled appealingly around her face. One day, Savannah prayed, Emma would just give up trying to ruin herself. One day, she'd just snap out of it.

"I'll tell you the absolute truth," Savannah said. "Life is glorious. Love is spectacular. If anyone tells you differently, they're blind. Happiness is a choice you have to make every morning."

Emma snorted again, and went back inside for more coffee. She drank it on the front porch, too far away for conversation.

Savannah sat on the stoop and didn't turn around. She took what she could get now, even if it was only a twenty-foot intimacy. Half an hour later, the mailman walked up the hill. He handed her a stack of catalogs, and a single letter on top. "Not a bill in sight," he said, and smiled as he walked away.

Savannah looked at the Prescott, Arizona, postmark and dropped the letter into her lap. Her mother had scrawled the address in nearly indecipherable purple ink, and something in Savannah's stomach curled up, rising high and tight against her lungs. A sane person would have just burned the letter, but Emma was behind her, staring so hard the back of Savannah's neck burned, so she blew on the envelope once for good luck, then slit it open.

*Savannah,*
*Your father's dying, but before he does it, he's decided to go insane. He's gotten it into his head that he has to have another bench for his garden, as if he hasn't spent half his life building worthless things already. He wants it to be some kind of testament to his life, and*

*there's no telling him how pathetic that
sounds, a man fitting his whole, tiny existence
onto a single slab of wood. He's hired a psycho
to do just that, for a price that would make
your skin crawl, let me tell you. Frankly, I
wouldn't be surprised if the man takes a
chainsaw to us the second he gets his money.*

*Nevertheless, your dad says he needs your
help with the bench, and what that really
means is he would like to see you one more
time before he dies.*

*Mom*

Savannah squeezed her eyes shut. She'd gone
home only a few times in fifteen years, to show off
Emma as a baby and young girl, before—she hoped—
any damage could be done. She hadn't been back in
six years, hadn't even seen this house in Prescott her
parents had retired to. In the last two years, they had
stopped asking her to come.

Yet her father had planted a fig tree the day she
was born and held it upright for three hours during a
ravenous spring flood. He'd been the one she hadn't
wanted to leave. Her fortune had just come true—the
Eight of Swords had issued its warning, and if the
Three of Swords was her father dying, then of course
she had no choice.

All of a sudden, Emma was beside her. "What
is it?"

Savannah opened her eyes and handed her daughter the letter. Emma read it over, then crumpled it in
her hands. "So what does this mean?"

"I guess it means we're going to Arizona," Savannah said.

"For a few days?"

"For as long as we're needed."

"Oh no. No way. I'm going to the dance next Friday. Diana is having her sixteenth-birthday party in two weeks."

"Emma, he's dying."

"Well, I'm sorry, but you're the one who never cries at funerals, who's got the guts to smile at sobbing widows. You can't just yank me out of school. There's only a month left."

Savannah stood up, but Emma backed away. "You can finish up the semester in Prescott. It's a pretty town. I heard it's a big retirement community now." She saw the look on Emma's face and touched her arm. "Emma, he's my father. He worked as a buyer for an electronics firm all his life, but I always thought he must have doubled as a spy. Whenever I slept beneath his roof, I never felt the slightest threat. I thought he was made of lead."

Emma jerked her hand off. "Well, goody for you. You had a dad around."

"Emma—"

Emma folded her arms across her chest. "Let me stay at Diana's. I'm fifteen. You know I can handle it. Trust me."

"I do trust you," Savannah said quietly, then turned away before her daughter could see her eyes. Obviously, she'd taken up lying without warning. She'd given Emma unqualified devotion and as much freedom as she thought safe, and she'd still ended up with a daughter she could not predict. Emma had taken up smoking just when Savannah thought she'd sign up for track. She'd picked friends Savannah would never have chosen in a million years.

But that wasn't what frightened Savannah most. No, what scared her was how much energy Emma put into being miserable—reading only suicidal poets and watching the movies where everyone dies at the end.

Savannah had never monitored the foods Emma ate or what she wore out in public, but she'd made sure her daughter knew luck was everywhere. Heads meant a wish would come true and tails gave you three more wishes. Sudden rain always brought good fortune, a penny in your pocket was a sign of a visitor, and three clouds in the western sky meant you were about to fall in love.

Now it turned out it had all been wasted effort. Emma hadn't believed a word she'd said.

"Then let me stay," Emma said.

"I need you with me. This is important, Emma. It's family."

"Great. Fine. Let's uproot our lives for the sake of some family you can't even stand to visit. I'm calling my dad."

She walked into the house. Savannah heard the beep of the phone, then a long pause, then Emma crying.

Savannah hung her head, but not before she saw the shadow of that wolf again, first rearing up, then lying down at her feet. She stood up and walked into the house.

"I can't believe this," Emma was sobbing into the phone. "I thought you, of all people, would be on my side."

Savannah walked past her and started packing. Every day, she thanked God for something, and today she decided it would be for Harry, for the fact that he had never given in to spite.

By the time Emma got off the phone, Savannah had stuffed most of her dresses and a few hats in a suitcase. Emma walked into her room and threw herself on the bed.

Savannah snapped shut the suitcase, then walked into Emma's room. She looked at her sobbing daugh-

ter, then out the window. "We've got a life here," she
said. "We'll come back." Emma only cried harder, as if
she'd seen what Savannah had just seen—Savannah's
shadow getting up after that wolf, then following him
west, as far as he would go.

Savannah called the office and arranged a leave of
absence. Emma did not say a word for the two-day
drive to Arizona. Her only pleasure came from the
Holiday Inn in Barstow, which had free HBO and con-
ditioner. Somewhere in the Mojave Desert, the sky got
so wide and light, bees could not spot land. Crows sat
on the tops of telephone poles and plucked the frus-
trated insects, one by one, out of the air. Outside
Needles, the temperature hit one hundred degrees
and kept climbing. Savannah licked her lips and
tasted salt.

Once in Arizona, she stopped the car to point out
the first saguaro. Emma just shrugged. She would not
get out of the car.

"There's a story about these trees," Savannah said,
stepping out of her light blue Honda.

"Here we go," Emma said.

The sun took up half the sky and was the color a
child might use, Lemon Yellow or Tangerine Dream. It
was scorching and added a tang to the air. Even if a
woman broke her heart, it would be too hot to cry.

"A long time ago," Savannah said, "the saguaro
lived on the edge of the forest. Believe it or not, he had
skin as smooth as silk and, at night, the moon spirit
took him in her arms and they waltzed together over
the mesa."

She walked along the car, drawing her name in the
dust on the hood. "But the desert kept creeping in on
him," she went on, "cracking the earth around his
roots. He began to yearn for rain and the smell of grass
and the chance to live higher up, where the pines grew

and the air had a chill to it. He even envied the fact that when there was a fire, the pines all went down together, while he survived alone."

The stories came like breath to her now. Inhale, a tale of moon spirits, exhale, the love story of the mermaid and the sea. She believed every one of them, because not to believe would have made the world too magicless to contemplate, it would have reduced true love to chemicals.

"The saguaro grew so bitter and angry," she said, "he hardened his own soul, turned his bones brittle. He covered himself in thorns so when the moon spirit came down to swing him in her arms, she pricked herself instead. Betrayed, the moon spirit cast the saguaro far out into the desert, to live alone forever."

She looked back at Emma, who was staring at the largest saguaro, one of its stumps sheared off by pranksters. There were Pepsi cans on the desert floor, and Burger King wrappers twisted in cacti.

Savannah got back in the car and started the engine.

"And the moral is?" Emma asked.

"Learn to love what you've got."

"Ah. Right. I should love leaving everything I know for a dying stranger."

Savannah drove the last two hundred miles to Prescott with the radio on loud. The temperature dropped to the eighties after they entered Flagstaff, and when they dipped down into the thick stands of ponderosa pines near Prescott, Arizona, the air smelled surprisingly of vanilla. She stopped at the first Mobil station in town to ask directions to her parents' house.

She knew the place halfway down the block, because of the garden. Her father would never settle for a lawn and junipers. He had planted a pair of Juneberry trees along the curb, and their branches sagged beneath clusters of pink flowers. Honeysuckle vines and akebias wound up the porch columns; the front garden was a sweet curl of chamomile and lily-of-the-valley and bitterroot, names she had rolled across her tongue as a child.

Savannah pulled into the driveway and cut the engine. She had hoped her first sight would be of her father, working in his garden. But the yard was empty, so she just sat there.

"Aren't we going in?" Emma asked.

Savannah tucked her hair beneath a baseball cap and got out of the car. Her emerald green dress was light as tracing paper, but wherever it brushed her, she felt little pinpricks of pain. When they reached the porch, she ran her hand down one of the columns and came away with a clump of honeysuckle blossoms. They smelled like the summer mornings of her childhood, when she'd left open her window so that the first thing that touched her would be something borne by her father.

She was reaching out to knock on the front door when a huge gray and white Husky bounded around the corner of the house, barking furiously. Savannah went still, except for an arm she swung out around Emma. The dog charged them, teeth bared, and Savannah used the only weapon she had—the white blossoms in her hand. She threw them at the dog and they fell in a flutter in front of the beast's eyes, so much like rain the dog stopped suddenly to shake herself dry. By then, Savannah had crouched down menacingly; by then the dog only rumbled.

"Just give it up," Savannah said. "You don't scare me."

The Husky still came on, and when she got within biting distance, Savannah reached out and slapped her nose. The dog was so shocked, all she could do was lie down and whimper. She curled into a pitiful ball at Savannah's feet.

The door opened and Maggie Dawson stood there. She had one hand on her hip, the other clutching a meat mallet. She looked down at the dog, then up at Savannah.

"One of the psycho's dogs," she said. "She'll eat anything human if you give her half a chance."

Savannah reached down and stroked the dog's fur. It was soft as angel hair. The dog's heart thundered in her chest. "She's just scared."

"Scared, shmared. She's a psycho too."

Savannah stood up. "Well, we made it."

Her mother tilted up her chin. Maggie Dawson was five feet four, with dark brown hair cut in a bob. She lived in the MesaLand retirement community and no doubt played bridge every Tuesday, but she still had the meanest gray eyes Savannah had ever seen.

"I can see that," Maggie said. "You should have gotten here before he started dying."

"Mom—"

"Don't talk to me. I'm not interested." She rubbed her hands over her arms, which were covered in goose bumps. A frigid blast of Lysol-scented, air-conditioned air streamed out of the house behind her. Maggie looked at Emma, still hiding behind Savannah's arm. "The last time I saw you you were nine years old, and your mother kept you in a motel. I couldn't even hug you, that's how afraid she was I'd contaminate you."

"Mom, don't," Savannah said.

Maggie squared her shoulders, then picked up the meat mallet. "Your father's out with the psycho, cutting trees for the goddamn bench. You can wait for him in the garden." Then she went back in the house and slammed the door.

Emma stepped forward, then jumped back again when the dog growled. Savannah tapped the dog's mouth until she quieted.

"Shit," Emma said. "Welcome home, Mom."

Savannah turned, ready to apologize, then realized there was no point, because Emma was smiling.

# TWO

## THE EMPEROR ❧ WAR-MAKING TENDENCIES

THE EMPEROR.

**M**aggie Dawson was shaking as she closed the door on her daughter. Nevertheless, she walked across her blue slate entry and turned the thermostat down another two degrees. The foot-thick stuccoed walls of her house vibrated with the pulse of air-conditioning that would run until October. Prescott was a mile high, and in summer it rarely got above eighty-five degrees, but the day Maggie had turned fifty, she'd vowed to get her hair done once a week and never be hot again. Let the students over at Prescott College smolder in their stifling dormitories, worrying about energy conservation and how to pay the summer electricity bill; they were young and slim and headed for six-figure incomes in business and computer science. Maggie was fifty-five years old, prone to hot flashes, and she'd paid her dues in Phoenix. She'd spent fifty summers there, wolfing down Wheaties so the milk wouldn't curdle halfway through, and crushing scorpions who got into her laundry basket and pantry and once, amazingly, a carton of milk, looking for a cool place to sleep.

Prescott was a dream compared to that, but Maggie still kept the thermostat at sixty-two or under, day and night. Her husband wore red wool sweaters and slept beneath a down comforter, but that was because now that Doug had gotten sick, he was cold everywhere, even in steaming hot baths. He would no longer drink Coca-Cola, his favorite, because he complained it chilled him going down. He had joked that all his hair falling out was a blessing, since it saved on haircuts and hers cost fifty bucks a pop. "You're wiping me out," he'd said, after she came home one afternoon with a new auburn tint.

She walked into the living room she'd redecorated in blue six months ago, right after Doug's biopsy. She'd chosen an indigo leather sofa, plush turquoise carpeting, and two seascapes for the walls. You couldn't walk into the room without shivering, and that was just how Maggie liked it. She'd bought the thickest drapes she could find, a quarter-inch of royal blue velour, and rarely opened them. This might be a mountain town, but twenty miles outside the city limits, forest turned to scrub. One more El Niño year and Lynx Lake would dry up, the pines would go down in a horrific forest fire and never reseed themselves. She'd be living in desert all over again. As it stood now, Arizona was little more than sand and crows, hot tempers and white-slacked widows staring pleadingly at an alarming expanse of sky.

At five thousand feet, there might be trees, but the sun was devastating. It sucked the burgundy right out of the gazanias; plants and animals blanched to the color of concrete. Heat-loving pomegranate trees wilted, pet iguanas left on the patio were fried crisp as barbecued potato chips, then devoured by crows. Doug's garden was the only thing that had flourished in the MesaLand retirement community, because he'd put in drip irrigation and knew how to Xeriscape; all the others were brown fescue lawns and junipers. Everybody else had just given up.

Maggie Dawson parted the drapes just enough to peek through. Her long-lost daughter was walking through the garden. Savannah had on an emerald green dress and black velvet sandals. Maggie would never have added that ugly baseball cap, but on her daughter it looked surprisingly chic. Of course no one, least of all Savannah, would ever give Maggie credit for her daughter's fashion sense. Maggie was responsible for every tear and heartache—no doubt for war and famine, too—but never for Savannah's successes, for her creativity and flair and the fact that she was happy.

Maggie gripped the curtains. Savannah was pointing out plants to Emma. Incense cedar, akebia quinata, ginkgo biloba, beard tongue, names Maggie knew but intentionally mispronounced, should anyone ask. Thirty-six years ago, Doug had taken his first gardening class at the community college. One morning he was hers, and that afternoon, poof, he was in love with begonias. He came home loaded down with sunflower seed packets, sorry-looking hibiscus cuttings, and a brand-new set of trowels, and she never saw him again. He knelt down in what passed for soil in their Phoenix yard and first replaced the burnt fescue with fairy duster and African daisies, then put in lemon and grapefruit trees for shade, dwarf pomegranate and cape weed for color. He bought mushroom compost by the truckload, then started making his own fertilizer out of coffee grinds and rotted onion skins. He planted fig trees and lantanas; he even went so far as to carve out a lily garden, which came back stronger every year, the flowers white as moonlight. His garden became the prize of east Phoenix; every evening, their neighbors gathered beneath Doug's bougainvillea-covered trellis and dreamed themselves right out of their hot, rotten lives into the green forests of Canada, or at least anywhere north of there.

When Doug announced he was accepting his company's early-retirement package and moving to Prescott, the women in the neighborhood knelt in his garden, sobbing. The men tried to bribe him to stay, offering to order him those twenty-two rare species of orchids he'd been eyeing, vowing to pay his water bill for life. Doug might have wavered, but Maggie was determined to get them out of that desert hellhole. She had chosen a house in Prescott with a dull but passable garden, hoping that Doug wouldn't have the energy to start all over again. But while the movers were still unloading their furniture, he had dug down three feet in the front yard to see what kind of soil he was dealing with. That evening, he pored over tree catalogs and ordered the rare pink-blossomed Juneberry trees, both of which had grown four feet a year.

Just like in Phoenix, everyone in the MesaLand retirement community loved the garden. Widows crept into the perennial bed and clipped bunches of sweet rock jasmine; old men got a little bit shaky, claiming they hadn't seen such shades of lavender in years. The neighbors loved Doug, too, because he was as bright and peppy as his garden. He said the same thing to every person he met: "Hello. Wonderful to see you. Beautiful day." Even if it was raining. Even if he was dying.

He hadn't always been such a fraud. On their wedding night, he had made love to her like a man on fire. For weeks after, he'd left the office exactly at five and taken her straight to bed. He'd spent hours encircling her wrist with his thumb and forefinger, marveling out loud at her exquisiteness and his luck.

He had not been afraid of anything then. He'd run across a park during a summer lightning storm just to pick her a wild daisy. When lightning struck the mesquite tree behind him and melted the rubber off the bottom of his sandals, he ran his fingers through his charged hair and laughed. He left the gooey remainder of size eleven Birkenstocks on the grass and snapped his fingers, sending sparks six feet in the air.

And then Savannah was born. Maggie remembered the morning they brought her home, because it was the first time she heard Doug Dawson cry out loud. He sat in that nursery for an hour, his head in his hands, just bawling. Then he wrapped his daughter in three layers of bunting and went out to buy safety bolts for every door. From then on, he jumped at thunder and refused to watch the news. He never ran full speed again. He loved that child past the point of passion and straight on into immobility. He discovered the horror of loving something he could not bear to lose.

Doug had a soft spot for children and weeds; he didn't have the heart to discipline either. He had never ripped out anything with his bare hands, and he figured he didn't have to. As far as he could tell, his garden was a miracle—not a single morning glory or azalea had ever died. That was because Maggie never let them. She was at war with Doug's garden, but she also knew what her husband could and could not stand. If it had been up to her, she would have planted a few fruit trees and been done with it, but nevertheless she found herself on her knees at three in the morning, replacing the blueberry climber that had suffered from an unusual frost with a new five-gallon transplant from Putnam's Nursery. She filled in the bare patches in his walkway with plugs of chamomile and replaced every one of his wilting prize roses before he could see exactly how much damage had been done.

Her husband had never had to wake up to anything short of perfection. He drove her crazy and had never realized a woman needed as much tender loving care as a fussy rhododendron, but that didn't mean she would break his heart. That didn't mean she would stop shielding him from the truth only she could bear: Death came easy. It came all the time.

Years ago, Maggie had had many talents, but the best of these was fashion. She had become addicted to silk at the age of thirteen, when a momentary boyfriend bought her a topaz scarf. She didn't give it back to him when she ditched him a week later. His awkward caresses hadn't come close to the feel of silk against her skin.

Other teenagers spent their afternoons roaming the mall or having sex behind the new subdivisions going up on the east side of Phoenix; Maggie spent her free time at the fabric store, running her hands over bolts of silk the color of the things she wanted—the deep green of northern lawns and money, the glittering silver of skyscrapers built half a continent away.

She could dress, that's what even the snobby cheerleaders said about her. Maggie designed and sewed her own silk dresses. She wore pantsuits of ebony velvet, regardless of the heat. She had one hundred designs in her portfolio. Slick, stunning dresses that could turn the mother of three children into a sexy woman again, silk skirts that even wild men would cling to.

As a senior, she was voted most likely to make a million dollars by thirty, and she accepted the award, even if it was a bit of an understatement. On the day of her high-school graduation, she had five thousand dollars in savings and a one-way ticket to New York, leaving in December.

Then she met Douglas, the best friend of her older brother, Michael, and right away she knew he was trouble. His fingers were the first things that felt better than silk; when he slipped his hand beneath her blouse and played with the lace hem of her bra, she couldn't conjure up a single dress design, she couldn't think of anything but him. In early summer, the two of them hiked to the top of Superstition Mountain and the gods took over. There was no other explanation. Maggie knew she was in the middle of her cycle. She knew she was risking every one of her plans, but love was a good-looking terrorist: He hijacked her whole life, then charmed her right out of her outrage. One kiss and she forgave him everything. One soft word and he got her thinking she'd been headed his way all along.

They were married in October, before she started to show. Doug was already working at the electronics firm he would stay at for the rest of his life, and had saved enough for the down payment on their tract house in Phoenix. Maggie sold the ticket to New York to a starry-eyed actor headed for Broadway, an actor who later went on to make action movies for two million dollars apiece.

She sold her one-way ticket, but the day before she went into labor, she boxed up her sketches and sent them off to Delorosa's, her favorite East Coast designer. Exactly one week later, they came back unopened, and later on Maggie would remember that rejection as the only one that didn't hurt. She was rocking Savannah to sleep when Doug brought the package in warily, and she felt a strange calm wash over her. She leaned down and kissed the top of Savannah's silky head. She rubbed her cheek across a shoulder of smooth pink skin, and understood about what lasted and what didn't, about the things that truly satisfied a soul.

The problem with epiphanies is that they have no staying power. By morning, she couldn't believe what she'd been thinking. Was it so awful to want something of her own, something not every woman's body could do, but a unique creation of *her* mind, of Maggie? She woke up to Savannah's pre-dawn cries and took only half-breaths, painful little gasps in rhythm to her daughter's tears. Her breasts were heavy and sore, she was bone tired, and it would be years before it got any better. A daughter was a ruthless blessing. From the start, Maggie felt so weak from devotion, she couldn't hold on to the things that had once mattered most—time, quiet, order, solitude, even a subsistence level of self-respect.

For a while, though, she refused to give up. A few days after that first rejection, she wrote out a new address label, this one to Robespierre's, and sent off the package again.

She sent the designs off to the twelve biggest New York designers, and all twelve sent them back to her. Two didn't even bother to look at her creations; they just scrawled *Return to Sender* on the box. The other ten sent her form-letter rejections. The last one came back on Savannah's first birthday, and by then Maggie was wearing terry-cloth robes like every other mother on the block. By then, the room she'd once vowed would be her studio was Savannah's playroom, decorated with Lincoln Log forts and Barbie's spring collection ensemble. By then, she'd pushed her silk dresses to the back of the closet, because she refused to have them ruined by spit-up milk curds and regurgitated Fig Newtons, which meant she would never wear them again.

The afternoon of Savannah's first birthday, after Maggie settled her daughter into her high chair with a chocolate cupcake topped with jelly beans, she read the last form letter. It didn't take long.

*Dear Sir or Madam:*
*We regret to inform you . . .*

She tossed it into the garbage can beneath the sink. She tried to kiss the top of Savannah's head, but her daughter pulled away to jam more cake in her mouth. Maggie left the room and went into her bedroom closet. She grabbed the whole lot of silk dresses and took them out to Doug's Spanish moss lawn, the only moss in all of Phoenix. Then she went for the lighter fluid.

She saturated every scoop neckline and double-stitched hem. She stood a little too close when she threw the match, and the hem of her robe caught on fire. If she hadn't heard Savannah crying in the house behind her, she might have just let it go. She was only twenty years old, after all, still young enough to do something dramatic, to give up and go up in flames. But she no longer had the right to do something deadly. She was a mother, her daughter might be choking on a jelly bean, and there was nothing to do but tear off the robe, toss it on the pile, and run back to her daughter.

When she found Savannah simply banging her fists for another cupcake, Maggie knelt down in her stained nightgown and sobbed into her hands. Doug came in behind her, soiled gloves in his hands. He just stood there watching her cry.

"The mothers all flock to me because Savannah's

so pretty and sweet-natured," she said. "But I want them to flock to me because of *me*. I can offer more than a good baby. Can you understand that?"

She could see he didn't.

He went into his new garden and clipped the first rose of the season. "See now," he said, bringing it back to her, "just take a whiff of that."

She looked at him, incredulous. All she wanted was an extraordinary existence, while Doug was happy with an unacceptable life. Really, it was amazing they had anything to say to each other. Sometimes it was all she could do to keep from screaming, to remember he was not one of her regrets. She heard the rotten things that sometimes came out of her mouth, but that didn't mean she had control of them. If she could force him to passion, perhaps even break his heart, then she could piece it back together. If she couldn't have greatness, then at least she ought to have a life with some *drama* in it.

But Doug did not rise to the bait. He never got promoted, never made a million dollars, never fulfilled his dreams and got to Europe, and yet he walked into his garden every morning whistling. She had replaced half a dozen of his torch lilies over the years, but sometimes she thought the wilting plants would have survived anyway. Sometimes she thought plants grew in Doug's garden simply to please him. If her husband had spent half as much effort on her, she would be a different woman. She might have forgotten the things she'd once wanted. Maybe she would have wanted only him. If he'd put in a few lemon trees and been done with it, if he'd stopped gardening before the wicked Phoenix sun got ahold of him, he might not have a hole in his forehead the size of a golf ball, and cancer running right into the core of his brain.

Her granddaughter, Maggie was glad to note, did

not care about the garden. She was not listening to a thing Savannah said, but glancing back at Sasha, the psycho's dog, who was still growling menacingly from the porch. Emma glanced at the front window and Maggie dropped the curtain. She breathed deeply and counted to ten, then opened it again.

Emma had disappeared and Savannah had reached the mermaid fountain Doug picked out right before his death sentence. Every time Maggie passed it, she spit into the copper bowl.

Savannah had gained a little weight over the last six years, padded her hips and stomach, and added an armload of bracelets. Nearly twenty years ago, when her body was still under Maggie's control, Maggie had grounded her for getting her ears pierced without permission.

"I won't let you ruin yourself," Maggie had said. "You'll thank me someday."

Savannah had stared at her. "I'm absolutely certain that I will not."

Maggie squinted at her daughter now. It was true, Savannah had not thanked her, not even when she turned out lovely, the one design that didn't come back rejected. She had moved away and become a success in advertising. She pretended she was too busy to visit. Maggie told the young people in Prescott to consider not having children at all. She meant it; motherhood had wrecked her. Thirty-six years later, she'd ended up with one hand locked in a fist, the other reaching for the hair her daughter wouldn't let her touch anymore. "Kids will suck you dry," she told them.

She walked to the phone in the kitchen and pressed the Speed Dial button. All the numbers were listed—Wendy Ginger, Maggie's best friend two doors down, Putnam's Nursery, Ben Hiller, head of the

MesaLand Homeowners Association. All except number 9, which Maggie pushed.

"Williams-Sonoma," a friendly voice said. "How may I help you?"

"It's Maggie. Is Angela in?"

They put her on hold to elevator music, and Maggie scanned her cupboards—gold-rimmed place settings, porcelain gravy boats, twelve crystal flutes, Lladro salt and pepper shakers for eighty bucks apiece. She'd been on a high for a week over the cappuccino cups she'd gotten at the Dansk outlet, but that was fading. It was unnerving how quickly her purchases now turned to junk. Sometimes within hours; occasionally, even, while she was still standing at the cash register. A salesperson would be wrapping her brandy glasses in tissue, and a cold hand would reach down Maggie's throat and snatch the air from her lungs. Sometimes, in the middle of the housewares department, with everything she could possibly want within reach, Maggie Dawson couldn't even breathe.

Finally, Angela came on the line. "What can I get for you today, Maggie?"

Maggie reached behind the phone book on the counter, where she stuffed her catalogs. She opened the Early Summer edition of Williams-Sonoma. Every page was dog-eared, two or three items circled in red, but believe it or not, she had some self-control. She would get only the essentials.

"I need towels. Page forty-eight. The flour-sack towels? Are those as good as they say?"

"Better," Angela said. "Super-absorbent. You could pick up, like, a whole cup of spilt coffee with one."

"All right then. Two sets of eight. And I was looking at that electric food slicer. Page twenty-seven? That's something."

"It's a definite must. You can cut your meat deli-thin. You know, most stores will give you a discount if you buy a whole side of roast beef, rather than having them slice it. You'll make the money back in no time."

"The only thing is where I can put it. It's not exactly something I can tell Doug we've had all along."

"I'm telling you, Maggie, once you start making him paper-thin bologna and cheese, he won't care how much you spent. And it's only two hundred. That's a steal, in my mind."

Maggie thought it over, though she didn't have to. Already her mind had cleared off the counter space. She hardly ever used that eight-slot toaster she'd bought two months ago, after Doug's first round of chemotherapy turned him pale and breakable as chalk. He might be able to stare at an oozing mole on his head and think everything would turn out fine, but she needed an occasional pick-me-up. He could go in for radiation five days a week, for six weeks, come home every day slightly blue and too tired to trim a single, leggy daisy, and still laugh during his favorite *Seinfeld* rerun, but she felt better only after she bought something nice. Doug never woke up terrified because the person in bed beside him paused between breaths, but she did.

"Let's do it," Maggie said at last.

"By the way," Angela said. "The crepe pan you wanted is still on back order. But let me read you the telephone specials."

She rattled off a list of special-priced steamers and cutting boards, all of which Maggie was fairly certain she needed. She held back, though.

"Ship everything to Wendy, like always. Bill it to my—"

She heard a throat clearing behind her, and whirled around to find Emma leaning against the doorjamb, one sandaled foot crossed over the other.

Emma wore a stained T-shirt two sizes too small, showing off a concave stomach that made Maggie's throat tighten. Her toenails were painted blue, her jeans ripped at the knees and flared at the bottom, and Maggie knew for a fact that if she'd made it to New York all those years ago, she could have saved this generation's fashion debacle.

"—Discover card," Maggie finished and hung up.

"Sorry to interrupt," Emma said. "Can I get a glass of water?"

Maggie could see right away that Emma was trouble; from clear across the room, Maggie could smell the lingering aroma of clove cigarettes and tangy rebellion. Emma had cut her fingernails to a sharp point, and tracked in two sandals' worth of mud without thinking twice. Her eyes were such a light silver, so heavily made up in blue, they'd give some people the heebie-jeebies. If she were *her* daughter, Maggie would force her into the bathroom and scrub her clean. She'd put her into some decent clothes and, while she was at it, go through her drawers for signs of marijuana.

But she also noticed that this fifteen-year-old girl didn't have an ounce of fear in her bones, and that was something Maggie admired. She was coming to believe that fearlessness was the only attribute worth having, in the end.

Emma had already taken two steps into the kitchen without being asked, and was heading toward the sink.

"You heard nothing," Maggie told her.

Emma looked at the phone, then at her. She tapped her right ear. "What? What's that you said?" She smiled—a smile that made Maggie forget, for a moment, that a fifteen-year-old girl should not be wearing that much lipstick.

"Whatever she told you about me," Maggie said, "don't believe it. I'm actually quite nice."

"Believe it or not, Mom's never said a bad word about you. She never says a bad word about anyone. She's, like, insane or something."

Maggie laughed. She went to the cupboard Doug never looked in, the one with the new cut-glass stemware she'd bought at Dillard's in Phoenix. She filled a crystal flute with water and handed it to Emma.

"There's not much to do here for a fifteen-year-old," she said, "except get into trouble. Let me warn you right now, I see all, hear all, know all about the children living under my roof."

Emma drained the water, then put the glass in the sink, and raised her chin. "I'm not staying here."

"Oh no?"

"You know what's really pathetic about my mom? It has never occurred to her that I'll run away."

Maggie stepped back. She looked out the kitchen window, where Savannah was walking up the cobblestone path toward the kitchen door.

"Where will you go?"

Emma squinted at her, then abruptly swung back her shoulders. "Everywhere."

Savannah walked in then and smiled. "I see you're getting to know each other."

"This place sucks," Emma said.

Maggie nearly cackled, but managed to squeeze it down. She was not above wishing Savannah a little misery, not after all she'd been through.

She started taking down old dish towels. When Doug asked if she'd gotten new ones, she would look him straight in the eye and tell him she'd just used bleach.

"Emma, please," Savannah said. "Mom, tell me about Dad. What happened to him?"

"That sounds exactly like a daughter who cares," Maggie said.

"Mom . . ."

Maggie slapped the towels on the counter. "The garden, that's what happened to him. How many times did I tell him to wear a hat? You heard me. 'Put on a goddamn hat, Doug,' but no, he liked the feel of the sun on his head. He liked desert sun, if you can imagine that. He'd like hell, if you sent him there. He'd tell me the people are just misunderstood."

Maggie paced around the kitchen. "Then, bam! A mole shows up on his forehead and starts growing like crazy. Pretty soon, it's the size of a quarter and bleeds every time he touches it. He goes to the doctor and, just like that, they tell him it's malignant, and what the hell was he thinking, staying out in the sun all goddamn day? They cut a hole the size of a baseball right in the middle of his head, and without even giving us a chance to breathe, they radiate the hell out of him. Then as if that's not enough, they start him on chemotherapy that makes him sick as a dog, and tell us to hope for the best. The best! You tell me, Savannah, what is the best I can hope for now?"

Savannah had backed up with each word, until she had flattened herself against the far wall. "He loved his garden," she whispered, holding a hand over her throat. "I would bet he'd say it was worth it."

Maggie whirled on her. "Then he's a selfish bastard, because it sure was not worth it to me."

Maggie noticed Emma in the far corner, rocking up and back on her feet. Maggie had no doubt her granddaughter had never heard rotten language her whole life. Savannah would have suffocated her with that positive-thinking crap and not prepared her for the slightest trauma. The first time she got her heart broken, she would no doubt split in two.

"When is Dad coming home?" Savannah asked.

"God knows. The psycho could have killed him already."

"You haven't changed a bit," Savannah said quietly.

Maggie put her hands on her hips. "No, I haven't, and you know why? Because life has come out exactly as I expected. I never got to New York, not even on vacation, my only daughter went north and forgot me, my husband isn't expected to live out the year, and I'm stuck in this goddamn retirement community when I'm only fifty-five years old! I should be taking cruises and visiting my grandchildren. I should be snuggling beside my husband every night instead of being afraid to touch him, in case he starts bleeding again."

"You got the life you expected to get," Savannah said. "You would have been unhappy no matter what."

Maggie turned away. She was not going to cry, not anymore, not when it did so little good. She slapped a towel down on the counter. As soon as Savannah went out, she'd call Angela back and order a steamer. She'd buy Emma seventy-dollar jeans from J. Crew.

Savannah walked over to Emma. She put an arm around her, but Emma jerked it off. Then they all heard the truck in the drive.

"That's Daddy," Savannah said, and took off running.

Maggie watched her go, then let out her breath. It was true, she had expected the worst and had not been disappointed. But what she had not expected, and didn't deserve, was never to be the one her daughter ran to.

Doug might have been the nice one, but he was also the one who had gone speechless whenever Savannah had gotten a cut, or soiled her underwear, or needed help with the school bully. Doug had known how to hug his daughter, but not the way to the pedia-

trician's or tactics for fighting back against the school-
yard thug. He'd never had any clue how to threaten
and cajole and scream until his child brought her
grades up enough to pass eleventh-grade English, how
to use guilt to keep her from smoking pot and killing
brain cells. He had no idea of the tricks and ruthless-
ness required to get a child through. But in the end,
what did he care? He got what he wanted: He was the
one who was loved.

# THREE

ACE OF WANDS, REVERSED ❧ FALSE START

Jake Grey would have been pleased to know he was
referred to as the psycho. Because of the knives he
carried and the dogs he'd never tamed, he was considered one mean son of a bitch. The story went that he
hid away on Kemper Peak not because he liked the
solitude, but because, in a crowd of people, he went a
little crazy. He could not be held accountable for his
actions and worse yet, Cal Bentley, the senior Yavapai
County sheriff, was his best friend, so there was no
sense calling the police when he snapped. You were on
your own. Standing six two, with a black beard and
eyes as cold and blue as glass, Jake looked like a man
you could shoot and shoot and never kill—only make
extremely mad.

On an afternoon in early May, when the air swept
in from the desert pre-warmed and gritty, Jake drove
back from Flagstaff, occasionally glancing at the man
sleeping soundly beside him. Doug Dawson had a few

tufts of hair left and bruises all down his arms. Jake turned onto Sage Street, where a thousand newly hatched gnats floated in the steam rising up from the asphalt. He pulled up in Doug Dawson's driveway and cut the engine. Doug woke up immediately, and turned around to look at the logs in the back.

"My wife doesn't know it yet," Doug said sleepily, "but she's going to love this bench. After I'm gone . . ." When Jake said nothing, Doug merely touched the bandage he still wore on his forehead, though the incision had been made months ago.

Jake got out of the truck and Sasha, his husky, came bolting for him. She reared up on her hind legs to kiss him.

"Down, girl." He scratched the belt-strap scars behind her ears until the dog no one would come within three feet of nearly purred.

He let Rufus and Gabe, his chocolate Lab and golden retriever, out of the truck bed and glanced at the sky. There wasn't a cloud in it, and that put him on edge. He liked a little cloud cover. All the thunderstorms in the area started on Kemper Mountain, where he'd built his cabin. Legend said that was where Lalani, the thunder god, lived; drunk talk said Jake spiked the sky with his own electric spite. Actually, it was the thermals along the summit, combined with the moisture that rose off the alpine lakes, that brought rain nearly every summer afternoon. Down here on the valley floor, it was dry as sand, and already Jake's lips had split in the corners.

Sasha sniffed the sawdust and chain-saw oil on his fingers and growled. Jake never took the husky woodcutting. The first time Sasha had heard the chain saw, she'd jumped through the sliding glass door of his cabin and run for miles, bloody and razor-sharp with glass. She'd mowed down everything in her path—full-grown elderberry shrubs, stunned white rabbits and, finally, Lowell Dresher, a two-hundred pound logger and Jake's nearest neighbor three miles down the road.

By the time Jake got to her, Sasha had clamped her mouth around Lowell's neck. She could have broken the man in two at any time. As Jake approached, she growled from deep in her throat, from a place Jake hadn't even known about. Lowell was not making a sound, but Jake could see the whites of his eyes. He flapped his huge, helpless hands on the ground.

Jake had laid his hand on the back of Sasha's neck. For a moment, she'd clamped down harder, then suddenly she let go. She was shaking so badly, her legs went out. She lay on her belly and pressed her nose against Jake's leg, and Jake could actually hear her losing her will to him. It was like the cracking of a twig, a snap, and then she was his, she was going to do whatever he said. She would love him whether he deserved it or not.

He drove Lowell to town, while the man's teeth chattered loud enough to be heard over the engine of the Ford. "You've got to put her down," he managed to get out.

"I'll keep her away from you. You have my word."

"I'm telling you, she's wild."

"That's exactly why I'm keeping her," he said. "What else is going to make me feel human?"

Now, he started unloading the lodgepole out of the pickup. The woods around Prescott were filled with ponderosas, but for Doug's bench, he had decided to use the straight grain of lodgepole, which grew in thick stands up around Flagstaff. Jake had let Doug come along wood-cutting, though he preferred to go alone. He had also agreed to craft the bench at Doug's house, so the man could watch over the progress. Jake had agreed to a lot more than he usually did, and he was regretting it more each minute. How could he deny a dying man anything? He had made beds for spoiled movie stars and never once given in to their tantrums, but for Doug Dawson, who was paying only one thousand dollars for a garden bench, Jake had already gone far beyond the call of duty.

"Beautiful," Doug was saying, helping him slide out the lodgepole. Then a woman ran around the side of the house. She had on a green ankle-length dress, a Dodgers baseball cap, and bracelets all up one arm. But the most amazing thing about her was that, when she reached the pickup, Sasha came dutifully around the truck and lay down at her feet. The dog put her head on her paws and started to whimper.

"Daddy," the woman said.

"There's my girl." Doug hugged her. "I knew you'd come."

When she wrapped her arms around him, she must have noticed there were bones where there ought to have been flesh, and a rank odor seeping out of the man's pores, but she still pressed her cheek against his chest. She overrode the stench anyway, with a mixture of lemons and Juicy Fruit gum.

"Wait till you see what Jake and I are making," Doug went on. "It'll be beautiful."

She pulled back to look at him. Jake watched her gaze pass right over Doug's fuzzy pink scalp and the bandage, then land on his mouth, which she smiled at.

"How long are you staying?" Doug asked.

"As long as you need me."

"Well, . . ." Doug said, toying with the edges of the bandage. "I could keep you here forever that way. You just stay as long as you want. I insulated the garage, did you know that? Put in air-conditioning, a little refrigerator for my plants. You can stay there. Or, of course, in the guest room in the house, though

Maggie uses that for a library. There isn't even a couch."

He was toying with the bandage so much, one side of the tape slipped off. Then Jake understood why he had kept it covered all these months. He'd been picking at it, and now a thin trail of black blood slid out.

"Daddy?" the woman said.

He retaped the bandage. "This? This is nothing. I scratched it again. The doctors tell me I can't scratch and then, of course, that's all I want to do. Scratch. Scratch. Scratch. Don't worry about it. Let me show you my ensete."

He led her to a huge, palmlike tree near the curb. Each leaf was nearly twenty feet long, so sturdy Jake was sure it could hold a man's weight.

"An Abyssinian banana," Doug told her. "Incredibly hard to keep alive. Every three to five years it flowers, then the plant dies down to the root. You've got to coax new shoots from the crown. Maybe it will live, maybe it won't. It's a toss-up. It's due to flower again. Maybe it will do it while you're here, and then we'll see if we've got any magic left."

"But Dad?"

He walked over to another tropical plant, this one with glossy, fanlike leaves. "A Japanese aralia. You can grow these in the Northwest or in Phoenix, believe it or not. They'll take full shade or sun. An amazing plant. It'll be getting flowers in the fall, then these little clusters of black fruit. Marvelous. Did you see that wisteria?"

The front door opened and Maggie Dawson stood on the porch, her hands on her hips. "For God's sake, Doug, she doesn't want to hear about every goddamn plant."

"As a matter of fact," Savannah said, "I do."

Jake turned back to the truck. He pulled out the

lodgepole and stacked it next to the drive. It was too hot in this valley. He didn't see how people stood it. The air was thick enough to choke on, stuffed with exhaust smoke and perfume and boiled eggs.

He was having trouble breathing, though he couldn't blame that entirely on the glutted air. It was always that way when he stayed in town too long, or when he saw a woman way out of his league. His skin began to itch and, for the life of him, he could not think of a single thing to say to anyone.

He'd always been quiet, but a long time ago it had not been considered a sign of something sinister. He'd simply been shy and big for his age, picked first for basketball because of his height and intimidation potential. It got worse after his father died of a heart attack when Jake was only eight. No one could think of a single thing to say to him, especially after he was spotted in the local Smitty's buying enough frozen dinners to last him and his mother a month.

Jake knew then that he was never going to be popular, so he settled for being smart. Nine years later, he ended up with a scholarship to Arizona State University and, as it turned out, with Joanne Newsome, who was smarter than he was, and certainly more beautiful.

They met on Central High's cross-country track course, a cemetery in the summer, with runners in various stages of asphyxia and dehydration sprawled across the dusty path. Joanne Newsome, though, was known for running five miles every afternoon, even when the mercury climbed to one hundred and twenty. She was famous for downing three gallons of bottled water a day and looking so sweat-sheened and hot, guys had been known to pass out from the strain of wanting her.

She was easy to spot. Not only was she tall and thin and the only thing moving on summer afternoons, her hair was flaming red. She was the only color in the desert, and when she jogged past the Central High front lawn, where Jake was studying calculus, he immediately gave up on antiderivatives and decided to join the track team.

He could never catch her. Halfway across the track she'd be coming back the other way, still flying after five grueling miles. First, she wouldn't even look at him. Halfway through the semester, he was lucky if she smiled. One day, though, she stopped cold. He licked his lips when he saw the sweat trickling down her neck into the shadowed crevice between her breasts.

"You know," she said, "you could just ask me out. It would be much easier."

"Will you go out with me?"

"Absolutely not. You can't even finish this course."

She jogged off, laughing, and for the first time that semester, Jake finished the course—though by the end of it he was one of those prostrate bodies, his legs and lungs on fire, but his heart burning for more.

He ran the course all season, until the day before state championships, when he was fast enough to catch Joanne's shadow. Her hair slapped his forehead, and he was delighted to find it smelled like burnt sugar. She showed up at his locker half an hour later. "All right," she said. "How about Friday?"

"Are you serious?"

"Yes. I just wanted to make sure you were."

They went to Trudy's Kitchen, where Joanne ordered everything in sight. Double cheeseburger, onion rings, strawberry milkshake, grilled cheese. Jake just ordered a salad.

"I can't keep weight on," Joanne whispered, then glanced around to see if anyone had heard. "Don't tell

Jill Eardly I said that. My God, she's crazy about her weight. Throws up after every meal, I swear to God."

"You going to be a professional runner?" he asked.

Joanne laughed. She had a deep, gritty laugh, as if she'd taken in more sand than she realized on those jogs. "God, no. My parents . . . they're *the* Newsomes, you know. My dad's CEO of At-Tel Electronics. My mom's, like, this force."

Jake nodded, even though he had no idea what she was talking about.

"Anyway," she went on, lunging at the food when it came, "they want me to marry well. That's, like, their only ambition for me. They think I'll be studying art or home economics at ASU, but I'm actually signed up as a business major. By the time I graduate, they won't have a clue what hit them."

She laughed again, then finished her hamburger in three minutes flat. She started on the onion rings, eating each one whole. Jake couldn't eat; it was too much of a marvel watching her.

"I know it," she said. "I'm hideous. But Mom won't let our cook make anything that isn't healthy. Did you know there are thirty-six hundred ways to prepare eggplant? My God, it's sickening."

Jake reached across the table and grabbed her hand. It was oily and warm. He was about to let go when she squeezed him back.

Joanne never prodded him to say more or talk about his feelings. After they'd dated for three months, she told him she wanted to hear only one thing.

"That I love you?" he asked.

"Oh, please. I'm not thirteen. Tell me it will last forever. Tell me this can never end."

At the time, he had not hesitated. Now, for the life of him, he couldn't figure how he had been so certain, but back then he'd had no reason to doubt his good fortune. He'd seen a lifetime in one skinny girl's eyes. "This will never end," he said.

On Valentine's Day of their sophomore year at ASU, he asked her to marry him. She said yes, with stipulations.

"First, we both have to graduate. Then you go to law school wherever I work. *Then* we tell my parents, and they'll have no choice but to give us the finest wedding in the history of the pathetically rich New-somes. And never, ever, do you tell me you're too proud to take their money. Because believe me, they've got gobs of it, and I'm entitled to some, for putting up with them all these years."

"None of that matters to me," he said. "As long as I can love you forever."

Joanne uncoiled her fists, and leaned over to kiss him. "Oh, Jake. You are a real doll."

Now, when a desert wind blew up his mountain, it sometimes reeked of what he'd thought happiness was, of burning sweetness and optimism and wanting. But whenever he swallowed, it went down bitter. It left a bad aftertaste that lasted for weeks.

He unloaded the rest of the wood, then gathered his dogs into the bed of the pickup. Sasha was still mooning over the woman, and Jake touched her head.

"She put a spell on you, girl?" She turned away, as if she didn't want him to see her eyes.

He got in the truck and turned over the engine. He had backed halfway out of the drive when Doug and his daughter knocked on his window. He stopped and rolled it down.

"You can come in if you want," Doug said. "I'm going to see my granddaughter for the first time in years. And you haven't met my daughter, Savannah."

Jake looked at the woman. She was nervous, that's what he picked out first off. She stood the way he'd stood for fifteen years, legs set apart, one foot in front of the other, one fist clenched—the stance of someone who was thinking about running. But when she looked at him, she was all smiles.

"It's nice to meet you," she said.

He nodded. He'd run out of conversation three hours ago and, besides, the only thing he could think to say was that a girl had shimmied up one of the Juneberry trees and was sitting precariously on a skinny limb. Jake watched her in his rearview mirror. He didn't give away anything, not even when she began tearing leaves from the branches and mashing flower petals in the palm of her hand.

"Let the poor man go," Maggie said, coming down the drive.

"Can we start on the bench tomorrow?" Doug asked.

Jake turned away from the yearning in his eyes. "This weekend. I'll call you."

He hit the gas and skidded out of the driveway. In his mirror, he saw the girl jump from the tree, scaring the daylights out of her grandparents. The woman looked after his truck, as if she regretted not hitching a ride. He nearly slammed on the brakes and went back for her, then wondered what he was thinking, assuming she'd have any desire to be with him.

He turned the corner and took a deep breath. When a group of girls playing hopscotch saw his truck and bolted for the porch, he felt a little better. Long ago, he had decided he was only good for scaring people, and he'd spent the last fifteen years proving it. He'd befriended Cal Bentley, the country sheriff, for one simple reason: It was only a matter of time before the man found him out.

\*  \*  \*

Emma jumped out of the Juneberry tree onto the concrete. The bandage was loose on her grandfather's forehead, but that was not what made her start crying. It was the color around him, black as dried blood. For as long as she could remember, she'd seen colors around people—a deep blue shimmering around Ramona, an orange so magnificent clinging to her friend Diana she could hardly bear to look at it. Her grandfather's, however, was the first one that reeked. It stunk like the deepest part of the compost pile, like something being eaten away.

"Oh, honey," Doug said. "Don't you cry."

He held her and that was worse. Emma didn't even know him. She wasn't about to start caring for someone who was only going to die. But whether she knew him or not, his arms felt familiar. He had the same awkward hooked grasp her mother had. He made the same clucking noise between his teeth. And though her mother had sworn Ramona and her friends from school were their family, that they weren't missing anything, Emma knew now that Savannah had lied. A real family made her cry when she'd thought she'd been perfectly happy. Pretty soon, they'd get her shouting for no good reason and missing what she'd never even known.

Emma pulled back. She couldn't look him in the eyes. He had two blond tufts of hair that stood up straight from his scalp; the rest was just pink, mottled skin, like the flesh of a baby whale. She looked straight at the sun, until she saw red. That didn't stop her from noticing that her grandmother's aura was even redder—red as blood, red as rage. It sizzled and sparked around her head; one streak flew straight to the top of the Juneberry tree and spooked the crows into flying. That stopped Emma's tears. That was wonderful. Maggie's meanness was like an alien creature, a monster she wanted to hide her eyes from, but couldn't, it was so marvelously awful. Emma had been set on running away tonight, as soon as the moon dipped behind Kemper Mountain, but she decided right then to stay awhile, because it was obvious something was going to happen.

Her mother's aura was the same as always, lavender, the color of a dreamer. Wisps swirled out from her to curl around Doug's shoulders.

"This is so wonderful," Doug said. "And all because of this little thing." He gestured to his forehead as if it were nothing, as if they all couldn't see the blood slipping out around the bandage.

Emma pressed her arms to her sides. She had expected a lot of things to happen when she turned fifteen. She figured she'd finally start filling out her bras and maybe get a chance to French kiss. What she had not been prepared for was the way she would slowly stop believing in everything. First in luck, because every boy she showed the slightest interest in fell in love with her best friend, Diana; and second in God, after her classmate Benjy Martinez was kidnapped from his own front yard, taken to the top of Mt. Tamalpais, and beaten senseless. And, just lately, Emma had stopped believing in her mother.

Savannah had raised her on laughter and stories; every cloud had been a guardian angel, every sudden rain had meant good fortune. Now all that seemed ridiculous. Life couldn't possibly have so much luck.

Her mother reached for Doug's hand. "It's going to be fine now. I can feel it. Let me read your fortune. I'll prove it to you."

"Oh no," Maggie said. "Don't even think about it."

"Mom, it wouldn't kill you to open your mind a little."

"It's open all right. Open enough to know it's all a bunch of garbage."

Another thing that happened to Emma when she turned fifteen was that she started wanting her mother to be like everyone else. She wanted her to get a little mean when she was tired. She wanted her to stop getting that look in her eyes when Emma cried, like it was killing her. She really hadn't expected to get what she wanted, but now it looked like she just might. This wasn't Savannah's world. She stood so still not a single bracelet jingled, and took shallow, short breaths, as if she was close to choking on something.

Emma realized everything wrong with her life was her mother's fault. Savannah was the reason food had suddenly lost its flavor; she hated health food and still fried everything, even though Emma had told her a thousand times she was on a diet. Her mother was the reason Emma cried every time she saw a rainbow or found a four-leaf clover, because she'd wished for a thousand things, for true love and a million dollars and for her dad to come back, and not a single one of them had come true—contrary to her mother's promises.

"You know what the tarots are?" her mother asked Maggie. "They are an act of trust in the universe. Selecting cards at random and trusting in their judgment is an acknowledgment that we're not always in control here. There is a power greater than anything we can imagine."

"My God," Maggie said. "You're worse than I thought."

Doug laughed. "I wouldn't mind a reading. I could use some good news."

"And what if it all comes up death?" Maggie asked. "What if you're going to die tomorrow?"

Doug took his wife's hand and massaged the knots out of each of her fingers. "Then I won't believe it."

"You'll believe the good things but not the bad?" Maggie said, tears in her eyes. "You can't do that. That's not how life works."

"That's how my life works."

"Then you're not being fair to the rest of us."

Emma turned away. Three clouds were gathering in the western sky, and below them a worked-over sports car came screaming down the road. The driver skidded to a stop in front of the house, then hopped out through the car window.

"Hey," he said. "Jake here?"

"You just missed him, Eli," Doug answered.

The young man nodded. He started to get back in the car, then stopped. He had long brown hair that completely covered his face, and he reached up to part it. Emma could make out two things: a flash of green, and the fact that he was staring at her.

She wrapped her arms around her waist and looked at the sky. Diana Truff had been the beauty of Mission High School—all blond hair and blue eyes and a C cup by the time she was twelve. No boy had ever shown the slightest interest in Emma, so now she hugged herself and made believe that life could swing on a stare. When those three clouds merged and suddenly thickened with rain, it seemed entirely possible that desire could sweep up out of a clear blue sky, that everything could change in an instant.

# FOUR

## THE MOON ❧ UNKNOWN ENEMIES

THE MOON.

**S**avannah had four weeks of accumulated vacation and sick time, and she had every intention of going back to San Francisco before they were over. She spent her first few nights in Prescott dreaming her father well, but in the mornings found lumps of his hair on his pillow. For days, she felt nauseated at the thought of what would happen if he died, but he felt worse; he spent his mornings in the bathroom, vomiting up everything but cream of mushroom soup. She unpacked her bags and hung her hats on the walls.

When she drew a card for herself and came up with Strength, she decided this was the perfect opportunity to try her fortune-telling full-time, and to stop being afraid of Harry's attorneys. She placed an ad in Prescott's *Daily Courier*. AMAZING FORTUNE-TELLER— KNOW YOUR FUTURE. CALL SAVANNAH. 645-1297.

The ad appeared Monday morning and by Monday afternoon, she got her first call. Unfortunately, Maggie answered the phone and told the young pilot out at Embry-Riddle University he was out of his mind. "What if she tells you a train's headed right for you? Do you want to live your whole life in fear? And why would you believe her anyway? Who made her an expert on your life?"

"I just thought—"

"No, you didn't think. That's the trouble with you young people. You're not thinking at all."

Savannah was standing in the back of the kitchen, and she headed for the door.

"You will not put up any signs!" Maggie called after her.

Savannah went to the converted garage, where she and Emma had moved in. Her father had apologized for the rakes on the walls and the exposed plumbing; he had never seen their house in the city when the housekeeper failed to show. Savannah would rather invite Ramona over for margaritas than dust her furniture. In her opinion, people who stenciled their hardwood floors needed some time in Tahiti.

She put on her Panama hat and grabbed her checkbook. She went to the phone company in person, to get a second line put in the garage.

When she returned, her father and mother were just pulling up in the driveway, after Doug's radiation treatment. This was his second round of treatments, scheduled five days a week for six weeks, and it was doing nothing but killing him. His hair was all gone and even when they left the windows open in his room, there was a yeasty smell there that could make a woman as tough as Maggie Dawson curl up in a ball and cry.

Savannah started across the yard, but Maggie stopped her halfway. "You go on," she said.

"I just want to help him in." Savannah looked past

her mother to the car, where her father sat frighteningly still. The only sign of life was his trembling bottom lip.

"You think he wants you to see him this way?" Maggie whispered. "You think this isn't killing him?"

Maggie's voice quivered, and Savannah looked up. It was obvious who this was killing, and that shocked her. She had thought her mother would be just fine.

"I'm sorry," Savannah said, and walked back to the garage. She was trembling, but she made herself walk normally. She quieted the throb in her throat with a stick of Juicy Fruit gum. She took a deep breath and climbed the ladder above the garage door. While Maggie slipped a strong arm around Doug's waist and half carried him into the house, Savannah nailed her fortune-teller sign to the wall. She glanced up occasionally at her father's window, but it was half an hour before she saw any movement, and then it was just her mother pulling down the shade.

At dusk, when the sidewalks filled with strolling widowers in pressed sweat suits, timing their heart rates, Savannah waited in the garden for one to come for a closer look at her sign. When the streetlamps snapped on at eight, a good hour before dark, a man did. Maggie watched from the kitchen window, smiling, because the man was Ben Hiller, head of the MesaLand Homeowners Association.

"There are covenants against this sort of thing." Hiller gestured at her sign with the sharp white point of his elbow. He was tall, silver-haired, and thin as a pear sapling. He wore all white, which only highlighted the fact that his skin was the color of macaroni and cheese. From the smell of his breath, she was sure that was all he'd been eating for weeks.

"Come on in," she said. "Let me give you a reading."

He had to bend his head down to look at her. She could smell sadness a mile away, and it reeked to high heaven on him. She put a hand on his arm, right over a liver spot shaped like a bird. He studied her bracelets a moment, then pulled away.

"We will not have any businesses run on our properties. We're here to live out our days in peace and quiet."

Savannah adjusted her hat. "I don't read to rock music. You won't even know I'm here, unless you come for a reading. I could tell your fortune right now. I'll do it for free, just to get the word out."

"Young lady," Ben said, "I've lived on that corner for twenty years. I think I know a thing or two about my neighbors. They're already scared enough, for one thing. They're not going to be lining up here so you can tell them they've got only two more years to live."

Savannah drew back as if he'd insulted her. "I'd never say that. The tarots are not fortune cookies, you know. They're not so much a prediction of the future as a way to get in touch with your own intuition. A way to see things clearer. Did you know the tarots go back to Egyptian times? The cards are based on mythical archetypes. The major arcana correspond to the twenty-two letters of the kabbalah. I'm telling you, I am not messing around here."

Ben Hiller stepped back and grasped the black string around his neck. It held two silver wedding rings, a woman's and a man's, which he tucked beneath his faded white shirt, against his heart.

"That is not the issue," he said.

"I'm not going to tell anyone they'll get in a car crash or have a heart attack," Savannah went on. "There's nothing in the cards for that. But four Fours often means a journey is near at hand. And there is no doubt about it, the Two of Cups means you're going to fall in love."

"No one on this block wants to fall in love again. I guarantee you."

Ben looked through the lemon stamp of lamplight at his house on the corner, the one with an overwhelming expanse of blue fescue, like an ocean he'd have to cross just to get to his front door. He stepped back, right into the path of a blueberry climber Doug had planted along the walls of the garage.

"Young lady, you take down that sign and don't even think about practicing your witchcraft here."

Savannah put a hand over her heart. "I swear I will not practice witchcraft."

Ben Hiller squinted at her. He was trembling, and they both heard the wedding rings slapping against his chest. He stepped back, until he crushed a blood-red tulip, which had just opened up. It was a well-known fact that crimson tulips from Canada to Texas bloomed on the same day, as if by magic. On that night, mothers put their toddlers to bed early and asked their stunned husbands to dance, girls pricked their fingers and said a boy's name one hundred times, and hard men cried. But Ben Hiller just scraped the blossoms off the bottom of his heel.

Savannah touched his shirt, above the rings. "What was her name?"

Ben Hiller stepped back and put a hand over his chest, as if she'd burned him. The wind curled around their shoulders and arms, but went no higher; it never rocked the top branches of the trees, it did nothing to deter the flight paths of crows. It was a wind for land-locked humans, and tonight it swirled around a widower's shirt collar, then collapsed into his pocket, where it trembled against his chest.

"Helen," he said. "She died sixteen years ago this summer."

Savannah suddenly felt unsteady, and reached for the wall of the garage. Husbands and wives ought to grow old together, not leave one another hanging. Life ought to reward true love, and if it didn't, then she didn't want to know about it. She looked at the blueberry climber and the darkening sky, everywhere except at the pain in one old man's eyes.

"Well," she said. "Thanks for the warning."

She left Ben Hiller standing in the garden and went back inside. She didn't even think about taking down the sign. But a few days later, she knew Ben had warned the neighbors, because no one in the Mesa-Land retirement community would come near her. Even after the ad appeared with her new phone number, she got only three calls, all high-school girls wanting to know how to win back their ex-boyfriends. Her neighbors hung up on her whenever she phoned with offers of a free introductory reading. They crossed the street when they saw her coming. Ninety-year-old Mark Ridley went so far as to ask his grandson to move in, just in case something funny should happen.

Savannah ignored this entirely. She read for the high-school girls and tried to stop dreaming of her old life—her corner office overlooking the Bay Bridge, and the dodgeball games her writers would be playing in the conference room. She tried to stop thinking Arizona was making her another person. Outside her father's garden, there was not enough color, so she wore nothing but crimson dresses and sapphire rings. She still woke up humming, but sometimes it took her awhile to figure out a tune. Sometimes, in the middle of frying up bacon, she couldn't think of one more note.

After two weeks, when her father had turned a

paler shade of chalk, she began to get a little nervous. When she was down to five days of sick leave, she ignored Emma's lethal stare and called her boss.

"I can't go back now," she said.

Taylor Baines was one of the most successful ad agencies in the city, second only to the Goodby Silverstein agency. There were a hundred people standing in line to take her job, but she couldn't consider that. Not while her father needed help getting from his bed to the bathroom, not while she heard her steely mother crying in the middle of the night.

"You could take family leave," her boss said. "Your position will be waiting for you when you come back."

He suggested freelance copywriting just to keep her finger in the business, and she found such work writing newspaper ads for Fulsom Foods, an independent supermarket chain in decline. Though the work was minimal, some days she found it harder than her job at Taylor Baines.

"Shop with experience," she said out loud. She was stirring up another batch of homemade cream of mushroom soup in her mother's kitchen. "Freshness *and* experience. No one can beat our quality and service."

"I got food poisoning from one of their tomatoes," Maggie said, coming into the kitchen.

"You did not."

Maggie went to the cupboard. "I most certainly did. Besides that, I prefer the new Smitty's. Have you seen the size of their deli? They've got a sushi chef on staff, if you can believe that."

Savannah stirred the soup, while her mother found a wineglass. Beyond the glasses, there was an inordinate amount of frying pans and utensils, and a cutting board to die for, none of which appeared to have ever been used.

"I'll get going with the fortune-telling anyway," she said. "This could all be fate, you know."

"You're a successful woman. Don't ruin it."

"I'm not ruining anything. I'm trying to follow my heart."

"Do you know what I would have given for a life like yours?"

Savannah looked at her mother's hands clenched tightly around the stem of her wineglass. She turned away. "We are two different people, Mom."

"So you'd like to think." Maggie unpeeled the tag from the wineglass, then filled it with chilled Chardonnay. She took a good, long sip, then finally turned to Savannah. "You won't do any fortune-telling business here. My neighbors already know their future. It's cream of mushroom soup."

Savannah's hand shook as she poured the bone-colored soup, but she wasn't about to start falling for doomsday thinking now. She took the soup on a tray to her father, but he had already fallen asleep. She put the tray down on the side table and pulled the blankets up under his chin.

She pressed her face into the crook of his neck, and breathed in deeply. She ignored the stench of illness entirely—the bitter breath and moldy sweat—because beneath that he still smelled of himself, of citrus and fishy soil and rose petals. Of the only cherry tree in all of Phoenix. He still smelled of the living, and she swept that up into her heart.

She pressed her cheek firmly against him. She adored him, but his dying was not bringing out the best in her. In fact, it had made her selfishness crystal clear. She didn't care what else he did, he just couldn't leave her. She could walk away and never come back, she could break his heart in two, but a father was meant to be there. He didn't have to say a word; he just had to last.

This didn't speak well for her, but she knew what she had to do—read her father's fortune and, if it came up badly, stack the cards. A child had to have some power, after all, and hers would be to make him live.

She sang a song she'd made up years ago, when she'd spent her nights on that back lawn in Danville, Emma tucked against her, her palms unfurled.

> *My lover went to sea,*
> *to sea.*
> *His heart he gave to me,*
> *to me.*
> *I stored it in a treasure chest,*
> *the key tucked near my breast,*
> *my breast.*
> *But still the sea swept it out to rest*
> *at the bottom of the sea,*
> *the sea.*

She stroked her cheek against her father's arm. The hair had fallen out there, too, so he now had skin like a baby's, so smooth and pink it brought tears to her eyes. She cried the way she laughed, from the pit of her stomach, from way down deep. And while she cried, she realized she had married Harry Shaw not only to escape her irascible mother, but also to get away from the goodness of her father, from loving someone so much, losing him would make her another person. She might suddenly forget the things he'd taught her—how to ride a bicycle and do long division. Worst of all, with her champion gone, she might start looking at the world differently, as if it were a predator and had been after her all along.

She felt a hand on her hair and looked up to find her father awake, staring at her. He stroked her hair and tried to smile, but his bottom lip split with the effort. She reached for the washcloth by the side of the bed and wiped off the blood.

"It's always darkest before the dawn," he said.

He had said the same thing every time she lost a boyfriend, or Maggie yelled, or a friend moved away. She had clung to those words, she had believed them, but now she was not so sure. She thought it might very well be darkest right before midnight, when there was still a whole night of darkness to get through.


The second Emma stepped onto the grounds of Prescott High, she knew she had made a mistake sticking around. Mission High in San Francisco was a small charter school devoted to the arts, and the students were even more bohemian than the artists south of Market and the witches who gathered on misty Tank Hill. The boys wore ponytails and backpacked all summer, the girls read Keats and hardly ever fell in love. Popularity was based not on athletics or looks, but on which part you got in *Othello*, on whether or not people cried while you sang a Tracy Chapman song.

Emma had been Desdemona in *Othello*, she had had friends hanging on her every word. Now, though, she was frozen solid; she was hideously out of place. Prescott High was double the size of Mission High, sprawling, nondescript, a vague brown. People had way too much land to play with out here, they had entirely too much access to concrete and computer-aided design. The school was a fortress of cement, with every window locked tight—a security measure since a boy in neighboring Flagstaff went crazy with an Uzi during homeroom. She was supposed to find room

203 for History, but she wasn't going anywhere, not any farther than the flagpole near the front gate.

A clique of girls in tight blouses and short skirts walked past her and snorted at her clothes—she'd worn her favorite ankle-length gray skirt, oversized gray blouse, and sandals. One of them said something about foreigners and the others laughed.

Emma picked up a handful of dirt and flung it at them. The girls yelped and turned around, but Emma was already picking up another handful. Ramona had taught her how to throw a hex. Emma spit on the dirt for luck, then hurled it at the tallest girl's eyes, all the while cussing like there was no tomorrow.

"Fuckshitgoddamnyoumotherfucker."

She must have done it right, because long before the dirt wad hit them, the girls were running. They flung themselves inside the Science building, where they hugged one another and sobbed. Emma slapped her hands clean, satisfied.

"Good aim," someone said.

Emma turned around to find a band of punks behind her. They were too old for high school, nineteen or early twenties, with cigarettes in their pockets and mean, ugly haircuts. The boy she'd seen drive up in front of her grandparents' house had already taken a step toward her.

"They had it coming," she said.

"No doubt."

He lit a cigarette and squinted when the smoke flew past his eyes. He was hard and audaciously thin, a lean coyote who has the guts to nudge open a kitchen door, looking for food. Long brown hair fell over his eyes and a nasty scar ran down his left cheek. He sucked on his cigarette but, as far as she could tell, never exhaled.

"What's your name?" he asked.

"Emma Shaw."

*"Emma Shaw. Emma Shaw."*

She did not know if he was singing her name or mocking her. The others passed around a joint and didn't bother to put it out when a woman in a blue linen suit slammed out of the administration building. Emma recognized her as Principal Harris, whom she'd met when she enrolled.

"Eli Malone," the woman said, "I told you if I caught you here one more time, I was going to call Cal Bentley. You'd better get moving, because he's already on his way."

"I'm shaking. I'm shitting my pants."

The boys all laughed. They passed the joint to Eli right in front of her.

"Haven't you got anything else to do?" the principal asked.

"We're just friendly, that's all," Eli said. "When Cal comes, what's he gonna pick us up for? Loitering? We'll be out in an hour. We'll pick up Rick and Pippen and come back even stronger."

Eli walked up to the principal and rested his head on her shoulder. "Principal Harris? You hear about that shooting during homeroom up in Flagstaff? You hear how that boy just snapped?"

The woman was at least thirty years older than Eli, with crusty brown lines fanning out from her eyes, but she leaned back, out of his reach. Behind her back, she crossed and uncrossed her fingers.

Eli laughed, then looked at Emma. He stared at her so hard, Emma had the feeling he was working some kind of magic, taking something from her even though she wasn't quite sure what it was. Principal Harris must have felt the force of that gaze, too, because she put a hand on her shoulder.

One of the boys held the joint out to the principal,

then laughed when she glared at him. Emma snorted. Big deal. In San Francisco, these guys would have to do a lot worse to get noticed. In a city where almost everything and everyone was accepted, it was frustratingly hard to be bad.

But here, where high-school girls either got scholarships or knocked up, and their brothers went to bed at eight o'clock or not at all, Emma could see right off she definitely had to choose her corner. Raise her standards or raise havoc, but either way decide early, so people would know how to treat her.

Emma squeezed her hands into fists. Though her skin was burning hot, she nevertheless turned toward the principal. She didn't dare look into Eli Malone's eyes. She wasn't the type of girl who suddenly started screwing up her life.

"Remember me?" she said to the principal. "I'm Emma Shaw. It's my first day."

"Well, don't start it with these boys. They were kicked out four years ago, and we haven't been able to get rid of them since."

The sheriff drove up then, but instead of scattering, the boys planted their feet. They weren't total fools, though; when the cop got out of his car, they threw the joint into the ivy.

The sheriff was built like a slab of concrete. He was taller than Eli, and had to weigh twice as much. His hair was cut short and going silver, but it was the lines around his eyes that held Emma's attention. That was where his color seeped out, a strangely luminous yellow, a surprising color for a man with hands the size of T-bone steaks.

"This is what I'm gonna do," the sheriff said, putting a hand on his gun. "I'm gonna push this up a notch and call it trespassing. See? Then the school gets a chance to sue. Then we're talking civil suit, in addition to criminal. And if that doesn't work, I'll get a warrant. I'll bet I can get each of you for possession right now. That's a felony, boys. That's the big house."

The others all looked at Eli, but he just leaned back on his shiny black boots and smiled. "Jake will never let you book me."

"Jake's got no say in this."

Eli shrugged. "I'll call your bluff."

Cal Bentley nodded and slipped a pair of hand-cuffs out of his back pocket. Eli turned around and held out his hands behind him. He smiled at Emma, and she took a step toward him before she wondered what she was doing.

By the time Cal had the handcuffs fastened, the other boys had scattered. "Looks like you're on your own," Cal said.

"What else is new?"

The sheriff led him to the car. The principal, who Emma had forgotten, squeezed her shoulder.

"You stay away from them," she said, leading her toward the school. "They're nothing but bad news."

Emma nodded. But she looked over her shoulder and saw Eli staring at her out of the backseat of the cruiser. His eyes seemed capable of burning holes straight through the glass, not to mention the thin lining around her heart.


The dogs started howling when the car was still a mile away. When Jake came out of his workshop, they leapt into the air and took to snapping at each other. Rufus, the chocolate Lab, went a little crazy chasing his tail, until he finally fell over, winded and dizzy, on the gravel driveway.

Jake walked up the pebble path to the drive. He got all the way to the top before the hair on the back of his neck stood on end. He'd had some warning, but still when he turned around and looked where the metal roof of his cabin peaked by the chimney, his heart skipped painfully. His hallucinations had taken solid form; his worst nightmare sat smoking a cigarette, his leg draped over the eave, a big black boot tapping against the log post. Jake closed his eyes. When he reopened them, the nightmare was gone. Then he heard a twig snap behind him.

He turned around in time to see a vague form disappearing into the woods. A shadowy man, with black hair and teeth the color of creamed coffee. Jake had had plenty of time to think of something profound to say, and it all came down to this: "Go to hell."

The wind through the pine needles sounded exactly like laughter.

When Jake had first built his cabin, the apparition had been no more than an occasional glow between the trees. The problem was, Jake had not denied the vision outright. He probably could have put a stop to it immediately, if he'd had the guts to turn away, like the spirit was nothing, not even worth his worry. Instead, he stared at the ghost's bloodshot eyes too long. He remembered the living man's black boots and, bam, the ghost was wearing them. He showed some signs of panic, and the ghost got high on his own power, which put a little more meat on his bones.

Give a ghost an inch and he'll take a mile. Pretty soon, he wouldn't be afraid to cross Jake's doorstep or perhaps even sleep in his bed.

"Get out," Jake called after him. "I mean it. Get fucking lost." He charged into the woods, but found nothing except a blackened hedge of bitterroot, as if something had burnt the life out of it.

He was being haunted, all right, but sometimes it was difficult to tell if it was by a ghost or his own bad dreams. For one thing, the ghost had never spoken, not in fifteen years. It was an awesome kind of power, holding back all the things he could say. Silence was as good as a firearm; when it finally broke, it would go off, right between Jake's eyes.

He started to walk out of the woods. The car he'd heard was closer now. He recognized the deep hum of Cal Bentley's squad car, just a hundred yards down the winding road.

He was friends with Cal Bentley for two reasons: because the man knew how to be quiet, and because every time he drove up the dangerous road to Jake's cabin, Jake assumed he had figured out everything. For fifteen years, Jake had been waiting for someone to find him out so he could finally confess. Not to murdering a man—that much was obvious—but to being glad he'd done it.

He was tormented by his own satisfaction. When the nightmares came, he was appalled at himself for waking up smiling. He was abominable, a man he would never want to know, because what he regretted most was not what he'd done, but the things he'd lost—his family, his woman, the certainty that deep down, he was a good man.

Guilt had eaten at him all right, guilt at ruining his own life. So he left out clues for Cal, like the picture of his mother and stepfather on the mantel, the only personal thing in his cabin, a thing he never referred to, not once. And the rifle in the locked gun cabinet, a spattering of blood still on the handle. And when he reached for one of his home-brewed beers, he always reached with his left hand, the one with the scar in the middle, the size of a dime.

If Cal Bentley noticed these things, he gave no sign. He seemed content to let Jake come to him, which despite everything, Jake was never going to do.

He had learned a few things in fifteen years, and probably the worst was this: If given half a chance, even a man who despised himself couldn't help wanting to survive. Throw a monster into a lake and he'll sputter to the surface. For some reason Jake could never understand, he got up each morning and started breathing.

When Cal Bentley's cruiser finally came into view, Rufus and Gabe were on it, leaping onto the trunk and down again, twice even vaulting over the roof, their nails on the metal sending chills down Jake's spine. Sasha flung herself at the passenger door, leaving scratch marks all down the white paint, which Cal had stopped patching years ago, when Jake first got his Husky.

Cal stopped the car and got out. Sasha snarled at him. "Good afternoon to you too, sweetheart," Cal said.

He looked at Jake and smiled. "Got a present for you." He opened the back door and yanked out Eli Malone, still cuffed. Eli looked at him through a part in his long, greasy hair.

"What is it this time?" Jake asked.

"Trespassing. The school might sue."

Jake said nothing. Cal thought him a fool for hiring Eli, and he was probably right. Jake, though, hadn't been able to stop himself. Eli was a runaway of a different sort, an escape from his own family, and he was getting ready to snap, anyone could see that. Jake never touched anyone but his dogs, but whenever he got close to Eli, he nearly took the boy in his arms and told him he knew exactly what it felt like to live inside a body you hated, in a world that didn't want you anyway.

"All right," Jake said at last. "Uncuff him."

The boy had thrown back his hair and was doing

his best to look rotten all the way through, but his left leg kept skidding out beneath him. While Cal uncuffed him, Jake walked to the side of the house and picked up the ax.

"Two cords," he said.

"Ah, fuck."

"After that, hike to Shafer Peak and find me a three-inch sapling, twelve feet long, for the rock star's bed. Drag it back without doing any damage and then we'll see if you'll have a job in the morning."

"You're gonna kill me, man," Eli said, but he took the ax. Sasha followed him, snapping at his heels as he walked to the woodpile at the side of the cabin.

"He's not worth saving," Cal told Jake.

"So he tells me."

"I found his dad behind Teton's last night. Wes had so much vodka in his blood, he was pissing it."

"Eli's no drunk," Jake said. "He's never even tasted my beer."

"Would you, if Wes was your father?"

They walked into the cabin Jake had built by hand ten years ago. When he had surfaced in Prescott fifteen years ago, he'd taken a job he had never considered in his other life, as a carpenter's assistant. He had tried to hate the work, but the truth was he took to wood the way he figured a mother took to a child. He wrapped his fingers around a smooth trunk and thought, *Now this has possibilities. This is something I might be able to make right.*

He started making pine furniture on the side, and was so good at it he soon had enough orders for lodgepole beds to go into business himself. He found this property on the back side of Kemper Mountain and, after studying a few log cabins in the area, decided to build one himself.

He was meticulous about the logs he chose, because he liked them marred—knotted, lightning-struck, shredded by bear claws. He handcrafted every support beam, joist, and table in the house from damaged wood. The floors, loft, ceiling, and walls were all scarred pine, and over the years the floors had gotten even worse, gouged out by the dogs' toenails. Only five small windows and a sliding door broke up the expanse of bad wood. On cloudy afternoons, he could hardly make his way down the steep stairs from the loft without a flashlight. If he took a deep breath, he got a little woozy breathing in so much natural fiber at once.

From the highway to Jake's cabin was a forty-five minute drive. He was separated from his nearest neighbor by one air mile, or three hazardous driving miles, where the slightest miscalculation could send a car plummeting down a ravine that appeared to have no end.

Cal and Eli were the only people with the guts to come up here now, and even they must have wondered, more than occasionally, what the hell for. Even they must have smelled the tobacco and spite in the air. Since they'd never seen a ghost, they probably thought it was all coming from Jake.

"You still working on that bench for Doug Dawson?" Cal asked. "How's he feeling?"

"The man's dying. He just doesn't know it yet."

He walked out onto the back deck, where the air was yellow and thick with pine pollen.

Cal came out behind him. His weight, along with Jake's, made the large deck sway. "You got anything to say?" Cal asked.

Jake sucked in hard, until his chest burned. Cal asked the same question every time he saw him. He must have smelled the bitter stench that rose out of Jake's chest, where he'd stuffed down what he'd done and what had been done to him, and let it rot.

What Jake could say was that fifteen years ago, his life went into cardiac arrest. He walked out the door one morning as one person, and could never come home again because sometime before nightfall, he became someone else. He could say it was entirely possible to walk around without a soul, because he'd done it. He was made up of little more than guilt and regret, both of which he wouldn't wish on anyone, not even his ghost. He could say he'd killed a man out of sheer rage, and lost everything he'd ever wanted.

But all he said was, "Nope."

Jake picked up one of the many rawhide bones he kept on hand for his dogs and flung it as far as he could. The three of them bounded off the deck, snapping at one another for the lead. Jake sat down in one of his uncomfortable Adirondack chairs, the same kind he sold for four hundred dollars apiece to Montana actors.

"You all right?" Cal asked. There was no sound except a few early-bird crickets and Eli's curses as he split wood. Jake was not all right; he figured that much was obvious.

"You see that woman?" he asked. "Doug's daughter?"

"I saw the granddaughter at the high school," Cal said. "I'd suggest you keep Eli here when you go down to work. He's no Romeo, but then, when you're that bad, you don't have to be."

Jake nodded. When he'd picked up the paper that morning, he'd seen the ad for the amazing fortune-teller. He never used to believe any of that stuff, but he'd had time to change his mind about everything. It was no longer a stretch of the imagination to think a gypsy might have the key to his future, so he had called her.

"Come any night after six," she'd told him. "I'm in

the MesaLand retirement community. On Sage Street. The house with the garden."

And then he'd known who she was and something else too. He'd known if she read his fortune, she would find herself in it. He remembered the look on her face when he'd driven off, and how he'd felt he was making the worst mistake of his life by not taking her with him. But he made terrible mistakes every day of his life; he was a master at messing up every possible good fortune. So when he found himself in the middle of his lonely woods, wanting something for the first time in fifteen years, he just hung up on her.

"You interested in her?" Cal asked.

Jake looked up. Cal had a wife and two grown kids, one a pediatrician, the other just finishing her masters in physics. He was from another planet, one Jake did not have access to. Jake still had no idea what he was doing here.

"I'm not interested," he said.

Cal fished a cigarette out of his pocket and lit it. "You should be."

# FIVE

## KNIGHT OF WANDS ❧ RISK

**J**upiter's Beard was so aggressive, Doug could watch it overtake his chestnut rose in a single afternoon. Two years ago, he had planted a two-inch seedling along the back wall and now it was twelve feet around. Like everything else in his garden, it was lush, colorful, and totally lacking in form. His neighbors might admire his jungle display, but master gardeners would cringe at his use of invasive crown vetch to fill a hillside. They'd berate him for not cutting back his leggy clematis to its roots each winter, and for failing to master the art of vase-shaped pruning.

The worst he had ever done was take out a row of raggedy crape myrtles. He'd never had the stomach for hard gardening, and luckily there had never been a need for it. When he'd tried to thin out his purple coneflowers, they'd merely sprouted across the street, in the cracks beside Wendy Ginger's lap pool. When he'd made up his mind to cut back the faded torch lilies, his wife beat him to the task, sneaking off to the lily bed in the dead of night.

Standing at his bedroom window, he scratched his forehead, then stopped when he picked off another piece of scab. He looked down at his bloody fingers, more stupefied than anything else. Despite lying in a hospital bed every Wednesday for a month with cold chemotherapy dripping into his vein, and now getting radiation treatments five days a week, he sometimes did not believe it. Sometimes he felt so good, he wanted to take Maggie to dinner and stay until they finished a whole bottle of wine. Sometimes, no kidding, he just stared in the mirror and did not know the chalky man who stared back at him, a creature frail and spindly as silver sage. Sometimes the sight of himself was worse than the cancer itself.

He was a gardener, never in much of a hurry, and now it looked as though he'd run out of time. He hadn't done half the things he'd set out to do. He hadn't made it to Europe or taken Maggie to New York yet. He hadn't tackled the Pacific dogwood, a tree that hated garden watering, fertilizer, pruning, and sunburn, a tree that was spectacular if you didn't kill it. If you did everything exactly right.

The door opened behind him and Savannah came in carrying a tray of cream of mushroom soup. She had brought him a tray that morning too, loaded down with eggs, bacon, and thick wedges of cantaloupe. He had sucked on the bacon to humor her, but she must have noticed him gasping when the salt burnt the tender roof of his mouth.

Maggie came in behind her. "Sit down, Doug," she said. "For God's sake."

Doug sat on the bed, though he hated the smell of his sheets, his own appalling odor sunk deep into the cotton and coming back at him. In his most fragile moments, a pillow under his head made him want to give up then and there.

He was grateful that the garden was self-sufficient. He'd installed a drip irrigation system before planting a thing. He had not wanted to do it; he had loved those evenings in Phoenix when he'd come home from work, eaten a few bites of steak, then had gone outside to hold a hose to his azaleas. He had watered till midnight some nights, until he'd tuned his humming to the same frequency as the shrill cicadas, until each root was mistaking desert soil for farmland.

But the day they bought this Prescott house, he'd gotten a funny feeling in his gut. An uneasy impulse to order three-year-old Juneberry trees instead of two, and put in pampas sod rather than sowing from seed. A sudden, desperate need to stop wasting time.

"Eat your soup," Maggie said.

Doug looked at the food and felt his stomach flip. When Savannah put the tray on his lap, though, he managed to take one spoonful.

"I've got two appointments for tomorrow after work," Savannah announced. "High-school girls."

Maggie snorted, but Doug reached for his daughter's hand. "Will you read my fortune now? I'm thinking it's got to be good."

Savannah looked at Maggie, but for once Doug's wife was silent. Savannah clapped her hands and went for her cards. When the door closed behind her, Maggie took a good, long breath.

"I don't want to hear it when the Death card comes up," she said.

"It won't come. You'll see."

He looked out the window. Whenever he'd gotten excited over a new strain of pear tree or daylily, Maggie had looked at him coldly and said, "That's great, Doug. Another goddamn plant." But it was never just another plant. He only bought plants that reminded him of her. Deceivingly delicate-looking bamboo that could stand up to hurricanes, narcissus that smelled so good, he took one whiff and couldn't think straight for hours. Tay blackberry, with its long, thorny vines that hid huge clusters of fruit. When he was knee-deep in soil, when he had his back to his house, he was really thinking of Maggie. She was in his roses, in the first shoots of ivy, in everything.

He fell in love with her the first time he saw her. He and his best friend Michael had planned a road trip to Santa Fe, and at the last minute, Michael's younger sister joined them. Maggie had sat silently in the backseat of Michael's stuffy Oldsmobile while he and Michael talked about the lack of a professional football or baseball team in town, the dearth of datable girls, and the merits of Budweiser over Coors. They smoked constantly and, after six hours, Maggie stuck her head out the window and screamed.

She pulled her head back in and glared at them both. "You are so simple."

Michael swerved to the side of the freeway and cut the engine. "You're a goddamn baby. You're the simple one. You and your stupid fashion designs, your pathetic dreams of going to New York. I'll bet you one million dollars right now you'll never make it west of the Mississippi."

Maggie didn't look at him, not until the end, and then she sneered, "It's east of the Mississippi, you fool."

"Whatever."

She reached into her purse, took out a small mirror and lipstick tube, and put on a fresh coat of passion pink. She did not say another word, and she didn't have to. Doug was already lost. When she glared at him, he saw something he'd never seen in a woman, something fierce and unknowable. He would never crack her code, and he didn't want to. In thirty-six years of marriage, he had never even thought of cheating. Why would he, when he woke up every morning beside a woman he could not predict?

Not everyone, of course, saw Maggie in the same light. The widows on the block avoided her. His best friends had sometimes squeezed his shoulder in pity, and Doug had laughed out loud. Maggie shouted for both of them, but only when she had an audience. In private, she said his name while she slept and sneaked into the garden when she thought he wasn't looking. In private, she watched the designer fashion shows on cable, then dared him to say a word about the tears in her eyes. Doug was no fool; he'd learned his lesson years ago. He didn't say a word or try to cheer her up with flowers. He just held her hand and prayed he'd been enough to make her happy.

Savannah had fought Maggie on everything from cereal choices to the meaning of love. She had fought until she must have been bloody inside. Right before she went off to marry Harry, she'd said, "God, Dad, why do you love her?"

Doug had not slapped his child; instead, he'd walked to the garden and ripped out the first of six crape myrtle trees. Savannah had followed him, and he had whirled on her.

"Remember your prom dress, the one your mother said came from Nordstrom's? Did you really think we could afford that? No girl looked as beautiful as you did that night, and that's because your mother swallowed her regret and bought two bolts of white silk. She sewed that design from memory. She wouldn't look me in the eye for days."

Savannah had blinked and blinked. "Why didn't she tell me?"

"God only knows, Savannah," he said. "Your mother's a complex woman. Half the time, I haven't a clue what she's thinking."

"She's not fair with her kindnesses."

"Maybe not, but that's her way. Stop fighting what she is, Savannah. She's your mother. She never once let you cry yourself to sleep. What more do you need to know?"

"She's mean," she said.

"And you're strong."

Savannah came in now wearing a fuzzy brown bonnet and holding up her cards. They were slightly larger than playing cards, beautifully decorated with suns and medieval princes and sorcerers. Savannah handed them to him and he spotted the Death card sitting close to the top. He turned them over.

"Think of what you want to know," Savannah said.

What Doug wanted to know was whether or not he'd be able to shuffle the cards. The strangest things had gone out on him. Not the muscles and senses closest to the tumor, not his eyes or hearing or the tendons in his neck, but the feeling in the tips of his fingers, the ability to curl his toes. The very best things had gone, like being able to dig his bare feet into two inches of cool, composted soil.

He turned away slightly and prayed his hands would work. He divided the cards, but he couldn't curl his fingers, and the cards all fell out beneath him. He glanced up at Maggie, but she'd turned her back on him. She stood stiffly by the window, her arms crossed over her chest.

Savannah reached out and gathered the cards. "Just swirl them around," she said softly. "They'll know what to do."

He took a deep breath. He put his hand over his daughter's briefly, to stop them both from trembling, then swirled the cards around on the bed like a three-year-old.

He thought of the poem he'd written thirty-six years ago, on his wedding night. He'd hidden in the bathroom of their hotel room and scribbled it on toilet paper. Later, he'd rewritten the verse, along with all the sonnets and love poems that followed, onto parchment. When he stopped writing a few years into his marriage, he had a shoe box stuffed with sentimentality no one else had ever seen.

He was amateurish and mawkish with words, untutored in rhyme scheme, but that wasn't what had made him give up the poetry. That happened the day he and Maggie went to a dinner party, and in front of twenty people, a man named Fred Feinstein proposed to the girl of his dreams. Fred was three hundred pounds and a hopeless stutterer, but nevertheless he got on one knee and haltingly recited all the reasons he adored this woman who had ne-ne-ne-never noticed his weight or sp-sp-speech problem. While every other woman had tears in her eyes, Maggie went to the buffet table and piled her plate with cold cuts. "I give it six months," she whispered to Doug. "One year, tops."

If Maggie had read his poem on their wedding night, she would have broken down laughing, then flushed the drivel down the toilet. Yet he still remembered that poem, word for word.

> *Before you blew in,*
> *all sirocco and sandstorm,*
> *I could see clear to the edge of my desert.*
> *Stone sky, blanched sand,*
> *subsistence level desires,*
> *I was colorblind.*
> *You were technicolor lightning.*

*Electric gray eyes,*
*lips purple passion,*
*breath white hot irrational.*
*Thunderstruck,*
*I looked into the eye of your storm*
*and saw the color of forever—*
*not sky blue or heaven's gold,*
*but a calloused, freckled ivory,*
*palm-sized,*
*tips painted hot pink.*

"Are you concentrating, Dad?" Savannah asked, because he had stopped swirling the cards. He started up again and thought about the only question he really wanted answered: How much more time would he have with the woman who couldn't hide the soil beneath her fingernails, who resorted to midnight trickery in order to protect him from grief? How much more time would he have with Maggie?

"All right." Savannah took back the cards, sat down on the bed and laid them out.

They looked all right to him. No Death card, no Devil. Savannah's hat dipped over her eyes as she studied them.

"This is the Hierophant." She pointed to the first card she'd drawn. "It can mean a spiritual leader, or too much reserve and timidity."

"Ha!" Maggie said from the corner, but she did not turn around.

"You see this?" Savannah pointed to the second card. "This is the Four of Cups. This is what crosses you. It is the card of weariness. A struggle."

"What about that?" Doug indicated the card to the right of the four, a man sitting on a throne, the King of Swords.

"That's your distant past. You've been exposed to a controlling person. That is what has shaped you."

They both looked up at Maggie. "So now I'm to blame," she said.

"Look at this, Dad," Savannah continued. "Your future is the Knight of Wands. I've always loved that card. It's the card of journeys. Advancement into the unknown without fear. It is a card of risk."

Doug looked over Savannah's shoulder at his wife. She stood stiff as stone. He knew, if he tried to touch her, she would pull away. She would tell him she didn't need his pity and it would only be later, when she thought he was asleep, that she would sneak into the bathroom and turn on the water so she could cry in peace.

She would have planted nothing but common, spiky juniper if it had been up to her; she abhorred softness and anything she had to work too hard to know. She believed he had kept something from her all these years, that his feelings were some kind of buried treasure in his garden. He had never refuted this, because it was better than the truth: He was not a deep man. He didn't want to be. He didn't philosophize or analyze his feelings. The only time he'd ever thought things through was when he wrote his poetry, and he'd given that up years ago. He had not liked those midnight sessions, when he'd surprised himself with his own ferocity. When he realized there were parts of himself he didn't own. He hadn't liked the way loving someone that much had turned his stomach inside out, made him almost angry. Better were the mornings when the desert sun seemed capable of burning the passion out of anyone. Better to plant a strawberry tree and watch it grow slowly, rising just ten feet a lifetime, and taking so little water it wasn't a drain on anything.

Maggie turned suddenly and stared at him. Her eyes were so dry he knew they stung her.

"What's there to risk," she asked, "if you're already dying?"

Doug leaned back. The doctors said the cancer had gone from his skin to his lymph nodes to his brain. They said it was unclear how much radiation and chemotherapy could do at this point, but there was no alternative, save letting him die. Treatment, however, would be a kind of poison. It would eat up the good cells along with the bad. There was the potential for horrendous side effects, including damage to the heart, kidney, bladder, lung and nervous system, nausea, vomiting, and debilitating fatigue.

What they hadn't told him was that the cancer would also spread to the coating around his heart. His ventricles fluttered now when he least expected it, when he was doing nothing more than looking at his wife. His aorta flip-flopped when he thought of leaving her behind with no one to be strong for, his pulse stopped cold when she got up beside him at dawn and watched the sun rise over his garden, tilting her head back, so her tears wouldn't run down.

Radiation had burned a hole right through the trapdoor at the back of his throat. Maggie was absolutely right: What did he have to risk when he was already dying, except those few things that cancer could not devour, the bittersweet poetry of his soul?

He breathed deeply, and his voice didn't break until halfway through, and by then it didn't matter. If he was already dying, then the least he could do was go about it flying through thin air.

He began:

*"Before you blew in,*
*All sirocco and sandstorm,*

*I could see clear to the edge of my desert.*
*Stone sky, blanched sand,*
*subsistence level desires,*
*I was colorblind.*
*You were technicolor lightning.*
*Electric gray eyes,*
*lips purple passion,*
*breath white hot irrational.*
*Thunderstruck,*
*I looked into the eye of your storm*
*and saw the color of forever—*
*not sky blue or heaven's gold,*
*but a calloused, freckled ivory,*
*palm-sized,*
*tips painted hot pink."*

He could hear his daughter crying, but Doug didn't take his eyes from his wife. He wondered if she would laugh, if she would even believe it of him. He hadn't shown any sign of passion or raised his voice in years. But now, he found himself thinking everything depended on whether or not Maggie thought him capable of poetry. All of a sudden, he had a million ways to say he loved her, and he had to get them all down on paper.

Maggie walked across the room and knelt by the side of the bed. She laid her head in his lap. She hadn't appeared to be crying, but immediately his pants were soaking wet. "You idiot," she said. "You sweet, simple fool."

After a few afternoons helping Jake at the Dawsons, Eli Malone had the place cased. The house itself was a fortress—deadbolts, security system, and that crazy woman who packed a stun gun in her purse. But the garage apartment was another story. Savannah Dawson never locked the front door and often left the windows open at night. She let in total strangers who, more often than not, listened to their fortunes, then stiffed her.

At midnight, he sat in his car across Sage Street, smoking a joint. If he were a fortune-teller, you could bet he'd get his money up front. Hell, for twenty dollars a pop, he could tell the future too. Beware of love and marriage and rules, because they were all things just asking to be broken. Get the best dope you can find and never care for anyone, just in case it turns out they have something you want.

Eli was not in danger of that. He was a sieve when it came to people; they could pour their hearts out, and it would go right through him. His father was a sober brute and a drunk fool, and both had no effect on Eli whatsoever. The last time his father had beaten him, it had been one hundred and five degrees, but when Eli packed his bags and left for good, he didn't sweat one drop.

He crushed the joint and stepped out of the car. The girl was in the garage; that might have stopped another guy, but it didn't dissuade him. Emma Shaw was pretty, but what did he need with that? Look at him. He was a mess. He owned two pairs of jeans, three T-shirts, an aging Corvette and two-year-old Reeboks. He had a two-inch scar on his left cheek, compliments of one of his father's sober rages, but which he told everyone was from a knifing. No decent person came within ten feet of him. He'd lived on his own since he was sixteen, in a shack up Boulder Creek, and not even deer came through his garden anymore, that's the kind of stink he gave off. Other guys based their worthiness on grade point averages and touchdowns; he based his on how many hubcaps he stole a night. Pretty girls were for Romeos and college boys. He'd slept with six girls, and they'd all been as ugly as he was.

So he wasn't going to think about the girl, or anything else. He took a step toward the garage, then flew to the ground when the door suddenly opened. Savannah Dawson stepped out and walked through the garden. She wrapped her arms around her stomach and the lamplight exposed the tears that slipped down her cheeks.

He hadn't expected that, but so what? So the woman was capable of sorrow. Big deal. She deserved a little; everyone did. She had been getting on his nerves anyway, with that really obnoxious good mood.

She headed out of the garden toward the corner, her dress swiping the neighbors' lawns and sending up clouds of moths. Eli waited until she'd disappeared around Forest Drive, then he crept through Doug's garden, a garden so well tended it was like a dressed-up baby, a garden he could not understand. He'd gotten up early one morning last week and crept into the perennial bed to toss salt through it, just to see how fast things could die. Unfortunately, that turned out to be the one day Doug felt well enough to get out of bed at dawn; the old man found him with the blue can still in his hand, the rock jasmine wilting at his feet but ready to rebound at the first hint of water. Instead of screaming, Doug had simply put an arm around Eli's shoulders. "You know, son," he'd said, "one day you're going to tire of all this hate. It'll seep right out of you, so it might not be a bad idea to have a backup plan."

Eli had blinked and blinked and blinked. And then he'd looked at Doug like he was crazy.

Now, Eli tromped through the garden and didn't breathe in. He wasn't about to be swayed by the tender aromas of honeysuckle and sage, or tempted to soft-

ness by the caress of velvet lilies. He put his hand
around a shoot of beard tongue and yanked it right out
of the ground. He tossed it in the mermaid fountain,
then crept up to the garage door.

Of course it was unlocked. If the gypsy couldn't
figure out on her own that it was a bad world, then
maybe she just had to be shown. Maybe he was doing
her a favor.

Silently, he opened the door and shut it behind
him, then waited until his eyes adjusted to the darkness. He made out Emma's shape on the bed in the
corner, all curled up. He had told himself he'd go
straight for Savannah's jewelry which, after he pawned
it, would bring in enough for a quarter of the latest
Colombian. He had told himself he'd be in and out in
seconds, but instead he walked over to Emma. Her
back was to him, a wave of pine-colored hair swept
over the pillow. He leaned over just enough to make
out the sweep of her nose, the long, brown lashes on
her skin, a funny red freckle in the center of her
cheek.

He reached out, then snatched back his hand. He
didn't know what he was thinking. He was not about
to start wanting anything now. Especially not a girl
who would take one look at him and run.

He turned away. On the window ledge were half a
dozen rings, and he slipped them all in his pockets. He
scooped up the bracelets just lying on the nightstand,
two dozen gold and silver strands. Then he walked into
the makeshift kitchen to look for cash.

They had set out a Coleman stove for cooking,
along with an old wood-paneled microwave. There was
a bowl still half-full of popcorn, and Eli stuffed a
handful in his mouth. Then he hit pay dirt. On the
sink, ridiculously in plain sight, was a glass canister

filled with cash—ones, fives, and tons of change—as if the world wasn't full of crooks.

The jar jingled when he lifted it, but Emma didn't move. He slipped the canister beneath his arm and headed for the door. The jingling of the coins was loud, so he bolted. He managed to get his hand on the knob, but no farther.

"She works hard for that," Emma said.

Eli went still. He had no luck. His father had started punching him when he was three, to toughen him up. It must have worked because, by third grade, not even the bullies would come near him. By the time he dropped out of school seven years later, there wasn't a person in the city, besides Jake, who wasn't afraid of him.

But toughness had nothing to do with luck. During a forest fire two years ago, his had been the only shack to get burned. He might as well wear a bull's-eye; he was a disaster waiting to happen.

So it was no surprise that Emma caught him. She got out of bed and came up right behind him. She put a hand on his arm.

He turned around, his eyes blazing, not because he'd gotten caught, but because her hand was soft as silk, because it was just plain stupid for a guy like him to feel what he was feeling.

"Look, I need it, all right?" he said. "Your mom can just con some more people, but me . . ."

"You can't just steal."

"Oh, can't I?" But what he was thinking was that no, he couldn't, not anymore, not when she was looking at him like that. He was thinking her eyes were the color of river rock, and something deep inside him was breaking apart.

"Eli," Emma said, stepping up to him, and he thought for a moment that she would kiss him, but all she did was take the canister out of his hand. She walked back to the kitchen and put it on the counter. She flipped on the overhead light.

It was one of those long fluorescent tubes, and its intensity shocked them both. Eli jammed his hands in his pockets, where he still had Savannah's rings and bracelets. He closed his fists around them.

"Are you gonna tell your mom?" he asked.

Emma looked away. She wore an oversized Mickey Mouse T-shirt that fell to her knees. Her hair was mussed, and she was so thin she looked like a child, but all he could think about was how she was going to have to push him to get him to leave now.

"No," she said quietly. "I guess not."

He stepped forward, then stopped. Everyone had assumed he'd moved out of his parents' house at sixteen to escape his father's beatings. But that hadn't been it at all. Fists he could take. It was his mother's crying every morning that had done him in. It was pity he'd run from. It was caring.

Nevertheless, he walked across the room. When he reached Emma, he lifted the jewelry out of his pockets and put it in her hand. He was still bad luck; probably he was bad all the way through. But for this one moment, for reasons unfathomable to himself, he found himself incapable of meanness. He was shocked by who he might become.

"Eli?" she said, but he was already out the door. He was through the garden in seconds, which was just as well, since it smelled sweeter than anything he'd come across in years.

Savannah watched the boy run through the garden and hop into his car. The Corvette peeled out, and Eli

Malone was halfway down the street before he remembered to turn his lights on.

She sat on the curb in front of Martha Williamson's beige stone house. The woman was nearly deaf and Savannah could clearly hear Humphrey Bogart telling Katharine Hepburn to get the hell off his boat. The light was still on across the street, in her garage, then suddenly it went out. Savannah took a deep breath.

She reached into her pocket for the pack of cigarettes she'd slipped out to buy. She had smoked years ago with Harry, then quit easily, much to the disgust of Harry, who needed hypnosis and four weeks of hysterical rages to accomplish the same feat. The trouble was, she could start up again as easily as she'd quit. Since she'd come to Prescott, she'd had cravings for menthol Virginia Slims.

She lit one and looked down the street. The neighbors still wouldn't talk to her, Ben Hiller had called to say if she didn't take down her sign, there would be legal action, and her last client, a twenty-year-old boy headed for boot camp, had laughed in her face.

"This is shit," he'd said, after she'd laid out two Fours and three Queens and told him to be ready for deception by a woman.

She had lifted her chin. "That's what the cards say."

"Lady, you're out of your mind. Look at me." He'd stood up to his full height, six foot four, well over two hundred pounds. "Do I look like the kind of guy who gets duped? I'm going into the Navy, for Christ's sake. They're sending me to the Persian Gulf. I'm not going to see a woman for months."

She had glanced down at the cards, and her head hurt a little. She couldn't make out anything else.

When she'd left the house for a smoke, she had been figuring how quickly Taylor Baines would hire her back. She was thinking how nice it would feel to slip into her apartment on Nob Hill, stretch out in her bed, and sleep for hours. But then she'd looked up at her father's window and had seen his silhouette in the chair, his baby skull. The truth was, love was a trap, and most people willingly walked into it. If her father had really been kind, he would have given her a reason to hate him. He would have known all she needed was a single excuse to walk away.

She heard an engine and looked down Sage Street. A truck turned the corner, then pulled up in front of the house. Jake Grey stepped out stiffly, and even though she sat in the dark of the curb, he came right for her. Savannah's stomach tightened. She had no doubt that if she laid out the cards for herself now, she'd get a whole lot of Swords. The Swords ruled change; they weren't necessarily bad, just impulsive, like teenagers or anyone falling in love. When they came up in droves, one crisis was often cured by the creation of another.

She narrowed her eyes. The man had hardly uttered two words to her in three weeks, but she'd felt him studying her.

"It's a busy night," she said. "Your assistant has already been here."

"Eli?"

She said nothing more. He was a different man without his dogs. They did most of the talking. With all their barking and yelping, they had probably given him the illusion, all these years, that he was making normal conversation.

He made no move to come down to her level, so she stood up. That did little good; he was nearly a foot taller. She didn't like the looks of him, not one bit, so she blew smoke straight into his eyes.

"Stop trying to scare people," she said.

"I don't try. I just do."

"Well, you don't scare me."

He smiled a little, she thought, although it was hard to tell with his beard. "I'm just here to get my tools. Left some of my chisels."

"My God. Tragedy." She had no idea why she was feeling so mean, except that the air was still and thick enough to trap a woman whole. She dropped her cigarette and stomped it out, while Jake just stood there.

"So go," she said. Still, he just stood, and she started to feel uneasy. There was no moon, and suddenly the streetlamps went out. She gasped, though she'd known this was by Ben Hiller's order. All streetlights were set to turn off at one A.M., to save electricity. In this kind of darkness, Jake Grey was all shadows. He did look like a psycho.

"You know," she said, "some people have enough to worry about without running into someone like you. You could shave your beard. You could show a little enthusiasm for the human species. You could say hello every now and then. It wouldn't kill you."

She poked him in the chest, then snatched back her hand. He was hard as concrete. He took a step toward her. "You're right," he said softly. "Hello, Savannah."

He walked across the street and disappeared into the garden. He returned in a moment, chisels in hands, and held them up. In the darkness, they glittered like knives. He got into his truck and turned over the engine. In less than a minute, he was gone.

Savannah stood on the sidewalk, listening to the distant rumble of his truck and the beating of her heart.

She hurried back across the street, already accustomed to the slight slope of the pavement, the variations in her father's cobblestone walkway. She didn't want to know why Eli had shown up tonight, but she was still going to pull a blanket up over Emma. In theory, a mother ought to trust her daughter, but she was still going to start locking the door.

# SIX

**S**hielded from the porch by a clematis-coated trellis, and sweltering beneath a blistering white sky, Jake could very well have been hallucinating the laughter. It came in staccato shock waves, then disintegrated into giggling. The mind played funny tricks, because it sounded very much like Maggie Dawson.

"All right," she said. "Let's see what you can do."

There was the tinkling of ice cubes against glass, then the beeping of the cordless phone. In a moment, Emma's voice rose up. "I'd like to place an order."

Jake saturated a tenon joint with carpenter's glue, then fit it in the mortise. He turned over the bench and set it down for the first time on three-inch thick legs. Doug had not specified an arm or leg design, and Jake wished he had. Because left to his own devices, Jake might very well carve in the point of an elbow and sculpt bracelets around slender wrists. He might taper the legs and chisel feet into the bottom. If it got any hotter, he might paint the tips ruby red.

Every weekend and every evening, Savannah Dawson went straight to the garden. She hiked her skirt up around her hips and dug her bare feet into rich soil. Every few minutes, a note would sail down from the upstairs window, and she would pick it up. *Cut back the lily of the valley*, Doug Dawson would have written. *Use fish fertilizer on the chamomile, diluted to two tablespoons per gallon.* For a moment, Savannah would hide beneath the shade of whatever hat she was wearing and cradle the note as if it were the last healthy piece of her father. Then she would raise her face to the bedroom window and smile. She would pick up the pruners and go get it done.

Sasha followed her everywhere, out of her mind with devotion. By nightfall, her silver fur smelled of lemons and Juicy Fruit gum, and on the drive home Jake let her ride in the cab. He ignored fur heaps and ripped floor mats just to breathe in that unlikely mix of tang and sweetness.

"Twenty-four in turquoise blue," Emma said. "Absolutely. Overnight them."

Both Emma and Maggie laughed, then there was the tinkling of more ice. Jake stepped out around the trellis, and Maggie jerked her head up and eyed him suspiciously.

"How long have you been there?"

Both she and Emma were holding tall, frosted glasses of lemonade. Emma had on short shorts and a tank top; above her eyes were two striking curves of blue eye shadow. She was glaring at Jake, too.

"I was hoping I could get something to drink."

Actually, he wasn't the slightest bit thirsty, despite the heat, but he wouldn't mind a little of what they were having. It was obviously making them giddy.

Emma turned her back on him and spoke into the phone.

"One more thing. The birdbath mailbox. Again in blue." She listened, then looked at Maggie. "There's a twenty-dollar additional shipping charge."

"That's outrageous. They're bleeding me dry."

"That's all right," Emma said into the phone. "Bill the Discover card."

Maggie stood up. "I'll get you a glass," she told Jake, and went into the house.

Emma hung up the phone and turned back to him. She rolled the frosted glass along her forehead. "Grandma says you're a psycho."

Jake laughed as he walked across the patio and sat on the stoop beside her. He was impressed when she didn't even flinch. They both heard Savannah from somewhere in the front garden, making up jingles. He wished she would just stop. Lately, he'd found himself mumbling refrains of "flowers blooming, sunshine's looming," until he was certain the ghost was laughing his guts out.

"What do you think?" he asked.

She checked him over from head to toe, then finally stared right in his eyes. "I think you're in love with her."

Jake went absolutely still. If he strained really hard, he could hear Sasha moaning in ecstasy whenever Savannah stroked her, which she did every few minutes. He was fairly certain he heard his own heart skipping.

"Don't be ridiculous," he said.

Emma snorted, then stood up. She walked to the trellis and ripped off whole branches of jackmanii clematis. She made a point to walk on the tender thyme between the flagstones, squashing them flat. She was out to ruin something, that much was obvious, and at her age the real danger was that it would end up being herself.

"Look," she said, "I don't give a fuck, all right? But if you want my advice, don't go anywhere near my mom. One day with her and you'll feel like you've gorged yourself on too much cotton candy. She's not real. You know what I'm saying? She can't fall in love with you, because that would mean there'd be nights she'd stay up late worrying if you'd make it home all right. She'd have to cry herself to sleep every time you left without saying you loved her, and Mom's not gonna do that. Not for a million bucks."

Maggie came out with a glass of lemonade and set it down beside Jake. "Isn't she something?" she whispered. "I tell you, I love that girl."

Jake took the glass and stood up. All of a sudden he was parched. He downed the lemonade in one gulp, but it was sour, and it left him thirsty for more.

He whistled for his dogs and Sasha, as always, was the last to come. Jake waited by the truck until she trudged up next to him, her head down and pouting.

"For crying out loud," he said, but he still let her sit in the cab. He was going to retreat to his mountain and not come down for a week. He was going to get away before Savannah cast a spell on him, too.

He was clear to his driveway before his lips lost their pucker from the sour lemonade. He took a deep breath of cool mountain air and held it in until it stung. He was just starting to feel better when he walked into his cabin and saw the locked gun cabinet standing wide open. The rifle had not been moved, but all of a sudden the hair on the back of his neck stood on end. He whirled around, expecting to find an intruder behind him, but all he found was his old wallet, the one he'd tossed into the bottom of the cabinet thirteen years ago, thrown open on the dining room table.

The dogs were outside howling, and he knew why. The ghost was out there blowing smoke in their eyes. He'd sidled up next to them and now they were on their backs, rubbing off something awful. The ghost was trying to drive them all crazy, and it was starting to work.

Jake walked across the room and picked up the moldy wallet. Amazingly, it still reeked of fish and stale water after all this time. The single credit card and laminated driver's license were stuffed in the flap, along with a yellowed letter.

Even before he looked at the fireplace, he knew the key to the cabinet would still be hanging on the hook by the mantel, undisturbed. He knew, if he checked the cabinet for fingerprints, he would find only his own. He listened to his dogs howl, then he picked up the letter that his mother has forwarded him thirteen years ago.

> *Dear Mr. Grey:*
> *I found your wallet in December, washed up*
> *in Mesquite Cove. I swear all the money had*
> *disintegrated. There was nothing in it but*
> *your driver's license and the credit card, along*
> *with the oddest thing, a cream-colored tooth.*
> *There's been some crazy things going on*
> *here lately, but I ain't no busybody. I'm not*
> *asking any questions, and I'm not saying*
> *anything, unless, of course, somebody asks.*
> *Sincerely,*
>
> *Donald Reed*

The dogs stopped barking. They came in one after the other, their fur standing on end. Jake put the letter back in the wallet, then the wallet in the gun cabinet, and locked it.

Probably, he'd opened the gun cabinet during a nightmare last night; he'd done it before, though not in years. If the ghost had really been set on haunting him, he'd have managed to get a hold of that tooth Jake had flushed down the toilet thirteen years ago. He'd put a bloated body on the front doorstep. He'd stop messing around.

Jake walked out to the driveway and looked up. The ghost was not on the roof, but the air still reeked of tobacco. There was a godawful chill to the air.

He had one hell of a headache, and it got worse when the phone rang. He didn't go to answer it; he'd never bothered with an answering machine and sometimes, if he was lucky, whoever was calling just gave up. This time, though, the ringing wouldn't stop. Finally, he walked back inside and picked it up.

"Jake Grey," he said.

"They're draining the lake," a woman's voice said.

Jake leaned against the wall. "Mom?"

There was no answer. Whoever was on the other end had already hung up.


Cal Bentley liked to say he'd grown with the town. Back in 1959, when Prescott had one hardware store and less than ten thousand people, he'd been twenty-two years old and one hundred fifty pounds. Fresh out of the police academy in Phoenix, he'd been amazed society trusted him with a gun. He came from a long line of cops, but he was also young, and so in love with the prettiest girl in Prescott, anything could happen. If she left him for a richer man, he might lose his head and go on a shooting spree. If she stopped loving him, he might very well turn that gun on himself.

With thoughts like that, he was often amazed disaster never struck. If anyone had told him at twenty-two that he was going to get everything he wanted, he would have told them they were crazy, that no one had such luck.

He married Lois Akerman on June third, 1960. He gained weight right along with her when she got pregnant with their boy, Mike, and two years later, their girl, Lanie. She exercised most of hers off, but he grew accustomed to her blueberry pies, and he just kept growing. Now, nearly forty years after he showed up as a deputy sheriff in Yavapai County, he was chief of police and two hundred fifty pounds. Lois had tried to get him on all kinds of diets—all-protein, high-carb, Slim-Fast, Jenny Craig, but the truth was, being big worked to his advantage. Most of the punks he picked up for drunk driving or possession of marijuana knew he could smash them flat if he chose to, and because he hardly said a word, they could never read his intentions. They had no idea he wished they'd just go home and sleep off whatever was happening to them. They had no idea he felt guilty just looking at them, because the only difference between him and them was love and circumstance and plain old-fashioned luck.

He'd put away kids for life who were no worse than his own, and watched slick rapists walk away free. Forty years ago, he'd known black from white, he'd flashed his gun half a dozen times a day. In the last three months, he hadn't taken it out once. He was cutting people slack left and right and if someone asked him why, he'd have to state the truth: He wanted to even up the playing field. Everyone was a little criminal, even himself.

He started going bad two years ago, when he went to arrest a sixteen-year-old for prostitution. She'd been hanging out by Teton's Bar, propositioning anyone who looked like he could pay her twenty-five dollars. Cal had shown her his badge as soon as she got in the car, and she hadn't even tried to get away. She just slumped against the door and said "Fuck."

Her legs and arms were spindles, but her stomach was already melon-sized and hard. He estimated she was six months along.

"You got parents?" he asked.

"Not as far as I'm concerned."

Cal nodded. He had been fifty-nine years old at the time, and aiming to retire at sixty-two. He didn't need this shit anymore. Both his kids had gone to college, married decent people, and made the trek home for Christmas every year. He knew how good life could be when people did what they were supposed to.

He drove to the corner, parked, reached over and opened her door. "Get out," he said.

"You serious?"

He sat staring straight ahead until she'd gone. Then he drove back to Teton's, ordered an iced tea, and made sure she didn't come back.

Since then, he'd let everyone from dope fiends to graffiti sprayers to runaways go. He was risking everything, his ample retirement and the respect of every sheriff on the force, and he didn't give a damn. The problem was, he'd spent too much time with criminals. He'd begun to see their side.

In forty years on the force, he'd shot only one man, and even then he'd just knocked the automatic out of the thief's hand. In the hospital afterward, the man, a forty-year-old accountant who'd orchestrated a string of burglaries in the area, had flipped him off with his bandaged finger.

"Some cop," he'd said. "Can't even shoot straight."

Cal had leaned over the man and his nostrils flared. He'd smelled the same rank breath hundreds of times before, the kind that came from way down deep, where a man had begun to decay. It rose up on the breath of people who would never amount to anything and knew it. Men who based their lives on get-rich-quick schemes and women who hoped a man would save them. Every time Cal got a whiff of them, he thanked God for Lois and the kids. He thanked God he'd been lucky enough to live a long, boring life, and he worried that he was due for catastrophe.

"You're a sorry mess of a man," he'd said. "You're not worth the stain I'd get on my conscience from killing you."

Cal had a tally of arrests while on the force. Three hundred twenty for rape. Thirty-three hundred burglary charges. A remarkable ten thousand two hundred DUIs. It sounded bad, but in nearly forty years, in a county that had grown to one hundred and fifty thousand, it was about average. He'd closed every case in town, except one, and that one wasn't on the books. It was the mystery of Jake Grey.

Cal had met the man when he showed up in Prescott fifteen years ago and went to work for Ivan Olak, the cabinet maker. Lois had wanted new cherrywood kitchen cabinets, and he'd gone to Jake's apartment on the edge of town to pick up the estimate. When Jake opened the door and noticed Cal's uniform, he held out his hands, as if he were under arrest. His palms were up, revealing a scar on his left hand, puckered and blue. It had never been tended, that much was obvious. When Jake turned his hand slightly, Cal saw the scar on the other side too, a nice clean bullet wound, from the looks of it.

Over the years the scar would fade, but so would the man. Cal would watch Jake slowly cover up his face with a beard, and his life with dogs and deadwood, with no clue how to stop it.

"You're Jake, right?" he asked. "Ivan sent me out for the estimate."

Jake dropped his hands. He went for the estimate and held it out with his damaged hand.

"That's quite a scar there," Cal said.

Jake looked up. He wasn't scared, as far as Cal could tell. He was waiting. And in fifteen years, Cal had not changed his mind about Jake. The man was still waiting. More than anything, it seemed, he wanted to be found out.

Cal had tried to oblige him. He'd run him through the computer and come up with a social security number, previous jobs, driver's licenses. He'd discovered Jake had been born in Phoenix to Cheryl and Paul Grey. There was a death certificate on file for Paul Grey in 1972, cause of death cardiac arrest. Jake would have been eight at the time. Cheryl Grey remarried ten years later, her new husband a plumber named Roy Pillandro.

There was one outstanding bill on Jake's account, to Smith's Jewelers in Glendale. A half-carat diamond ring had never been paid off, and was eventually repossessed from its owner, Joanne Newsome.

The only other interesting piece of information was the missing persons report filed on Roy Pillandro in 1985, the year Jake turned up in Prescott. Roy was last seen on his forty-foot houseboat on Wawani Lake. He'd taken a single suitcase with him, and had not been heard from since.

Cal might have mentioned this, but that would have spoiled his afternoons at Jake's cabin. If there was something bad in his friend's past, he just didn't want to know about it. Better to stand silently on Jake's deck listening to the wind boomerang off Kemper Peak. When lightning flared, he didn't run for cover. He didn't even consider the fact that he could lose everything. He just stood on the highest point of Jake's deck and drank one of his friend's beers in pure silence. He watched the maniac dogs run in circles. When the fireworks fizzled at dusk, and hummingbirds swooped in, mistaking his old high-school ruby ring for nectar, he was struck by the truth: He was a lucky man.

"What is he to you?" Lois often asked him. "What on earth do you do up there, because I know for a fact, Cal Bentley, that that man never says a word."

Cal couldn't answer, because if he did, he would break his wife's heart. Jake was the man he would have been if he hadn't fallen in love with her. He did not tell her that sometimes, despite all his luck, he looked in Jake's eyes with pure envy.

So that was why the fax still sat on Cal's desk. He stood with his back to it, staring out his office window at a day that had begun with frost on the ground, and was ending in steam rising off the high desert floor. Earthquake weather, they called it in California. Here in Prescott, though, only people got shook up. Within a few hours, when the storms moved in off Kemper Peak, the calls would start coming in about juveniles terrorizing the neighborhood and honest men up and leaving their wives. If dry lightning sprang up, it was entirely possible all hell might break loose.

The fax was from Dan Merrill, a deputy assigned to Wawani Lake now that they were draining it for the new Desert Sky Reservoir. Desert Sky would provide water for homes from Phoenix to Las Vegas, turn the desert into a sea of green lawns and golf courses. Cal had never said a word about this, but when he'd picked up two environmentalists on charges of tree spiking up by Thumb Butte, he'd listened to their plan of dynamiting the new reservoir, and set them free.

Cal walked back to his desk. He picked up the paper and his stomach began to churn.

Lake draining turning up some interesting
things. Found an inordinate number of dead
dogs. Beer bottles. Condoms. Nobody's
swimming anymore, I can tell you that, but
the kids are hanging out, doping up,
searching for wreckage. Best of all, found
one of those ID bracelets, pretty corroded,
but could still make out the letters, ROY.
Records show a missing persons report filed
fifteen years back. Roy Pillandro. Once we
fill up the new reservoir and drain this baby
out, I have a feeling we're going to find our
man.

Dan

Cal dropped the paper. He'd burn it, if he thought it would do any good.

Instead, he picked up the phone and called Jake. "Have you got anything to tell me?" he asked.

Jake must have heard the tension in his voice, because for a long time, he didn't say a thing. Then one of the dogs barked, and he told him to be quiet.

"No," he finally answered. "Should I?"

Cal heard thunder cracking behind him, a storm swirling up out of nowhere. He picked up the fax, then unlocked his top drawer. He slipped it inside and relocked the drawer.

"Not for now," he said.

The old man's garden was a riot of scents; it either threw a dog into a frenzy of sniffing ecstasy, or just made her mad. Sasha fell into the latter category. She thought only two scents worthwhile: urine and food. One to mark territory, the other to satisfy desire. Anything else just complicated things, so every time Sasha padded through the old man's redolent garden, she didn't even grace it with her pee. Instead, she urinated on the concrete sidewalk, so at least one thing would be clear: Come closer only if you dared.

Today, Sasha followed the hat woman around the garden. She was that sweetest kind of human, smelling not of chemicals, but of what she'd eaten last, usually candy. As Sasha followed her, the garden lost its scent of confusion. It was no longer rock jasmine and chamomile this way, blueberry and a Doberman's urine over there; it smelled only of the woman, of peppermint sticks and Juicy Fruit gum.

The woman stopped and arched her back. She took off her sun visor, ran her fingers through her hair, then put the visor back on. She glanced at Sasha. "Come along then," she said.

They walked into the gazebo, and the woman sat on the redwood floor. Sasha circled her, feeling for indentations in the wood, the give of the floor. Finally, she chose a spot beside her and stretched out her aching legs.

The other dogs were in the street, chasing down a UPS truck. In seconds, Gabe was nipping at the brown bumper. He had no idea a shaggy mutt like him should not be able to run like that. It was some kind of gift from God. He leapt onto the van's bumper, then jumped off. Leapt on and jumped off again. Once the van turned the corner, Gabe threw back his head and howled into the air.

Sasha pressed her nose into the hat woman's pink belly. She wore a short halter top and skirt, with a gap of skin between so rich and moist, Sasha's head swam. Dogs did not believe in love at first sight. A dog's love had to be earned, but once it was, it couldn't be beaten out with whips or kicks or the meanest words. Nevertheless, Sasha was here, in love for no reason at all, pressing her nose against that belly, until the woman scratched her behind the ears and laughed.

"Greedy," the hat woman said. "That's what you are." She reached into her skirt pocket and pulled out a peppermint candy. She unwound the wrapper and held out the mint.

Sasha took it in her mouth and swirled it around her tongue. The sugar rush brought on the hallucination, because right in front of them, in deep shade, a pair of shadows crept toward them.

It was the woman and the good man. She was dancing and he was standing, then just when he started dancing too, she walked away. Sasha crushed the peppermint between her teeth and swallowed it.

"Well," the woman said. "Don't get me started on that."

Seven years ago, when Sasha had lived with sixteen other sled dogs in a ten-by-ten concrete kennel, she'd spotted the good man peering through the chain-link fence. The next day, the man scaled the fence and tossed each dog a steak bone. The day after that, he cut the fence with a pair of steel loppers. He cracked the chains shackling all sixteen sled dogs, and every one of them bolted for the woods. All except Sasha, who'd had to pull a twenty-mile trek that morning in subzero weather and at last turned on her owner, biting him through the neck before he beat her bloody for it.

The good man had picked her up gently and carried her to the cab of his truck. He had put a blanket on the seat inside, along with a bowl of water. He drove an hour without stopping, then finally pulled to the side of the road. Sasha bared her teeth when he reached for her, but he was either too stupid or brave to care. He found the single patch of her fur that wasn't bloody or scarred and stroked her there. He leaned his face down to hers.

She would have torn him to shreds, if she hadn't smelled the strange scent of his tears—fishy and rank, like sulfur. She had no pity, not since her owner beat it out of her, but nevertheless she licked the thin trails of tears at the corners of his eyes. He was ashamed to be human, and that was enough for her.

Back then, the good man talked very little, but when he did he yelled. He took his rifle out of the gun cabinet and jumped in his truck, the sweat on his arms charged with spite. Then for some reason he just stopped. He got out of the car and ran six grueling miles to the top of Kemper Peak. He ran until his heart was straining, and he was gasping for air. He let out a sound she hadn't known humans could make, the sound sled dogs made when they couldn't run anymore, but a man kept driving them forward anyway. The sound they made when they wished he'd whip them harder, so they could just die.

Despite the good man's kindnesses, Sasha occasionally thought of escape. When wolves passed through, she stood at attention on the deck, imagining running until her paws were bloody, taking down a rabbit and flinging it side to side in her jaws to break its neck. Then she heard the good man's quiet breathing in the cabin behind her, she felt the pull of him, almost like a tug on her collar, then like a caress. She turned her head away and let the wolves pass. She felt their scorn and understood it; nothing wild could understand that she could be trapped and content at the same time. Nothing untamed could comprehend that once she'd seen a man cry, she no longer needed adventure. She lived on love alone.

Rufus came to them the next year. Sasha was the first to notice him roaming the woods, so thin the first frost would kill him. Wherever he went, he left a trail of blood-lined feces and regurgitated grass.

The good man started leaving out food. First kibble on the ground, then rawhides on the stone steps, then a T-bone steak on the deck, which Rufus lunged at. Sasha let him eat the entire steak, bones and all, then she bolted out of the cabin and nipped his ear. Rufus cried out, then threw himself on his back—a good thing—or else she would have had to draw blood to show him who was in charge. He had welt marks on his nose, scabs on every inch of his paws and belly. When the good man saw the scars, he looked the same way she had when the wolves had passed through. As if he was debating the kind of man he wanted to be. As if he could go either way.

Six months later, they picked up a brown heap on the side of the highway, with its leg pointed in the wrong direction. Gabe was a mangy mess, and when Jake brought him to the vet, the woman said it would be kinder to put him to sleep. The good man didn't do anything but step forward, but the vet ran for her splints. After that, Gabe could run like the wind, like there were villains on his heels.

Sasha could still make them cower just by growling, but she could no longer outrun them. In the last year, her legs had started shrinking at different rates. She was off-kilter now, her front paws shorter and curled inward. She hurt all the time, and though she wasn't afraid of dying, she was afraid of leaving behind the one man who needed her.

The good man was in the back garden now, his face in shadows. She pushed herself to her feet. The pain whistled through her bones, but she was the meanest dog in town, so she didn't show it. She stepped off the gazebo and walked over to the good man. She pressed her snout against his leg and he reached down and stroked her. She had spent the last seven years trying to make him believe he was worth loving, but she had not succeeded. Every dog spent his or her life doing the same, but people were so stubborn; they saw their own greed and bitterness and cruelty and never bothered to look deeper, to their goodness, to the only parts of themselves dogs paid any attention to.

When the good man looked at her, she tried to tell him everything through her eyes: It was enough for one being to love you. Without him, she would have been another creature, she would have been vicious.

But he didn't see this. He never had. She watched his eyes harden and by the time the hat woman reached him, he was a man who could frighten anyone, if they didn't know he was really scared to death.

Savannah stood behind Jake as he attached the second arm to the bench without the benefit of nails. He used some intricate puzzle pattern, wood biscuits and glue. The sky reflected onto the sweat on his neck, turning his skin blue and glistening. His face, when he turned, was hard as stone.

She wandered around the garden, gathering clusters of pink flowers from the Juneberry trees. It was said the tree bloomed in April when the shad were running in the rivers, but this year, the fish must have been lazy. The flowers hadn't come up until May, and the leaves were just now turning from purple to green.

Since no one was interested in her fortune-telling, she had been spending her days extolling the lusciousness of Fulsom tomatoes, and her nights in the garden. It had gotten so she could dig down two feet and name a plant by the feel of its roots. She could identify a smell—jasmine, hibiscus, or freesia—ten feet away.

The other dogs raced back from the street now, tearing out black clumps of chamomile. They practically upended her as they passed, stirring up sawdust and leaves.

"You should get them under control," she said.

Jake didn't turn around. "How?"

Savannah snapped her fingers, and Sasha left his side for hers. She pressed her nose into Savannah's thigh.

"Impressive," Jake said. "But the others couldn't care less."

It was true. Rufus was peeing on the fussy rhododendrons, Gabe was running in circles around the mountain silver bell, cutting an ugly path through the Boston ivy.

Jake stood up. "They disappeared once for five days. When they came back, their paws were bloody. They wouldn't eat anything but raw meat for a month."

"You think that's impressive? A bit of wildness? Seems to me the real challenge would be to go beyond what you were born as. To discover what makes you exceptional."

She bent down to stroke Sasha's throat, and heard the rock music of the dog's heart. Out of the corner of her eye, she watched Jake's arms, and in the hush that followed, the muscles there tensed.

"I'd rather be ordinary," he said finally.

Savannah looked up. He was the kind of man she'd do well to steer clear of, because he had obviously never been loved right. He looked like someone she'd have to spend a lifetime rehabilitating with long, slow kisses.

"What about you?" he asked. "What's your area of greatness?"

Savannah was thankful for the diversion, and for the easiest question of all. "Emma," she answered.

She walked around the garden, touching the velvet tops of the lilies. She stole glances at Jake, watching him hunch forward over his work.

"How long have you told fortunes?" Jake asked suddenly.

She snipped off a pure white lily and held it up to her nose. "I learned the tarots right after high school. In one way or another, I've been trying to make a go of it ever since."

"What does your husband think of that?"

"Ex-husband," Savannah said automatically. "He thinks it's a crock of shit, but that's because he was always drawing the Moon."

Jake crouched down on his heels, like a catcher. He was not working now, just staring at what he'd done. "What's the appeal of fortune-telling?"

"Are you kidding? I can change a person's life just by letting them know good things are coming. It isn't sorrow that kills people. It's thinking the sorrow will never end."

"What if you're wrong?"

"Oh, I'm never wrong. Good news comes to everyone eventually, especially when they're looking for it. I tell my clients to make ten wishes a day. God likes that kind of greed. The more you want, the more you get. The more you get, the happier you are. The happier you are, the more God likes it. So wish, wish, wish. Out of ten wishes, one is bound to come true."

Jake stood up straight and stiff. He had not wished in years, anyone could see that. His hands were closed tight, so that even if a falling star headed straight for him, he wouldn't be able to catch it.

"Here," she said, "let me try something."

She put the flower in her pocket and walked to his side. She took his left hand and had to pry it open; even then his fingers kept curling back down protectively. He had a three-quarter-inch scar in the middle of his palm. She ran her finger over it, then across the domed calluses. He tensed, but when she looked up he was staring past her, into the setting sun.

"I'm not very good at this," she said. "My friend Ramona is the palm reader, but she's taught me a few things." She traced her finger along his lifeline. "You've had to change course. You see this break here? You went in a new direction, while your break went on its own path. You see? It will swing around and meet you again. You will come full circle."

When he finally met her gaze, she couldn't tell a thing about him. It was entirely possible he was the madman people whispered about, but she thought it was just as likely he was someone in desperate need of kissing.

She didn't think, just rose up on her tiptoes, and even then she only reached his bottom lip. He didn't even kiss her back for a moment, that's how stunned he was. Then he slipped his arms around her waist and lifted her up to meet him, and something raw slipped out of his throat.

She had never been careful who she kissed. Most men needed kissing, in her opinion. But she might have made a mistake kissing this one, because once he started, he wasn't about to let go.

But suddenly he set her down and stepped back, out of touching distance. She wanted to pull him back, but he gestured toward the house, where her father was coming out, a sweatshirt pulled on over his pajamas.

Doug was waving a piece of paper in his hands. "The first carving for the bench," he said.

He weighed one hundred thirty pounds now; three months ago, he had been one sixty-eight. He had lost all his hair, but at least the radiation treatments were over and he could make it to the garden for a few minutes now and then. Every morning, Savannah read his fortune, and she didn't even stop to consider all the Swords and Fives she'd taken out of the deck. The cards would find a way to tell the truth even without the worst cards, but what her father needed now was not close calls, but the World or the Ten of Pentacles. He needed extravagant possibilities. He needed to be assured, absolutely, that everything would be all right.

Doug held up the piece of paper. The skin on his wrist bubbled with gooseflesh, though it was over ninety, and even the black-eyed Susans were bending over in the heat. He started across the cobblestone walk, teetering on the uneven stones, but Jake bridged the gap in seconds, in three huge steps. He steered Doug to the porch swing, the one Doug had painted in bright yellow, and helped him sit down.

"See?" Doug said, oblivious. He held out the drawing. "I've finally come up with the perfect thing. The first carving ought to be of Superstition Mountain." He turned to Savannah and smiled. "That's where I asked your mother to marry me. That's when my life began."

Savannah stepped up on the porch. She sat beside him on the swing, while Jake studied the drawing.

"It was late in the day," Doug went on. "Everyone else had already headed on down the mountain, but your mother wouldn't leave. She held her arms up to the sky, and I swear, she caught the setting sun in her hands. Her hair turned this blistering shade of copper. I tell you, I think she swallowed the sun."

Savannah smiled and took his hand, though she didn't believe a word of it. Her mother closed her drapes against the sun every day. She didn't hike any farther than the outlet mall.

"How could I not ask her to marry me then?" Doug asked. "She was made of fire."

"And she said yes."

Doug laughed. "Oh no. She said, 'No way. Not until I start fashion school and hitch up with Delorosa's in New York and then start my own line. Maybe ten years down the road.'"

"But it didn't happen like that, because of me."

"You made it better."

"She never got what she wanted."

"Well, that all depends on how you look at it," Doug said. "It depends on how much Maggie is willing to admit on a given day."

Savannah looked up at Jake. He tucked the drawing into his shirt pocket, then stared right back at her. He had eyes as blue as ice, and he didn't blink.

"I'll get going on this carving," he said.

He walked around the side of the house. She hadn't swallowed the sun, but she still felt on fire. Already, she had forgotten how cool fog could be. She was having trouble remembering why she'd wanted to avoid Jake in the first place.

"Nice man," Doug said.

Savannah tensed, but when she turned to her father, his eyes were closed. She might have even thought he was sleeping, if a smile hadn't crept slowly across his lips.

# SEVEN

## THE FIVE OF WANDS ❧ CRUEL BOYS

When Emma came out of English composition class, Eli Malone was standing in the hall, deftly twirling a lit cigarette around his thumb and forefinger. Girls covered their throats when they passed him, tough boys dared each other to say hello. Only Ron Braverman, a punk in his own right who pulled a knife on a gym teacher last year, managed a mumbled, "Hey." Mrs. Coffman, Emma's English teacher, bolted her door. She used her cell phone to call security.

"You're not so tough," Emma said, though her palms had gone sweaty. The closest thing to a hoodlum Mission High had was Johnny Lazarus, a senior who played Iago with stunning wickedness. Outside the theater, though, he was all show. He pretended to run people down with his motorcycle, but always stopped five feet away, ten if they were children.

Eli Malone, on the other hand, had a deep purple aura, the color of a bad bruise. Beneath the fluorescent hall lights, he did not cast a shadow. And when he dragged on his cigarette, she heard it hiss going down.

"So," he said. "You got another class?"

"Who's asking?"

Eli shrugged. The bell rang, and the far doors to the hall opened. Two armed security guards, hired after boys started demanding less homework with loaded .38's, started down the hall. Eli tossed his cigarette on the vinyl floor and ground it out with his black boot.

"Whatever," he said, then started for the door.

"Wait!"

Emma had egged a few houses in Danville, but beyond that she'd never done a bad thing in her life. She didn't know how to go about it. She'd never been in love before either, and she could not believe what she was feeling was the start of it because it felt like nausea. A swirl of the Diet Coke and Twix bar she'd eaten for lunch, a light panic that turned her skin green. She thought she could just as easily hate him.

"Yeah?" he said.

The security guards were running now, so the decision had to be made in a split second. But falling in love, she figured, was not something she could take time considering. She'd just have to do it. Drop her Peechee folder, take his hand, and run.

Eli flung open the doors and pulled her across campus, zigzagging around buildings until they lost the guards. He held her hand until they got to the parking lot, then he abruptly let go. He unlocked his Corvette, but didn't open her door for her, as if he were giving her one last opportunity to turn and run. Instead, she hopped in and strapped on her seat belt. When he peeled out, it was all Emma could do not to cling to the door or beg for mercy. She dug her fingernails into her jeans and didn't say a word.

He drove toward Granite Mountain at breakneck speed, the radio on so loud Emma could not tell what was playing. The interior of the car smelled of marijuana, but it had also been restored—a new leather dash, thick black fur seat covers, eight premium speakers in the back.

Eli took a sharp left off Granite Basin, then another left on an unmaintained dirt road. Five jarring minutes later, he pulled up in front of an old cabin.

"Home sweet home," he said, but he did not get out of the car.

Emma stared at the shack. It was burnt on one side, with a sagging corrugated-steel roof. The walls were a mix of weathered two-by-fours and cast-off plywood. There was only one window, and it was too dirty to see through. A red steel door had been jerry-rigged into the frame; it must have been ripped off someone's fancy house.

She couldn't look at the shack without crying, but she knew he didn't want to see that. She stopped her tears, threw off her seat belt, and got out of the car.

The front door was unlocked, the interior so dark, she could make out nothing except a nauseating stench of bacon. She ran a hand along the wall for a light switch. As soon as she flipped it on, she wished she hadn't. The whole place was little more than a single room, pitched precariously downhill to the right. The floorboards were rough cedar, and the second one she stepped on cracked beneath her feet. An old woodstove, coated in dust, squatted in the corner. Everything inside looked a thousand years old, except for the stereos and televisions still in their original boxes, stacked along the far wall.

For a long time, she just stared at the stolen goods. Her two feelings wouldn't jibe, the rush of protectiveness she felt for anyone living in a place like this and the desire to turn him in.

Eli leaned against the doorjamb, his hands in his pockets. She tried to figure how a person got to this point, but she couldn't do it. That was the trouble with being loved and well cared for; it often made disasters seem improbable, when actually they happened every day.

"So?" she said. "What now?"

Eli took his hands out of his pockets. He flicked back his hair and, for a moment, seemed unsure what to do. Then he shrugged. "Come on. I'll show you the view."

They hiked to the top of Granite Mountain, where they had a clear view down to Granite Basin Lake and the summer campers, living in more luxury while they roughed it than Eli did normally. Emma picked up a stone and tossed it over the edge, but it got lodged in a tree halfway down the slope. Eli picked up a hand-sized rock and heaved it over. It cleared the tree and kept on falling. In a minute or two, it might scare the bejeezus out of some kids roasting marshmallows, it might whack a perfectly nice woman on the head.

Emma lay down in the moist grass, while Eli sat beside her, torturing the blades. He plucked off the brown tops, then yanked whole clumps of sod out by the roots. He tossed his victims one by one over the cliff.

"How'd you find this place?" Emma asked.

"What's to find? Nobody else will live here."

"How long have you been here?"

Eli glared at her. He picked up a rock and stuffed it down a snake hole. Emma held her breath, wondering if next he'd take to killing small animals with his bare hands, just to show her how unsalvageable he was.

"Look," he said, "just listen around town and you'll hear what they say about me. My dad's a drunk, and my mom keeps pushing liquor on him 'cause that's the only time he's nice. It's in all the papers."

"What about you?"

"Don't you get it? I'm bad blood. I'm bad all the way through."

Then she couldn't have stopped herself if she tried, which she didn't. She sat up, grabbed his hand, and held on tight. She fell in way over her head. She'd dreamt about falling in love all her life, and gotten everything wrong. Turned out it had nothing to do with what was good for her. Already, her losses were mounting—half a day of classes, the desire to be with anyone else—and it was only going to get worse. In love's twisted way of thinking, Eli Malone was the most beautiful thing on this earth. She leaned forward and kissed him straight on the mouth. His lips were cold as river water, and that just made her love him more.

She pulled away long enough to tell him, "Don't you believe what they say about you. Don't believe anyone but me."

He looked like one big ball of pain, so she kissed him again, harder, until he uncurled right into the palm of her hand.

Savannah was ripping up lettuce in her mother's kitchen when she heard the squeal of the Corvette. It came around the corner on two wheels and sent the crows shrieking. Eli Malone bolted into the driveway, cigarette dangling from his lips, and cut the engine. Emma was in the seat beside him, looking enraptured.

Maggie set down the carrots she'd been peeling and glanced at the clock. "Three hours and twenty minutes late," she pointed out, as Eli and Emma stepped out of the car in a cloud of smoke. "Don't tell me you haven't been worried sick."

Savannah said nothing. She'd had a lump in her throat for three hours, but she wasn't about to admit that. She dropped the lettuce in the bowl, turned her back on her mother, and walked outside.

Jake was crouched by his bench; he only glanced at her, then went back to his work. He'd already etched out a slim crescent moon, and now he carved deep into the spine of Superstition Mountain. Savannah walked past him and through the jasmine-twined gazebo. Emma and Eli had sat down on the small patch of chamomile and when Emma leaned her head back, Eli reached out to pull a pine needle out of her hair.

Savannah's throat went dry. She didn't need her cards to realize that sometime between this morning and now, Emma had slipped right through her fingers into someone else's palm.

Eli saw her coming first, and tossed back his hair to reveal bloodshot eyes. When she got close enough, she could smell the marijuana still clinging to both of them, and then she regretted every single joint she'd smoked, because that left her with very little room to argue.

She looked at her daughter, who was suddenly enamored with the furry texture of chamomile leaves. "Where have you been, honey?" she asked.

"School," Emma said, not looking up. "Eli brought me home."

"You're a little late."

"We went driving," Emma said. "No big deal."

Eli lit a cigarette, and inhaled and exhaled without removing it from his lips. Savannah imagined young girls and senior citizens fainted from the mean look in his eyes. She imagined he thought himself gangster material. But teenage boys did not scare her. When they had come to her house for fortunes, they usually demanded she tell them they were going to make a million dollars, or lose their parents in plane crashes. Instead, when she laid out her cards and said that, actually, this one would find the girl of his dreams, and that one's mother's cancer would go into remission, they usually got real quiet. When one of them started crying, she didn't say a single word.

So now, she just bent down and plucked the cigarette from between Eli's lips. She crushed it beneath her sneaker.

"I inherited only one thing from my mother," she said, "and that's eyes in the back of my head."

"So?"

"So watch yourself. Emma is fifteen. Anything you do with her is quite possibly a felony."

"Mom!" Emma stood up, outraged. Well, maybe Savannah was outraged too. Maybe it was her worst nightmare to sound like her own mother, and she never would have if Emma hadn't started something neither one of them would be able to stop.

"How old are you?" she asked Eli.

He got to his feet. "Nineteen." He was thin and nervous as a jackal. Even from two feet away. Savannah could hear the beat of his heart, fast and frantic, the kind bound to wear itself out early.

"I don't think you should be bringing my daughter home," she said.

"Oh, Mom, come on," Emma broke in. "He was doing me a favor. Jake vouches for him. Don't you, Jake?"

Savannah turned around to find Jake behind them. She hadn't even heard him come up. When he looked at Eli, the boy, whether he knew it or not, shrunk a good two inches. His heart slowed to the beat of a ballad. Jake could have squashed him flat, but all he said was "Yes, I do."

Savannah wrapped her arms around her waist. "Well, then, that settles that. Go on in, Emma. I'm sure you've got a lot of homework."

Emma glanced at Eli, then turned and ran to the garage apartment. As soon as she was gone, Eli lit another cigarette.

"Emma says you tell fortunes," he said.

"Yes."

"You believe in that crap?"

Savannah's mouth twitched. "If you mean by crap that there's a force in the universe greater than ourselves, then yes, I believe in it."

"Jesus." Eli shook his head then started after Jake.

"You are the Five of Wands," Savannah called after him. "Don't think I don't understand."

Eli stopped, then turned around slowly. "What's that supposed to mean? Stop trying to freak me out."

Savannah walked up to him, until she was just inches from his face. Before he could even consider she might be a worthy opponent after all, she was twisting the skin of his arm.

"I give Emma the benefit of the doubt," she said, "but you're another story. I've got no reason to trust you, and believe me, I don't."

She let go and walked to the garage. Later, when Eli was helping Jake with the bench, she would lay out her tarot cards on the porch, Five of Wands on top. She would wait until he was sweating, until he had that card in hand, before she told him the Five of Wands was the battle of life—unsatisfied desires, the struggle to overcome losses. It was a mimic of warfare, and if played right, it could very well mean victory. But if played wrong, it often meant that boys who weren't rich or smart or popular often could think of nothing else to be but cruel.

Mabel Lewis was the first and only person to win a fight against the MesaLand homeowners board. The covenants were clear: All exterior paint colors had to be neutral and non-offensive, harmonious with the landscape (meaning brown), and approved by the ten-member architectural committee of the MesaLand Homeowners Association—all retired widowers with nothing better to do than bicker over the exact composition of ecru. Noncompliance would result in financial and legal penalties and, if still unresolved, a lien against the property.

Mabel Lewis had never read the covenants, and even if she had, she still would have painted her bungalow limestone green with banana cream shutters. She'd lost her husband three years ago and, with those chest pains she'd been getting recently, she was probably only a few years, maybe months, from joining him herself. What was the point of being non-offensive now? She would never get back her singing voice, or fill a young man with lust again. She might as well be a troublemaker.

The day of her official hearing, she wore her first miniskirt. She was seventy-two, with hair white as bone, but she'd swum a hundred laps every day for fifty years—it was about time her legs did her some good. She sat down in front of Ben Hiller and Dave Tripp, president and vice president of the board, and hiked up her skirt.

Ben Hiller just about keeled over in his chair. At one time, Mabel would have gotten a rush from that. At one time, she had found Ben interesting. There had been talk, when he and his wife Helen first moved to

MesaLand, of the two of them buying a boat and sailing around the world, or him going alone to Everest, to become the oldest man to reach the summit, preferably without oxygen. Then Helen had gotten sick, and Ben had stopped playing golf and walking the mall. The day after Helen died, he sold his car, and now wouldn't even ride the bus anymore. He paid some teenager to pick up his groceries, and he talked to all his relatives via E-mail. He only got revved up about the homeowners board, so Mabel decided she'd give him something else to think about, namely her.

She had splashed herself with that new Calvin Klein perfume, and already Ben's eyes were watering. She hiked her skirt up another inch.

"When Ed died," she said, "I thought I'd remember everything about him. I thought I'd be haunted by him, and that was some comfort, but now I can't even remember the color of his eyes unless I'm looking at a photograph. They were this funny kind of green, real light, like limestone."

She looked at Ben and saw she was not getting through. He had already raised his pen above the form that would start costing her hundreds of dollars a day in attorney's fees. She hiked her dress up one more time.

"And besides," she went on, "I just wanted to do something a little bit bad."

Ben Hiller dropped his pen. He turned to Dave Tripp, but Dave was beet red and coughing up phlegm. Ben picked up the complaint signed by twenty-eight homeowners and ripped it in two.

"Maybe we could have dinner sometime, Mabel," Dave said, once he'd recovered from his coughing fit. Mabel stood up. She smoothed down her skirt and smiled. She still had all her teeth, and thankfully she'd never gotten latte-mad like Wendy Ginger, so they were relatively white. She decided on the spot to wear miniskirts every day for the rest of her life, and also to turn down all offers. She adored being called baby and mistaken for a fifty-year-old, but she had also loved Ed Lewis with all her heart and she just didn't want anyone else touching her.

She might be within five pounds of her high-school weight and a looker in three-inch heels, but she had cried herself to sleep for three years straight. Not even her children would guess she hadn't slept on her own side of the bed since Ed died. She wore Ed's pajamas and slept in the indentation he'd left behind. Right around midnight, if she was very quiet, she would swear on a stack of bibles she heard Ed's heart beating inside her own chest.

Ed had died of a stroke at seventy-eight. Their three children, split among the big states, California, Texas, and Florida, had told her they were thankful he'd lived a good long life. Her children were fools. They hadn't lived long enough to know seventy-eight was nothing. Ed had just been getting started. He'd finally gotten over his fear of water and had booked them on a cruise to Fiji. He had taken to making love to her on the back patio, at noon, when anyone could come by and see them.

The evening after the hearing, Mabel changed to a firetruck-red miniskirt and stepped out her front door. Simon Wasserstein, watering begonias next door, dropped his jaw, but she didn't even wave. Mabel walked down the street, making the widowers groan from their porches. She sashayed down Sage Street and up the garden path to the sign that read *Amazing Fortune-teller—Know Your Future*. She glanced behind her, hoping one of the harpies from her bridge club would see her, so she'd start a scandal.

Two days ago, all the bridge ladies had talked about was Savannah Dawson.

"The nerve she has," Carol Vicenzo had said. "Preying on old people with that New Age mumbo jumbo."

"She's from San Francisco," Wendy Ginger joined in, after gorging herself on a vanilla latte. "They'll let anybody live there. Hippies, homosexuals, Jerry Brown, they don't care."

"Have you seen the way she dresses?" Carol went on. "Those dresses you can see through?"

"And what's with the hats?" Barb French chimed in. "Is that some kind of West Coast thing? I don't understand why Maggie Dawson hasn't done something. It's shocking."

Mabel had gone to her liquor cabinet and poured a hefty snifter of gin into her tea. Then she stared them all down.

"Don't talk to me about shocking," she'd said. "Shocking is when someone ups and dies on you. Shocking is going to a funeral every other weekend, the way we do, and then still getting together for mahjongg, as if it isn't killing us. That girl . . . that girl is just lovely."

Now, she smoothed down her miniskirt and knocked on the garage door. She didn't even look at the main house. She knew Doug Dawson was dying, and this was a thing she could not bear to see again. Four of her friends had lost husbands since Ed had died, and they had all assumed she'd be the first one to comfort them, that she'd want to spend hours having tea and crying. They were wrong. She did her grieving at night, while lying in Ed's imprint. Her grieving was between her husband and her.

Savannah Dawson opened the door. The girl was dressed in a blue gauze dress that fell to her ankles. It was so sheer Mabel could make out the dark swirl of her navel, a fact that would have horrified her neighbors, but which, for some reason, perked Mabel right up.

"I'm here about the fortune-telling," Mabel said. "I don't have an appointment."

Savannah had already swung open the door. "Oh, that's all right. Come on in. Jiminy, just let me clear a place."

Mabel walked into the garage apartment and laughed out loud. Flamboyant clothes were draped over a foldout cot, hats took up every bit of counter space. The table was heaped with newspaper grocery store ads, but Savannah swept it all aside.

A girl slept on a cot in the corner, her yellow hair spilt over the pillows. Mabel was fairly certain she'd seen her before. She squinted, then placed her. She'd been one of the girls in Eli Malone's Corvette, one of the girls who had no idea she was just one of the girls.

"You're one of my neighbors," Savannah said.

"Mabel Lewis. Two blocks over. The green house."

"Oh, the green house! I love that place. You come around the corner and, pow, you let out a breath you didn't even know you were holding."

Mabel sat down. Savannah was diving deep into a mound of hats on the counter. "I've got my cards right here," she said, although all she'd come up with so far were purple pillboxes and a feather-coated bowler.

Mabel had woken with a headache—that was how she'd known change was coming. Up until then, she'd had only two headaches her whole life—the day she met Ed at the horse races, and the morning he died. This new one stumped her. What could possibly happen to her now, with her husband in a grave, her house paid off, and her children so busy they couldn't be bothered to visit more than once a year?

Savannah finally located her cards on the bottom. "Ta-dah!" She handed them to Mabel and sat down. "This is so great. Just shuffle and think of what you want to know."

Mabel shuffled the cards and tried to focus on her future, but all she kept thinking about was Ed—how he'd been the slickest bettor at the horse races that day she'd met him, fifty-five years ago. He'd sized up each race, then bet on long shots, winning two out of every three. He started with one hundred dollars and ended with fourteen hundred. He came alone and ended the day surrounded by a horde of people who considered him their best friend.

He had pushed past them all to come sit beside Mabel, who had been spending her first day at the track with her parents. Luckily for her, her parents had just gone to get the car.

"You want to know the secret?" he'd whispered in her ear. She'd gotten shots of pleasure all down that side. She fell in love in two seconds flat.

"Sure."

"Multiples of seven," he said. "First race, one times seven is seven, right? So I picked Chariot. Seven letters. Then second race, two times seven. King of the Track."

"What if there are no multiples of seven?"

"Multiply by seven, divide by three, forget the leftovers. Sometimes add seven again. Fourth race. Four times seven divided by three is nine something. That's Jokester."

"Jokester has eight letters," Mabel pointed out.

He looked down at his winning ticket, then up at her. He burst out laughing, revealing a quarter-inch gap between two front teeth that she would never let him fix.

"Well," he said. "That's marvelous. Looks like I'm just lucky."

Mabel smiled now as she handed the cards back to Savannah. "I want to know what's going to change."

Savannah nodded. She reached back on the counter and chose a gaudy lace bonnet, with two purple feathers sticking out the left side. She put it on her head. Then, with ruby-red fingernails, she turned over six cards. Mabel saw men with swords, naked women, suns.

"Your distant past is the Queen of Pentacles." Savannah pointed to a woman on a silver throne, holding a gold star. "You were influenced greatly by a noble soul. A rich and generous person."

Mabel reached out to touch the card and winced: The plastic was red hot. She glanced up at Savannah, to see what kind of trick this was, but the woman had moved on to the next card.

"More recently," Savannah went on, "you suffered a great loss. You have the Nine of Swords here. Nines often mean the culmination of things, sometimes an ending. Together with the Queen of Pentacles, my guess is that you lost the one you loved."

Mabel drew her hand away. It didn't take a genius to guess that. Half this community was grieving widows. Still, her fingers tingled. She ran them through her white hair and the ends curled up. Savannah was looking over the cards, so polite she did not say a word about the purple haze that had suddenly appeared above the table, strung out like taffy. The girl in the corner, though, had woken and was sitting up. She looked where Mabel looked, right beneath the pizza-parlor lamp, where the haze became a purple cloud a foot thick.

"This is what crosses you," Savannah said. "The Tower, reversed. That's entrapment. Following old ways, even when they're outdated. See, you have to read the cards by their relationship to each other. If you add your future . . ."

"What's my future?" Mabel asked, tearing her eyes from the purple cloud, which was billowing out and coming her way.

"The King of Cups. The card of a professional, and a pleaser. You know what I think? I think you've been doing things because you thought you were supposed to. But the Tower is telling you it doesn't have to be like that. You can make some serious changes. The King of Cups often comes to artists or scientists, someone enamored with their career. What's your career?"

Mabel sat back. She could feel the prickle of that cloud above her head. A purple tentacle slipped under the curl on her forehead and stroked her skin. It had fingers like warm ice. She could feel that girl watching her.

"Emma, honey," Savannah said. "Could you make us some tea?"

The girl got up slowly, then walked into the makeshift kitchen. She had on a white silk blouse that was glowing purple, and Mabel did not understand why no one remarked on this. While the girl opened a tea packet and lit a match to the Coleman stove, that cloud swirled around and tickled the back of Mabel's neck. It was some kind of trick, it had to be, but Mabel was crying anyway because the cloud smelled like mint, like Ed's favorite cologne.

"My husband always wanted me to go back to school," Mabel said. "I stopped for the children. You know how it was. And then I was fifty by the time they all left home, and it would have been silly. I wanted to be a molecular scientist. If I started now, I'd be dead before I got to graduate school."

Savannah was looking right at the tendrils of that cloud, but she didn't even blink. Perhaps it wasn't a trick, just an old woman losing her mind. Suddenly, she couldn't get the tune of "My Girl," Ed's favorite song, out of her head.

Savannah dealt out four more cards. "This card puts you in perspective," she said, pointing to the first. "It is the Six of Cups, the card of memory. Things that have vanished."

Mabel cried harder, which she knew looked horrid on a woman her age. She turned her head away, but by then Savannah had gotten out of her chair and come around beside her. She knelt down and slipped an arm around Mabel's waist.

"What was his name?" she asked.

"Edward."

"Well, look at that. The card for secrets and fears is the Hanged Man. That's the card of sacrifice. It means he'll go now so you can move on. The Hanged Man is a life in suspension, Edward's life, and now it's time to let him go."

Mabel looked up and, that quickly, the purple cloud was gone. She knew, even if she listened as hard as she could tonight, she was not going to hear Ed's heartbeat. Savannah kept hold of her, which was a good thing, because she felt capable of tumbling right out of her chair. She felt capable of believing in just about anything.

"Your final result," Savannah said, pointing to the last card, "is the Three of Cups, the card of solace. Whatever happens, it's going to be all right."

By the time Emma brought the tea, Mabel had cried herself dry. It was mint tea, and that could have explained the scent in the room, but no one could convince her of that, not for a million dollars. She drank the tea and touched each card. They were only warm now, and when she got home, she had no doubt that imprint on Ed's side of the bed would be gone. It wouldn't matter which side she slept on, and she'd probably just sell the bed anyway, because college dorms came furnished.

When Savannah walked her to the door, Mabel reached into the tiny pocket of her miniskirt and took out a fifty-dollar bill.

Savannah shook her head. "I haven't got change."

"I wouldn't give you a penny less."

They stepped out into the garden. The streetlamps had already come on, and the air brushed against them like velvet. A pair of crows streaked out of the eastern sky, and Mabel jumped.

"Don't listen to what people say," Savannah told her. "There is no bad luck in nature. When you hear a crow squawking, it's a sign you'll soon be finding your heart's desire. Black widow spiders on the windowsill mean faded love is about to get a polish, snakes in the bathroom are telling you to expect adventure."

"This is all crazy," Mabel said.

Savannah laughed and pushed her ridiculous hat back up on her head. "Well, sure. But that doesn't mean it isn't true."

By the time Savannah got back inside the garage, that bit of fog, or whatever it had been, was gone. She flipped the light on and off, to see if it had been some kind of wiring malfunction. She walked to the drapes and held her fingers up behind them, to see if something strange could sneak through.

"You saw that?" she asked Emma, who was sitting in the corner.

"Saw what?"

Savannah dropped the drapes and stared at her

daughter. When Emma was seven, she had sneaked Savannah's tarot cards into her bed every night and fingered the Sun so much she had worn out the edges. She had fallen in love with the whole suit of Cups.

But the other day, she had scoffed when Savannah drew the pregnant Ace of Wands for a girl from Prescott High.

"She's only going to be a sophomore," Emma had said. "Nothing meaningful can happen in high school, believe me. It's some kind of rule."

Since school had let out, Emma had taken to drinking lemonade with Maggie on the back porch and catalog shopping like mad. Now, when something magical happened right in front of her, Emma was not about to admit it.

"Don't be so hasty to get cynical," Savannah said. "You've got plenty of time."

Emma shrugged and sat down on her cot. She picked up a bottle of blue nail polish and started to paint her toes.

Savannah gathered up the cards. She put the Swords and the Devil back in every morning, after she'd read her father's fortune, so Mabel Lewis had gotten a fair reading. Now, while the room still smelled of a man's minty cologne, she shuffled them quickly. To get at her heart's desire, she couldn't think at all. Fast as she could, she spread the cards out on the table and sat down to read her own fortune.

Her crossing card was still the Eight of Swords, bad news coming. She rapped her knuckles on the table; for the first time, she got a little mad at what she'd dealt.

"Come on, come on."

She actually considered reshuffling and starting again, but that would have been worse than removing the bad cards, that would have made all her readings suspect. She laid out the rest, ending with the Ten of Pentacles, the card of bad odds, a gamble with potential for great losses.

"Emma?" she said, without turning around. "I think we ought to go home."

All of a sudden Emma was standing beside her. "I'm not going anywhere," Emma said, and it was obvious she wasn't. If she could have, she would have sunk herself half an inch deep in the concrete floor.

"I thought you wanted to go back."

"Well, I don't." Emma stepped right onto one of Savannah's hats, a green beret, and smashed it flat. "You know what I think?"

Savannah realized she did not. This girl wearing a silk blouse mail-ordered from Nordstrom's was a stranger. She wore blue fingernail polish and never spoke unless spoken to, and then she did it with such truculent words, Savannah wished she would just stop.

"I think you're afraid things might get a little ugly here," Emma said. "I think you're looking for a place to hide."

"I'm not hiding."

Emma raised her voice. "That's all you ever do. You're chicken. Stop taking out all the swords. You're not fooling anybody."

Savannah stood up slowly. Emma was already taller than she was by an inch and would just keep growing. Very soon, she would be entirely out of her reach.

"I'm scared of one thing," she said. "That something might happen to you."

"Well, don't be. I'm fine. I'm capable of taking care of myself."

"This is about Eli, right? You want to stay because of Eli."

Emma didn't answer. She didn't have to; her skin was flushed with longing. Savannah sat down again. She was afraid for her daughter, all right, but the real reason her throat tightened was that she had never looked as radiant as Emma did now. She had never grown luminously pale, miserably beautiful. Moonlight did not lust after her, following her into dark houses or behind the shadows of oak trees.

"The thing with Eli is . . ." Savannah began.

"What? That he's poor? That nothing's ever gone his way? I know what you think. You think happiness is a choice, but that's only true until your luck sours. Until all your gods and angels leave you and you have to stand alone, the way Eli has. Just wait, Mom. Just wait until your luck leaves you."

Savannah didn't say that it already had. When she reached out for Emma, her daughter was already halfway across the room, her heart even farther, out there somewhere in a boy's black Corvette. Savannah's luck had left her as soon as she started wishing for a nice boy and easy life for her daughter, because to a fifteen-year-old, that was a threat. That was the moment she got a mutinous look in her eye, and went looking for exactly the opposite.

# EIGHT

### FOUR OF PENTACLES ❧ YEARNING

O nce school let out for the summer, Emma's life became a complete and utter waste. She could have stayed in bed all day, and it wouldn't have made any difference, except she would have had to put up with the crazy old people. Since Mabel Lewis and the purple cloud scam, her mother's business had gone hogwild. Savannah took an hour a day to publicize grapes for a dollar a pound, and spent the rest of her time with pathetic widows hoping to talk to dead men.

Emma didn't believe any of it. Her mother had staged some kind of trick, that's all, to get the fortunetelling ball rolling. Indoor clouds were made with steamers, an old man's aftershave bought at the five-and-dime. Didn't these fools know her mother wrote lies for a living? Everything she did was accomplished with a lot of chutzpah and a trick of the light.

Still, it was just as well her mother was busy; otherwise, Savannah might want to talk. Emma had nothing to say, not a single word that wouldn't sound dangerously demented. She had not thought it possible to go stark raving mad from wanting someone, but now she knew it could happen. Eli had not come around for two weeks, and her mind and body had started to decay without him. She couldn't form any sentence that didn't begin with his name. She cried at the drop of a hat, at the swish of her mother's dresses, at lightning that died out just as she was getting used to it. And she was racked with fever, one hundred and three morning, noon, and night. Her mother told her to rest, but that was worse. When she slept she dreamed of Eli, of kissing him enough to make up for every waking hour he was denied her. When she woke, she was worn down and raw.

She was not the only one. Every day, her grandfather sat in a chair by his bedroom window, puckering his lips at every brown-tipped leaf. He'd been able to make it to the garden for a week or two, then suddenly turned frail again. In the last few days, his aura had gotten blacker, and though she would never say this out loud, she thought it might be better for some people to just die rather than dragging it out forever. She thought a man should be able to get to his own garden, and if he couldn't, well then, that was telling him something.

Lately, the only thing that had made Emma even remotely happy was shopping. Her grandmother had entrusted her with a credit card, and she'd ordered four hundred dollars' worth of jeans and shirts from Eddie Bauer. She was in one of her new pima cotton T-shirts when she woke one morning to knocking. She threw on a new waffle-weave robe and beat her mother to the door.

When she saw her father standing there and felt only disappointment, she realized she had not only

changed beyond recognition, she'd turned into someone she didn't particularly like. She leaned against her
father's chest and started crying.

"Well, pumpkin," Harry said, "I'm glad to see you
too."

Her mother came up behind her. "You could have
called."

"I did. I spoke to your mother yesterday."

Savannah glanced at the house, then walked back
to the makeshift kitchen, where she was flipping bacon. Emma kept her face pressed into her father's
chest.

"Come on, honey," Harry went on. "What is it?
What's wrong?"

Emma could only shake her head. She was not
even a real person anymore. She was made of glass
and shattering fast.

"She's emotional," Savannah said. "It's my dad."

"How's he doing?"

"Better. That second round of radiation finally
kicked in. And I read his fortune. He'll beat this."

"I'm really glad." Harry squeezed Emma tightly,
until her tears subsided, then he ran his fingers
through his hair. He opened his mouth and closed it
again. Emma stiffened a little. Her father had been car
dealer of the year for three years straight. He never
had trouble with words.

"Dad?" she said.

He didn't even hear her. "Savannah, I'd like to talk
to you."

Her mother didn't look up from the sizzling bacon.
"I've got a full slate this morning. Business is finally
picking up."

"I heard you're reading fortunes again."

Savannah turned off the burner on the stove and
put her hands on her hips. "Don't start with me,

Harry. I'm not bringing crazies into Emma's world. When I go home, I'll get my old job back. I'll go back to wearing suits and writing slogans for cereal. I won't shame you two."

There were tears in Savannah's eyes, and Emma could not believe it. She had blamed her mother for almost everything, except the one thing she felt guilty for. Savannah did not embarrass her. In fact, she did just the opposite; she seemed too good to be true, too much to live up to.

"I didn't mean that," Harry said.

"I think you did."

"Look, I just want to talk. Not about that. About . . . well . . . I'm having trouble again, Savannah. I'm getting that empty feeling in the pit of my stomach."

"Oh, Harry."

"Can we have dinner tonight?"

"You're too old for this," was her reply, but she also agreed to meet him.

Emma's father turned to her. "Let's go for a walk, princess."

Emma dressed in a new pair of slim-fitting jeans and a T-shirt, then met her father outside. The wind was already sweeping off Kemper Peak, whirling up newly cut grass and shavings from her grandfather's incense cedar. She was close to crying again, so she turned her face to the sky and stared straight into the sun.

"I'm sorry I missed your call the other day," Harry said. "Melinda told me you sounded upset."

"It's just . . ." She breathed deeply. "Don't listen to what Mom says. Grandpa's dying, Dad."

Harry led her down Sage Street to Red Rock Lane, past houses with three different floor plans, all painted in shades of brown. They didn't hit color until they turned the corner and reached Mabel Lewis's limestone-green bungalow, which now had a Sold sign on the lawn. Three widowers had bid on it in a single afternoon, one for twenty thousand over the asking price.

"I'll take you hiking this afternoon," Harry said. "You pick the trail."

Emma shrugged. Since the fever had begun, she'd had trouble moving uphill.

"Emma," Harry went on, "you ever feel like you don't know what's going on? Like you haven't got a clue how to be happy?"

Emma stopped. She didn't like the sound of this at all. She had no desire to become her father's confidante. It had been so much easier to admire him and do what he told her when she was little and thought he was perfect. Then one night she came in on him dead drunk and passed out on the table, one afternoon she actually heard him telling a neighbor he'd be damned if he'd let a black couple move in across the street. There was no question of her loving him, but if he wanted her to like him, he ought to just shut up.

She kicked a rock, aiming for the base of a telephone pole, but instead hit a mesquite tree ten feet away. Not only was she losing her ambition and appetite, she was losing the things she'd always counted on, like good aim and faith in her parents' common sense.

"Dad, go home to Melinda."

Harry ignored the disgust in her voice. "See, that's just it. Melinda's so good to me, it only makes me feel worse. She supports me every time I stake out a new dealership to buy, she looks great in a Donna Karan suit, but sometimes I wonder if I've made a terrible mistake."

"You're crazy. You've got everything you want."

"Jesus, Emma, no one's got that. Especially not me. I want a little sunshine now and then, a nicer car, definitely a house farther up in the hills in Whidbey Heights. I want some inner peace. I want to stop dreaming about your mother."

Emma walked across Mabel's browning lawn. Since Mabel had moved to California, Emma had spotted the MesaLand widows walking past her yard at all hours of the day and night. They pocketed blades of grass and ran their hands over her fading rhododendrons, hoping whatever secret charm she'd used to woo Ed Lewis back from the grave would rub off on them. By the time they got to Savannah's table, they reeked so badly of yearning, Emma had to leave the room. It didn't seem right, so much wanting streaming out of chalky bodies like that.

"You shouldn't be talking about this," she said.

"Absolutely not, but I can't help it. I dream of her every night. The way she laughed, her head thrown back and her mouth so wide I could see clear down her throat. She'd laugh at anything, stupid movies, your silly jokes for the hundredth time, and usually I'd tell her to be quiet. I'd tell her she was making a fool of herself."

"Dad—"

"What else was I supposed to do? She was so happy, it was like a direct assault. I couldn't compete with it, I didn't even admire it. Joy is unambitious and blind."

He ran his hand along the back of his neck, then suddenly seemed to remember Emma was there. He put his arm around her and kissed her forehead.

"Forgive me, Emma. I'm delirious. I caught a flight out here before I could even think. Let's talk about you. You don't have to wait until August for your visit. Why not come early? You can stay the rest of the sum-

mer, if you want. And if, in the fall, you feel like going
to school there, you know you can stay."

Emma turned away. She'd made the hour trek to
Danville every summer for the past seven years and
she despised it. It was too pink and phony over the
hill—all storybook castles and perfumed dogs and people doing one thing while dreaming about doing something else. It was one colossal waste of time.

"Did you know you loved Mom right away?" she
asked. "Like, in an instant?"

Harry dropped his arm and stepped back. Emma
wished he would take off all his rings and forget about
hair gel. She wished they were going backpacking
again soon, just the two of them, yet even as she
thought this, she knew she would only lie beneath
those stars and dream of Eli. She knew that simple
pleasures like solitude and stargazing and nights alone
with her father had been ruined the moment she
kissed Eli Malone.

"Well now," he said, "maybe not right away. But I
proposed awfully quick. She was  .  .  .  Your mom's different, you know? She's like the warm part of the
world, and sometimes, in winter, you just crave her.
I've been craving her, Emma. But I'm no fool. I know
she can drive me crazy, too."

"But you still want her."

"Maybe I do. Maybe everyone's got to want at least
one thing they can't have."

They started walking again, and when they came
around the corner of Sage Street, Emma stopped
short. For the first time in two weeks, Jake's truck was
there. Her eyes widened, and her stomach rose clear
to her throat when she spotted Eli in the bed, handing
Jake his tools.

Before she even knew what she was doing, she was
halfway down the block, running hard.

"Emma!" her father called.

She had to stop, but she tapped her foot on the sidewalk. Every second she had to wait for him chipped off another chink of her devotion. She hadn't thought he would ever get this old. He looked like someone a woman would be crazy to love.

Harry finally reached her. "Jeez. Give your old man a break."

"I just remembered," she said, looking past him. "Grandpa asked me to talk to the psycho about the bench."

She tried to pull away, but her father caught her arm. "Excuse me? The psycho?"

"That's just what Grandma calls Jake. He's the furniture maker, the one Mom's falling for."

Then she tore away and started running. He called out after her, but she didn't stop. No one had control of her now, not even herself.

She reached the truck just as Eli hopped out of the back. He rose up straight and stared at her. He had no idea he was this close to being her sole purpose for living.

"Tomorrow night," he said. "Pierce Park."

Emma had felt faint for two weeks, and now it got worse. She wrapped her arms around her stomach and held on tight. By the time her father reached her, she was light-headed, but also sure of one thing. She wasn't going to be standing on someone's front lawn when she was seventy, yanking out blades of grass and still yearning. She was going to get what she wanted now, when she was still young and brave enough to enjoy it.


That night, Savannah and Harry met at Luigi's, a small Italian restaurant downtown on Cortez Street. Harry asked for the back booth, the one up against the faux brickwork, and ordered them a bottle of Chianti.

"Nice place," he said, though she could tell from his tone and the way he eyed the red-netted candles that he wouldn't have been caught dead here, if not for her. He had to shout to be heard over the Italian opera tunes that someone in the back was singing along with.

Savannah tapped her fingers on the table, waiting for the wine. The last time she'd gone out to dinner with Harry, he had been telling her how easily he'd fallen out of love with her. She had been drinking hard then, straight bourbon if she recalled. Not to numb herself, but to trigger tears, to tickle up some regret, because no marriage ought to end with a casual list of complaints and no heartbreak on either side.

A handsome waiter brought the wine and smiled at Savannah while he poured it. She drained half her glass at once. She liked this restaurant, not only for the music and gorgeous waiters, but because the place was so dark everyone was cast in shadows. That way, she didn't have to take Harry's shadow seriously, the one that sat huddled against the faux brick wall, crying.

"How did Emma seem to you?" she asked.

Harry sipped his own Chianti. "Distracted. I took her hiking up Granite Mountain, and she kept stopping to rip off blades of grass."

Savannah said nothing. She was not going to start in about Eli. Whenever she woke up during the night and found Emma sitting by the window, her knees curled up to her chest, she reminded herself she had been in love with forty different boys in high school. Love was like desert lightning at that age, dramatic and threatening, but dying out as soon as the sun went down.

"She's glad to see you," she said.

"Well." Harry set down his glass and reached across the table. He hadn't touched her for so long, Savannah just stared at his hands. His fingers had puffed out and whitened with age.

"Are you glad to see me, too?" he asked.

She tapped his hands, then pulled away. "Of course."

He grabbed his Chianti and downed it quickly. When he started twisting off his rings and staring at her as if she were a new-model Ferrari, she knew she should have picked a brighter restaurant, one where he could have made out all the reasons he had left her in the first place.

"Melinda reads the stock page every morning," he said, yanking hard on his pinkie ring. "She highlights all our gains in yellow, the losses in pink. Whenever she walks into my office, she's always got some plan on how to buy a new dealership or sell those old Troopers we can't give away. I am telling you, Savannah, every time I see her it's like looking at myself, and it's not pretty."

He put down every ring in a row between their water glasses. She couldn't take her eyes off the jewels—one fat ruby, an emerald, two sapphires, a two-carat diamond.

"What's it all for?" he went on. "I mean, with bonuses now I'm making close to two hundred thousand a year. That ought to make me happy. That ought to be enough. Will you tell me, please, when I'm going to have enough?"

His voice broke, but before Savannah could respond, their dark-haired waiter returned. Savannah ordered baked lasagna, though she wasn't going to eat a bite. She had lost her appetite as soon as she realized she would have to break somebody's heart.

After the waiter left, she took Harry's hand. She massaged beneath the knuckles, along the tan lines from his rings. Once, she had dreamed of Harry; now, she only dreamed of the meanest man in Prescott. When she woke every morning, she fully expected to find burn marks on her neck and black hairs on her pillow from his beard.

"You want someone to make you another person," she said softly. "I already tried that. It doesn't work."

He looked up. Tears piled on his lower lashes, but they weren't going to fall. "Every morning when I look in the mirror, I despise myself. The trouble is, that doesn't stop me from putting some fresh-faced newlyweds into a car they can't afford, just so I can make enough bonus points for an all-expense-paid trip to Bermuda."

"Harry—"

"I'm sick of it, Savannah. The whole thing. The money and the worry about the money. I could never have enough. Every time I get what I want, I just want something more."

Savannah could think of a million things to say, but eight years with Harry was enough for her to know he wouldn't listen. There were certain people who had to be miserable, or they wouldn't feel alive. There was no talking them out of it.

"Melinda's good to me," Harry said. "Too good. I wake up every morning knowing I don't love her enough."

Savannah moved next to him and kissed him on the cheek. He tried to turn his lips to her, but it never worked. They got tangled in noses, they were still all wrong.

Harry pulled away and poured more wine. He put his rings back on. Savannah covered his hand with hers and squeezed tightly.

"Here's the secret, Harry. Pick one person and love her for all you're worth."

"It's not that simple."

"Yes, it is."

She returned to her seat on the other side of the booth. They were silent for a long time. The food came and got cold. Harry finished the bottle of Chianti. His gelled hair came loose on one side and hung in a clump above his left eye. Finally, he tapped his rings on the table.

"Emma told me you're interested in the psycho."

Savannah snapped her head up. Her mother had been spending way too much time with Emma. "He is not a psycho. He's a furniture maker."

Harry stared at her, as if he were sizing up her weaknesses. She hadn't gotten through to him at all.

"So," he said, "are you interested?"

She looked away. She stabbed at her lasagna, then left the fork standing there. "I'm going back to San Francisco. There's no future for me here."

"Maybe you should tell the psycho that before you fuck him."

Savannah might see the good in people, but she was no fool either. She'd lived with Harry long enough to know love could turn to hate, just like that. Before Harry even blinked, she lunged across the table and twisted the slick fabric of his Armani suit between her fingers.

"You know what your problem is, Harry? You've forgotten how to be kind." He blinked twice, then she shoved him away and stood up.

"You pay," she said. "You've got the money." Then she put on her fedora and walked out.

*   *   *

Harry Shaw drove to Sage Street and stomped through his ex-father-in-law's overgrown garden. Within seconds, he was attacked from all sides by dogs. A chocolate Lab threw himself at his knees and some kind of retriever mutt took him down by the ankles. Once on his back, a Husky leaned over his neck, growling from deep in her throat. She had rotted teeth and breath that smelled of fresh meat and feces. She snapped her jaws, and Harry just lay there, whimpering.

"Off!" a man yelled.

Suddenly, the dogs were gone and the psycho was standing over him, holding out his hand. The man was as large as some of the foreign cars Harry sold, and certainly better built. His hand was the size of a steering wheel.

"You stay down any longer," the man said, "and Sasha will mistake you for kibble."

Harry took his hand. It was cool to the touch and heavily calloused. The man hoisted him up, and a quick burst of wind covered them both in sawdust. Harry immediately brushed himself off.

He had a world-class headache, and it got worse when he realized he ought to be home. He was grasping at straws here, but he didn't see a way to stop. He swore he had holes in the bottom of his feet, because everything he professed to love just went right through him. It had been so long since he'd been truly happy, he couldn't even remember what it felt like, if it was simply the lack of heartache, or something more.

He wished he was already on a plane home. He might not be happy there, either, but at least no one went crazy in Danville, or if they did the police pulled them off the street before they could disturb anyone's sleep. There were no thunderstorms there, only interminable drizzle, and no one got lost in the mountains because they weren't mountains at all, only hills, fenced off and reseeded yearly. Right now, Melinda was probably opening up a bottle of Pinot Noir and ordering out.

"You're Savannah's *ex*-husband," the psycho said, turning back to his bench.

The dogs were behind him again, growling. Harry drew himself up to his full height. Maybe he had been grasping at straws with Savannah, but that didn't mean he was going to let her fall into animal hands. That didn't mean he'd leave her and Emma to the wolves.

"And you are . . ."

He waited, but the man said nothing. On the bench, the psycho had carved in the outline of what looked like Superstition Mountain, beneath a crescent moon. At the top of the mountain were the silhouettes of two people, facing each other. Harry had no intention of being moved by primitive art, but he couldn't deny the chill down his spine. This was not the kind of thing he expected a madman to be capable of.

The man took one of the smallest knives on the grass beside him and chinked away a crevasse in the mountain. "What I'd like to know is why a man lets a woman like that go?"

"Look," Harry said, "you don't know anything."

"True."

"It was years ago, all right? I wanted to move up. She wanted . . . God only knows what Savannah wants. Sometimes I think she doesn't want anything. You know how hard that is to live with?"

Harry marched around the cobblestone courtyard. "You know the trouble with Savannah? She looks good in the beginning. I mean, what's not to love? She's happy, she's beautiful, she sees only the good in things. But then what happens when you have a bad day? What happens when your dog gets run over or you lose a huge sale and you just want to curl up and die? You can't turn to her. She'll just tell you to sparkle up. She's good for parties and fortune-telling, but I'm telling you, when it comes right down to it, there is nothing substantial there to hold on to."

Harry had walked to the other side of the bench without realizing it. He was now staring the psycho in the eye. When the man said nothing, Harry continued, more shakily this time. "Look, you can do what you want with Savannah. But when it comes to my daughter . . ."

He stopped. He took a good, long breath. He was a mess of a man, but not so pathetic that he couldn't see the one clear thing. He was worthless without Emma. She was the one person on this planet he would sleep on the ground for; when they were backpacking, he never noticed rocks beneath his sleeping bag or the biting cold. At ten thousand feet, he got a little dizzy, but not from thin air. He was high on his daughter, on the kind of man he might have been if he'd been able to keep her all these years. It occurred to him that Emma was the only person who could save whatever was left of his used-car salesman's soul.

He planted his feet. "Let me be clear about this. My daughter's not going to live in some shack in the middle of the woods with wild dogs. It's always been my intention to bring Emma to Danville, to give her a chance at a normal life. You get serious with Savannah and, frankly, you'll give me all the ammunition I need to take my daughter home with me. You'll play right into my hands."

The psycho stood up. He rose well into the air, but there was no way Harry was backing down now. He turned his back on the dogs and walked to the garage apartment. He knocked on the door and in a moment

Emma opened it up, bleary-eyed. He took her hand and led her back to the sleeping cot in the corner.

He tucked her in and brushed her hair with his fingers. She tried to keep her eyes open, and he would always be grateful for that. Because for the few minutes before she fell asleep, he got to look in the one pair of eyes that saw him as something more than a huckster.

He leaned down beside her as her lids finally closed in sleep. He put his lips to her forehead and just left them there. "Here's the secret," he said softly. "Pick one person, and love her for all you're worth."

# NINE

**M**aggie stepped out her front door into a line four fools deep. She put her hands on her hips and glared at her neighbors, but since they'd all sworn they hadn't believed Mabel Lewis, none of them would look up from their fold-up lawn chairs and meet her gaze.

"Have you all gone crazy?"

Sitting beneath someone's beach umbrella, they were dressed in the clothes their dead husbands and wives had loved best, their white, pasty hands clutching twenty-dollar bills. Only Dick Leoni had the guts to speak up. He had on half-inch-thick glasses and extra-wide white sneakers without a stain on them. In his jacket pocket was a red carnation, the kind he'd bought for his wife, Francine, every single day of her life. "Well, now, Maggie, if you'd heard Mabel before she left. She swore—"

"Mabel has always been one trunk short of a tree."

"That may be, but she swore on a stack of bibles

Ed was talking to her through the cards. And you know, I got to thinking it would be worth twenty dollars to get a chance to talk to my Francine again. I mean, twenty dollars, Maggie. That's nothing. What have we got to lose?"

"Your minds, for one thing. Your reputation. Your hard-earned money. Your self-respect." She would have gone on, but the door to the garage apartment opened and Sally Trabelli came out, red-eyed. They all stood up, but she shook her head.

"He never talked to me when he was alive," she told them. "I don't know why I thought it would be any different now."

"There, you see?" Maggie said. "Mabel was delirious."

"Not just Mabel," Savannah said, coming out after Sally. Maggie did not know what to make of her daughter. Savannah wore a peacock-blue dress and rings on all her fingers. Somehow she had managed to convince Maggie's unsuspecting neighbors that with enough faith, anything was possible.

"You know that nice man from Thunderbolt Road?" Savannah went on. "Vern Wilson? His wife died eight years ago, and since then he hasn't let himself even look at Lucy Frish, even though it's common knowledge she lost her heart to him years ago. He was shuffling the cards and then all of a sudden we smelled this marvelous lavender perfume. After that, he got all Cups. I swear to God, every card a Cup, the suit of love. His wife was telling him it was all right. He could fall in love again. I'm not making this up, Mom. I wouldn't have the slightest idea how."

Maggie's head hurt. The idea that a wife would wait until she was dead to tell a husband all the things he needed to hear made her blood run cold. "You will not bilk my friends out of their social security money."

"I'm not bilking anyone. I couldn't conjure up Sally's husband. Her fortune was to stay away from enterprising men. If I was conning people, don't you think I'd make it work every time?"

"I don't even pretend to know the game you're playing."

Savannah pushed back her feathered hat and looked Maggie in the eye. "As a matter of fact, I am trying to make people happy. You should try it." She walked over to Dick Leoni and took his hand. "You ready?"

He took the carnation out of his pocket and handed it to her, along with his twenty.

Maggie tapped her foot. "This is outrageous. You're giving them false hope."

"There is no such thing."

"Savannah, you're breaking my heart."

"Well, good. Maybe it will mend itself correctly this time."

Maggie stared her down. "That is just plain mean." She glanced at her neighbors, sitting in a line like sheep. "Go on then. You deserve to be bilked, every last one of you."

She clutched her purse and headed to the car. She'd gotten only to the first Juneberry tree when she spotted the paper stabbed through one of the lowest branches.

At first, she thought it a teenage prank, perpetrated, most likely, by those Dunbar boys who sideswiped mailboxes and spray-painted pentagrams on the garage door of any girl who wouldn't go out with them. Then she caught the handwriting. It was Doug's wavery, post-cancer script, and for a moment she just stared at it. For a moment, she had herself convinced she could go right past it and not be taken in by whatever strange sentimentality Doug had gotten into his head this time. She took one step toward her car even, before she stomped back and ripped the paper from the branch, slicing it in two.

She took both pieces to her car and started the engine. She had backed halfway out of the drive before she slammed on the brakes. "Son of a bitch," she said.

She lined up the pieces. It was another of Doug's poems, poems she had not known about until he got sick, as if it was all right to let her go on for thirty-six years thinking he was someone he wasn't, as if failing to mention he had a heart was just a small oversight. Maggie had already decided she detested his poetry, but nevertheless she started reading.

This one, she saw right away, had been composed recently. She cursed him the whole time she read it, because he had to have known it would break her heart.

> *I can't die*
> *while you love me,*
> *so you must love me forever.*
> *I can't leave you*
> *until you realize my garden*
> *was for you.*
> *The woolly thyme and gray sage*
> *to sweeten your air.*
> *Sweet alyssum and freesia*
> *to brighten your table.*
> *And the Juneberry trees*
> *to stand in my place,*
> *thick enough to wrap your arms around,*
> *strong enough to keep you.*
> *I cannot die*
> *until you know the secret of my garden*
> *was you.*

Maggie closed her eyes. She was a fool to love this sentimental man. She was a fool to love anyone. It would only end in heartache.

She opened her eyes and backed out of the drive. If Doug was going to die and leave her, then she was going to spend every last penny he'd ever made before he went. She was going to get in way over her head. Something should be happening to her along with him; at the very least, she should have a comparable terminal disease—AIDS maybe, or even better, Alzheimer's, so she could forget all this was happening. Every day he woke up retching while she was feeling fine was a mockery of what marriage ought to be.

She drove the ten miles to the outlet mall, but once she got to the parking lot, she just sat there.

*I cannot die*
*until you know the secret of my garden*
*was you.*

That was ridiculous. The secret of Doug's garden was time, time spent away from her. Time when he could have been telling her these sweet things years ago, when she'd been unsure of his love and needed to hear them. Who was he to start getting sappy on her now? She was an old, bitter woman; she needed a hand up the stairs and more dinners out, not poetry.

Nevertheless, she couldn't get out of the car. She stared at the Dansk outlet, at the marvelous display of white porcelain plates and hand-crafted goblets, and could not move an inch. The sun heated the interior of the car to ninety. She liked the idea of one of those nose-ringed salespeople from the Levi's outlet finding her decaying body tonight after closing, but nevertheless, she started the car and was back home in seven minutes.

The line to Savannah's scam was now eight fools long, and she ignored them all. She got out of the car and found Doug in their bedroom, trying to put on his pants. He'd gotten down on the floor to do it, the way a two-year-old does, and now he could not get back up.

If he hadn't been dying, she would have killed him for what he was doing to her. But things being what they were, she simply knelt down in front of him and helped him on with his pants. She kept her head down, her concentration focused on the buttons.

"It's these buttons," he said. "My fingers . . ."

"Just be quiet, Doug. Don't say another goddamn word."

She was shaking so badly, she could hardly pull him to his feet. Once they were both standing unsteadily, she just held on. "I swear to you, I'll let the garden go to weeds. I'll let the dandelions take over. I'll never water a damn thing again, so you'd better work a little harder staying alive."

"Maggie—"

She pushed away from him. No one would ever know this from looking at her, but after slipping socks on Doug's icy feet, she'd cry her eyes out. After buying him a book he might never finish, she actually felt herself going to pieces.

But she didn't tell him that. He was not going to get better by having to take care of her. She walked to the bathroom, turned on the water, then let it run while she cried. She watched the most precious thing in this desert go right down the drain.

Doug came in behind her. "Maggie."

She squared her shoulders, stopped her crying, and stared at him. He was slim as a boy now and fragile as parchment. He was dying right before her eyes.

"I don't want any more poems," she said. "You're

killing me, Doug. These are the things you should have said to me years ago."

He lowered his head, and when he lifted it again there were tears in his eyes. "You are my breath and soul, Maggie. I couldn't stop the poetry if I tried."

"You're insane," she told him, but nevertheless she turned off the water and clutched him to her. When he fell asleep an hour later, she taped the poem back together. She fingered it until ink began to come off on her fingers.

Emma waited until her mother went to sleep, then crept out of bed. She was out the door and down the street, and by the time she reached Pierce Park, her heart was thundering against her chest and leaving bruises on the other side. Eli was leaning against his Corvette, his denim jacket frayed at the wrists. He said something when he saw her, but with the ringing between her ears, she couldn't tell what it was.

She could not see his eyes through his hair and he never once unclenched his fists. He was bad enough to rip someone's heart out, but Emma had already come this far, so she just walked right up and kissed him.

He tasted of smoke and fury. His arms came around her hard; in the morning, she would find bruises the color of his purple aura. He ran his fingers through her hair, then pushed her away.

"You're a kid," he said, then pulled a pack of Camels out of his pocket. He lit one and blew the smoke in her face.

She didn't flinch, didn't even get nervous. That's how certain she was this was meant to be. "You may be right. But then again, I'm free until morning, and I'll go anywhere you've got the guts to take me."

Years ago, her mother had told her the fortune of love. The Sun and the Moon, brother and sister, had once stood side by side in the sky. The Sun was mesmerized by his sister's pale skin and gentle tug on the oceans. He grew jealous of the men who sailed in her light and sang to her beauty, so one night, without warning, he tried to seduce her. From that moment on, the Moon started running, and from that moment on, the Sun followed her, destined to wander in her wake forever.

Emma had loved that story as a child, but now she knew it was dead wrong. Love did not run from anything. She took Eli's hand and put it on her breast. She would stand there until she made him another person. She was in love, but she wasn't a fool. He was not fit for love. But what was love, if not the ability to change someone's life for the better? What was love, if she couldn't make Eli give up everything for her?

They drove to the liquor store off Union Street. "Wait here," Eli said, opening his car door. "Don't move."

She watched him walk into the store, his jacket hunched up to his ears. He headed straight to one of the back aisles, and Emma didn't even have time to fix her lipstick before he was running out, a six-pack beneath his jacket, and a furious, six-foot clerk running after him.

He dove into the car. Emma didn't have time to think, so she was staring right at the clerk when he took the handgun out of his pocket and aimed it at her head. She screamed, and Eli pushed her down in the seat. He sped off, his head thrown back, laughing.

"Chickenshit didn't even take a shot," he said. Emma was still on the floor beside him, her head tucked over her knees. Eli made a quick right, then left, then pulled to the side of the road. "Come on,

Emma. It's over. What did you think, that I'd let you get hurt?"

When he held out his hand, she realized this was her last chance. She could walk away now, still relatively intact. She could hike back to the liquor store, tell the clerk who had stolen from him, and continue to have what passed for a life.

But when she touched Eli's hand, she knew if falling in love was a choice—which she was beginning to doubt—she'd already made it. She was in way over her head and hoping to stay that way. She was halfway to throwing up and halfway to laughing, and when Eli hoisted her into her seat, laughter won out. He handed her a beer and she drank down as much as she could stomach in one gulp. In three seconds flat, she was warm all the way through.

They drove ninety miles to Wawani Lake, arriving at two-thirty in the morning to a crowd of fifty—drunk boys, mostly, with beer and shovels. Since they'd started draining Wawani Lake, the greatest sport for miles was coming to await what the lake would spit out. According to the papers, a fifty-year-old woman had stumbled across a rusted coffee can filled with solid gold Canadian coins. An eight-year-old had picked up a live hand grenade and had his right arm sheared off, which was all the incentive bored teenagers needed to sneak out at night and tempt fate.

Eli led Emma across the sand. They sat down by a dirty dune and he took two Camels out of his pocket. He lit them both, then handed one to her.

They smoked and listened to drunk talk—boys boasting they could swim across the shrunken lake in one breath, that they'd driven one hundred miles an hour the whole way here while their parents, the fools, thought them asleep in their beds. Emma looked up at the gritty stars. There were billions of them, but not a single one was red.

Eli took the cigarette from her fingers and put it out in the sand. Then he was on her, sinking her into the beach, his tongue in her mouth. He was trying to scare her, but all she did was twine her hands through his long hair and pull him closer. She might never have stopped kissing him, if someone hadn't started to shriek.

Suddenly, the drunk boys were hooting. Eli jumped up, but Emma was slower. She kept looking at the stars, feeling Eli's lips on her.

"Come on." Eli pulled her to her feet. "Let's check it out."

By the time they reached the crowd, half the bones had been found. Two femurs, a tibia, sternum and clavicle. Two of the drunks were tossing a skull like a baseball. Emma backed up, but her heel caught in a rib cage. She screamed and yanked out her shoe, then stepped on an arm bone poking out of the sand like a flag.

"Excellent," Eli said.

When two of the boys started playing swords with femurs, Emma took off running. By the time Eli started after her, she was halfway around the shrinking lake. She threw up over what had once been lake floor, fifteen feet down. Eli finally tackled her by a rock formation that had ripped the bottoms out of half a dozen boats over the years.

She fought against him, until he laid his body out over hers on the moist sand. He pressed his lips into her pulsing neck. "Stop, okay?" he whispered. "Just stop."

He kissed the pulse beneath her ear, then her ear lobe, then her bottom lip. He slipped his hand up beneath her blouse and covered her breast. She breathed in so deeply, she'd never get the scent of him out of her lungs. When he started unbuttoning her jeans, she was as helpless as this lake, watching itself be sucked into another body.

"That was a person," she said. "Don't you get it? It was a living person."

"Shhh. Don't talk."

He kissed the tears at the corners of her eyes. When he slipped inside her, contrary to what she'd heard, it didn't hurt at all. It just sealed her fate. It made her his then and there.

Savannah slept late, her morning dreams filled with wild dogs who turned to wood when she touched them. When she woke, she still smelled the scent of fur and pine. Then she opened her eyes and realized the smell was real; her window was open and Jake Grey was in the garden, already at work on her father's bench.

She walked to the window. Jake crouched beside his creation, studying yesterday's work. He'd finished Superstition Mountain and begun Doug's next design, an intricate bird-of-paradise, which Doug had planted the day she was born, and which had never become the small shrub most people knew, but instead grew into a twelve-foot tree.

She turned from the window and picked up her cards. She was ready for disaster, even for the Three of Swords, but not for what she laid out. Today the cards issued a warning, the Page of Wands as her crossing card, which can mean either a faithful person or a man who would probably break her heart.

She looked over at Emma's bed, but there was no movement there yet. "Emma," she said, "rise and shine. Shake a leg."

She cleaned up her hats and jewelry, then looked over her shoulder at Emma's bed again. "Come on, lazybones. Get a move on."

She walked across the room and was about to brush back her daughter's hair when she realized Emma was not there.

For a long time, she just stared at the pile of blankets and deceit. At first, it wasn't panic she felt so much as disbelief. She would have let Emma stay out all night if she'd known where she was going, if Emma had only asked. But obviously, it wouldn't have been the same if she had asked. It would have sucked the thrill right out of it.

Savannah leaned against the wall. The Three of Swords had not been her father dying after all. It was the future of every parent of teenagers. Sorrow, disappointment, opposition. The Three of Swords was that moment when Savannah realized it really had been better fifteen years ago, when Emma's colic had kept her so sleep-deprived, she couldn't form a single coherent sentence. Then, at least, she had known where Emma was. No matter how miserable they were, the bottom line was they both were safe.

She started to get shaky, but managed to walk out the door and around to the back yard, where Jake was carving the frond leaves of the bird-of-paradise.

"Is Eli with you?" she asked.

He stood up straight. "Should he be?"

"Emma's not in bed. Probably, she hasn't been there all night."

She sat down on the porch stoop, her legs suddenly flimsy as paper. Sasha came to lie at her feet and she buried her hands in the dog's silver fur.

Jake looked toward the street, then set his knife down on the bench. He came and sat beside her. His big hands tapped his knees, then slid off to the concrete stoop. He didn't seem to know what to do with them when they were not holding some kind of tool. He certainly had no clue what to say to a woman or, worse, to a mother who was fighting for control and losing, whose hands were clenched in tight, terrified fists.

"Savannah—"

"Tell me about this Eli of yours," she said, trying to talk instead of cry, to keep herself in what passed for one piece.

"He's not my Eli. He's a boy who needed a job. I thought it might keep him out of trouble."

"Has it?"

"Not yet."

Savannah nodded. She felt the panic now. It seeped beneath the skin and turned her blood icy. It numbed the tips of her fingers and toes. She knew, too well, the things teenage boys did for fun. They raced cars through steep, one-lane canyons. They dared each other to drink a pint of tequila in five minutes flat. They drove girls to the desert, screwed them in the sand, then left them there.

Jake reached over and took her hand. "She'll be all right."

"How can you know that?"

"Because I've known Eli awhile, and he's never looked at anyone the way he looks at her. He's not about to let anything happen to her."

That did not soothe her. Love was more cruel than teenagers, teasing girls with little bits of rapture, then vanishing into a deep, bottomless hole. Emma could very well end up like Savannah's heartbroken clients, women who had once been beautiful, but now were thin and pale as night moths. Women who would wear nothing but the faded shirts their lovers had left behind.

She pulled her hand away and stood up. She walked to the end of the courtyard and back again. There were a hundred things that could have happened to Emma already, and each stabbed at a different part of her. Her head ached with the horror of fatal car accidents, her stomach clenched around brutal police arrests. She didn't know how other women stood motherhood, because it was clearly killing her. She'd walked straight into the trap of loving the one person who could do the most damage to her.

Something awful must have escaped her throat, because Jake came up next to her. He cradled her in his arms and whispered "Hush" into her hair.

"I should have left weeks ago," she managed to say.

"Absolutely."

"You don't even know how to laugh." She pressed her face into his chest and breathed in deeply.

He wrapped his arms tighter around her, even while telling her, "I'm worse than Eli."

"I'm not fifteen."

"You don't want to know me. I'm not from your kind of world."

She leaned back. "Maybe I can make you happy."

"Maybe I'm not capable of it."

Savannah tapped her foot. "Don't talk to me that way. It's as bad as swearing."

"You can't close your eyes to ugliness, Savannah. It's everywhere. Just listen to the news, figure out where your daughter is, take a history of my life."

Savannah would have told him he didn't scare her if Eli and Emma hadn't driven up then. Emma stepped out of the Corvette with bite marks all over her neck, and sand still clumped in her hair. She raced across the garden and, without a word to anyone, ran into the garage and slammed the door. In a heartbeat, Savannah became the mother she had always sworn she wouldn't be, the mother no woman can help being if she is going to do the job right.

She felt light-headed relief, but only for a second, and then she was furious. She started for Emma, then changed her mind and charged Eli. He was leaning against his car, lighting a cigarette, and he smelled of fish and Emma. Savannah jabbed a finger into his chest and might have hit a boy for the first time in her life if Jake hadn't reached around her and grabbed Eli by the scruff of his collar.

"You're fired," he said, then shoved him away. For the first time, a little of the boy broke through that tough veneer. Savannah saw a flash of scared green eyes.

"Hey," Eli said. "Come on, Jake. It was an accident. It got late. There was this body—"

"A body?" Savannah said. "You took my daughter out to see some body?"

"We went to Wawani Lake. They're draining it, you know? For the reservoir? And this body washed up. All bones now, and then the cops came, and it was like the first real thing that's ever happened to me. It was the first time cops talked to me without hauling me in."

Savannah jabbed him in the chest again. She kept jabbing him and jabbing him, until he started giving way. "You stay away from my daughter. You hear me?"

Her voice was high and shrill; she hadn't even known she was capable of the sounds. Eli glanced at Jake, then Savannah noticed him too. He'd gone absolutely still and the dogs had started whining. Sasha was pressing her head against his thigh. When he didn't move, she threw back her head and howled.

Savannah shoved away Eli and went to Jake's side. His left arm was limp and cold as ice.

"Jake?" she said.

He was falling so slowly, Savannah and Eli had the chance to get beneath him. When he took them all to the ground with him, Savannah saw that his face had gone pure white. She cradled him in her arms while Eli crawled out from beneath him.

"I'm all right," Jake whispered, but it came out mostly like a sigh.

"Call an ambulance," Savannah told Eli. "Hurry."

# Ten

## The Devil ❧ Self-Destruction

Things did not start to go Cheryl Pillandro's way until both her husbands were dead. The first thing she did was stop living in dumps. She moved out to the classy Tucson suburbs, leased a two-bedroom condo, and started reading novels. She cut off nearly all her hair without worrying that someone would turn over a table because of it. She didn't just throw out her high heels and short skirts, which her second husband, Roy, had forced her to wear, sometimes at knifepoint; she took one of Roy's knives and slashed the clothes to rags, then used them to clean out the engine of her car.

Without a man around, she never watched hockey or bought beer, which was a good thing, because the smell of Budweiser made her go cold all over. Sometimes, of course, she missed a man's arms around her. She missed someone taking out the garbage and scaring off door-to-door salesmen and stumbling into bed at night. She missed that old sense of martyred superiority, when she had known that even if no self-respecting woman would look her in the eye, she was still better than the creature who drank too much and swung a mean right hook.

Now, she couldn't date a man more than twice, or else he would find out he was too good for her. The men she went out with drank Cabernet and held doors open; they would never call again if they knew the things she had once stood for. What Roy had said fifteen years ago was true: He'd ruined her for anyone else. No other man would want her once he saw the marks Roy had left, once he knew the pain Roy had gone through to make her his.

Roy might have been right, but what he hadn't reckoned on was that one day Cheryl would discover she didn't need a man around at all. With her job at Dillard's and the sale of her Phoenix house, she had enough money to pay the rent, even eat out occasionally. Why would she want a man choosing tacky restaurants, or getting violent over the color of her hair? As it stood now, she ate salad for lunch every day and hadn't heard a cuss word in fifteen peaceful years.

Up until the time the sheriff showed up on her doorstep, Cheryl Pillandro actually thought her life might turn out fine.

"I'm Sheriff Merrill," the man said. "I'm afraid I've got bad news about your husband."

Cheryl walked back into her house. She picked up her water glass, then immediately spilt it. The sheriff took it out of her hands and went into the kitchen. He came back with a rag and the glass full of gin.

"Drink," he said. When she finished it, he got her another, then sat down beside her.

"Your husband's remains washed up from Wawani Lake last night. We're doing an autopsy. We've already pulled the missing person's report you filed fifteen years ago."

She set down the glass and stood up. She had no mementos in this house. Not a single photograph of either of her husbands, or one of her son, Jake. When her first husband, Paul Grey, had died of a sudden heart attack, she had worn his sweatpants and slept in his white work shirts. She didn't cry until his smell went out of them, and then she didn't stop for three weeks.

After Roy, though, she bought all new sheets and towels. She burned every pair of his underwear and held a garage sale for anything he might have touched—furniture, plates, even canned goods. She took pennies, if that was all she could get. After Roy, she slept thirteen hours a night and slowly but surely stopped ducking when a man reached for her, but now she was having trouble looking the sheriff in the eye. If she wasn't careful, she'd start jumping at the sound of footsteps again, she'd start attracting trouble and figuring she deserved it when it came.

She tried to meet the sheriff's gaze, but couldn't. "Do you need my permission or something?"

The sheriff stood up. He was a good six feet, but tall men didn't scare her. Tall men didn't have anything to prove. No, what scared her were men who had flunked algebra and never been good in sports. Men who had known, early on, that they would never amount to anything and had better make other plans for getting what they wanted. Worthless men were the worst sort of mean; they had nothing to lose by taking a woman down with them.

"What I'd like, what would save us a whole lot of time, is for you to tell me the truth," the sheriff said. "Roy Pillandro didn't disappear. Someone smashed his skull in, and what I'd like to know is who."

Fifteen years was a long time. Long enough to forget the tinny taste of fear and all the reasons she'd let a man do the things he did. When she looked back now she was just stupefied; she couldn't come to any conclusion except that she'd been weak and stupid. She'd made the wrong choice years ago, when her son had stood outside her door in the rain, and she hadn't let him in. She'd never forgotten the sound of her grown boy crying.

Cheryl Pillandro had a good life now, except that she regretted every minute of it.

"I have no idea," she said. "As far as I know, Roy disappeared. He was a mean, drunken bastard, but if you're asking if I killed him, no, I did not."

"You have no idea who did?"

"That's right."

When the sheriff finally left, Cheryl sat down at her kitchen table. She drank three more shots of gin, but did not feel the slightest bit drunk. Then she walked into her bedroom and started to pack.

When she was through, she sat on the bed and ran her hand over the canary-yellow comforter. Roy would have detested the color, along with the four-poster bed and the baskets she'd hung low from the ceiling, so that anyone over five seven would crash into them. She had gone to work in the lingerie department of Dillard's to help pay for this place, and Roy would have detested her work ethic, too. He had met her when she was nearly catatonic, and he had done his best to keep her that way.

The day after her first husband died, Cheryl quit her job and began sending her eight-year-old boy out for the essentials—toilet paper, Hostess Cup Cakes, which she served for breakfast, and frozen dinners. She let the lawn die and never got the Buick serviced. It chugged along for six years, then simply stopped one afternoon at the intersection of Fifth and Central and refused to start up again. She had it hauled to the junkyard, where she got fifty dollars for parts.

She left the house only for Jake's school plays, and then no happily married woman could bear to look at her. All of her so-called friends stopped calling a year after Paul's death. They couldn't drive past her house without weeping at her broken fence and dead lawn. Because of Cheryl, no man on the block got a moment's peace. Their wives followed them everywhere, into bars and their sanctified garages, making sure they didn't collapse in some dark corner, the way Paul Grey had.

Cheryl might have stayed locked up and shunned forever, if her water heater hadn't blown. Her one pleasure was her afternoon bath, and when she stepped into a tub of ice-cold water, she knew she'd have to get help. The repairman was a thirty-year-old named Roy Pillandro who, after he'd replaced a gasket, plopped himself in Cheryl's kitchen and refused to budge.

"I could use a glass of water," he'd said. Cheryl had gotten it for him, careful not to touch his thick fingers as she handed him the glass. He had dirt under his fingernails. The top three buttons of his gray shirt were unfastened, revealing a bush of wiry black hair. She backed up until she was flush with the counter.

"And a bagel or something." Roy Pillandro tapped those fingers on the table and stared at her. He had wavy black hair and ripples running down both cheeks. He had teeth the color of creamed coffee, which she would find out later he drank by the gallon. But when he smiled, which he did a lot, at least in the beginning, he made her itch in Paul Grey's clothes.

While she was spreading cream cheese on Roy's bagel, Cheryl caught a glimpse of herself in the toaster—the thick wad of bangs in her eyes, the purple caverns beneath her eyes. She started shivering then and there. Roy got up from the table and put his hand on her shoulder.

"See now," he said, "I happen to specialize in broken hearts."

They were married one year later, and for the wedding Cheryl dyed her hair jet black, Roy sang his wedding vows in a deep, luxuriant voice. No one could have convinced her she wasn't the most beautiful woman in the world that day. Or the luckiest.

Roy moved out of his mobile home and into the shambles of her house. Immediately, he threw out Paul Grey's clothes without asking. He walked through the rooms turning around pictures on the walls.

"Can't have him watching us. You have any idea the things a ghost can do?"

When he left for work the next day, Cheryl stored every picture of Paul Grey in a box in the attic, but still, a week later, she came home to find Roy ripping out the daylilies Paul had planted along the back concrete wall. The dead lawn was smeared with pulverized gold petals, Roy was up to his elbows in soil and plant guts, but Cheryl didn't feel more than a ripple of fear. She thought it was kind of sweet, actually, the way Roy was jealous of a man who was dead as dust.

After Jake started his second year at ASU, Roy sold his classic Mustang and bought a used forty-foot houseboat. He quit his job and called a realtor, all in one afternoon. He strutted into the kitchen and grabbed Cheryl from behind.

"Pack your bags, babe. We're heading to Wawani Lake for a life of leisure."

"But this house . . ."

"Fuck this house. We're selling it. We'll make a ton."

"It's *my* house," she said. "I'm not—"

She didn't see it coming. In the early days, she never did. She thought he was just leaning in to hug her. By the time his fist landed in her stomach, she was already puckered for a kiss.

The force slammed her into the cabinet. She didn't lose her footing, something she would always do later, when she discovered it was harder for him to hit a low target. She grabbed the countertop for support, then Roy punched her again, this time in the ribs.

"You've got nothing without me," Roy whispered, rubbing his fist as if she'd done him damage. "You got that?"

She couldn't breathe well enough to answer, so he took that for a yes. He drove her to the real-estate broker's office that afternoon, but when he left to go to the bathroom, she ripped up the paperwork. "I'm not selling. My boy's going to stay in that house and go to college. I'm headed for a life of leisure."

That life of leisure turned out to require a huge amount of work on Cheryl's part. The houseboat was rank and barely floatable, the closest supermarket an hour's drive away. Though Cheryl scrubbed down the toilets daily, mosquitoes still grew in the tank. The thin orange carpeting sprouted dark green mold in the corners. Roy could not understand why she didn't do something about it.

"Lower the asking price on your house," he said one night, when his foot went right through the decking and halfway down the rotted pontoons. A couple of belly-up fish floated by, victims of the highest level of contaminants in any lake in the western United States. "Why the hell hasn't it sold?"

Cheryl managed not to smile. It was her only victory, fooling Roy into thinking she'd give up one more thing for him. Her house had never been on the market. Jake lived there, drawing on his father's life insurance policy to pay the mortgage and taxes.

"The market's slow," she told him. "Give it time."

"Time," Roy spat out. "Why should I wait around for a few luxuries? I like things nice, you hear me? I'm a man with some *class*."

He turned so fast, she didn't have time to react, and even if she had, she wouldn't have known what to do differently. He slapped her hard across the face, so hard the mark of his hand would last for days. So hard she saw stars, thousands of tiny white lights that had to be a consolation for something.

"Now fix this." He stormed off the boat to the dock, and in a moment, she heard the squeal of tires.

She lay on the deck without moving, just breathing in the stench of stagnant water and dead fish. By the time Roy came back, with flowers and plywood to fix the hole, the sun was up over the brown hills and he was crying.

"God, Cheryl," he said, kneeling down beside her. "Why do you make me do this? Don't you know I love you?"

He put his head in her lap and she stroked his hair. The flowers were wild daisies, the kind that grew like weeds on the hills surrounding the lake. They were already dying.

The next night, when she overcooked the spaghetti noodles, he hit her again. A week later, when she changed the channel from one of his hockey games, he grabbed the scissors and cut off her hair at the shoulders. She started sleeping on the very edge of the bed, trying not to breathe, until he hit her for that, too.

She couldn't leave him; he would only come after her and beat her for it. Besides, where would she go? Her son was in college, better off without her, and Roy had made certain she'd lost all her friends. Roy was slowly killing her, sure, but without him she would have died a long time ago. She would have curled up in Paul Grey's house and willed herself dead, but now she cleaned that awful houseboat, fixed Roy his rotten meals, and despised him so much her body crackled with animosity. Hate woke her up in the morning, so she could spit into Roy's bowls of cereal. Hate straightened her spine while she made Roy double margaritas, to cover up the taste of the trout guts she'd mixed in. Hate carried her to the store, where she'd gone as far as buying a box of rat poison, which she kept beneath her bed. Hate made her stand up to almost anything, because someday she would have her revenge.

Then one night, after noticing another water stain on the carpet, Roy grabbed her right arm and yanked it back until it snapped.

"I could kill you," he said.

"Well then do it! Although, frankly, it won't make much difference."

He let go. Her arm was burning, but she wouldn't rub it in front of him. That was the game they played; he pretended he wasn't a monster, and she never let on how much damage he'd done.

"Look what you've turned me into," he said, and she thought he might cry.

After he left, she made a sling out of one of his shirts; by the next morning, her arm was gray and lifeless as the lake. She felt almost giddy from the pain, from how much she could stand. Every time he hit her, she sent Roy one notch deeper into hell.

By noon, when Roy was out fishing, she lost sensation from her hand clear to her neck. She drove one-handed all the way to Phoenix Memorial, where she wrote on the admitting form, "Broke arm falling." The doctor looked at her skeptically, but said nothing as he reset her arm. When he was done, he put a prescription in her hand.

"A two month supply of Vicodin. It'll help with all kinds of bruises and pain."

Cheryl didn't cry in front of Roy anymore, but after the doctor left, she curled up on the examining table and sobbed until she was hoarse.

Later, she drove past her house. She intended to go right by, but then she noticed the new sod Jake must have put in. The freshly painted yellow trim made her put her good arm on the steering wheel and weep. All the place had needed, she saw now, was to get rid of her.

She got out of the car and let herself in the front door. She heard the sound of pages turning in the dining room. She walked in to find Jake taking notes from his pre-law books.

Then, too late, she remembered her arm. She had avoided Jake for months, not wanting him to see her bruises, so of course his gaze went first to the cast, then to the discolorations on her arm and neck. There wasn't a place on her body that hadn't been damaged, but she was so adept now at avoiding mirrors, she hadn't realized how hideous she looked until she saw herself through her son's eyes. She hadn't even thought herself a victim, until Jake looked at her with a horrid mixture of pity and disgust.

"What the hell?"

"Just listen," Cheryl began, but Jake would not. He was circling her, unable to touch her anywhere without brushing a scar. His hands were already clenched into fists. "It's not what it seems."

Finally, Jake stopped and looked right at her. Her son was six two, with serious eyes and a deep laugh she had to pry out of him. He was his father's son, though he'd never had the opportunity to know this.

"Look at me and tell me he didn't do this to you," he said.

Cheryl opened her mouth. She had every intention of lying, but Jake cocked his head a certain way, the same way Paul had, and the truth just slipped out. "He did it."

He was gone in a split second. She hadn't even breathed before she heard his car speeding away. By the time she ran to the door, he had turned the corner, and she knew that even if she drove as fast as she could, she would never catch him.

Now, though, Cheryl was quicker. She was no longer weighed down by bruises and twisted thinking. What her son didn't know was that she had tracked him all these years. She knew exactly where he was and what he had suffered. She snapped shut her suitcase and walked out the door. She could get to Prescott in three hours, if she drove like a maniac. She was not about to let disaster strike twice.

When Jake awoke, he prayed his heart would keep on burning, because it had brought a beautiful woman to his bed. She held his hand tightly, her fingers twined through his. Her rings bit into his skin, her bracelets jingled when she smiled at him.

"Well finally," she said. "A little heart attack and you think you need to sleep forever. You've got to get a move on. My dad wants his bench."

Savannah laughed, which must have meant the pain in his chest was nothing to be afraid of. Maybe he'd been struggling for breath all his life. He looked around the hospital room, painted in pale blue, its single window facing another wing. He didn't remember a thing. One minute he was standing in Doug's garden, the next he was waking up here. He didn't want to remember, he knew that much.

"What are you doing here?" he asked.

She walked to the window, her topaz dress sweeping the floor, the peacock feather in her hat dusting her cheek. He still didn't think he was entitled to anything, but he couldn't stop himself from wondering what it would be like to feel her curled into his chest, her tiny hand tucked against his neck.

"The doctors said it was a mild heart attack," she told him. "You'll be out in a few days. But I read your fortune anyway. You want to know what it is?"

And then Jake remembered. The kids at the lake, the body. His stepfather's body. It was only a matter of time before they identified it. Only a matter of time before someone figured out what had happened. At least he knew now he had a weak heart. It was entirely possible something catastrophic would happen before Cal Bentley showed up with a warrant, before he lost one more thing.

Savannah didn't wait for an answer. "I'll tell you. Your distant past was Death, which usually means a huge transformation or change, and your recent past the Four of Swords, which is some kind of exile. What I'd like to know, Jake Grey, is what you're running from."

She took off her hat and set it down on the table. Then she eased herself on the bed beside him and curled up against his chest. She pressed her lips into the pulse of his neck. She actually kissed him and he closed his eyes. Her skin was white hot, her scent sweet as peppermint, and for the moment he was grateful for every single minute of his rotten life, because it had all led here.

He kissed her hair and she slipped a leg between

his. "I'd be doing you a favor," he said, "if I kicked you out of here."

"So don't do me any favors."

"Savannah." The name stuck in his mouth, made him tongue-tied. She leaned back and just waited until he could go on. "Those bones the kids found. I put that body there."

And then he waited. He didn't blink, because this was what he'd been waiting for—losing, once more, what mattered most. But all she did was look at him.

"You didn't ask what your future was," she said.

"I know my future."

"If you do, then you know it's the Four of Wands. That's rest after a long struggle. That's when you lie here and tell me everything, so you can finally let it go."


Jake was twenty-one when his mother showed him the bruises, and a twenty-one-year-old has many attributes, but caution is not one of them. He'd already shown he was capable of snapping. When his father had died, he'd gone out walking the day after the funeral and hadn't come back for six days. He left with two hundred dollars, came back with twenty, and had very little recollection of what happened in between—except that it had involved rotten personal hygiene, the muddy irrigation canals used to turn the desert green, and pure fury. He was eight years old.

Even then, he'd known it was an unjust world. He could love someone to the best of his ability and still lose him. He could disappear for nearly a week, and that fact would not shatter anyone but himself. When he finally walked in the door again, his mother, who had snapped too, simply looked up and asked where he'd been.

So years later, when his mother came in with bruises, Jake was hardly surprised. In an unjust world, a woman could lose her first husband to heart failure and get beaten by her second, while the woman across the street married her childhood sweetheart and had three beautiful children who never caused her a moment's grief. In an unjust world, he could speed all the way to Wawani Lake, on a highway usually crawling with cops, and not get stopped by anyone.

When he pulled up to the dock, it was just after dark, the time when lake moths rose up by the millions and got tangled in fishing nets and hair. They beat their velvety wings against his windshield, and a fine white powder rose up. Jake sat there, trying to come up with alternatives, but as far as he could tell, there weren't any. He got out of the car and must have given off some kind of merciless odor, because the moths nearest him all took flight.

He walked down the dock to the houseboat. When he flung open the door, Roy Pillandro was sitting on a chair, a rifle resting on his knees.

"The boy," Roy said. "She fucking gets the boy."

Jake wasn't about to start explaining that he hadn't been a boy since the day his father died.

"This is between your mama and me," Roy went on. "You just hightail it on back to college, boy. Go get yourself a fancy education and marry that debutante. I'll just wait here for your mama to come crawling back."

That's when Jake started to smile and couldn't stop. He couldn't think about his exam the next morning, or Joanne and all their plans for getting married after graduation. All he could think about was how he needed to smash something, and that something was going to be Roy's head, and it was going to feel good.

So he smiled, and Roy raised the gun. "You smiling at me, boy? You think this is funny?"

Before Roy could do anything, before he realized he ought to be wary of a smiling twenty-one-year-old, Jake charged him. He grabbed the rifle and tossed it out of Roy's hands. Then he went straight for Roy's throat. He landed a punch there that sent the older man crumpling to the ground.

No one could have stopped him. He became something he would never live down, a man who lost control not only of his fists, but of his whole life. It sailed up and out Roy's window, and was quickly devoured by moths.

He punched Roy so hard, his own knuckles bruised and bled, his head got a little dizzy. And all the while he was saying, "If you ever touch her again, I'll kill you. I swear to God I will."

Finally, he realized the thing he was beating was not moving, and that the sobs he heard were his own. He stood up straight. He unclenched his fists and found a bloody tooth in his palm, one of Roy's coffee-colored incisors. He stuffed it into the wallet in his pocket, and put his hands over his eyes.

He waited until he got his breath back, then walked out of the houseboat into darkness. He had reached the end of the deck when he heard the cock of the rifle.

Years later, he would wish he had just stood there and taken the bullet in the back. He might have survived the shot, he and Roy might have called it even.

But he was twenty-one, his adrenaline was racing, and he wasn't about to let a stupid brute win. When he heard the arming of the gun, he ducked and whirled. A shot sailed over his head and, as Roy struggled to recock the gun, Jake grabbed it by the barrel. He smashed the butt into Roy's head, and a shot went off.

The bullet passed right through the palm of Jake's left hand, but he hardly noticed because Roy had gone over the side of the boat.

Jake dropped the gun. Some woman called out from a neighboring houseboat. "Roy? You all right? You need me to call 911?" She turned on her flood-lamps, and Jake was blinded for a moment, before he came to his senses and jumped back into the shadows. She said again, "Roy?"

Jake looked down at his bleeding hand, then at the bubbles that were coming slower where Roy had gone down. Then in a voice so smooth it would become the monster voice in his dreams, he answered the woman, "No, thank you. Roy just went a little crazy with a firecracker. We're fine."

He had to wait until he heard the click of her door before he jumped into the water, and by then, of course, it was too late. The body he found on the shallow sandy bottom was full of water and for as long as he lived, Jake would never forget the effort it took to bring it to the surface.

He hoisted Roy over the deck of the houseboat, then climbed up after him. He was crying so hard, his cheeks were on fire. He kept opening and closing his mouth, but all that came out were cuss words, "Goddamn" and "Fuck it all" and "You son of a bitch."

He blew air into Roy's vicious mouth. He thumped on his chest, tried to squeeze the water out of his good-for-nothing lungs. And all the while he kept crying, because he knew none of it would do any good.

Finally, he sat back on his heels, his left hand bleeding and throbbing. He wished it hurt more, enough to cloud his thinking. Instead, his mind was sharp. When he finally stopped crying, all he could think about was how to save himself.

He started up the houseboat. He eased out past

the buoys into open water. A few houseboats were anchored in the middle of the lake, their yellow lights bobbing on the surface. He went past them, to Mesquite Cove, where years ago the artificial lake had covered up an old mesquite grove, where a man's body had every chance of getting stuck in the decaying branches and never coming up again.

He looked at Roy's body a long time. He felt only two things: hate and more hate. Three lives ruined in one day, because a man didn't know how to walk out of a room when he got angry, because a woman didn't leave the second a man punched her. Because a boy had not yet realized he couldn't change people, not even by force.

It took only a second to push Roy's body overboard and ruin his own life. As soon as he heard the splash, he took ownership of Roy's soul, whether he liked it or not. Roy would not materialize for years, but right away he would haunt him through his nightmares. Jake would go to sleep and dream of fishing, of how fast he could down a six-pack, and of a fury that swept up out of nowhere.

Over deep water, Jake got out the bleach and scrubbed away bloodstains. He vacuumed up telltale signs of hair. He took off his bloody shirt and tossed it over the side, not realizing until later that it had his wallet and Roy's tooth in the breast pocket. Then he drove the houseboat to the far side of the lake and docked. He took an armload of Roy's clothes out of the closet and stuffed them in a suitcase, and grabbed the rifle he was afraid would be too buoyant to sink. His hand was throbbing as he locked the door to the boat and prayed.

It would take hours to walk back around the lake to his car. It might take days for anyone to notice Roy's houseboat wasn't around. It would take months, he hoped, for people to realize Roy was not coming back.

He saw a tent up on the beach, but heard no signs of life. He put his head down and started walking. After an hour, his hand stopped bleeding. He tried not to breathe too deeply, because when he did he smelled fish and blood and violence. He would smell the lake on himself for years.

It was raining by the time he got back to Phoenix, but when he reached his front door, his mother wouldn't let him in.

She looked through the screen door at his ravaged hand, the hole in the center of it, then at his face. "No," she said.

"He's in the lake. He's never coming back."

"No. No. No. How am I ever going to salvage myself now? He was mine to finish, Jake. Whatever he was, he was mine." She backed up. When he started to open the screen, she slammed the door. He heard the click of the dead bolt.

The rain was streaming off his cheeks and chin. "I did it for you," he cried, but even as he said it, he knew it was a lie. He'd done it for himself, so he could go on believing in justice and God, so he could go on.

"Mom, please." He laid his head against the door and cried. He pounded his forehead against it, but she never unbolted the door. She never let him in.

Finally, he went back to his car and slept in the backseat. In the morning, she would let him in. But in the morning, her car was gone, and there was a note on the front door that read: *Get your things and go*.

He did not get his things. He drove to Joanne's and held out his bloody hand. She took one look at it and his tear-stained face, and pulled him into her arms.

"My god, what happened?"

She led him into the kitchen and forced him to sit down while she bandaged his hand. Finally, he leaned his head against her breast and left it there.

"Whatever it is," she said, "we'll get through it."

And then he told her. He told the whole tale, even when he felt her stiffen. Even when she jerked his head off her. When he got to the part where he pushed Roy into the water, she was standing clear across the room.

"Oh, Jake. You've gone and ruined everything."

He stood up slowly. "I love you," he said, and it was the last time he would say it to anyone. From then on, the words would sit in the bottom of his stomach, like inhaled lake water, and make him ill.

"This will hang over you for the rest of your life," she went on. "Even if they don't find the body right away, you'll always worry. There will always be the threat of being found out. You think I deserve a life like that? Waiting for some awful bomb to drop? What about the children we might have had? What would I tell them when their father is carted off for murder?"

Her voice grew more and more hysterical. "God, Jake, you've ruined it. We could have had everything. And now there's only this." She gestured at his bandaged hand. "This . . . stamp of what you've done. Why didn't you just go to the police? Why did you have to be a fucking hero? Why . . ."

He walked out before she could finish. He drove to ASU, then right past it. He turned northwest and kept driving. He dumped Roy's suitcase in a trash can outside Mayer. He didn't stop until he smelled pine.

It never occurred to him to go back to school and pretend nothing had happened. Something had happened, all right. He'd proven out his theory: It was an unjust world. The people you loved could turn on you in an instant.

Now, Savannah lay beside him, her tears soaking his shirt. He tensed, waiting for her to leave. He wanted her to prove the world was the enemy, that he'd been right hiding away all these years. But all she did was cry as he should have but had never been able to.

She took his chin in her hand and turned him toward her, and then he was lost. She was all he wanted. She kissed him softly and his aching heart ached more. Sometime during that kiss, with some kind of magic trick, she plucked a tear from the corner of his eye, and then another. One sleight of hand and he was crying for all he was worth. A few soft words and he got his forgiveness, whether he deserved it or not.

# ELEVEN

## THE KNIGHT OF CUPS ❧ ATTRACTION

Doug left the light on at night now. He was not afraid of the dark, but of waking up in the morning surprised by vomit on his pillow, or a bit of blood on his collar. He liked to be prepared for things, that was all, the way he prepared for May frosts with a coating of shredded straw and waterwheels for his tomatoes. He left the light on so that, if there was blood, he could find it before Maggie did. While she slept, he soaked all his stains in cold water to keep them from setting.

Besides, he hardly slept at all now. This spring, the top branch of the mountain laurel had reached his bedroom window, and the hours from two A.M. to six found him in the chair by the window, breathing in the apple-like scent of the blossoms and writing love poems.

He had not expected to start writing again. What did he have to write about except that he could no longer get rid of chills? They lasted for days and left him rickety. They were like long, slow earthquakes that appeared to do no damage until he looked under the house and found the foundation gone.

He sat in his chair now, shivering. He would have given everything he had just to walk down the stairs and make his wife breakfast. French toast sprinkled with cinnamon, thick-sliced bacon and cantaloupe. He would have given anything for the look on her face when he started taking care of her.

Maggie, though, did not want breakfast in bed; she wanted to know what he was feeling. But even if he'd had the words, he wouldn't have been able to tell her. He was nearly mute with exhaustion; his breath no longer reached his lungs, and asking him to say more than a few words at a time was like asking him to stop being melodramatic and just get well already.

So instead he took up pen and paper and tried to write of how he sometimes felt death in bed beside him, a cold black mass in the spoon position, its knees tucked up against the back of his calves. He tried to write of the pain that rocked his bones, no doubt causing bruises in his marrow, how his teeth ached and the high-pitched ringing in his ears seemed like a scream coming from the heart of the tumor. He tried to write that his bladder burned, but he couldn't relieve it, because it hurt even more to urinate, and that a shower just about killed him. It chilled him right to the bone. He tried to write that he was furious; he ought to be able to lie beside his wife at night without his odd-smelling sweat offending her, without her reaching for him, then pulling away when she touched the sharp bone of his hip. He tried to write that every time he looked on a healthy man he thought God a traitor, but all that came out were love poems. Tonight's went like this:

*I've always had good soil.*
*A place where roots grew deep*
*and the things I loved best bloomed quick and*
    *long,*
*like they were supposed to.*
*I've been happy as a deep-rooted honeysuckle,*
*because the column I curled my tendrils around*
    *was you.*

He couldn't help it, and he'd stopped trying. He just wasn't made for melancholy or deep philosophical debate. He'd been made to write sappy poems and to love a complex woman, and that was enough for him.

He tucked the poem into his pocket, then curled his hands around the arms of the chair. He checked that Maggie was still sleeping, because there was no need for her to see what he had to go through to stand. He slid to his knees, then rested his head on the chair seat until his arms stopped shaking. He pressed his elbows into the seat, gritted his teeth, then slowly hoisted himself to his feet.

The blanket dropped from his shoulders, and his shale-like skin prickled. The cold hurt, but then, so did everything. He worked his way around the chair arm to the wall, then along the wall to the door, always gripping something, steadying himself on tables and lamps, like a thirteen-month-old desperate to walk.

There were sixteen steps down to the kitchen, and tonight he had to slide down them on his rear like a child. After he'd done it, he opened the back door to his personally planted heaven. The first scent to hit him was the syrupy aroma of the honeysuckle, then the blue bite of sage, then at long last the jasmine. There was nothing sweeter in this world than jasmine tangled up in a warm summer's night. It was the only thing that got rid of the chills; it was like being enveloped by a soft, fleshy woman.

He stepped out into the garden and saw where Maggie had replaced a withering, rare purple salvia with the more common blue variety. She had done her best to prune it to form, to cover up all signs of her work, but he could still make out her handprints in the soil. He knelt down and put his hands where hers had been. He was the only person on this planet who knew what she went through to keep things around here living, and he was glad. Marriage was not only a vow; it was also a privilege. The right to see what no one else could see—both the tender and the ugly, the many faces of a woman who did all her wooing in secret.

He stood up slowly. It took another fifteen minutes to work his way to the partially carved bench beneath one of the Juneberry trees. He sat down and leaned against Jake's carvings. He had already decided on the next one. A vegetable patch, with carrots and potatoes pushing their way out of the desert soil no one else had had the nerve to plant in. He had never been in a fistfight in his life, but he'd planted peas in Phoenix. He'd grown all his daylilies from seed. That ought to count for something.

He steadied himself on the arms of the bench, then climbed up on his knees. Ten minutes later, he got to his shrunken, pale feet and clung to the lowest branch of the Juneberry tree. This time, he wanted to spear the poem on the topmost branch. He wanted it to touch the heavens awhile before he coaxed Maggie into looking up.

He wrapped his arm around the branch, then tried to hoist himself up. He didn't even get close. His arm gave, his foot slid out, and just as he was falling, large hands encircled his waist and planted him back on the ground.

Doug turned around to find Jake Grey. "You should be in the hospital," Doug said.

"I broke out. Anyway, I could say the same for you."

They looked at each other, then Doug laughed. "Look at us. Some kind of men."

Jake stepped back and ran a hand over his beard. He glanced at the garage apartment, where men frailer than Doug had been pacing for the last three days, waiting for Savannah to take a break from the hospital and Jake, to read their fortunes.

"You all right?" Doug asked.

"Sure," Jake said, though his face was pale, and his left hand fluttered every now and then.

"You up for climbing?" He handed Jake the note. "I want to spear it through the top branch."

Jake glanced at the poem, then tucked it in his pocket.

"You can read it, son," Doug said.

But Jake didn't. He grabbed the same branch Doug had been hanging on and hoisted himself up. He hovered atop the strong limb for a moment, breathing hard, but Doug didn't worry about his heart. Tough men died young, but not while they were wrapped up in a woman, not when they were waking up wanting something for the first time in their lives.

Jake climbed to the top branch and speared the poem through the limb. By the time he got back down, Doug was sitting on the bench again, his shoulder curled along the rim of Superstition Mountain.

"Your daughter," Jake said, but Doug held up his hand.

"You don't have to ask my permission. I'll tell you, though, she'll make it impossible for you to be miserable. You'll wake up one morning not even knowing yourself."

The night wind swirled, slapping them with lily petals and lime-green gingko leaves, but when Doug looked up, the poem was still there.

"Why don't you come up to the cabin for a while?" Jake said suddenly. "All of you. The fresh air will do you good. We can finish the bench in peace."

Doug looked at him, and it was the strangest thing. It was like seeing himself in those blue eyes. His dark twin, twenty years younger.

"I'm no bed and breakfast," Jake went on. "Everyone cooks their own food, makes their own beds. The cabin's small, but it's got a loft. There's no one for miles, and the water out of my well is clean as rain."

Doug tried to hoist himself to his feet, but he was bone tired. Jake helped him with an unsteady hand, another damaged body to lean against. Doug knew how hard it had been for Jake to offer, as hard as giving away a piece of his own soul. "I'd like that," he said. "Very much."

The next evening, Maggie listened to Doug poke at the sheets. Usually, he lay still as stone, trying to get her to believe he was sleeping. Well, mister, she was down to two hours sleep a night herself. She could fake steady breathing as well as he could.

Finally, she stood up and yanked up the shades, filling the room with dusky light, soft and purple, like Doug's swollen veins. "All right. Out with it."

She'd found another of his poems in the Juneberry tree that afternoon. She'd had to get it down with the extension pruner, and now she could not get it out of her mind. If she'd been the column he'd curled his tendrils around, then she must have been rotting from the start. Otherwise, he would have grown strong by now. He would have smothered her years ago.

"Jake asked us up to his cabin to stay a while."

She breathed in deeply. She understood exactly what he was saying. If he went, he would not come back.

"It's hard for me here," Doug was saying. "Seeing the garden, but not being able to work in it. The fresh air . . . Well, stranger things have happened. It's not out of the realm of possibility that I might get well up there."

Outside the garage, a line was forming. Technically, Savannah was still writing copy for the supermarket, but even Maggie could not deny that her real job was here. Her neighbors came day and night now. An unusual purple light streamed out of the garage window, and Maggie thought she heard crying.

"He'll want Savannah to come along," she said. "He's in love with her."

"Well, sure."

"This one's got disaster written all over it, too."

"Ah, Maggie. Give them a chance. You never know."

When she turned around, Doug was sitting up straight. Despite his bald scalp and skin as flaky as pie crust, she sometimes refused to believe he was dying. Perhaps, through her eyes, he never would. Perhaps, if she never took her eyes off him, she could make him live.

"So what do you say?" Doug asked.

She wouldn't say anything, just to put a little drama into it, but she decided right then that she would go to the cabin. Even if she had to put up with no air-conditioning and those psycho dogs running loose, at least they were doing something. They weren't just going to sit in this house and rot.

In the morning, while Doug did what little packing he could, Maggie found Emma in the garden, dressed in cut-off shorts and a stained tank top. She was slinking around the mermaid fountain, picking out the change Savannah's clients had thrown in for luck.

"Mom's in there with another one," Emma said. "That woman with the red hair."

"Marie Albert?"

"Whoever. She's in there wailing about some guy she was in love with before she met her husband, like forty years ago. I mean, I'm sorry, but like, get over it."

Maggie smiled. She adored this child. She would give her anything she asked for, if she would only ask.

"I take it you don't believe in your mother's powers."

"Mom's got no powers. If she did, we'd be millionaires. We wouldn't be living in your garage. No offense."

She walked around the fountain, stepping on the cobblestones hard enough to chip off the edges.

"I saw that . . . thing when Mabel was here," Emma went on. "I don't know what it was. It could have been the ghost of Christmas past for all I know. But, I mean, if her husband wanted to get in touch with her, he should have just done it. The fact that he had to wait for this two-bit psychic to help him is really pathetic."

"You're in love with that boy, aren't you?"

Emma jerked her head up. Her eyes were like silver fire, passion oozed out of her pores with a lilac scent. With so much lust to spare, Maggie wished she'd share some. She'd give anything to go back to the days before she'd decided to be miserable, when wanting had been the only cancer, eating her up from the inside out.

"I know what you all think of him, but you don't know anything. I'm not giving up."

"Well, let's hope not."

Emma eyed her, then leaned back against the fountain. "Grandma, sometimes I think you're messing with my mind."

Maggie threw back her head and laughed. "We're all going up to Jake's cabin to stay a while. Eli goes up there quite a bit, doesn't he?"

Emma went still for a moment, then threw herself into Maggie's arms. "I love you, Grandma."

Maggie sniffed. "I should hope so."

They were still hugging when a sedan pulled up in the driveway, and a trim, white-haired woman stepped out of it. She spotted Maggie and Emma in the garden, and cut right through the rhododendrons.

"I'm Cheryl Pillandro," the woman called over to them. "I'm looking for Jake Grey. I was told he often works here."

Maggie squinted, but it was Emma who jumped in. "He had a heart attack, like right where you're standing."

The woman stopped and put a hand over her heart as if she might do the same, and Maggie glared at Emma. She took the woman's elbow and steered her to the half-carved bench.

"He's all right. He's back at his cabin. Just needs to take it easy a while."

The woman caught her breath, but Maggie could feel her whole body trembling. "I'm his mother. It's vital that I talk to him."

"Well, if you want to see him, you'll have to go up the mountain. You can come with us. Your son asked us to move in."

Cheryl looked at her closely for the first time. "Really?"

"Go figure," Maggie said, turning her face up to the sun. "It's mostly about my daughter. She could be anything she wants, but instead she's turning into a flimflam artist. Let me tell you right now, there's no chance in hell it will work out with her and Jake."

"I don't think I understand."

"What's to understand? They're horrible for each other. Someone's going to get their heart ripped out, and maybe it will be Savannah. Maybe she'll finally start seeing some sense."

Emma was giggling. Cheryl rubbed her forehead, as if she was regretting leaving the safe confines of her car.

Maggie took pity on her. "Come on. I'll make you some tea. Or would you rather have a gin and tonic? God knows I would. I need every drop I can get to watch my daughter walk around without her feet touching the ground. A woman's got to get some soil between her toes. She's got to *experience* things. Believe me, getting your heart broken is not the worst thing." Maggie looked at Emma deliberately, but then Cheryl Pillandro grabbed her hand.

"No," she said. "The worst thing is breaking someone else's."


Jake came home from Smitty's with a sack of groceries, frozen foods mostly, and cream of mushroom soup for Doug. He stepped out of his car and looked up. Mountain fog had rolled in, but not thick enough to hide an arsenal of pine cones stacked neatly on the roof.

He was on Carvedilol to strengthen his heart, and huge amounts of Avapro to lower his blood pressure, but nevertheless he set the bag on the porch, grabbed the corner post, and climbed to the roof. When he looked over the edge, he found the metal roof littered with piles of ashes that could very well have come from the chimney. He heard laughter and then knew he'd crossed some invisible line, because the ghost was as real as he was, sitting on the far end of the roof, tapping out ashes from his cigarette.

Jake pulled himself up and sat down. He was too woozy to try to catch a ghost, and he should have realized years ago that it was impossible anyway.

"Just go," he said.

A light mist started to fall and went through Roy's head and out his toes. When the downpour began a few minutes later, Roy lit up a new cigarette.

The ghost made his way across the roof, the metal creaking beneath him. His feet were still clad in fifteen-year-old black boots, his ruby pinkie ring now a dull black. He knelt down beside Jake.

Jake reached out a finger and was sure he touched a bony knee. He must have gone right over the edge, because everything was clear as day to him now. Love and meanness were the two things that could turn a dead man into a ghost, but only meanness turned him solid. Only viciousness let him point a cigarette toward a man's eyes so he could feel the heat.

Roy smiled, and thrust his tongue through the hole where his gold-capped tooth had fallen out. He was still smiling when he said his first words in fifteen years. "I'm not going anywhere. So shoot me."

Roy laughed uproariously, but Jake just climbed down the porch column. His dogs were running in circles, howling. He grabbed the sack of groceries and went inside, but right away he got a sick feeling in the pit of his stomach because the house reeked of cigarettes.

He opened all the windows, then put away the food. By the time the Dawsons' car pulled into the driveway, the smell had dissipated and the ghost was gone. Maggie and Savannah helped Doug out of the car, while Emma lingered in the downpour. She didn't step up on the porch until she was thoroughly drenched, chancing pneumonia. One more woman still sat in the backseat. Jake had never expected to see her again, so it was a long time before he recognized his mother.

His heart throbbed painfully as he walked out into the rain. Cheryl Pillandro rolled down her window, and Jake took a good, long breath.

"Mom," he said.

"The police found the body. The sheriff came to my house."

He nodded. He was not even remotely surprised. All he felt was that this had been a long time coming, and in truth, he was a little relieved.

"You called me a while back." He felt the rain sink through his shirt and drip coldly down the muscles of his back. His skin prickled, then he started to shiver. He had a feeling it would be hours, maybe days, before he'd be able to stop.

"Yes. When they started the draining. I wanted you to have time to run."

He invited her in, then went to the loft to put on a dry shirt. By the time he came back down, the dogs were running around the living room in tighter and tighter circles, barking wildly. Jake banged his fist against the wall.

"Take it outside."

The dogs obediently went out onto the back deck. Emma went with them, then stood on the edge, where the rain poured out of the gutters in thick surges. The Dawsons all surveyed the downstairs.

Jake had not wanted to make the cabin beautiful. He hadn't sanded down any of the logs, had not put a single coat of urethane on the floors. He'd chosen the roughest, knottiest wood he could find, but now, when

Savannah turned around, her eyes shining, he knew he had failed.

"Nice," Doug Dawson said. "Really nice. I think I'd like to lie down awhile."

Jake showed him to the bed upstairs. Above it was a single, triangular window he had salvaged from an old Victorian house in town. He was afraid the ghost might hang his feet outside the glass, but all that was there now was rain.

Jake helped Doug into bed, then turned to leave. "Jake," Doug said softly. "You all right with this?"

Jake turned around. If his father had lived, Jake's whole life would have been different. Yet when Paul Grey had died, the last thing he'd told his wife was "Thank God it wasn't you." That was the thing with fathers; they had no idea how vital they were. They had no idea a child just went to pieces without them.

"I'm not all right with you dying, no," he said. Already the loft smelled sweeter, as if pieces of Doug were coming off in the air. He went to the window and propped it open. "But if it has to happen, then you ought to do it here."

He looked back and Doug was smiling, his eyes closed. Jake walked down the stairs.

Cheryl, Maggie, and Savannah all sat around the dining-room table, whispering. They stopped cold when they saw him.

"I suppose you told her," he said, gesturing to Maggie. "What's the point of being an escaped murderer, if everyone's in on it?"

He walked out onto the deck. The rain had finally let up and the air was cold and charged. He threw a rawhide for the dogs and sparks flew when it hit the ground. He heard a throat clearing and turned around to find Emma standing there, glaring at him.

"As a matter of fact, I hired Mr. Malone back. He'll be here tomorrow afternoon."

Her sudden smile startled him, and it would bring Eli Malone to his knees. A boy like that never expected a girl like this to fall in love with him. It was out of the realm of possibility. It could shake a whole world.

She ran off into the woods after the dogs and, a few minutes later, Cheryl came out. She put her hand on his shoulder, then quickly dropped it.

"I didn't say a word to the police," she said. "I swear I didn't."

"It doesn't matter."

"Of course it does. Everything matters now. They've identified the body, Jake. They think I did it. And since I didn't, there's nothing to worry about."

Jake turned to her. He did not laugh, because it would have hurt too much.

"You know why I left?" he asked.

Cheryl looked away. There were tears in her eyes and he was glad. He'd waited a long time to hurt someone back.

"It wasn't because I killed him," he went on. "It was because I hadn't done it sooner, before he'd tainted you."

Cheryl grabbed his arm with the hand Roy had broken all those years ago. Today, her nails were smooth and polished in pale pink. She had a ring on her middle finger with a sapphire blue stone.

"You can hate me," she said. "I can take that. But what I can't take is you giving up. Just letting them get you."

"It doesn't matter."

She dropped her hand and stepped back. Her hair was cut clear above her ears, a style Roy would have beat her for.

"I was crazy then," she said, running her hand

along the wet deck railing. "I lived on hating Roy. I know you can't understand that, but it's the truth. I woke up every morning holding my breath, hoping my heart would just give out."

Jake turned away. He had waited a long time for this day, but now he was disappointed. It was too hard to hate a person. It took more energy than he had. He wished Savannah would come out and lay her head on his shoulder. He wanted her to stand beside him until the sun went down, and then point out every constellation and tell him the myths behind the stars.

"You can't understand it," Cheryl went on. "I know you can't. I can't, not now. There are very few things a woman can't forgive herself for, but one of them is not standing behind her son."

"It's all over now," Jake said, but of course it wasn't. It was just beginning. The thing with hiding out was that nothing got done. Time would stand still until someone found him out.

Cheryl leaned against him, crying. He closed his eyes. He tried to work up some kind of loathing, but the woman in his arms was too much of a stranger, and strangers were easy to forgive.

"It's all right," he said. "Don't worry about it. I've done fine."

Cheryl pulled back to look at him. She wiped her eyes and glanced up at the roof, where the ghost had materialized out of the blue and was watching them steadily. His mother saw nothing. She turned around and fingered the buttons on her silk blouse.

"I sold the house. I've been working at Dillard's. In lingerie. They're moving me up to the women's nine-to-five department."

The ghost slid down the gutter behind her. He was smiling, but in a second his grin stopped cold, and even Jake, who was always expecting a fight, was not ready for the fist when it came at his mother.

Roy swung at Cheryl's head, but the blow went right through her and landed on the side of Jake's chin. Jake put his hand to his skin, expecting to find blood. His fingers came away clean.

"Jake?" Cheryl said. "Is something wrong?"

The ghost seemed as surprised as he was. He stared at his hand, twisting it right and left. He tapped the porch railing and Cheryl whirled around at the sound.

"Woodpeckers?" she asked.

Roy threw back his head and laughed.

"No," Cheryl went on, "robins. Definitely robins."

Jake took a deep breath and realized something would have to be done. It was entirely possible he would have to kill Roy Pillandro twice.

He looked back at his mother, but she was just smiling, looking out at the woods. "It's beautiful here," she said. "I'll give you that."

For a moment, she looked half her age. She looked like a woman who wouldn't hesitate to fight back. Jake looked for the ghost, but Roy must have noticed the same thing, because he was gone.

"It took me thirty days to get up the nerve to go back to the lake," Cheryl said. "You know the first thing I did when I got there? I leaned over the pier and spit on that son of a bitch's grave."

Jake reached out and touched her white hair. When she pushed her cheek against his hand, he remembered why he'd killed a man. He remembered why he'd been glad.

"I'm happy you've found someone," his mother said.

Jake looked through the window into the cabin. Savannah and Maggie were sitting at the table. Savannah had laid out her cards, but Maggie refused to look.

"I haven't found anyone," he said. "She's not staying."

"Why not?"

"She's not the staying type."

"So you'll go with her."

"I can't go anywhere. Not anymore. What will happen will happen. I don't really care anymore."

Cheryl grabbed his hands. "Oh, you care. Don't think I don't understand what you're doing. Your father was the same. He'd get all quiet and stoic when inside he was dying. He never told me a thing about that heart of his until it exploded on him. That was just plain cruel, Jake. I didn't even know where the checkbook was. I couldn't get his damn stick shift out of the driveway."

"Mom."

"You care," she said. "And if you don't, I'll bet that woman in there does. I saw the way she looked at you. You better care, Jake Grey, or you're going to break that woman's heart in two."

"I think that it will be the other way around."

Cheryl stayed for the night, but the next morning had to get back to work in Tucson. Jake walked her out on the porch, which during the night had been dusted with a slick coating of pine pollen.

"I've got a bedroom this color," Cheryl said, swiping a finger through the yellow dust on the railing. "I'm in a book club, too. Did I tell you that? We meet every Wednesday night. We read John Irving, if you can believe that."

Jake smiled. "That's great, Mom."

"I'll come back the second you need me. I'll quit if I have to. One won't make up for the other, but nevertheless, this time I'm doing it right."

After she left, Savannah met him on the deck. The morning sky was closing in, smelling of rain again, and birds seemed to fly at them out of nowhere. A pine cone fell right out of the sky, or maybe from off the roof, but Jake wasn't about to turn around to check.

He stood stiff as wood. He might never have held her, if she hadn't held him first.

"I can see why you love it here," Savannah said quietly. "I fell asleep the second my head hit the pillow. I dreamed of vanilla ice cream." She laughed and leaned into him.

When he had asked them to come, he had not considered that Savannah would ruin his cabin for him. Now he'd never be able to stand in this spot without wishing for something soft to hold. He'd never sit in front of his fire again without craving ice cream. He'd be relegated to the few spaces she hadn't touched—his woodpile, the basement, the dim corners of his workshop.

"The sheriff came to my mother's house," he said.

She nodded. She flicked at a mosquito hovering around her face, then turned to him. "There's no way they can link you to that body. And even if they could, you did what you had to do. It's been fifteen years, Jake. No one's going to pursue this now."

"Like hell they aren't." Maggie had come out onto the deck with a cup of coffee.

Savannah stepped out of Jake's embrace. "Jake doesn't deserve—"

"It doesn't matter what he deserves," Maggie said. "Jake understands this."

He nodded, because he did. Life unfolded as it would, whether you were good or bad. If he ever learned to pray again, he'd pray for luck, not love or money.

"He's suffered enough," Savannah said. "God can't hold this against him."

"God can do whatever he damn well pleases," Maggie said, "if he's even there. God does not pay very good attention, if you ask me. People are falling through the cracks left and right."

She walked off the deck toward the woods, scattering the morning grasshoppers, who leapt out of the way of her sneakers. She left deep, dark footprints in the soggy ground.

"She's right," Jake said.

"Please don't side with her."

He heard the plea in her voice, and reached out to touch her cheek. "How do you do it? I've seen your deck. It's full of swords and turmoil. It goes against logic and fairness that good things could happen all the time."

Savannah walked into the cabin, then came back out with the cards. "Shuffle and pick one," she said.

"Savannah—"

"Just do it. If you already think bad things will come, then you certainly can't be afraid."

He shuffled the cards, then turned over the top one.

"The Seven of Swords," she said. "New plans. Confidence. Proof that not all the swords are bad. Pick another."

"This is ridiculous."

"No, it's fate. Pick."

He reached into the middle of the deck and drew Strength. "Self-explanatory," she said. "And good, I might add. Pick again."

He chose the Knight of Cups. "That's attraction. Sometimes falling in love, often a challenge. Go again."

Jake picked twelve cards, and to all twelve, she had

a promising future in store for him. "How do I know you haven't stacked the deck?" he asked. "How do I know you're not cheating?"

She yanked the cards back and flipped them over. He saw, very clearly, that the bad cards were in there, but they had all sunk to the bottom with his shuffling.

"Magician," he said.

"I didn't touch the cards. You did. So don't you tell me you have no luck, Jake Grey. Don't you dare tell me this can't all work out all right."

She placed the cards back in his hands, then closed his fingers over them. When she turned and walked into the house, all his dogs followed her.

Jake breathed in the vanilla morning air and squeezed the cards tight. Then he opened his fist and picked one out of the middle. It was the Ten of Pentacles, a man, woman and child all dancing, an old man reaching out to pet a dog. He quickly threaded it back in the deck. It was some kind of trick, and he wasn't falling for it. Only a fool wished for the one thing he really wanted.

# TWELVE

## THE SEVEN OF WANDS ❧ COURAGE

Savannah knew the superstitions. Kill a cricket in the house and bad news will come to your door. Rip the wings off a bee and you'll lose everything you treasure within a month.

So when she hiked the trail to Kemper Peak and stepped on an anthill, smashing it flat, she said a prayer not only for the ants she'd annihilated, but for herself. Earlier, she'd swatted a fly without thinking twice and flushed a gargantuan spider down the toilet. How many more signs did she need? Obviously, something bad was about to happen.

No doubt it had to do with the boy in front of her. Eli Malone, along with Emma and Jake, were showing her the path to Kemper Peak. Savannah never saw the bald granite mountain ahead; instead, her gaze stuck on Eli Malone's back. His brown hair was tied in a ponytail, bobbing from one shoulder to the other. Jake had given the boy his job back, but had promised to keep him away from Emma, if that was what Savannah wanted. The problem was, Savannah didn't know what she wanted. Since Jake had collapsed in the garden, nothing was a sure bet, not heartbeats or Emma's happiness or even her very own desires.

Jake was the last kind of man she ought to fall for, all silence and misery, a festering heap of neglect. But when she'd been holding him, waiting for the ambulance, she'd known she was falling then and there. When she had looked up and seen Eli crying, she'd known she didn't have the heart to keep him from her daughter. Sometimes, you just fell for the wrong person, plain and simple. Sometimes, you just had to ride it out.

Emma walked in front of Eli so he could watch her every move. She kicked up rocks and dust, sliced breezes in two with the sway of her hips. She snatched up dandelions and blew the cottony seeds in his path. Because she didn't turn around, she never knew Eli snatched them right out of the air and tucked them into his shirt pocket. She never knew just how much effect she had.

The summit was still a half-mile ahead, a jagged boulder that jutted into the air like a fist. The peak was the site of the biggest avalanche ever recorded in Arizona. The slide had taken off fifty feet of mountain and killed every tree but one. The north face they were maneuvering through now was a minefield of granite debris, with a single, stunted ponderosa growing in a three-inch deep pocket of soil.

Savannah watched her daughter and Eli scramble toward the summit, kicking up landslides of their own. Above them, three clouds were brewing, and the air smelled of smoke, from a controlled burn that had immediately gotten out of control and was now threatening a ritzy new subdivision ten miles up the road.

Every once in a while the wind changed, and Emma's voice floated down, or rather the new Emma's voice did, because Savannah didn't recognize a single strain.

She turned to Jake, who was walking slowly now, his initial adrenaline at breaking his doctor's orders withering beneath the hot sun and obvious chest pain. She put her hand on his arm.

"What does this prove?" she asked.

He wiped the sweat off his neck. "Nothing."

She kept hold of him to make him walk slower. By the time they reached the summit, Emma and Eli were lying on their backs on the rock, the tips of their fingers touching. Emma was telling the story of Agamano, an Indian girl—a story Savannah had created the first time they hiked the Sierras.

"The Indians lived in these mountains a long time ago," Emma was saying. "This peak, they said, was the sacred temple of the sky god. If the Indians got too close, the mountain grabbed them with its claws and fed them to the sky."

Savannah and Jake sat down, while the dogs raced past the boulder and down the ragged south flank, hunting for squirrels in the rock.

"One day," Emma went on, "Agamano, a young squaw, decided it was all superstition. She set off up the mountain alone and, halfway up, no claws had grabbed her. Ten feet below the summit, she was sure she was going to make it, and that's when a shadow fell over her and a stone claw rose up. It grabbed her in its tentacles and lifted her to the sky. The clouds opened up, and behind it a huge, gaping mouth. The sky ate her whole, and the rain turned red with her blood."

Eli had been throwing rocks off the side, but now he stopped. "Shit, Emma."

The first raindrop fell on Savannah's left hand, the

second on Jake's beard. Savannah looked up; those three clouds had abruptly merged and turned the color of charcoal. In the time it took to blink, the last bit of blue was swallowed up with a rumble and a lightning bolt that struck Alpine Peak to the north.

Savannah stood up quickly. The blood rain was Emma's addition, and Savannah wasn't sure she liked it. She didn't like this storm, either. It went from drizzle to downpour in seconds, and the rain was cold and sharp as ice.

"Come on," she said. "We have to go."

Lightning struck the far peak again, and in the distance they heard a tree splinter, then fall. The dogs came charging up the mountain, their fur standing on end. Savannah grabbed Jake's hand, but Eli and Emma just laughed. Eli jumped up and pulled Emma with him.

"Uh-ya-ya-ya," he sang, patting his mouth the way he'd seen television Indians do it. The sky god must have heard him, because the rain came harder and lightning struck that single tree they'd passed, splitting it in two.

"Emma!" Savannah shouted, but Emma was oblivious. She was dancing with her face toward the sky, so certain love was more dangerous than a mountain lightning storm that she'd dare anything now. Probably, she was hoping lightning would strike her, so she could prove she would survive it.

Then, as quick as it came, the storm let up. The lightning drifted right over them and hit Whitmore Peak to the south, then disappeared completely. The rain stopped all at once, and behind it came cold mountain air and an eerie quiet. Eli and Emma stopped dancing, and Eli reached out and took Emma's hand. Savannah leaned against Jake, but that was worse, because she could feel his heart pounding off-kilter, one beat here, one long, painfully quiet second, then two beats there.

"Eli," Savannah said sharply, and the boy dropped Emma's hand. "Walk with me." She started down the mountain. When he reached her, Savannah noticed how small his hands were. Little-boy hands. Hands that might have been made for delicate surgeries, except that no one had bothered to tell him that.

"The Five of Wands," she said when they reached the tree line.

"Don't start that shit again."

Savannah shrugged. "It's a card of struggle, but that doesn't mean you won't win out. Reversed, it is the card of contradictions."

When they were deep in the thick of trees, Savannah looked back over her shoulder. Emma and Jake were still navigating the rubble, and when Emma stumbled, Jake reached out and took her hand.

"Look," Eli said. "I'm not gonna mess things up with Jake, so don't worry. I'm keeping this job."

"Why?" Savannah asked. "He works you to death."

Eli stopped. He grabbed a shoulder-high pine bough and twisted until it snapped. He started yanking out pine needles one by one. "He's the only person who ever trusted me not to steal from him, so I never have."

"Stealing just messes you up. Every time you take something, something's taken from you. Sometimes a dollar from your pocket, but more often a piece of your heart. Pretty soon, you're falling in love with innocent girls, you're getting married and settling down, and ending up just like your parents."

"I'll never be like my parents."

"Every single person says the same thing," she said. "And then we grow up and see it's not so easy. Worse, we see they just might have been right."

"You don't have to worry about Emma."

"Oh no?" she said, walking again. "Why is that?"

Eli dropped the mangled remains of the pine bough. "I love her."

Savannah didn't look at him, because the words were simple, honest, and most definitely a threat.

Jake worked and slept in his workshop, but even there, his quiet was spoiled. Doug slept most of each day, but Emma blasted hip-hop from the deck. Maggie drove down the drive at breakneck speeds, spooking the blue jays into chattering all afternoon. Savannah went to town every afternoon to drop off her copy and do her readings, then came back and took long walks. Strangely enough, her absences were the noisiest. Waiting for her to come back played like sentimental music in his head, the same foolish song over and over, and he got no peace.

He didn't get too close to any of them, especially Maggie, who was doing her damnedest to civilize the place. She cooked French cuisine and redecorated his living room with wildflowers and mail-ordered Berber rugs. Whenever Doug woke up, she made sure to smile at him. Because he looked so well rested, she told him she was having the time of her life. Every night, though, after Doug went to bed, Jake could see her through the window to his kitchen, her hand clutching the telephone, her face white and tight. After two days, his post office box started filling up with fruit platters and all-cotton percale sheets.

One week after she'd arrived, she came into his workshop. "I'm taking Emma to Phoenix. You are in desperate need of a new shower curtain."

"Maggie, you'll have to let me pay you for all these—"

She waved him off. "Consider it rent. She and I are going to do some shopping and go out to lunch, have a little girl time. Not that it's not exciting enough here."

Jake was working on one of his other projects, a rock star's bed. He could have sanded it blindfolded, but nevertheless he studied his work closely, because he didn't think Maggie Dawson would appreciate his smile.

"I'm going to call as soon as we get there," she went on. "If anything . . . He's been sleeping like crazy since we got here, and maybe that's what he needed. I wouldn't leave if I didn't think he'd be all right."

Jake set down his sandpaper and sat back on his heels. "Believe it or not, your devotion is obvious."

Maggie walked to the small window that looked out on the worst view on the property—the bare slope Frank Simmons had gouged out with a Bobcat, in order to level off a building pad. Jake had put his workshop window there on purpose, so he would never be distracted by the beauty right outside his door.

"Love is just plain cruel," she said. "I should never have given in to it."

"I didn't think any of us had a choice."

Maggie breathed deeply. She looked smaller up here, more vulnerable to wind and weather. He wondered if she realized the fight was seeping right out of her.

"I appreciate you letting us come here," she said, still keeping her back to him. "I know it can't be easy giving up your privacy."

"I'll survive."

"Well, it was nice. I didn't expect it of you."

Jake picked up the sandpaper again. "Psychos are people too."

She whirled around, smiling. "You know about that?"

"Doesn't seem to be much of a secret."

"You are a psycho, Jake Grey, and thank God. At least you're something."

She walked up the hill, where Emma was already waiting in the car.

"You're a psycho, too, Maggie Dawson," he said, as she skidded out of the drive, sending up smokestacks of dust and gravel.

An hour later, while Savannah was still in town reading fortunes, he went into his own house and didn't recognize it. His countertops held a minefield of hats and fluffy clothing, Maggie's new fruit platter was piled with more apples and kiwis than five people could possibly eat. His dining-room table had been turned into a cosmetics counter, with lipsticks and nail polishes ranging from ruby red to black, and a dozen shades of blue eye shadow. The air was steamy and lavender-colored, and smelled like the sweet, moist folds of a woman's skin.

He reached down to pick up a pair of Emma's sandals, then changed his mind and just left them there. His heart burned as he picked his way to the refrigerator. Who'd have known a man could feel whole just by walking through a woman's chaos? There were lipstick-smeared cups in the sink, and he just stood there, smiling. It had taken fifteen years for somebody to start living here, and even then it wasn't him. He found one of Savannah's rings on the counter, a surprisingly plain silver band, and slipped it into his pocket. Let her come to him to get it back. Just let her come to him.

He opened his refrigerator, then just stood there, stunned. Maggie and Savannah had gone to the deluxe supermarket in town and bought out the place. Mineral water, organic tomatoes, fresh sliced roasted turkey. Corn-fed chicken, Edam cheese, pre-washed salad and poppy seed dressing.

He'd withstood blood on his hands and hauntings, but the sight of fresh strawberries in his refrigerator nearly brought him to his knees. He was reaching for one when he heard a thump on the stairs. He closed the refrigerator and rushed to find Doug curled up on the top step, a red welt already forming on his forehead.

"A shower," he was saying. "I didn't know anybody . . . It's so hard on Maggie."

Jake lifted him up. The man weighed less than one of his dogs, and just went limp. Jake carried him into the bathroom, then set him on the toilet. Doug's pajama top clung to the C-curve of his stomach. Jake started on the buttons. There were eleven of them, and with each one his throat tightened more, until he couldn't have said a word if he tried.

He finally got the shirt off, and forced himself not to flinch at Doug's scent, humusy and damp. When he saw the goose bumps all over Doug's parchment skin, he reached up and flipped on the heat lamp.

"I can't get warm," Doug said. "Not ever."

Jake took off Doug's slippers and pants and underwear, and was glad then that he was a hermit with a thick beard and false eyes, because that way Doug couldn't read him. Jake would never be the one to break his heart. Doug hunched over, his hands the only things still their original size, spreading across a puckered knee and a half. A strange clump of hair had grown in on the back of his scalp, straight out and surprisingly gaudy, the color of Oriental poppies. His penis leaked continually, and the urine was cloudy, the color of cream of mushroom soup.

Doug tried to breathe deeply, but only shuddered.

Jake reached over and turned the hot water on full. Doug shuddered again, and had to rest his head against the counter.

Jake rolled up his sleeves and tested the water. When it was right, he lifted Doug up and set him down gently on his feet. "Hold on to me. Tomorrow I'll nail in a safety bar."

Doug held him around the waist. Jake ignored his drenched shirt and picked up a washcloth and soap. As softly as he knew how, he washed the man's back and stomach. Doug's skin flaked off easily, and the layer below was pale pink. He quickly swiped the urine off Doug's penis, and neither of them looked up. Despite the running water, he could hear Doug crying.

He washed the man's legs and arms and scalp, and the bathroom quickly filled up with enough steam to hide the worst of it. Finally, he turned off the water and grabbed the thickest towel he could find. He wrapped it tightly around Doug's body.

"Sit here," he said, putting him back on the toilet. "I'll get a fire ready."

He went out into the living room and filled the fireplace with kindling and six pieces of the wood Eli had split. He lit a match and waited until it was raging. The afternoon was destined for ninety degrees, but from now on there would be a fire in his hearth day and night.

He went upstairs and changed his shirt, then picked up a warm gray sweat suit for Doug. He took it into the bathroom.

"Figured we'd get dressed today. What the hell."

Doug managed a weak smile. He shivered when he dropped the towel, but Jake quickly helped him on with his clothes. After, he tried to lift him to his feet, but Doug shrugged him off.

"Thank you," he said, not looking at him. "I'd like to try to do it myself."

Jake stepped back while Doug ran his hands along the counter. He gripped the faucet and hoisted himself to his feet. After a moment's unsteadiness, he slid one foot forward, and Jake went into the living room and poked at the fire.

He didn't turn around while Doug shuffled from wall to side table to couch, where he finally sat down. When he was settled, Jake handed him some of his gardening magazines. He moved his own chair near the door, where he could get some air and work on a few designs. They didn't say a word for an hour, until they heard Savannah's car pull up in the drive.

"Thank you," Doug said quietly, without looking up.

"You're welcome."

Savannah walked inside. She stared at the fire, but only took off her baseball cap and wiped the sweat from her forehead. She walked over to the couch and kissed her father's clean forehead, hovering there for just a second, just long enough to breathe him in.

"Jiminy, I'm starving," she said.

She began singing some ridiculous tune about rabbits hop hop hopping on their way to meet the mouse, but not before she passed Jake's chair. Not before she put her hand on his shoulder and squeezed.

Eli parked by the Dansk outlet and lit a cigarette. Across the lot, by Fieldcrest Cannon, Rick Laufer flashed his headlights twice, then gunned his Mustang. Eli turned on his own engine, but not the lights. He clamped the cigarette between his lips, inhaled a lungful of black smoke, and hit the accelerator.

Zero to sixty in seven seconds. He aimed straight

for Rick's car and only, at the last possible second, swerved left. He did a three-sixty on two tires, leaving skid marks Prescott teens would be admiring for years. He laughed the whole time, because what the hell did he have to lose? If he didn't die young, he'd be stunned and, probably, disappointed.

Rick got out of his Mustang, a beer in his hand. "You motherfucker," he said.

They drank the Flagstaff wheat beer Rick had stolen from the local microbrewery and smoked half a dozen cigarettes apiece. When Jack and Pippen arrived, they didn't waste a second.

"We're gonna need a grand," Rick said. "Maybe more. This is serious shit. These guys have cousins in Colombia. Hell, if we play it right, we could be their local distributors."

Eli let the ashes from his cigarette fall on the back of his hand. He was hardly listening. He was thinking, instead, of meeting Emma a mile down the road from Jake's place, so the dogs wouldn't bark. He was thinking about her climbing into his car and filling it with the scent of lemons and longing. He was thinking about running his hands down her smooth, tawny stomach, and how many times, in an hour, he could make her smile.

It no longer mattered how many hubcaps he stole a night. He judged his worthiness now on how often he could make Emma Shaw laugh. The first time he'd kissed her, he'd also made his first wish. *Please, God,* he'd thought, *just don't let her hate me.* He was not a fool. He wasn't about to ask for more than that.

"So what do you think?" Rick was asking him. "You think she'll do it?"

"What?"

Pippen kicked his shin. "Shit. You've got sex on the brain. You think your girlfriend will help stick up Bob

Simon's liquor store? Simon's never seen her before. By the time he realizes she's in on it, we'll have the safe cleared out. We'll have the powder in our hands in less than a week."

Eli tossed his cigarette on the ground. Sometimes, swear to God, he wished he was another person. He wished he'd been born into one of those soccer-crazy suburban families, that he'd been some kind of nerd and gone on to college to study chemistry. He wished Jack and Rick and Pippen weren't his only friends in the world, that just one person expected more of him. Mostly, though, he didn't wish for anything, because he knew for a fact he wouldn't get it.

"I'll ask her," he said.

"Tell her, man. The girl's hot for you. Tell her."

That night, though, Emma kissed him so hard, he couldn't say a word. She sat on his lap while he drove them to Sage Street, and it was all he could do just to stay away from cliffs and telephone poles. When they sneaked inside the garage apartment, he wanted to say something, but she was quicker.

"Thank God," she said. "Thank God I met you."

Oh, he was done for, all right. *Thank God I met you.* She might as well have locked him in some cave only she knew about, because from that moment on, he was all hers. He wasn't going to lose control after all, he was going to give it up—hand himself over to her on a silver platter. *Thank God I met you* was the moment he realized how barren his life was, so he started living for her.

He didn't say a single word, just unbuttoned her shirt. He buried his head in her breast. She held onto his hair and hummed deeply. Even her breathing sounded like music, and though the guys would be furious if he didn't get her in on their plan tonight, he wasn't about to ruin this. No girl had ever come to him before. No girl had ever, really, wanted him. If he spoke, she just might change her mind. Better just to keep kissing her for the rest of his life.

Jake couldn't sleep. At midnight, he walked to his bench and worked on a chair ordered by a country singer in Nashville. Doug's bench sat in the corner, nearly finished, if Doug could only decide on the final carvings. Jake had never put so much time into a piece, and after this, he never would again.

He picked up a dozen strands of willow and twisted them into a chair arm. Rufus, the only dog who hadn't deserted him for the warmth of Savannah's feet, sat up abruptly, his hair on end. Jake reached over and calmed him. He knew what the dog had heard; it had been the same for seven nights running. Emma waited until she thought they all were asleep, then she sneaked out the front door of the cabin, her breath held in a tight ball in her chest. She wore no shoes, made no sound, and had no idea anticipation had an echo all its own, one that resounded like trumpet blasts in a lonely man's heart. Jake couldn't sleep for listening to it, and wanting exactly what she had.

He walked to the door and spied her running by, wearing jeans and a thin T-shirt. She saw him and stopped in her tracks. Her face was pale as moonlight, and she looked ready to cry.

"Come on in," he said, then turned around without waiting to see if she would follow. She took her time. He had already added another two strands of willow by the time she sat down on her grandfather's bench.

He didn't look at her. He couldn't look at her without thinking that love at her age was like bad cocaine. She thought it made her more beautiful and witty, but she was delusional. She was actually strung out and a little bit frightening; she was quickly becoming someone only other addicts could like.

"Believe it or not," Jake said, "love's not always good for you."

Emma snorted. She tried to pick up sawdust with her toes and kept glancing out the window. "What do you know?"

Jake picked up another band of willow and worked it through the loop of the chair arm. "I know Eli. You might want to watch yourself. That's all I'm saying."

"You hired him. You're, like, his only hero."

Jake looked at her. She was young and in love, but he was halfway dead inside, and he was able to stare her down. "That should be a clue to you about his state of mind."

"Look, just don't tell my mom, all right? This has nothing to do with you."

But it did, that was the trouble. Because even though love was bad for her, even if he could see with his own eyes that it was eating her up, wasting her away to skin and bones, he still sat there filled with envy. Because she, at least, was touching who she loved. She was kissing him until she lost her breath. She was loving him, with no thought whatsoever of the consequences, or all the things she could lose in the end.

"You be careful," he said.

He saw she had some quick retort, then decided not to speak it. She stood up and walked to the door. She looked over her shoulder at him.

"You know," she said quietly, "she's not sleeping either."

Jake looked up, but she was already gone, a slice of burning white light through the night.

* * *

Just before dawn, Maggie heard her granddaughter sneak back into the cabin. The girl crept past Savannah, who slept on a mat in front of the fire with the dogs across her feet, and curled up on the sofa beside her. In seconds, Emma's breathing went from hysterical to still.

Maggie had heard Emma sneaking out every night to be with that future convict, but she couldn't bring herself to stop her. If it had been Savannah at the same age, she would have hog-tied her to the bed. She would have served her only bread and water until she came to her senses. But she was getting old. She had to be because she'd started rooting for a teenager. The girl was a maudlin mess, in love out of her mind. Everything but Eli just faded to white, and still Maggie couldn't stop herself from looking out the window when Emma ran down the road and whispering, "Faster. Faster."

Now, Maggie curled on her side toward Doug. For the last two weeks, Doug had slept like a well-behaved six-month-old. Twelve hours a night, then another three-hour afternoon nap. He slept without spittle at the corners of his mouth, his breath did not bubble in his lungs, and he smelled, suddenly, clean as soap. She reached out for his cheek, then his hand was on hers. His eyes were wide open.

"Maggie," he said.

Before she knew what she was doing, she was kissing him. She pressed her body against his, and for the first time in months, it was warm. She hardly noticed the jut of his hip bone. She worked up the nerve to run her hand over his bare scalp, and it was not so bad. It was smooth as a baby's skin. He kissed her cheeks, her nose, the tears at the corners of her eyes.

"It's all right, love," he said. "You see? It's all right."

He slipped his hand under her nightgown. He wouldn't let her touch him, but he moaned when he ran his hand over her breast, as if that was, and always had been, just as good. She didn't expect him to, so it was that much sweeter when he slipped inside her. It had been so long, she cried out, but he covered her mouth with his. When she finally came, the climax rolled over her body, pulling her up and away from him, but she hadn't come this far to let that happen. She cut off the pleasure in midstream and clung to him tighter. She swore over and over that she would never let him go.

# THIRTEEN

## THE FIVE OF CUPS, REVERSED ❧ RETURN OF AN OLD FRIEND

**B**en Hiller, president of the MesaLand Homeowners Association, had seen many amazing things in his life—the battle of Iwo Jima, Boy George, Clinton elected not once but twice, but when the gladiolus his wife Helen had planted and watched die fifteen years earlier miraculously began poking through his lawn again, he just stood on his porch in stark disbelief. Helen had watered those flowers every day for a full summer, but they had still turned the color of diseased fruit and fallen over. He had dug up the rotten bulbs himself, thinking they might contaminate the roots of his imported blue fescue, but now there they were, stalks high as kneecaps, flowers the color of hot pink desire.

He just stood and stared and wondered what God was thinking, torturing a man with his dead wife's favorite flowers or, worse yet, letting him fall in love with her in the first place, when she was destined to die in her fifties. It was just plain cruel.

Wendy Ginger was the first to notice the blooms. She came out of her house across the street, dressed in her hospital candy-stripes, and asked the young driver from Dial-a-Ride to wait.

"You old romantic," she said, crossing the street. "What a wonderful tribute to Helen."

Ben didn't say a word. He turned sideways before she could spot the tears running down his cheeks, before she could ask herself in for coffee and expect him to think up something to say. The only woman he'd been able to talk to was Helen, and that was because she'd done all the talking; she'd decoded his nods and mumbles into poetry, she'd stunned him with who she thought he was.

The man from Dial-a-Ride honked. "Off to spread some cheer," Wendy said.

Ben stared at his lawn, a hum building in his throat. He was not much of a talker, but whether he liked it or not, now he had something to say. He was fairly certain he was being haunted. It wasn't just the gladiolus. In the last month, he'd started seeing Helen everywhere. A dozen times a day, she was walking down the street, kicking off her shoes on someone's lawn, or standing in their rose garden in a pair of lacy lavender socks. She appeared in the silky heads of butter lettuce in his crisper, as an anchor on the evening news; she had a tendency to poke her head out of his neighbors' car windows. He'd found himself running out his front door and putting his arms around old Marilee D'Annuncio, until she cried out that he was scaring her. Once he had wandered down his block and clung to a streetlamp, until a nice widow came out of her house in her slippers to take him home.

Deliberately now, he kicked off his own shoes. He

tossed one beneath the rosebush, the other in the center of his perfect lawn. Then he walked barefoot to his car. Everyone knew the way to Jake Grey's place, but until now, only the young people had had the guts to go there. At first, when he hit the forest road and then the huge drop-offs, he felt a little sick. After he breathed in enough vanilla-scented air, though, he actually drove a little faster. He hadn't taken a chance with his life in years, and that was ridiculous. Before he'd met Helen, he'd scaled every ten-thousand-foot peak in North America. He had taken his first free-fall skydive at the age of sixteen. He could understand growing more conservative while his children were growing up and Helen needed his steady paycheck, but now, hell, he ought to be jumping off skyscrapers left and right. He ought to be a madman.

He laughed out loud when he went around a blind turn at twenty miles an hour. He tapped the accelerator with his bare foot and picked up rocks from the rubber mat with his toes. It took him forty-five minutes to reach Jake's cabin, and then the dogs attacked. He sat in his car while the beasts leapt against the passenger door, scratching the deep blue finish of his Buick. Finally, Jake came out of the cabin and called off the dogs. By the time Ben got out, wincing when his bare feet struck gravel, Maggie, Doug, and the fortune-teller were standing on the porch.

Ben took a deep breath and looked at Maggie. "There were some lights on in your garage apartment the last few nights," he said. "Thought I should tell you."

Maggie stared at his bare feet. Savannah wrapped her arms around herself, but no one answered. The dogs were getting hysterical again, circling his ankles, taking whiffs of his toes and howling.

"I figured they were on a timer," he went on. "But there was a Corvette in the driveway, too."

"You came all the way up here for that?" Maggie asked. "You could have called."

"Well," Ben said. At last, the dogs got a whiff of chipmunk and took off in another direction. Then he thought, *What the hell.* He'd get himself a tarot card reading and let the gladiolus come up all over his perfect fescue lawn. He might never scale Everest, but if things went his way, he might be the next man on the block to paint his house limestone green.

"I came to see Savannah here." He smiled the smile that had won Helen over more than fifty years ago. "Would you do me the honor of reading my fortune?"

Savannah clapped her hands. She led him into the small cabin, which, contrary to Wendy Ginger, did not smell like blood. There were women's clothes draped over the sofas and chairs, hats and dresses and a pair of long white gloves with the fingers cut out. Eye shadows in every shade of blue were spread out on the dining-room table.

"Let's sit on the floor," Savannah said.

Ben had to bend his legs at odd angles to get down there. The retriever had given up on the chipmunk and come inside. He sniffed him thoroughly, then decided he was friendly. The dog nudged Ben's hand until he stroked him behind the ears.

Savannah found her cards and handed them to him. "Go ahead and shuffle," she said, sitting beside him. "Concentrate on your question."

Ben patted the dog, then took the cards. Helen had always said to him, "Ben, what are you doing with a little ol' southern girl? You're an adventurer at heart. Don't think I can't smell it on you."

She'd never had any idea loving her was more dangerous than a solo ascent of Denali. He might survive a hundred-foot fall, but he was certain he couldn't live without Helen. When she was out of his sight for even a day, he felt wobbly. A month after their wedding, he stumbled on the easiest section of El Capitan and never went mountain climbing again. He stopped taking chances. He double-bolted their door every night, but death came up from under the bed and slithered into a blood vessel in Helen's brain. What he wanted to know was how to stop hating God.

He handed the cards back to Savannah, and she laid them out. The others had come in and were watching from the kitchen table, but Ben paid them no mind. Because right away, he could smell the scent of Helen's lilac perfume. Right above the cards, plain as day, was a cloud the color of pink gladiolus.

"What crosses you is the Two of Pentacles," Savannah said. "This often signifies too much conservatism. Difficulty getting started."

Ben said nothing. He couldn't stop looking at that cloud. They all had to see it, yet no one said a thing. It twisted a little, took on the shape of Helen's face, as everything did. The blunt cut of her chin, the tender curl of her nose, the long, wavy hair, the style she'd worn when they met.

"Your past was a good one," Savannah said. "The World and the Sun side by side. You don't see that too often. That's love, joy, and fulfillment. You've been a lucky man."

Ben hung his head. He'd been lucky, then his wife died in bed while he slept peacefully beside her. He didn't even wake up to hold her hand.

"Your future is the Knight of Cups," Savannah went on. "That's an invitation or opportunity arising. A challenge."

Ben raised his head while Savannah laid out the

last four cards. The cloud was dissipating now, the smell of Helen's perfume fading; by the time he reached out, his hand swiped nothing but clean mountain air.

"This here," she said, "the Eight of Pentacles, puts you in perspective. That's effort and change. Sometimes upending your whole life. With the Two of Pentacles you got earlier, it seems to me you've got something to do."

"Helen, she . . ." He trailed off, but Savannah took his hand and smiled.

"The Knight of Swords is your dream card. Isn't that lovely? It's the strength and dash of a young man."

"See, I could just as easily go home and never come out of my house again."

"Well, sure. That's your choice. The cards just show your options. Either way, your destiny is the Five of Cups, reversed. That's the return of an old friend."

Ben held Savannah's hand in both his own. For a moment, it seemed those ruby-red fingernails shortened, her fingers widened and freckles rose up on every knuckle. For a moment, he had what he'd always wanted most, what he had never taken for granted, not once. Then Helen was gone, and Maggie was standing behind him, her hand on his shoulder.

"You believe all this, Ben?" she asked.

"Well, why not?" he said. "Wouldn't you?"

She didn't answer. Ben got to his feet and took a twenty out of his pocket. His hand was trembling as he placed it in Savannah's palm.

"What will you do?" she asked.

"I don't know."

But by the time he was backing out of the driveway, he did know. He didn't hate God; he hated himself without Helen. His wife had once announced he was passive-aggressive, with a borderline antisocial personality disorder, and it was obvious he wasn't getting any better. He was too old for mountain climbing or sailing the seven seas. He had lost all desire to see the wonders of the world, especially if he couldn't turn to Helen and say, 'Well, lookie there. A pyramid.' There was only one adventure left to him, and as he pressed on the accelerator he smiled, because he was no longer afraid of a thing.

As soon as Ben left, Savannah went looking for Emma. She found her in Jake's workshop, knee-deep in willow strands. She had untwisted the knots he'd made to keep them neat, and her hands were full of splinters. As soon as Savannah came in, she thrust the willow away. She stood up and tried to go past her, but Savannah put a hand on her arm.

"You've been sneaking out with Eli."

Emma jumped back and planted her feet. "I have not."

"Emma, don't make it worse by lying."

"I'm not. What, did Jake tell you he saw me? Well he's wrong, all right? I was going for a walk by myself. I'm not chained to the bed, you know. I can't sleep here, it's so quiet. It drives me crazy. I like to walk is all."

Savannah bent down and picked up the straightened willows. "Whoever undoes a knot undoes their own luck."

Emma glared at her, then yanked the willow out of her hand. "You don't scare me."

Savannah could see that was true. For weeks now, Emma had been standing on tiptoes, ready to fight anyone, prepared to do anything. She hadn't just fallen in love with a street punk, she'd sworn to never stop.

"That boy is trouble," Savannah said.

Emma walked to the window, then whirled around. "I love him."

Savannah could feel the implication clear to her toes. Emma was going to love Eli no matter what she did. She was going to love him to spite her.

"I'm glad," Savannah said carefully. "But you're fifteen, honey. You don't understand yet—"

"Oh yes, I do. I understand I scare the hell out of you. I know what I look like. I'm ready to explode, and you know what? I'm glad of it. I don't mind exploding. I don't care if this ends up killing me, just so I get to feel this now."

Savannah grabbed her hand. "I understand, believe it or not. But there's something you need to understand as well. This will pass, Emma, and then what will you have? A boy with no future, no talent, and not a single shred of hope inside him."

Emma yanked away her hand and folded her arms across her chest. "You're not listening to me. Not even when I tell you things from the very bottom of my soul."

"You're wrong," Savannah said softly. "I hear every word you're saying."

Emma walked to the door, then back again. "You know what I think? I think you never loved Dad. You couldn't have, if you let him go so easily. Did you cry when you married him? Did it hurt going down?"

"Emma, that's not love, it's surrender. It'll break your heart in two."

"So then break it. People walk around with broken hearts all the time, and that's kind of beautiful, if you think about it."

Savannah took a deep breath. "Emma, you can't see him anymore. I'm sorry, but he's the kind of boy who can only do you harm."

Emma stared at her, but Savannah didn't back down, just as her mother had never backed down. She was a parent, which meant she had to stand there and take her daughter's loathing. She had to do what was best, even if it meant Emma would never talk to her again.

Emma walked out without a word. Savannah picked up the discarded willow and tried to reknot it, but her hands were clumsy. She ended up with nothing but a palm full of splinters too.

Her mother came in soon after and put her hand on her shoulder. "There's no joy in motherhood," Maggie said.

"Oh, that helps."

"Nothing helps except time."

Savannah dropped the willow and turned around. "She hates me."

"And she should. You're stopping her from having the only thing she wants."

"I can't just let her go to him. That boy—"

"She wants to be free and you want to keep her safe, and there is no middle ground. The tighter you hold her, the more she'll squirm, until she flies right out of your hand."

"Mom, you are not comforting me."

"If I did, you wouldn't be prepared. Now listen to me, Savannah. At this very moment, Emma's figuring ways to get around you. She's plotting her little guts out, and you've got to be ready. This is just the beginning of years of being defied and despised."

Savannah stepped back. The worst part was not what her mother said, but that she was beginning to believe her.

"Just stop," she said.

"Why? Emma won't. She'll fight and plot and become more devious and mean than you can imagine and you know what? That's good. That's what you want. Those kids who never rebel, they're the ones who go crazy with machine guns in McDonald's. Emma's turning into a well-adjusted young woman."

"Mom," Savannah pleaded.

Maggie stepped back. "Listen to me." As always, when she said that, Savannah braced herself. She stood up straight and glared, but all Maggie did was turn toward the door. "This is when she starts mistaking your love for prison. When she starts swearing she never loved you at all. Don't believe her. I never did."

She walked out quickly, so neither of them could see the other crying, which was a ridiculous thing, after all this time.


Sasha was digging up the pea seeds the dying man had sneaked out to plant when she heard the grating of steel against granite. To humans, it sounded like nothing more than a snap, perhaps an old tree splitting in two in the distance, but the one thing Sasha hadn't lost over the years was her ability to hear trouble. The sound sent a pulse of hot pain down her spine, and she threw back her head and howled. She sped past the hat woman who'd just come out of the workshop, and made her brittle legs run.

She followed the scent of exhaust smoke and gladiolus. Around the blind turn, she spotted smoke. She hesitated on the edge of the ravine, where the side had given way. She could hear the woman and the good man behind her, calling her name and running hard. Sasha could easily outrun them, even when slowed from arthritis and plain old dying, and for a moment she considered the possibility. If she started now, she could reach the big mountain by nightfall. She could run until her heart gave out, the way every dog prayed to go.

But she was not so much a dog anymore, that was the trouble. The good man had been messing with her all these years, playing a subtle game of kindness that could drain the wildness out of any beast. He'd tricked her into craving kibble instead of squirrel meat, and going to sleep every night with a pillow beneath her head. She was so soft now she couldn't even run without checking to see that he was following her, so she waited on the precipice until the good man and woman came around the corner, then she started down the path of the slide.

She found the car hung up between two fifty-year-old ponderosas. She could smell the blood when it was still fifty feet away, and she howled again. A few flames shot out of the engine, then died out. That old man must have died on impact; he'd come halfway through the windshield, and still managed to keep his eyes wide open.

Sasha circled the car, peeing on all four corners to keep the wolves at bay. Already, crows were circling. A coyote approached stealthily until Sasha growled and ran him off.

The man and woman finally reached the wreck, but only the man really looked at it. The woman grabbed hold of a knobby pine and threw up. She held onto the tree and wept until Sasha's spine shivered. The good man closed the old man's eyes, then tried to hold the woman, but she acted like an injured wolf, the kind it was too late to help, who paced until he died.

"It was a blind turn," the good man said. "An accident."

But the woman was no fool. Sasha had known that from the start. She had the ability to look at things the

way a dog would, stripping them down until she found
the core of truth. She knew, for instance, that all men
were worth saving, and that this had all the makings of
an old man running until his heart gave out.

She looked straight at Sasha, and though Sasha
thought most of those words they uttered were wasted
effort, she wished she had some of them now. She
wanted the woman to know what else she had heard at
that first crash of metal on granite, the sound of an old
man cheering.

Instead, she walked over to her and pressed her
muzzle into the woman's thigh. The woman just
went stiff.

"Dear God," she said, "what have I done?"

When Savannah saw the blood on Ben's face, she easily could have sat down and never gotten up again.
When an excited deputy cordoned off the whole hillside with yellow tape, and a crane pulled up Ben's
mangled car, she thought about running and never
coming back. When word filtered down to town, and
the crank calls started that night, she might have
taken to crying, but instead let Jake take the phone off
the hook.

She vomited again after her mother made pot
roast, then late that night lay listening to her own
quick, scared heart. At midnight, still wide awake and
sick to her stomach, she walked out onto the deck.

That's when she smelled it, not clean mountain air
but stale cigarette smoke. She felt an unsettling cold-
ness at her ear.

"Murderers," she thought she heard. "The both
of you."

She whirled around, but all she saw was a thick

fog rippling over the deck like lake water. She felt a chill clear down to her toes.

She took a deep breath and walked right through the mist, holding down the desire to scream. Her skin turned ice-cold, the tips of her hair went temporarily white. She went inside and locked the door behind her.

The next morning, she grabbed her tarot deck and took out the Four of Swords, the card of exile. After breakfast, she wedged it between the slats on the deck, where the air still reeked of tobacco, where whatever had been there last night would find it as soon as darkness fell.

It wasn't only ghosts who were taunting her. That night, Eli and his punk friends chopped up the crime-scene tape and tied yellow flags to the antenna of Eli's Corvette. They must have dared each other all the way to Jake's house, because after they pulled up in the driveway, they got out puffed-up and mean. Jake took two steps down the porch, but Savannah stepped in front of him.

"No," she said. "They're here for me."

She walked across the gravel drive. The boys reeked of marijuana and beer, which had only made them meaner. Eli drifted toward the back, but the others elbowed each other. Finally, Rick Laufer stepped forward.

"Here's twenty bucks," he said, handing Savannah the cash. "Come on. Give me your worst. Drive me to suicide."

He laughed, until Savannah grabbed his arm. She'd been second-guessing herself all day, trying to figure which warning signs she'd missed, what she'd said wrong. She'd re-created Ben's fortune, then quickly scattered the cards. If she'd missed some ominous sign, she didn't want to know it. She was going to predict happy endings for everyone, even if she had to flat-out lie.

She yanked Rick Laufer into the cabin and shoved him toward a chair. Ben Hiller had been destined for that cliff long before she came along. Thousands of people were destined for cliffs; it was fortune-tellers who got them contemplating alternatives, unexpected fortunes and lovers coming from the north. At the very least, a gypsy could make a man wait a day to jump, just in case this was the day his whole life turned around.

"Sit down," she said.

Rick sat and tried to light a cigarette, but couldn't get his hands to stop trembling. The others stayed outside, howling like wolves. Savannah swiped the makeup to the side and dropped her cards in front of him.

"Shuffle," she said.

She stared him down until he dropped his unlit cigarette and shuffled. Bad coincidence made her tense and mean, and it seemed nothing could be done about it. She grabbed the cards back from this two-bit hood, a boy she could see in an instant would never be bad enough to be a gangster or good enough to settle down. He'd slip right through the cracks, this one, he'd never belong to anyone, and one day he'd simply lie down and die of a broken, lonely heart.

She laid out the cards for him. Her parents were upstairs, Emma out on the back deck with the dogs, but Jake came in and sat beside her. Beneath the table, he put his hand on her knee.

She looked down at the cards, all swords, all reversed. "Tell me, have you ever been happy?"

Rick laughed, but he could just as easily have cried, she thought. She had cried for an hour beside Ben Hiller's smashed car, and then she had looked at his hands, still grasping the steering wheel. On his finger was his wedding ring, the one he'd kept hung around his neck. He had flown back into the arms of his lover. She had to believe that, or else how could she go on?

"I'm fucking ecstatic," Rick said.

Savannah nodded. "Then beware. You've got the Five of Swords, reversed, in front of you. That's an uncertain outlook. The chance of misfortune for a friend."

"That's it?" Rick said.

"What else would you like me to say?"

"Shit, I don't know. You're the fortune-teller. What did you tell Ben? That he was doomed?"

Jake squeezed her knee, then put his fists on the table, where Rick could see the size of them.

"Come on," Rick said. "I want my twenty dollars' worth."

Jake just stared at him, and Rick pushed back his chair. "Shit. The misfortune of a friend. Who the fuck cares?"

He walked out of the cabin and slammed the door. Savannah breathed deeply. She pushed herself up from the table and gathered the cards.

"The cards don't make things happen," she said.

"Of course not."

"They just show us the options. They clarify. I told Ben he had something great to do. How could I have known he'd take to driving off cliffs?"

Jake stood up and gathered her in his arms, but that only made it worse. He kissed her slowly, little feather kisses to the corners of her mouth. He kissed the line of her tears, then held her face in his hands. She was not going to love him. He was the Page of Wands, with a bad heart, and he was trouble. He conjured ghosts and reeked of sorrow. He was everything she didn't want.

"This is not your fault," he said, and it was probably true, but still her throat tightened.

The boys were all howling in the yard. She walked out onto the back deck where Emma ought to be and instead found the Four of Swords ripped to shreds and scattered along the planking. Jake came out beside her. Despite the howling, she could hear him breathing.

He bent down to pick up a piece of the shredded card. It showed only a man's hands folded in prayer. He tucked the piece in his pocket and stood up.

Savannah took his hand, but then the dogs started yelping. They both ran around the side of the house, and found the boys hurling rocks at the dogs. Sasha led the countercharge, coming at the tormentors with her teeth bared.

"Emma?" Savannah said.

She spotted her beside Eli, a rock in the palm of her hand. Her daughter might be guilty of lying and bad judgment, but never of cruelty. Savannah would not believe it, not with the evidence right in front of her, not ever. Her gaze met Emma's, and her daughter dropped the rock to the ground.

All it took was one step forward from Jake for the boys to bolt. They leapt into Eli's Corvette, but not before Emma grabbed Eli and kissed him. Not until all the boys cheered.

After the car was gone, Jake looked over his dogs and found only a couple of scratches. Nevertheless, he took them into the cabin for first aid and steak bones. As soon as he'd gone, Savannah charged across the yard. When she reached for her daughter, Emma flinched.

"I'm not the one throwing rocks," Savannah said.

"Mom . . ."

"Come with me."

She didn't wait for a rebuttal. She started down the road, stopping at every elderberry bush to snip off a branch or two. By the time she reached the blind turn, where the yellow tape was now chopped in pieces and strangling the necks of sagebrush, she had an armful of limbs.

She waited until Emma was just a few yards back, then she started down the cliff. Where Ben's car had landed, there was nothing left but pulverized pine needles and the smell of gasoline.

Savannah glanced up the hill, where Emma was making her way down slowly. When she finally reached her side, Savannah handed her a few branches.

"Plant a twig of elder on someone's grave," she said, "and their ghost will be at peace." She kicked at the soil, then picked the richest spot. She spit on the bottom of her branches. "Put them in deep. Pray for rain."

The two of them knelt in the moonlight and planted twigs. Every now and then, Emma faded in the moonlight, her heart picked its way over Kemper Peak and Desolation Canyon into Eli Malone's shabby cabin, and there was nothing Savannah could do about it. The part Emma left behind was not even speaking to her.

Finally, Savannah stood up and wiped her hands on her dress. She led Emma back to the cabin and did not say a word about the bats that skimmed their hair. Even when Emma cried out, Savannah didn't soothe her about how many bugs bats ate an hour, or the myth of the prince who takes up residence in a bat's body in order to search the world for the woman he loves. For once, she just stayed silent.

She tucked Emma into her sleeping bag on the couch, then sat on the chair by the door. She waited patiently until Emma fell asleep, then she went to the closet.

One thing a fortune-teller knew was that when she started feeling things against her will, it was time to leave. When a daughter started throwing rocks at dogs who loved her, it was a clear sign that things were going down fast.

What Savannah did not expect was to discover that a ghost felt the same way. She opened the closet where she'd left her suitcase, and was assaulted by the stale smell of cigarette smoke.

She crept back to the chair and breathed deeply. Her shoulders tightened each time she heard a creak on the metal roof, but when she went outside and looked up, the roof was empty except for a scattering of pine cones.

She went back inside and packed her suitcase. So she agreed with a ghost. So what? That didn't mean she was doing this his way. She would stay through the night, just to spite him. She wouldn't leave until dawn, when spirits can't materialize, because if they do, they disappear into thin air.

# FOURTEEN

## THE LOVERS ❧ SACRIFICE OF THE SOUL

Emma fell asleep plotting ways to fool her mother. She'd tell her she was going to California to visit her father, then she'd hitchhike back to Eli. She'd simply never do another thing Savannah said. Instead of guilt, she felt high on the things she could possibly give up for love. Everything but Eli was up for sacrifice—good grades, friends, a healthy appetite, her mother's trust.

Tonight, as always, she dreamed of him. He was twenty years older and in some kind of sales job. He'd cut off all his hair and taken to wearing suits, and he kept cocking his head when she cried. 'Isn't this what you wanted?' he asked her.

A thump woke her. She was tangled in the couch pillows, her hair moist and sticky against her neck. It was just before dawn, the air purple and hallucinatory, so when a man pressed up against the sliding glass door, Emma at first thought him a lingering part of her dream. The skin along her arms puckered and burned, but the muscles themselves were immobile. The man had dark hair, and vertical lines down his cheeks. He had the foulest-looking smile she'd ever seen.

She screamed, but nothing came out but a hollow whistle. The man put his hand on the door and began to slide it open.

"Mom," Emma said. "Mommy?"

Savannah, who had been sleeping on the floor, got to her knees. Emma was shaking so badly, all she could do was point. But what she was pointing at had vanished, leaving behind only a white haze where he'd breathed on the glass. That, too, faded right before her eyes.

"You saw something?" Savannah asked. "I'll go look."

Emma grabbed her arm. "No. Don't go out there."

Savannah sat on the couch and tucked her up on her lap. Like a baby, Emma buried her face in the moist curl of her mother's neck.

"It's all right, honey," Savannah said. "There's nothing out there that can hurt you."

She kissed the top of Emma's head, then gently put her down. She stepped out onto the deck and didn't check the drive or shadowy spaces behind the cabin. She merely put her hands on her hips and looked up.

When she came back in, she sat beside Emma and held her hand tightly. "See, there's this ghost."

Emma closed her eyes. She was done, absolutely done with her mother and all her superstitions. She was not going to live in a place where ghosts could materialize. She was not going to live with a woman who believed in them. She felt something harden in her chest, so that from then on it would be a little tougher to breathe and to sleep without nightmares.

That was the price she'd have to pay for deciding she didn't want a mother anymore.

"He's trying to stir up trouble," Savannah went on. "But he won't be able to, once we leave."

Emma opened her eyes abruptly. She held her breath while her mother went to the door, where she'd already packed a suitcase. She started putting Emma's clothes into a sack.

Emma didn't say a thing, because she knew every word would come out like a sob. Her mother dropped the bag by the door. She gathered the makeup on the dining-room table and stuffed it in her purse. When it became obvious that Savannah was determined to go, Emma threw out the one thing that might stop her.

"Aren't you at least going to say goodbye to Jake? Can't you tell when someone's in love with you?"

Savannah put the last blue eye shadow in her purse and looked up. "Love is a stretch."

"I don't think so."

Emma gripped her pillow. She clawed her way clear to foam stuffing by the time her mother sighed and headed toward the door. "Go back to sleep," Savannah said. "We'll leave after dawn."

Emma lay back down, but as soon as her mother stepped off the deck, she jumped off the couch. She had tears running down her cheeks with no idea why. She got into her jeans and boots and grabbed her sack by the door.

Though the roof was creaking in the night breeze, she could still hear her grandfather's steady breathing. Ever since they'd gotten up here, Doug had been able to take deep breaths without shuddering. It was her grandmother who now moaned during sleep.

The dogs were all out with Jake. All Emma had to do was take this moment and run, but instead she caught a glimpse of herself in the mirror.

Something was happening to her, and it wasn't appealing. She no longer had any desire to finish school or play the lead in *Othello*. Her hair had lightened to the color of wheat, and her eyes, once dark gray, had been bleached to a light sandstone. Wanting was so bitter, lately she hadn't been able to keep down anything but honey and marmalade.

She walked to the counter and snatched her mother's tarot cards. She flipped through them quickly, until she found the Lovers, and then she stole it right out of the deck.

She didn't care if this skewed her mother's readings; she only knew she had to have that card. Love ought to be generous, but she had this feeling it was not. She was even worried that her own mother was taking her share. Whether Savannah knew it or not, she couldn't look at anything but Jake when he was in the room. He'd been sacked out in that workshop all these nights, waiting for her to come to him, waiting for a lot more than that. She could see it written all over him. He was eating only honey and marmalade too.

She picked up the phone. As soon as it started ringing in Eli's house, she took a good, long breath. Now that she was connected to him, she felt ten feet tall and full of light. She felt capable of anything.

"Yeah?" he said.

"Meet me at the mile marker as soon as you can." Then she hung up and ran. She was out and free in seconds. It was so easy, she only wondered why she'd waited so long.

She had no company from stars. The sky was blank and moonless as she ran, and she was not surprised when she found the mile marker empty. It was obvious she was now on her own.

Then she heard the distant roar of an engine, and

she tingled clear down to her toes. Eli pulled up next to her and got out of the car, and she flung herself at him. She stroked his hair and face, jammed her fingers into the pockets of his jeans. She had shoplifter's hands with him. She pocketed strands of his hair, loose threads on his shirt, the warm change in his pockets.

"What's up?" he asked.

His voice quivered, and that was lovely. People thought he was nothing but a druggie, a thug, a delinquent. They couldn't see the most obvious fact—Eli was a nineteen-year-old without a soul. Maybe he'd sold it to the devil, or had it snatched from him by his father's brutish hand; either way, Emma vowed to get it back for him. She'd kiss him until he'd just have to accept there was someone in this world who loved him, who wasn't going to leave.

She laid her head on his chest. "I love you, Eli."

He looked down at the bag by her feet. Even the crickets had gone silent to hear the racket of his heart, his jerky breathing.

"They're gonna call this kidnapping. You know they are. Shit, Emma."

Emma stepped back. She had expected anything but cowardice. She kicked at her bag, then at the front tire of his Corvette. When she dented the rim, she kicked harder.

"Jesus," Eli said, pulling her back. "What the fuck are you doing?"

"I'm doing something. Anything. And you should do the same, Eli Malone. You should fucking do the same!"

Eli stared at her, then brushed back his hair. He was so beautiful she wanted to hide him away some place he could never do damage to himself again. But instead she grabbed his hands and held on for dear life. "I'm running away. I'm coming with you. Don't even try to stop me."

"They're gonna come to me first thing."

"Then we'll just have to leave town."

"Where will we go? Emma, I don't have any money."

"What about all those stolen stereos?" she asked him. "I'd say now's the time to sell."

He stared at her, and Emma dropped his hands. She would have forced him to love her, if she had thought it would work. Instead, she jammed her hands into her pockets and wondered how anyone ever came through love in one piece. She wondered why more people hadn't gone crazy. If he didn't tell her he loved her soon, she was going to crack. She could feel her bones quivering, but she was a better faker than she'd realized, because on the outside she wasn't even shaking. She looked like the only kind of girl who could snare him, the kind who couldn't care less.

"I can sell some of the stuff," he said, "but there's a better idea."

"Good. You can tell me in the car. Let's get going. Just drive where they won't ever find us."

She threw her bag in the back and got in the car. Eli got in after her and turned on the engine. He drove them to the highway in silence, then turned east for five miles. He pulled over on an old logging road and cut the engine. He lit another cigarette.

"The guys have been thinking," he said. "There's this liquor store . . ."

By the time he was through, she felt no more hesitation. All she wanted was the chance to prove her devotion.

"When do we do it?" she asked.

\* \* \*

When Savannah walked through the door of his work-shop, Jake figured his heart had gone out and some mix-up had gotten him into heaven. He had gone to bed this very night telling himself to just forget it, to stop wishing for anything, but his dreams had betrayed him. They'd been full of jingling bracelets and Pan-ama hats.

Then he opened his eyes and it was real. She was there, naked, sliding into the sleeping bag beside him. She kissed his eyelids, his nose, the beard he'd cut shorter and shorter every day she was here, so that now it was just a shadow on his chin and tomorrow might be gone entirely.

His hand shook as he ran it down her neck and cupped his palm around her breast. "You know what you're doing?" he asked.

"Not at all."

She leaned forward and kissed him again. Jake ran his hand up her smooth back, traced the wings of her shoulder blades. Then he just held on.

He knew he was in trouble, because his fantasies had never gone beyond this. All he'd dared to dream about was holding her, and if she gave him more than that, he might not come away in one piece. He was in too deep, greedy for a woman, dependent on her lov-ing him when it was still unclear if she ever would.

She was the one who reached for his pants, who slid them down and climbed over him. She took him deep inside her, and out of the corner of his eyes, he saw a light at the window. He didn't blink when the comet streaked past, its tail crossing over the ladle of the Big Dipper, when he saw how lucky he really was.

But luck left. It was some time after he rose up inside her, after he sunk his fingers in the hot folds of her skin, that he realized she was really saying good-bye. She was fanning her fingers across his ribs to memorize them. When she came, she was kissing the corners of his mouth and saying his name, so she could remember it later, when she might regret what she'd done.

"You're not going anywhere," he said, and she just kissed him harder. Her tears dripped into the hollows of his neck.

He pulled away and sat up. She pressed her cheek against his back, and the truth was, being haunted by Roy's ghost would never come close to what losing her would do to him. The worst ghosts weren't enemies, but the people you had loved best, the ones you wished would haunt you but didn't. The ones who couldn't, or wouldn't, love you back.

"Try to understand," she said.

"Oh, believe me, I do. I'll bet this was how it was with your husband. You divorced him as soon as you started to feel something."

She sat up and yanked on her dress. He had to be mean to her. Meanness was the only thing that would get him through once she was gone.

"It was never like this with Harry."

"No," he said, unable to help himself. "He got a little more time."

She slipped on her sandals and turned around. "I don't belong here, Jake."

"Neither do I."

She tapped her foot on the floor. "You want the truth then? All right, here it is. My father could die any minute and if I manage to keep Emma safe beside me, she'll hate me for it. I'm not losing one more thing, you hear me? I'm going to fall in love with someone with no history of heart disease. I'll marry a twenty-year-old, someone who will outlast me by a decade. Will you look at me when I'm talking to you?"

Jake could not, because right behind her, her

shadow had split off and walked out the door. It blended into starlight, and that meant it was too late for words. All he could do was get dressed and give in.

He put on his pants and walked out the door. Savannah came out after him, but he wasn't going to look at her now, not when she was the most beautiful thing he'd ever watched walk away from him. He stared at the sky until he spotted what he wanted—a falling star. Then he made the most rational wish he could think of. He wished that the police would figure out who had killed Roy Pillandro and come for him already, because if he was going to lose the one thing that mattered, he might as well lose everything.

She finally took his hand. "I'm not crying over you, Jake, so just forget it."

"Savannah—"

"What happens when your heart gives out? What happens when you leave me?"

"I couldn't leave you," he said. "It would be impossible."

But Savannah was shaking her head. "There's a story about a shepherd named Stanko. He was a master flutist and one night he played so beautifully, he entranced the Vila, a forest spirit. Stanko loved her at first, but after a while, he felt mauled by her devotion. He asked witches to help him rid himself of her, but no spells worked. Even worse, the Vila began to beat him. She was out of her mind with love for him and knew it was that very love that had turned him from her. For years, Stanko was discovered on the tops of trees, gagged and bloody. Then one morning he escaped and drowned himself in a ditch."

Jake stared at her. "I imagine that's one you've never told Emma."

Savannah kissed him hard on the lips. When she pulled back, there were tears all down her cheeks.

"Love is a matter of degree. Too little and it's worthless. Too much and it will drive you to suicide."

"None of it and you turn into a hermit. Or a gypsy."

"I'm going," she said.

"So go."

He was holding tight to her hand, but somehow she extricated it. When she was halfway to the cabin, his throat was so tight, he could only whisper, "You're chicken, Savannah Dawson." Probably she didn't hear him, because she just went into the house.

Roy was up on the roof, cackling. Jake grabbed a rock and hurled it at him, but it just came tumbling back down. He realized he no longer cared if he was going to hell or not, as long as he got that son of a bitch off his property. He walked up the slope to the house, but before he could do any damage, he heard Savannah crying. He went inside and found her on the couch, her head in her hands.

"Emma's gone," she said.


Four hours later, when the sun was well up over Whitehead Peak to the east, Savannah was still on the couch, her elbows on her knees, rocking. Her mother was holding the telephone, but Savannah would not let her make the call.

"I cannot believe this," Maggie said. "You call the police right this second, young lady. You put out an APB."

Jake had returned from Eli's house half an hour earlier. He'd found the Corvette gone, the oil puddle in the drive already dry.

Savannah went on rocking. Her father sat beside her, his thin arm around her waist. He hadn't said a word all morning. Now, he stood up and took the phone out of Maggie's hands.

"She doesn't want to do it," he said. "Come on. I woke up feeling great this morning. I think I'm up to a stroll."

"No strolling." Maggie sat down beside her. She yanked Savannah's elbows off her knees and held her face firmly in one hand. "Go get your daughter back."

Savannah leaned forward and kissed her mother on the mouth. "No."

"What about Harry? You think he won't call in his fancy lawyers when he finds out you just let her go? You think this won't give him exactly the ammunition he needs to steal Emma away from you?"

"He can't steal Emma if she's already gone." Savannah stood up and grabbed her cards off the table.

"Doug, talk to her," Maggie said.

Savannah kissed her father's cheek, then walked out of the cabin. She was still psychic about Emma. She could see her running down this road, unwilling to turn around for fear of regret. She could see her with her face to the sky, where nothing would refute the belief that the more she and Eli suffered, the purer their love. She knew the feel of Eli's arms around her, both electrifying and exhausting.

She could see them driving east, holding hands so tightly they both felt a little numb. Very deliberately, Savannah turned west. She had to consciously make her feet move, but however she did it, she walked the other way.

She reached the bald summit of Kemper Peak by noon and sat beneath a sky too blue for what she was feeling, a sky meant for children and lovers, not for mothers who were down to praying simply not to make the wrong move. She sprawled the cards in front of her. They'd been rummaged through the night before, and now she looked to see what was missing. It took only a minute to realize it was the Lovers, a card that meant romance and love, but if drawn a little too often, also meant the sacrifice of the soul.

She closed her eyes. She knew exactly what she was supposed to do in this situation: Call the police, hunt down her daughter, then take her home or perhaps to her father's, until she could be tamed. And she knew what she was going to do, which was sit on this mountain awhile, and let the sun warm her through. If Emma was willing to give up everything for that boy, then, mother or not, Savannah was going to root for her. The strongest love charm in the world was also the hardest to invoke: She would have to take after her mother and do the most unlikely thing.

It was after two by the time she got back. Her father was knee-deep in the soil he'd asked Jake to haul up yesterday. He had a packet of spinach seeds in his hands.

"He should get a good fall crop," Doug said. "I just wish we'd gotten up here sooner. We could have planted those Roma tomatoes your mother loves."

Savannah knelt in the dirt beside him and laid her head on his shoulder. For the first time in weeks, his skin had a fine coating of downy hair. He hadn't even draped one of his usual blankets around his shoulders.

"There, there." He sprinkled the seeds in a shallow trench. "It'll all turn out all right. I've got this feeling."

She kissed his cheek and helped him cover the seeds. He looked past her, to the unfinished bench beneath a ponderosa.

She followed his gaze and spotted a sheet of blue paper tied to the back of the bench. "Another poem for Mom," she said.

"Not this time. That one's for you."

If he hadn't been kneeling there, smiling with anticipation, Savannah might never have moved. She had every reason to believe he was getting better; he'd managed to start the garden, even go for a short walk now and then. Yet every time she looked at the things he'd given her, the silver charm that read "World's Best Daughter" and a basket of vegetable seeds she had yet to plant anywhere, she got a queasy feeling in the pit of her stomach. She had to hold something more solid than the flimsy flesh of his arm.

She didn't want him to give her one more thing she'd cling to after he was gone.

Doug gestured for her to go on, though, so she went to the bench. She untied the paper and read it.

> *I am your soil,*
> *plain, but composted well,*
> *with only a few surprises*
> *if you dig down deep enough.*
> *Plant figs or acorns,*
> *and I'll cradle your roots.*
> *Grow tall and*
> *I'll hold you to earth.*
> *Your fruit will sustain me.*
> *I am your soil.*
> *I will never let you fall.*

She folded the page into quarters, then eighths. She didn't look up for a long, long time. Then she walked to her father and tucked her face into his neck while she cried her heart out.

Within ten minutes of their arrival at a motel off Highway 69, Eli and Emma were ratted on by the manager. Cal Bentley pulled into the parking lot and spotted the

Corvette immediately, but he didn't get out. That boy had no luck; he never had and probably never would.

Cal lit one of his contraband cigarettes and sucked in even harder when he thought of the tirade he'd get from Lois. She never made her usual Saturday night pot roast when she caught him smoking. Instead, she tried to balance the damage done by cooking tofu and falafel, two things no amount of mustard and Worcestershire sauce could turn edible.

He kept an eye on the dingy outer hallway. He'd just gotten off the cell phone with Savannah. If she wanted to let her fifteen-year-old daughter loose with a boy like Eli, that was her problem. His problem was making sure a boy on the run didn't do something stupid. His problem was harder.

Mistake number one: The kids hadn't gone more than fifty miles before stopping. Mistake number two: They'd pulled into a motel right by the side of the highway, where anyone could make out the black glow of Eli's Corvette. Mistake number three: They'd paid the motel manager by cash, which was always suspicious, and signed in under John and Jane Doe, which was just plain ridiculous. The manager had waited no more than five minutes before phoning Cal.

Cal had one hell of a headache. He'd had it since yesterday, when Dan Merrill had called to give him a list of houseboaters who'd lived on Wawani Lake at the same time as the Pillandros. Dan himself had located a man who, years ago, found Jake's wallet, along with a yellowed tooth, washed up on shore. Dan had wanted to bring Jake in for questioning.

"You've got nothing," Cal had told him.

"What about the hole in the dead guy's skull?" Dan had asked. "What about the fact that this skeleton was Jake's stepfather, and one son of a bitch to boot?"

"I'm telling you, get your facts in order first. You've got nothing here. You hear me?"

But Cal knew exactly what they had. The day before Roy Pillandro had disappeared, his wife, Cheryl, had been treated at Phoenix Memorial for broken bones, and then seen by a neighbor at her old house in Phoenix, where Jake was still living. And yesterday, Cal had checked on some of those names Dan had given him and spoken to Mrs. Alice Lane.

"Roy was a brute," Mrs. Lane had said. "An all-out animal. Cheryl never said a word, but I mean, how do you hide bruises all over your face? We weren't deaf, you know. We heard the screaming."

"Do you recall what happened when Roy disappeared?"

"Recall it? I was there that night. I was watching television, then all of a sudden there was shouting, then a loud bang. I ran outside, but when I called over, a man's voice said Roy had just gotten crazy with a firecracker. Ha! That was no firecracker. That was a gun going off. I caught a glimpse of the man who shot it, too. Tall, dark-haired, but just a kid. Twenty or so."

"Could you identify him now?"

"Oh, I doubt it. It was fifteen years ago. And he jumped back into the shadows so fast, it was hard to notice anything other than his dark hair. But when you find him, you tell him I'm glad he did it. That night was the first good night's sleep I'd gotten in years."

They had motive, mounting circumstantial evidence, and a probable witness, but Cal was obviously losing his mind because even if Jake had killed Roy Pillandro, he didn't particularly care. On top of that, he was sitting here in front of a motel, letting a couple of runaways think they'd gotten off. His heart just wasn't in it anymore. He'd gotten so old and soft, when Eli and Emma finally skulked out of their room, he decided then and there to let them go. When Eli took off his jacket and wrapped it around Emma's shoulders, Cal smoked his cigarette down to the stub. When they got into the Corvette and huddled together before peeling out, Cal turned on his radio to the oldies station and sang "Blueberry Hill" at the top of his lungs. When the song was over and the kids were long gone, he got on his cell phone and called Lois.

"Honey," he said, "slip into something pretty. I'm taking you out to lunch."

Eli was breathing hard as he skidded out of the motel parking lot. Cal Bentley was sitting in his squad car not fifty feet from them. Eli's hands slipped off the wheel as he turned the corner and drove toward the signal at the highway on-ramp. The light was red, and his lungs were on fire. Emma was pale as fresh paper, looking into the rearview mirror.

"See him yet?" Eli said.

"No."

"Fuck. He's playing us." He gunned the engine. The light was going to stay red forever. Finally, he just blew through it. He headed up the on-ramp and waited for the lights and sirens, but they never came.

He was doing sixty in seconds, then seventy, seventy-five. He swerved into the fast line, cutting off a Suburban loaded down with a family of blonds. He couldn't have slowed if he tried. Finally, Emma got up on her knees and turned around in her seat.

"He's not coming," she said.

"Yeah. Right."

Eli floored it. He was doing eighty-five and not about to stop. He had pawned a couple of stereos just to stay the night at that lame hotel, and now the cops were on to them. Fearlessness had kept his bones strong all these years, and now he could feel them splintering. He wished he had a home to go to. For the first time in years, he wished someone else was in charge.

"Really," she said, turning around. "He let us go."

Eli let up on the accelerator. He started shaking and couldn't stop. He didn't like this one bit. He fully expected himself to act crazy, but when cops started doing it, the whole system went to hell. Next thing you knew, Cal would be taking bribes, Eli's dad would be getting sober, and he'd be crying in Emma's lap. Everything they'd pretended to be would blow up in their faces.

"We'll go to Flagstaff tonight." He despised the tremor in his voice and sucked on another cigarette to stop it. "I've got a friend there who can put us up for a few days. Then we'll meet Rick. He thinks we can score at least a grand, maybe more, from the liquor store. That'll get Rick his powder and us out of this fucking state."

"Why do we have to rob that liquor store? Let's go somewhere out of town."

"Rick knows the combination to the safe. That's where the real stash is. His brother was a cashier there. We'll be in and out, Emma. No one's gonna catch us."

Emma nodded, but she kept looking over her shoulder, and he didn't blame her. The cop wasn't there, but that didn't mean something wasn't closing in on them fast. That didn't mean they weren't headed for disaster anyway.

# FIFTEEN

## THE FIVE OF SWORDS,
## REVERSED ❧ MISFORTUNE OF A FRIEND

The only evidence Doug had been in the garden was two shoe prints in the soil. When Jake called his name, Doug disappeared so fast into a thicket of pines, not even a hound could have tracked him. He pressed his back against the bristly trunk of a ponderosa and by the time Jake went back inside and slammed the door, he was covered in sap, and laughing out loud.

He had never thought he would be good at espionage, but maybe every man had a bit of James Bond in him, especially when it mattered this much. Jake wanted the last two designs for the bench, and no doubt he wanted his privacy back too. But Doug had already decided he was never leaving the cabin. He feigned sleep whenever Jake peeked into the loft, and escaped for walks when Jake came outside. He wasn't going anywhere, not when the air up here was pure oxygen, his blood running clean as Jake's well water, and on good days he could walk nearly a mile.

In fact, he had decided on the next symbol for the bench, and he would tell Jake in another week or two, to keep the man happy. He wanted the sun carved in, deep and dazzling. The blazing sun that had given life to his garden, then threatened to take his own. The sun he still couldn't get enough of, despite what it had done to him.

He turned his face to it now and wasn't blinded. He could stay out in the sun all day and not get burnt. The one benefit of dying was that nothing else could hurt him now. They ought to send him into battle; he could detonate bombs at close range and stop bullets with his teeth. Better than that, he would move the enemy to tears; one whiff of his spoiled breath and young, hearty men would start packing for home.

He was giddy, too. This morning, when Savannah had laid out her cards for him, he'd put his hand over hers. "Now," he'd said, "go get the other ones."

She had looked up quickly, then simply went to her bag and pulled out another third of the deck. She mixed them in with the others, then he reshuffled. She laid them out stiffly, but then she smiled.

"Oh, Dad. Do you see this? It's the Ace of Cups. That means fulfillment. A favorable outlook. It means you're going to be all right."

"I never doubted it."

And he hadn't. He was going to be all right, one way or the other. He hadn't gotten worked up over the cancer, and he wasn't getting worked up over this apparent remission. Sixty years in this world had taught him things were never as bad or as good as they appeared, and either way, life worked out as it should.

He walked to the meadow. He was not leaving, not when the sun was this warm and the grass waist-high and soft, and the old dog needed him. Sasha was right on his heels. When he lay down in the grass, in the blunt shadow of Kemper Peak, she lay down too, her gray muzzle on his chest.

They breathed in sync, in shallow, jerky breaths. When Doug fell asleep, he dreamed animal dreams. He had paws instead of feet and ran faster than he'd ever imagined, through forests so heavily timbered, his fur was scraped off by pine bark. He had amazing spring to his legs, he could leap over granite boulders twice his height.

He spotted his prey just a few yards ahead, a white rabbit, gone still with fear. He growled from deep in his throat, but when he went to charge it, he couldn't move. His chest was on fire; his paws twitched, then slipped out from under him. He fell to the ground, pine needles piercing his belly. His tongue lolled out the side of his mouth. He looked up to find a frail, while-haired man bending over him.

When Doug opened his eyes, Sasha was curled into him. His own chest rose and fell evenly, but hers labored, and her tongue hung out of her mouth. Doug reached over and scratched behind the ears.

"Nothing to be afraid of," he said. "Just a bit of dying, old girl."

She pressed her head against his hand, then dropped her chin to the ground. She shuddered, but when he put his ear to her chest, he could still hear the shaky beat of her heart.

He got to his feet, then reached for a tree to hold on to. He could walk a mile now, but the corners of his vision were going black. The tips of his fingers were numb. As he headed back to the cabin for Jake, he had to feel his way through, tree to tree.

Sasha saw colors now. Before, the world had been black and white, but now the good man's face was lavender and chartreuse and mustard and a marvelous lime green. He came in and out of focus, but when he got close enough, Sasha managed to lift up her head and lick his bearded chin.

She could hear the good man crying, saying her name, but she was floating now, dancing on air. Her bones no longer ached; in fact, she couldn't find her paws, or any fur to lick. She'd been snatched by the wind and carried up over treetops. She growled at a robin flying by, then looked down and saw her old body, which the good man was hugging fiercely.

She swooped down and looked up through her body's eyes at this man she loved. She was afraid to leave him, afraid he might not know how to love anything but dogs, but the air smelled of a hundred irresistible scents, all the colors were Day-Glo, and devotion didn't stop here, no matter what the man might think.

Her legs jerked in release, the man cried out, and she wished she spoke his language so she could tell him it didn't hurt at all.

The man's tears fell on her snout and slipped into her mouth. She drank them down, but her throat was still parched. The man clutched at her, but she was already floating again. Gabe and Rufus were circling her now, howling. They would mourn her for a day, then get on with things, the way dogs did. Life for a dog was too short to do otherwise.

Sasha sailed up past the detestable chipmunks, up over the hundred-year-old ponderosa that had withstood a dozen lightning strikes. When she looked down again, past the splintered crest, she saw the good man's bent head. She tried to swoop back to take him with her, but the air was too light and the colors too mesmerizing, and soon she was sucked up into the sky.

* * *

Jake crouched over his dog, his chin pressed into her fur. Savannah had come to the meadow with him and now she wrapped her arms around his shoulders. He must have let something awful out of his throat, because she squeezed harder, and Rufus and Gabe howled.

"This is your good world," he said. "You love one thing and then it dies."

Savannah squeezed him tighter. She was crying, too. He could feel her tears sinking through his shirt, but he made no move to comfort her. She was just going to leave him anyway.

She rocked him back and forth. She pried his hands out of Sasha's fur and looped her fingers through his.

"I loved her," he said.

"Well, thank God. You just stand here and thank God for that."

She was stronger than he'd thought; she yanked him right to his feet. She wore a red gauze dress and straw hat and, even through his grief, Jake knew she had him, like a pebble in her hand she could play with or toss away.

"We'll bury her on your mountain," she said. "That'll give Roy some unexpected company. Dogs are the best ghosts, you know. They come on full moons and bark like crazy. They don't take any crap."

He had the strangest thought: He needed her to make him real. He'd been only a shadow on his mountain and hadn't materialized into substance until she looked at him head-on.

"You never lose them, that's what I'm saying," she said. "You never lose what you love best. That's why I haven't lost Emma, no matter what she might think."

He was never going to get an invitation, he saw

that now. She wouldn't be able to stand the silence here much longer; she certainly wasn't going to stick around to watch her father die. She would return to sea level, where people didn't hallucinate about ghosts and love, where the air was so dense, no one could take a deep breath of anything. She would never ask Jake to come with her. There was no reason she should, no reason to think he could ever give up his little, damaged life. But if he just stood here, the ground might open up beneath him. The only way to keep from falling in was to hold on to her.

He leaned down and stroked Sasha's fur once more, then stood up as straight as he could. "When you leave, I'm coming with you."

She leaned back to look at him. If she didn't take him now, he would go into the woods and not stop walking. He would be one of those men backpackers found beside streams in the spring, the meat stripped from his bones long after he'd died of some mysterious hunger.

He wanted to state his case, to plead, but all he did was stand there. When she just went on staring at him, he looked into the sun. "Please. Say something."

She put her hands on each side of his face and pulled him down to kiss him.

Bronco Liquor was just outside of Prescott, off Highway 69. The owner was a sixty-year-old named Bob Simon, who had made the mistake, a few years back, of hiring Rick Laufer's older brother Phil, despite his felony record. Phil had worked at the liquor store for two years, with full access to the safe. He had repaid Bob Simon's trust by selling cocaine from the storeroom and, right before he was arrested for dealing, slipping the combination of the safe to his younger brother.

Late Thursday night, Rick sat beside Pippen in the front seat of his Mustang, waiting for the one car in the parking lot to pull out. Emma was in the back with Eli and Jack; she'd been smoking Marlboro reds non-stop for an hour. Her throat was raw, and that was just as well, because if she said anything it would probably be about right and wrong.

They all had purple auras, Rick and Eli and Jack and Pippen. Even worse, when they rolled down their windows, most of those auras blew away. Whatever those boys were, or wanted to be, was so weak the slightest breeze could change it. When their auras grew back again, they were just outlines and even darker, almost black.

The car finally pulled out, and Rick parked down the street. "Okay," he said. "You know what to do, Emma?"

She nodded. She had thought being bad might excite her, but it only made her sick to her stomach, and a little bit green. Eli grabbed her hand and brought it to his lips. Even though the guys would ride him later, he just looked right at her.

"You don't have to do this," he said.

That's when she knew she did. She had something to prove, and it wasn't that she was daring enough to rob a liquor store. It was that she was brave enough to love a lost cause. She was willing to give up everything.

She got out of the car and walked to the door of the liquor store. She turned around and gave the sign.

Then she took a deep breath and walked inside. She went to the back, searched for a six-pack of Michelob, and brought it to the counter. Just as they had known he would, Bob Simon took a good look at her and shook his head.

"Yeah, right. Not even a fake ID is gonna work, little lady."

She was able to smile right over the flip of her stomach. "Come on. It's just a six-pack. I'm not driving, I swear it."

He took the six-pack off the counter and walked back to the refrigerator. "No way. You know what the fine is now? I can't even sell you cigarettes."

"Look, I won't tell."

The man laughed. He looked a lot like her grandfather might have, if he hadn't gotten sick. Bob Simon was reaching out to give her a sympathetic squeeze on the arm when the guys, all covered in ski masks and carrying sawed-off shotguns, burst in.

One of them, Rick she thought, shot a round into the ceiling. "Give us the cash!" he shouted.

The man looked at her, but she couldn't meet his gaze. One of them came up behind him and jabbed the barrel of the gun into his back. "Hurry up, old man."

Emma looked from one to the other, but the worst part was, she couldn't tell which was Eli. They all wore jeans and black sweaters. Beneath those ski masks, all their eyes looked black.

Bob Simon was remarkably calm as he walked back to the counter. Rick had pointed out that Bronco Liquor had been robbed three times in the last year. It wouldn't even faze the old man, he'd said. Bob Simon pushed a few buttons on the cash register and Rick ran around behind him and grabbed the cash. "This is it?" he shouted, holding up a few twenties.

"You idiots," the man said. "You think I'm gonna keep a lot of cash on hand? I'm no fool."

Rick slammed the butt of the gun into the man's neck and Emma screamed. Bob Simon crumpled to his knees and one of the boys shot a hole through the shop window.

"Neither am I." Rick grabbed the man's arm and dragged him toward the back.

Emma fell to her own knees and started rocking. Suddenly Eli was there, crouched down and holding her. His eyes through the holes of the mask were not black, as she'd thought, but a deep, bottomless green. She looked over his shoulder in time to see Bob Simon get to his feet and press a button near the back door before he went through. His eyes met hers, but all she did was take a deep, long breath.

"This is crazy," she said, and then she was laughing. She was laughing so hard, urine seeped through her panties.

"Hold on," Eli whispered. "Just a few minutes more."

It wasn't just a few minutes. It was forever, time enough to change indelibly, before Rick ran out, waving the cash in the air. Bob Simon was not with him, and Emma laughed harder.

"Grab her," Rick said. "She's losing it. Come on."

Eli grabbed her arm and pulled her outside. The others were far ahead; Rick had already leapt in his car. Eli dragged her along, but her feet kept slipping out beneath her. Somewhere along the way, when they heard the sirens, she slipped right out of his grasp.

"Come on, Emma. Come *on*."

He ran faster, but she slowed. By the time Eli had jumped in the Mustang, she was a hundred feet behind him. She couldn't have moved if she tried.

She heard Eli screaming for her, but Rick just took off. Someone threw a twenty out the window and it landed right at her feet.

Bob Simon ran out then, his lip bleeding, but not suffering from any bullet wounds that she could tell.

He reached her side just as the police car pulled up. She expected the man to beat her, but all he did was hand her over gingerly to Cal Bentley and his partner.

"Got herself mixed up with the wrong crowd," Bob Simon said. "But that doesn't mean there's no penance, little lady."

Emma looked up at Cal Bentley's somber face. He had to know who was behind this, but he was never going to prove it, not if she had her way. She hadn't given up everything after all. She hadn't given up Eli.

"Come on." Cal escorted her to the police car. "I'm telling you, Emma, you've given me one hell of a headache."

Savannah and Jake planned to leave for San Francisco on Saturday. Sasha had been buried, and Savannah was not sticking around to bury anyone else. She was going to leave while her father seemed healthy, while there was still a chance everything might work out fine.

Jake was determined to go with her, but she noticed he didn't box up any furniture. Even though he packed a few suitcases, he still did not look like a man capable of going anywhere. He had lived at his cabin so long, he coughed up yellow pollen in springtime, and in autumn the tips of his dark hair turned gold. His skin had deepened to the color of fifty-year-old ponderosa pine, and probably his roots ran just as deep. Probably, if she tried to move him, he'd die.

She was only slightly better at pretense. She went through the motions of leaving without her daughter, of going on without any idea where Emma was or what she was doing, but only the childless were fooled. The mothers she passed in town took one look at her and burst into tears. She gave off some kind of panicky stink that made fathers clutch their toddlers and vow to cut back their hours and stop wasting time. There had been plenty of moments over the years when she'd bristled at being a mother, when all she'd wanted was her own life back. Well, now she had it and it didn't fit her. It was a twenty-year-old's life, tight and flashy, and she was a thirty-six-year-old with twenty extra pounds of devotion and a preference for loose clothes. The only kind of life she was interested in now was the type she could cut into pieces and serve as lessons and comfort to her daughter.

Early Friday morning, when her car was fully packed, she could have gotten behind the wheel, but instead sat down on the porch steps. Jake came up from his workshop, the dogs at his heels, moths and red earth clinging to his shirt, as if they could make him stay.

"He'll be one lonely ghost," he said, sitting down beside her. Savannah took a deep breath, because otherwise she was going to start telling the truth. She was going to look straight in his eyes and tell him this had never been meant to last. She could put him up in a whitewashed apartment in San Francisco, but he was still going to reek of despair. You can't cure a man of sadness, but worse than that, Savannah had the feeling heartache was contagious. Whenever she sat this close to him, she felt on the verge of either tears or loving him, and both were unpleasant, both stung going down.

The phone rang in the cabin and, after a moment, Maggie came out. When she called her honey, Savannah knew there was trouble.

"Honey, it's the sheriff," Maggie said. "He wants to talk to you."

Savannah ran into the house. She didn't need to look in her mother's eyes to know that whatever had happened, she would never live it down. Everything that followed would be her fault.

She picked up the phone. "Cal?"

"Now listen," the sheriff said. "First of all, Emma's all right."

Savannah went stiff. "Oh, God. What happened?"

He told her about the liquor store robbery, all the way to the point where he led Emma to a county jail cell. "She's in custody. She's not cooperating about who was with her."

"Oh, come on. You know damn well—"

"Right now I can't prove anything, and Emma's telling me it was some boys from Phoenix. Boys she didn't meet until a couple of hours before the robbery. Other than that, she's not talking, except to call her father. He's already caught a flight out."

Jake had come in behind her and put a hand on her shoulder. Savannah's head was pounding, and now the pain went right between her eyes. She dropped the phone and rushed outside. She got in her car, but had forgotten her keys. She looked up and found her mother standing beside the car, jingling her key ring.

"Move over," Maggie said. "You're in no shape to drive."

Savannah slid over, and Jake got in the backseat. Doug started toward the car, but Maggie shooed him away.

"Don't be crazy," she said. "This road kills you and you know it. I'll call you as soon as we know anything. Go rest."

He turned around petulantly and Maggie backed out of the drive. Savannah had forgotten she was wearing a beret, until it fell off when she put her head between her knees.

"You were right, Mom."

"Well, of course," Maggie said, "but there's no

sense going into that now. What you've got to do is go in there fighting. Your job is to get her out of this."

They got to the county jail in an hour, but couldn't see Emma until visiting hours at noon. While they were waiting in Cal's office, Harry burst in. He looked like the Harry she remembered, dressed in jeans and a crisp white shirt, ready to take on the world. There must not have been enough time to grease his hair or find all his rings. He hardly took a breath before he started yelling.

"How could you just let her go? Are you insane? What kind of mother lets her fifteen-year-old daughter run away? Why the hell didn't you call me? I had a right to know."

Jake stepped forward, but Savannah squeezed his arm. "It's what I would have wanted at her age," she said. "To be trusted."

"She is fifteen goddamn years old!" Harry said. "You don't trust teenagers. You rein them in. You protect them. You knew exactly who she was with. That boy is a menace. You can thank yourself for what happened."

"Mr. Shaw," Cal said, but Harry ignored him. He yanked Savannah's arm.

"You stupid fool," he hissed.

Savannah lowered her head, because even though he was crueler than he should have been, he was also right. She picked at her fingernails, but had already stripped off the last bit of ruby-red nail polish on the drive down.

Cal came around his desk. "Just calm down. You're both upset. I understand that. Let's just keep it calm."

"Oh, I'm calm," Harry said. "Calm enough to see that Emma doesn't need any more of this mystic mumbo jumbo. She doesn't need someone patting her hand while she's bleeding and telling her everything works out all right in the end. Emma needs someone who just gets the goddamn bandage and fixes the cut. She needs someone who can take over and get her out of this, now. Emma needs *me*."

Maggie had been standing by the door, but now she came forward. "I never liked you much, Mister Used-Car Salesman, and now I'm fairly certain I hate your guts. Emma made a rotten choice, that's for sure, but she's got the courage to protect that future convict, and if you can't see the beauty in that, then you're blind as a bat."

Harry just stared at her, then turned to Cal Bentley. "We must be able to do something here. She's no threat to society. You know that. She got swept up in somebody else's plot. I'll pay back the stolen cash, with interest. I'll get her out of town and keep her there. I'll take full responsibility."

Cal stepped back, but not before Savannah saw relief flicker across his eyes. Not before she knew she had lost. Harry was absolutely right. Emma did not need mother devotion or a tarot card reading telling her how things might turn out. She did not need any of the things Savannah could give her. She needed her father.

"I'll have to talk to the prosecutors and Bob Simon," Cal said. "In the meantime, Savannah can see Emma now. Mr. Shaw can come next."

He picked up the phone and asked someone to show Emma to the visitor's booth. Then he led Savannah to a narrow room with small windows and black phones lining either side. In the last booth, Emma sat hunched on a stool on the other side of bulletproof glass.

"My God," Savannah said, "is it necessary to keep her here?"

"It's a felony."

She picked up the phone. "Emma?"

Emma didn't even look up. She looked thin as a wire and already snapped.

Savannah whirled around. "Come on. Why can't you just go arrest those boys?"

"Talk to her," Cal said. "Right now I'm looking for four juveniles from Phoenix, none of whom have any outstanding features or names that she can recall."

Savannah turned back to the booth. She put her hand on the glass and beat on it until Emma looked up. She pointed to the phone and finally Emma picked it up. "Emma Shaw, don't you dare do this."

Emma looked at her head-on and said nothing, and Savannah could see that she did dare. Even if Savannah had the means to save her, it was plain as day that her daughter wouldn't let her.

"It's not doing Eli Malone any good to protect him," Savannah said. "Don't you see? You're not helping him."

Emma stood up slowly, then reached into her pocket and took out a crinkled, sweat-stained card. She held the Lovers up to the glass.

"I'll give this to the guard to give to you," she said. "I won't be needing it anymore."


Harry Shaw paced up and down the courthouse steps, whirling around whenever a police car drove up. Cal Bentley had been gone two hours—more than enough time to convince that liquor store owner to drop the charges. A dirty wind was picking up, slapping his ankles with leaf and newspaper debris, and a few smoky raindrops glanced off his forehead. A guard stood at the door, making sure he didn't go back inside. He'd been escorted out when he drove two clerks to tears with his ranting. When he glared at a couple leading their pale-faced teenage son inside, the guard walked down the steps.

"Take your hysterics somewhere else," the guard said. "You think you're special? Shit. This kind of thing happens every day."

Harry stomped across the street to a delicatessen. He wasn't hungry, but he could go for a black coffee. He had his hand on the door when he looked through the window and spotted Savannah, her mother, the psycho, and another woman sitting inside.

He started to walk the other way, then suddenly whirled around. That other woman had curly hair pulled back with a familiar gold clip. She had on a Donna Karan suit he had bought her last Christmas. He pushed open the door and walked in.

"Melinda?" he said.

His wife stood up. "I found your note and took the next flight out. I brought brownies." She gestured to a white box, the kind Grendel's Bakery in Danville used. "They're Emma's favorite."

Harry just stared at her. She must have had to rush like crazy to get here so fast, but she still looked polished in her green linen pantsuit. She'd been at the salon when he'd gotten the call from Emma, getting her ringlets cut to the size of penny rolls.

She held out her hand. Probably, she was waiting for him to tell her how grateful he was that she had come, but Harry was not grateful, not one bit. Her being here just made this whole disaster more real.

When he didn't take her hand, Melinda simply took his. "You poor thing. Sit down. I'll order you tuna salad."

Harry sat beside her and jumped whenever she patted his arm. He put his hands flat on the table, but they kept trembling anyway. Melinda ordered him lunch, plus a glass of Cabernet for herself, which came in a jelly glass.

"It was one hundred and eighteen at the airport in Phoenix," Melinda was saying when the waitress brought his tuna salad. "I can't understand how people live in that. You'd get heatstroke just going out for the paper."

Savannah looked up. "It's always best to fall in love in summer. You can't sustain lies in heat like that. Doubt just shrivels up."

They were quiet for a moment, then Maggie tapped her fingers on the table. "What kind of bull-shit is that? It was horrid. Phoenix is another word for hell."

Melinda reached over and touched Harry's arm. "What did you think when you lived there?"

Harry looked down at her hand, the mauve finger-nails, the red freckles beneath her knuckles. He honestly thought he might cry, but instead he just re-moved his arm. "The only thing I think," he said slowly, "is that this is a ridiculous conversation to be having when my daughter is in jail."

Melinda looked down at the table, but before any-thing else could be said, a spoon hit the bottom of Harry's chin.

"Hey!" he said.

Savannah had already stood up. "Let me tell you something, Harry Shaw. You can hire all the fancy law-yers in the world to get custody of Emma. You can get restraining orders galore. But if you can't learn to be kind, my daughter's not getting anywhere near you. I'll kidnap her if I have to. You understand me?"

She stormed out of the restaurant. Maggie was laughing as she got up after her. The psycho said noth-ing, just tossed a couple of bills on the table, certainly not enough to cover the tab, and walked out.

Melinda sat silently beside him. She was crying onto the white box of brownies.

"Look," he said. "I'm stressed, all right? My daughter's in a jail cell across the street. You've got to cut me some slack."

She turned to him so quickly, she didn't have time to right her face. For a moment, she looked no more familiar than an angry stranger on the street, the kind he'd always kept his distance from. She looked like a wife who'd had just about enough.

"I came all the way out here. I wanted . . . No more slack, Harry. I've been cutting you slack for years, and now I'm done."

"Melinda—"

"When you rode out here on your white horse, did it ever occur to you to ask me if I'd be willing to have a fifteen-year-old girl who can't stand the sight of me in my house?"

Harry sat back. The waitress brought two take-out boxes, then just left them on the table when she saw their faces.

"She's my daughter," he said. "I thought I didn't have to ask."

"Well, you do."

Harry began putting the tuna salad in the Styrofoam boxes, even though he would never be able to touch this food again and he was on a committee back home to ban Styrofoam.

"I'll tell you something," Melinda said loudly, stopping conversation in the booths around them, something she would never do back in Danville. "Just because a woman is in the Junior League and doesn't tell every stranger who comes along her troubles doesn't mean she doesn't have any. Being nice is not the same thing as being happy. I may not read fortunes, but I can tell you you have no future with me if things don't start changing right this second."

Harry went to twist one of his rings and realized he'd forgotten to put them on in the rush to get to Arizona. He wore only his silver wedding ring, the one he couldn't polish regularly, because he couldn't get it off his finger.

He pushed the food to the other side of the table. He waited until conversation around them had picked up again, then he took Melinda's hand.

"Look at me, Melinda," he said quietly. "How many chances am I going to get to be her hero?"

Melinda looked up, and he realized he had never seen her without makeup. He had no idea of the natural color of her hair. She'd been put together when he met her and she'd stayed that way. He had figured if she was unhappy, she would let herself go like everybody else, she would give him some sign.

"If you get her out of this," she said, "she just might hate you. Are you willing to take that chance?"

Harry stared at her. He had a rush of insight he knew he would never hold on to. Melinda was the only thing standing between him and being alone.

"Only if you are," he said.

Melinda stared at him a long time, then slowly lowered her head, until it touched his.


They got away with fifteen hundred dollars cash, which wouldn't even begin to cover the things Eli had lost. They doled it out in the middle of Desolation Wood, in the exact spot where two teenagers making love for the first time had been bludgeoned to death by the first woman serial killer in the state of Arizona. No one would dare come for them there; it was too haunted.

Whether from ghosts or his own crazy mind, Eli heard wailing the whole time Rick was dividing up the money. "What about Emma's share?"

"What share? You don't get a share if you get caught. That girl was out of her mind. A few more steps and she would have been free as a bird."

"Bob Simon saw her face," Eli said. "She never would have been free. They would have picked her up eventually."

"She knew the plan. I'm heading for Denver before she squeals. How about you?"

Eli didn't think. He just pulled back his arm and landed a solid punch in the center of Rick Laufer's nose. The jerk went down, hard. With any luck, Eli had done irreparable damage.

"You son of a bitch." Rick tried to get up to fight him, but Jack and Pippen held him down.

"Get the fuck out of here!" Jack yelled. "Are you out of your mind? Rick will fucking kill you!"

Eli might have lost his mind, because when he got home, he used two twenties to light his cigarette. He sat on his porch steps and waited for the police to come for him. He wondered what it would feel like to finally tell the truth, and realized he was looking forward to it. He would tell Cal Bentley it had been sheer misfortune that Emma met up with him in the first place. He would tell him the robbery had been his idea. He'd confess to everything, even crimes he hadn't committed, if Cal would let Emma go.

But it wasn't the police who finally drove up his dirt drive. Eli put out his cigarette and propped open his door, exposing the last of his stolen goods, before he went to meet Emma's mother. Savannah wore a green velvet dress and black beret, and when she got out of her car, her hands were closed into tight fists, the size of birds' eggs.

"She's still in jail," she said. "Bob Simon is thinking about whether or not he wants to press charges. If he doesn't, she'll either be tried by the county prosecutor or her father will take her to California. Either way, I doubt very much you will ever see her again."

She would never know if her words had the desired effect, because he didn't show a thing. Inside, though, he could feel his blood going cold, things shutting down. He had just lost the one good thing in his life, and there was no way he was getting it back.

"What the hell were you thinking?" she asked. "Did you suddenly come up with this brilliant plan to sacrifice the one person who loves you?"

Eli shrugged, but had to turn away, so she wouldn't see his eyes. He prayed she was almost through, because he would only be able to stand there so long. His left leg was already trembling. He looked up once and the sky was blue, but when he looked again clouds were forming. Like always, he was bringing in the rain.

Savannah closed the gap between them and grabbed his collar. "I've heard the stories about you. You've had it tough. Your parents are pretty messed up. But I'll tell you the absolute truth, Eli. You've got nobody to blame but yourself."

She pushed him away and walked into his house. By the time the drizzle started and he went inside, she had laid out her cards on the floor. She sat crosslegged beside them.

"I got out my Rider-Waite deck for you," she said. "I'm not cutting you any slack."

He nodded. He hoped she wouldn't. He hoped he would get only the worst cards.

She pointed to his future card. "The Empress. This is the feminine influence. A mother. Sister. Wife. Your intuition."

"Emma," he said.

"Oh no. Your crossing card was the Two of Cups, reversed. That's divorce. Separation. That's where you and Emma end."

Eli stood up and walked around his shack. The floor had given out in two more places, and the woodstove wouldn't burn wood anymore, only melt it down into carcinogenic ash. The worst part was not living in a place like this, or having parents like his, or dropping out of school because he was told he was stupid. The worst part had been accepting all that. It had been assuming life would not get any better. Because when it did, when Emma came along, he had not really believed it. He had known she'd have to leave him, and somehow he'd made certain she did just that.

"Look," she said, "you're still the Five of Wands." He looked at the card, five young men hoisting staffs into the air. It looked like warfare to him. "Even in the Voyager deck, this is the card of oppression. Any way you look at it, you're trapped."

Eli stared at her. "You don't need to curse me."

"I'm not. You're already cursed, though not from the reasons you think. You've just stopped looking for possibilities."

They both heard the truck then, but Savannah just stared at the cards. Eli went to the door and saw Jake driving up, only two of his dogs in the bed. Eli had walked out on every job he'd ever had, but he had never felt he let anybody down, until now.

Jake got out of his truck slowly and walked into the house. He didn't even glance at the stolen stereos. He looked straight at Savannah, and though no one would believe this, Eli could actually spot love when he saw it. He could also see when love was backfiring, twisting a man inside out.

"Are you all right?" Jake asked Savannah.

She stood up slowly. She was shaking, but Eli could tell she was not going to turn to Jake. There was something about mothers and daughters, something a man would be a fool to come between. Her eyes were firmly on Eli. "If you're interested, your final result is The Moon. That's the card of delusions, and it's also a card of movement and change. Believe it or not, Eli, you might very well become a different person."

She pushed past them both and walked out into the drizzle. She let Rufus and Gabe out of the back of the truck. The dogs knocked her down trying to kiss her. They competed for space in her lap, for the scratch of her fingers behind their ears.

In the cabin, Jake came up beside him. Eli didn't even brace himself. He wanted a punch that would land him on the floor. He wanted someone to finally put him in his place, but all Jake did was put a hand on his shoulder.

"Emma won't name you," he said. "But that doesn't mean Cal's stupid. Next time, evidence or not, he'll haul you in."

"There's not gonna be a next time." And as he said it, he knew it was true. The only thing he wanted to steal was in jail. "I suppose I'm fired," he went on.

"It doesn't matter if you are. I'm leaving with Savannah."

Eli stooped down and gathered up Savannah's cards. He shoved them toward Jake. "Pick one."

Jake looked at the cards. He started to take the top one, then instead fanned them out and took one from the middle. He hesitated, then turned it over. Neither of them needed Savannah to read it for them. The card was the Hermit.

"I'll be damned," Eli said.

Jake handed back the card and walked out. He walked up to Savannah and said something that made her snap up her head. He gathered the dogs into his truck and drove off.

Eli still had the cards in his hand when he came out a moment later. His presence turned the drizzle to a downpour.

"What did he say?" he asked.

She didn't even jump when lightning struck the tree behind his cabin, when she had to shout to be heard. "Sometimes the cards are wrong."

Eli handed her the cards, but she shook her head. "You keep them. I'm trying to freak you out."

Water dripped off her hat onto her chin, but she didn't wipe it away. She had cigarettes in her pocket and dirt on the curl of her cheek. He wondered if she even knew herself anymore.

"You told me before the cards are only our own intuition," he said.

"That's right."

"Then mine tells me I'm gonna get Emma back."

She stared at him. For a moment he thought she smiled, but he knew that had to be a trick of the dimming light.

After she drove off, he went in and gathered his money. By the time he came back out, the storm had passed. The air that followed smelled too good for a boy like him to believe, so he lit a cigarette. Then before he could think things through, he got in his Corvette and drove to Bronco Liquor.

Bob Simon hadn't missed a day of work and was behind the cash register when Eli Malone walked in. There was a new piece of acoustic tile on the ceiling and plywood over the bullet hole in the window.

Eli walked up to the counter, then just stood there. Bob Simon got a little skittish and reached for something beneath the register, but all Eli did was shove a hand into his pocket and come out with his share of the cash. He flung it on the counter, then rocked back on his heels. He could have taken off then, but instead waited for Bob Simon to pick up the phone and call the cops. He waited and waited, until the silence was as good as a scream. He slammed his hand on the counter.

"Well?" he said.

Bob Simon put the money back in the cash register, where it belonged. "Well, what? Are you gonna buy something or not?"

Then the toughest nineteen-year-old in Prescott put his head in his hands and cried.

# SIXTEEN

## THE HIEROPHANT ❧ FORGIVENESS

**B**ob Simon called while Cal was swallowing his seventh Advil of the evening. "Got a thief here who won't stop crying," Simon said.

Cal had wondered what Eli Malone would do. In Cal's mind, the boy had two options—either disappear or become another person. It wasn't as hard as people thought. All Eli had to do was look in a girl's eyes and turn into whatever she thought him capable of. He had to wake up one morning and decide never to disappoint her again.

"You still got the girl?" Simon asked.

"Yes. Won't tell me anything but lies."

"Tell her if she comes in here again, I won't show her any pity. Tell her to go get some kind of life."

Cal smiled for the first time that day. He was going to take Bob Simon out to dinner and send all his friends to Bronco Liquor for beer. "I will."

In another hour, he'd convinced the prosecutor to

drop the charges, as long as Emma left town. But even then, Cal didn't call Emma's parents with the good news. He broke yet another rule and let everyone sleep on it. He wanted everyone, himself included, to recognize how quickly a person could slip through their fingers, how much they all had to lose. He stayed at the station and didn't sleep all night. He kept walking to the girl's cell to check that she was breathing. At midnight, he pulled up a chair and leaned his head against the bars. Emma was feigning sleep but eventually turned around on the cot to face him.

"Everything's ruined, isn't it?" she said.

"No, honey. Not everything. Just give it some time."

At dawn, he called his daughter Lanie in Philadelphia. She was seven months pregnant with a baby she would call Katherine or Kyle. "Be careful," he told her. "Just do me a favor and be careful of everything."

"Oh, Daddy. Don't be silly. What could happen?"

He didn't go into everything that could; it would take him all day and, anyway, he had things to do. He called his travel agent next and booked an open-ended flight to Philadelphia for him and Lois in October. They'd bring a pastel layette set and black-and-white picture art. They would stay until Lanie got sick of them.

Cal set his retirement date for October first. That would give the office nearly two months to find a replacement. That would give Lois enough time to get ready for him, because once he was home, he was not going to read a single paper or watch the news ever again. He was going to sit by his wife's side and study the pattern of freckles across her nose. He was going to bask in the wonder of her hands.

At eight sharp, Cal made two more phone calls. Within the hour, Emma's parents were in his office.

He glanced at Savannah, but turned away before he could see what his words would do to her. He looked only at Harry.

"Here's the deal. We'll drop the charges." Savannah started to clap her hands, so he hurried on. "Mr. Shaw will take Emma out of state. If she runs away and shows up here again, if I see one glimpse of that face, I'll book her on felony robbery charges."

Harry breathed out long and slow. Savannah simply dropped her arms awkwardly to her sides. Neither of them had any idea Cal was bluffing; most people never did. Once Emma was gone, the case was closed, period. He'd be glad to get rid of it. He'd take Lois out to a good steak dinner. He'd get her a little bit drunk and maybe even get lucky.

Harry looked at Savannah. "She won't go anywhere. I can guarantee it."

Cal hesitated as he walked past Savannah, then reached out to touch her arm. She was trembling underneath, leaning north, and he tried to right her. "I'm sorry, but you know otherwise she'd end up with those punks."

"Yes," she said quietly. "Of course you're right." She surprised him by putting her hand over his. Her palms were moist, her nails short and bare. He wasn't about to look up and see what was in her eyes. He squeezed her arm, then got out of there as quick as he could.

He went to the cell for Emma. She was still curled up in the fetal position on the tiny cot.

"You have any idea the kids who rot in here?" he asked. "The ones who don't have any parent, let alone two of them, fighting for them?"

He could see she didn't, because when he led her to her parents, she backed away from their hugs. She wrapped her arms around her stomach and looked like she would scream if anyone said a word to her, so no one did. Cal had seen this a hundred times before, but he knew if he saw it once more, he'd go crazy. Turned out it wasn't a mass murder or grisly crime scene that made up his mind about retirement, it was the brittle-ness of a wrecked teenager. It was a fifteen-year-old's sorrow, raw around the edges and charged with des-peration. It was the panic on her parents' faces when they looked at this girl they didn't know or understand, panic that would not go away until she hit twenty and decided life was worth living after all. Until then, they would hide the aspirin and razor blades and blame each other for her melancholy. They would cry into their pillows and wonder how this could be, when they had loved her more than anything, probably more than a parent even should.

He walked them out. Emma stood stiffly between Savannah and Harry, curling her shoulders in when they got too close. Melinda was talking about a new literacy project she was starting up in Danville. She opened a white box and took out a brownie. "Come on, Emma. Chocolate always helps."

Emma looked at her like she was crazy.

"We'll ship your things later," Harry said when they reached his car. "Your mother and I have already decided you're going straight to the airport."

Savannah stepped up to Emma, but the girl raised an arm to ward her off. Savannah froze, then tucked her hands into fists against her stomach.

"It's for the best," she said, but she was crying. "Time heals everything."

Emma jerked back, as if she couldn't have said anything worse. She got into the backseat and slammed the door.

"Have a safe trip!" Savannah called after the car. "Harry, call me when you get . . ." She let the rest drop; the car had already turned the corner. There were tears all down her cheeks, and a sound Cal did not want to hear winding up at the back of her throat.

"Savannah," he said.

She let out the cry, and he ran his fingers through his hair. He looked anywhere but at her.

"She'll come back to you," he said, but he wasn't sure if she even heard.

She stared at the last place she'd seen her daughter, then wrapped her arms around herself tight. When one of those bold summer breezes dove down the collar of her dress, she turned her back on it. This was the kind of day that got tourists calling their bosses back east and saying they were never coming back, but Cal was actually thinking about moving to Miami. There, the crime rate was so phenomenal, a man couldn't get personal about any of it.

He turned to go, then thought better of it. "Now that this is over, you and Jake might want to head out. Fast."

Savannah stopped crying for a moment and jerked her head up, but he wasn't going to say more than that. He kept his silence all day, until he got off duty and found Jake in Teton's Bar, still apparently unwarned. Jake was at the usual back table, scaring the local gang members into whispers. Cal sat down in the chair opposite him. They didn't talk for forty minutes, just halfheartedly watched a Diamondbacks game on the satellite TV.

The part Cal hadn't told Savannah about was Bethany Appleton, the woman who had come into the office yesterday. She had been watching one of those local tabloid shows when they aired a story about the body found in Wawani Lake, and the mystery that ensued. She had walked right into Cal's office and ruined an already horrible day.

"I was camping in Mesquite Cove that night," she'd said. "Not fifty yards from where that man docked the boat. I might not have paid much attention if my boyfriend hadn't just left for beer. I mean, I was all alone there, and then this really tall, really spooky-looking guy comes off the boat with a suitcase and a rifle on his arm. He could have been a serial killer, right? So I was watching him real closely."

"Could you identify him now? It was fifteen years ago."

"I could identify him, all right. It's the kind of thing that sticks in your brain. He'd left the light on in the boat and I could see his face, all that black hair. He was bleeding from his left hand. Later, after he'd gone, I checked the beach. There was blood all over it."

"Why didn't you say something back then?"

"I was a kid. Sixteen. Who'd have believed me? And what was there to say? I didn't see anyone get hurt. No one said anything on the news. If there had been mention of a murder, I would have come forward. But now . . . well, now it looks like you guys need some help."

"And the tabloids pay real well for a story like that."

She fidgeted a second, then leaned back and shrugged. "Yeah, well, that too. But that doesn't mean I'm lying. I've just got a daughter to support is all. And I saw him. I could solve your case for you right this second."

Cal had stood up slowly, aching all the way down to his toes. He had led the woman to a conference room and taken her statement himself, something he rarely did. Then he filed it in his private cabinet.

He was going to retire, goddammit. He was done with people's private violence, done with warring families and spite. He was going to spend his life savings on a Winnebago and eat beef to his heart's discontent. But not before he led one more man to safety.

Cal looked at Jake's hands on the table, the scar beneath his knuckles he'd never tried to hide. "I told Savannah you two might want to head on out tomorrow morning. Tonight, if you can swing it. Take a tour of the country. Maybe head up to Canada."

Jake didn't take his eyes from the television, but the muscles along his shoulders tensed. Finally, he grabbed his beer and drained it.

"A woman's come forward," Cal went on. "She was camping the night Roy Pillandro disappeared. Says she got a good look at someone who stepped off that boat with a rifle and a bloody hand."

Jake stretched out the fingers of his left hand. "Well."

"We'll have to set up a lineup," Cal said. "I can hold it off for a week, maybe two." He fished into his pocket and took out a cigarette.

"When's your retirement?" Jake asked.

"The second that woman says it wasn't you."

Jake smiled, but not the way Cal wanted him to. Not the smile of a man who was going to do everything he could to save himself.

"I thought I could go with her," Jake said. "But even if this thing with Emma hadn't happened, I wouldn't have been able to leave. You just get to a point where you can't run anymore. You get sick of hating yourself."

Cal lit his cigarette. He had expected as much. Some men just aren't comfortable unless their heart is broken, unless they're paying for justifiable acts with their life. Cal put his hand on his shoulder, then got to his feet.

"Lois is waiting for me," he said. "See, she's got

this strange idea she has to take care of me. Cooks sensible meals and keeps them warm until I come home, no matter what time that is. Sometimes we don't say a word. We just sit there. But she never goes to sleep unless I'm in bed beside her."

Jake looked up. "I'm aware of what I'm giving up."

"I can't do any more, Jake."

"I know that. You've done more than I ever expected."

Cal paid for his beer. He squeezed Jake's shoulder once more before he left the bar.

Savannah sat on the bench in Jake's garden. The sky was bursting at the seams, glittering with blue meteoroids. All week, the news had been filled with the drama of the collision of Athens Fire and Taurus, two asteroids a mere one hundred thousand miles from Earth, a near miss. But this near miss wasn't harmless; in fact, it was full of potentially lethal fallout debris. Hour after hour, the newscasters talked of nothing but the rubble headed for Earth. They showed simulated meteorite hits, possible death rates, and the next-to-nothing chance a piece of rock and iron scrap could wipe out life on Earth. Then when real damage started occurring, they couldn't believe their luck. They sent live crews to every city in the southwestern United States, where the hits were centered.

A ten-foot wide rock had crashed through the eighteenth floor of the Bank of America building in Phoenix, narrowly missing four loan officers. In Amarillo, a whole stable of racehorses had been taken out by a pummeling of six-inch debris. Here, though, the only evidence of anything remarkable was the meteor dust that got into everything. It clung like blue ash to hair and hamburgers and the cleats of tennis shoes. It disoriented the robins, who mistook the ground for sky and kept barreling into it, knocking themselves out.

Meteor dust felt like ice melt, and at the cabin, it had brought autumn on early. A week into August, the aspens hugging Switchback Creek were gold at the edges. The chipmunks no longer stopped to chatter, but ran around ceaselessly, gathering blue-dusted acorns. Tonight, Savannah wrapped a shawl around her burgundy dress, and put on the first of her winter hats, a furry fedora.

Jake drove up at midnight. He'd been at Teton's Bar all night, but when he got out slowly and steadily, she knew he'd stopped at two beers. She tucked her head against his carving of Superstition Mountain, which he'd stained with henna. He had whittled away at the arms and legs, carving in wrists and ankles. Pretty soon, if her father kept avoiding him, the bench would mean more to him than it did to Doug.

He walked over and sat beside her. He smelled of beer and cigarette smoke, but beneath that, always, of his mountain. She put her hand over his.

"Cal said we ought to leave tomorrow," she said, and then he squeezed her hand. She looked past the meteor shower to the north and spotted the only red star. It was distant and faint, overshadowed by meteoroids.

"Savannah—"

"You're not coming."

He dropped her hand. "They're going to find me soon. I won't put you through that."

She stood up. It really didn't matter what he thought he could put her through, but how much she was willing to stand. She was jittery, and had been for days. She had to get out of the path of those asteroids. She couldn't live in a place where all anyone talked about was their chance of death by debris. If she wasn't optimistic about the future, then all her fortune-telling turned to threats.

She hadn't been breathing right all summer. Oxygen stopped just short of her lungs. The atmosphere up here was obviously too thin for clear thinking because she wasn't even sure if the tears in her eyes were from relief or regret or meteor dust. She only knew somewhere along the line she'd lost her smooth gypsy voice, and now even her simplest words cracked with emotion. Now just looking at the people she loved hurt.

"Now that Harry's got Emma," she began, then couldn't go on. The words numbed the corners of her tongue. She wrapped her shawl tight around her. "I don't want you to come anyway, if you're only going to leave."

He stood up beside her, but she could see he was not going to argue. He thought himself a hermit, a man running from his past, but that was not it at all. He'd simply been waiting for his past to catch up to him. He'd been waiting to turn himself in.

She heard a whizzing sound and ducked, thinking a piece of asteroid was falling from the sky. But it was only a pine cone bouncing off the eaves.

"I think we should just say goodbye now." She was surprised her voice didn't break, surprised that Harry had been right all those years ago. It was simply stunning that she could love someone this much and still be able to leave him.

Jake stared at her. He could be as still as one of his pine trees when he wanted to. He could not reveal a thing.

"All right then." He walked down the path to his workshop, then shut the door tightly behind him.

Savannah breathed in and out quickly. Her

mother had been spooking her all these years with talk of the terrible things that could happen, all the people she could potentially lose. But that was not the worst. The worst was being able to stand all the losses. The worst was the way a broken heart still beat.

She walked inside, where she left no note, only the Hierophant on the kitchen counter. It was hard to tell who needed to be forgiven; probably they both did. She tossed all her decks except the positive Voyager into the garbage. From now on, she would only work with a deck whose bad cards were opportunities for redemption.

She tiptoed up the stairs to the loft. Her parents were sleeping soundly, her father tucked against her mother's back. Savannah leaned over and kissed first her mother's cheek, then her father's. Doug's eyelids fluttered, and she jumped back into the shadows. She held her breath until he was still again, until she could get out of there without saying one more goodbye.

She took Jake's suitcases out of her car and put them on the porch. She was long past crying. She was going to miss him every day of her life, and that was just the way it would be. But at least she was going where the sky wasn't falling. At least she wouldn't be afraid to look up.

She got in the car and started the engine. She really didn't expect him to come after her, but when he didn't, she yanked off her bracelets. She tossed them one by one out the car window, leaving a trail she knew he would not follow. She reached the highway by two; by dawn, she was well on her way to San Francisco, where all the things she couldn't bear to see were hidden in fog.

\*   \*   \*

As soon as Cheryl Pillandro heard about the lineup, she got a leave of absence from Dillard's. Maggie Dawson insisted she stay at the Sage Street house, and Cheryl stopped there only long enough to change into the clothes she'd bought at a thrift shop. Torn jeans, red halter top, knee-high black boots, clothes she might have owned fifteen years ago. Roy's kind of clothes. She looked like white trash, like a middle-aged woman suffering from delusions of youth and garish beauty, and that was exactly how she wanted it. She wanted a man to look her in the eye and think her capable of all kinds of foolishness.

She arrived at the sheriff's office half an hour later, and raised havoc until a deputy showed her into Cal Bentley's office. He was seated beside his desk, digging into a supersized bottle of Advil.

"Sorry, Chief," the deputy said. "This is Cheryl Pillandro. Jake Grey's mother. She wouldn't—"

"It's all right," Cal said. "She can stay."

Cheryl waited until the deputy left, then took a deep breath and marched to Cal Bentley's chair. His eyes widened; probably he thought she was going to make a pass at him, but all she did was bend over, so he could see the blue scar along the back of her neck.

"Steak knife," she said. She put her foot on his chair and rolled up the jeans. "Golf club." She held out the arm Roy had broken. "Brute force."

She walked around the desk and sat down. She'd been sweating on the way over, but now she was cool as ice. This was the first time in fifteen years she hadn't hated herself, and she drew out the next words, so she could make the moment last.

"Roy Pillandro was a son of a bitch," she went on. "And I killed him."

Cal sat back in his chair. He tapped out three more Advils and swallowed them without water. He stood up and walked to the door to lock it. Then he turned around.

"I wish you had," he said softly.

Cheryl dropped her hands in her lap. By the time Cal got back to his desk, she was crying. He handed her a tissue.

"We've got witnesses placing you at your house in Phoenix the night Roy disappeared," he went on. "Bethany Appleton saw a man coming off Roy's boat, a *twenty*-year-old, with dark hair and a rifle. And it would have taken more than a hundred-ten-pound woman to smash in a man's skull."

Cheryl looked up. "I'm telling you, I did it. If you've got a confession, who the hell cares if it's the right one or not? Roy's not here to tell you different."

Cal knelt down next to her chair. When he touched her hands, she cried harder. She didn't want anyone's pity. She wanted a chance for redemption. She wanted to finally start acting like somebody's mother.

But all Cal did was squeeze her hands. "I'll do everything I can to keep him out of jail, but it's almost as if he wants that. I'm fighting him, more than anything else."

Cheryl stood up. She swiped at the tears that just kept coming. "I wanted to kill him. Roy had so many enemies, someone was bound to do him in eventually. He was dead either way. It shouldn't have had anything to do with Jake."

"I'll try . . ."

Cheryl walked out. She got in her car and drove back to the Dawson house, where the garden had turned wild in Doug's absence, the jackmanii clematis claiming a whole sidewalk, the ginkgo tree roots turning over cobblestones. She walked into the house and went straight to the telephone directory. She found a

Bethany Appleton on Diaz Street, and picked up the phone.

When a woman answered, Cheryl said nothing, just held the phone to her ear while the woman said, "Hello? Is anyone there? Who the hell is this?"

In the coming week, she would call every Bethany Appleton within a hundred-mile radius. After she'd worn them all down with silence, she would call one more time and do a perfect imitation of Roy. "Whoever condemns a man to hell," she'd say, "goes there with him." And then she'd hang up while they both were crying.

Maggie never invited Doug on her shopping excursions. It was hell on him to get down Jake's mountain on that sorry excuse for a road. But a week after Savannah left, when Maggie walked to her car, he was already in the passenger seat, waiting.

"I'm coming with you. Don't argue. I mean it."

Maggie got in the car. He had a blanket over his legs, but when she tried to tuck it in around him, he kicked it off.

"Don't go crazy now," she said.

"Why not? Why not now?"

Maggie got a chill up her spine and started the car. Since Savannah had left, the cabin had been eerily quiet. Jake had hardly come out of his workshop. When he did, he stomped along the front porch and threw stones at the rooftop, where they clanked against something hard, then came whizzing back down. He walked for miles, and only came back after sunset, when his legs were trembling and they couldn't see his eyes.

Maggie knew they had worn out their welcome, but she was not leaving. There was something in the air up here that was making Doug well, and if she had to lie, cheat and steal to keep it coming, she would. Whenever Jake asked their plans, she told him plans were for newlyweds, for people with all the time in the world. "All I plan for," she said, "is to get up earlier every morning, so I can have more time with Doug."

Her husband was eating meat and cuddling her in bed again, and she wasn't going to miss a second of it. She knelt beside him when he worked in Jake's garden, and never took her gaze off the rise and fall of his shoulders. Sometimes, when his breath shuddered a little, her stomach dropped out. She couldn't get her breath either and had to sit there until the spell passed.

She drove carefully down the mountain, then north toward the outlet mall. She parked in the handicap spot, though they had no sticker. But hell, she had an open bottle of wine in the back, too, which she sipped after shopping, on occasion. Rules were for people in their thirties who gave a damn.

She helped Doug into the Levi's outlet, and had him try on a new pair of 501's. They were three sizes smaller than the pair they'd bought six months ago, but when he walked out of the dressing room, he looked like everything she'd ever dreamed of. The hairs that were slowly growing back on his head were red, of all things. Red and soft as kitten fur. He looked so good in the jeans, she walked up to him and planted a kiss on his lips. A teenager looking at sweatshirts gawked at them.

They bought the Levi's, then went into Fieldcrest Cannon and found new sheets for Jake. They also bought him sixteen crystal goblets, which he would never use. At Crocodile Rock, Maggie bought a leather purse, and at the Lane store, Doug charged a leather recliner, which they had shipped to their house.

When they were through, they drove to Lynx Lake and brought out the open bottle of wine. They sat on the sand and drank Merlot out of Jake's new glasses.

Maggie closed her eyes and raised her face to the sun. She still thought life was horrible. God was unjust and downright mean. Then he did something crazy, like give her someone to love. He gave her a moment so perfect, if she didn't sit still and enjoy every last second, she'd be a goddamn fool.

Doug slipped his hand into hers, and the moment passed. She opened her eyes and looked right at him. His hair was coming in red all right, but the whites of his eyes had turned red, too. There was blood in his urine. It seemed only right that he buy everything he could get his hands on.

"Maggie," he said, but she shook her head. There was nothing more for him to say, and only a few words left for her.

"I love you, Doug," she said.

He smiled and squeezed her hand. "I've always known that."

She lowered her head, because if he knew that, then he probably knew the rest. That she was sorry for the things she'd said. That it was easier to be mean than tender. And that there was no way she could live without him.


When Savannah returned to San Francisco, she had two choices: Return to Taylor Baines or work the party circuit, telling fortunes with Ramona. After trying out a couple of parties, she realized it was no choice at all.

Something had changed, and Savannah supposed it was her. Suddenly people were lining up across ballrooms to hear their fortunes. After all these years, she'd discovered the secret of successful predictions:

People didn't want to hear how to be happy. They wanted her to promise them their heart's desire, assuming this was the same thing. Actually, it wasn't even close. A heart's desire was Emma's safety; happiness would have been keeping her safe herself. When Savannah sat parked outside of Harry's house, she had what she wanted, but she couldn't hold it in her hands. She could only hope for quick glimpses through an upstairs window, or a sudden, miraculous change of heart.

Most people, however, didn't care about this discrepancy. In fact, her business was on fire. After handing out business cards at a few parties, customers started lining up outside her house. Her first client on Thursday night was a man in his thirties with thinning hair. He was shaped like a bell curve, thin at the ends, soft and protruding in the middle, and when he sat across from her, she could feel the fingers of his sadness washing over her. She pulled down her beret and leaned away from him.

"Tell me what you want to know," she said.

He hesitated, then took the cards she offered. "I guess . . . I guess I just want to know how to get Julie back. Otherwise, I don't see how I'm supposed to go on."

Savannah sighed. Just once, she'd like to hear someone ask how to change the world. She'd like a man to come in hoping for swords, or the Voyager's Seven of Worlds, the card of breakthroughs. She'd like someone to ask her how he could be free of caring, so she could find out for herself if it was even possible.

The man shuffled nervously, then handed her back the cards. Sweat speckled his forehead. He sat with his hands in knots on his lap while she laid them out.

Instead of the Celtic spread, she now used an old

gypsy layout, a simple fifteen-card design that wasn't nearly so threatening. No crossing cards, no destiny. Just three cards to define the questioner, three for the past, three for the forces beyond his control. Then the last six for the future—three for the natural future, if nothing was done to change it, and three for the possible future, if he chose to get involved.

She liked it. It gave fate an out, and a man some alternatives, if he'd only take her up on them. This man got Art in his natural future.

"You'll be ruled by creativity, if you decide not to change anything. The Art card often means putting things together, using your artistic side to make yourself whole. Are you a painter, maybe? A writer?"

The man went pale. "No, but Julie wants to be a novelist. She's been writing something for the last seven years or so, a romance I think. I've been after her to send it out to publishers, but then yesterday . . . Yesterday, she said she couldn't work in our house anymore. Said it was stifling. She left me this."

He reached into his pocket and handed her a piece of crinkled paper. She opened it and smoothed out the wrinkles.

> There once was a man named Ned,
> dumb as a rat and no good in bed.
> His wife was no dummy,
> she took all his money,
> and found a young lover instead.

Savannah thought of her father's poetry. Every night, she put his poem to her between the Star and the Moon, then tucked them all beneath her pillow. Sometimes, though, she imagined she felt the rough edges of the paper poking her. Sometimes, she had to take them out so she could sleep.

"Oh dear," she said, handing back the poem. "But look at this." She pointed to two cards in his possible future, the Seven of Wands and the Emperor. "The Seven of Wands is courage. The Emperor builds an empire with planning and logic. Are you a businessman?"

"An electronic salesman, at Circuit City."

Savannah was getting a headache. "Have you ever dreamed of something more?"

"Like what?"

She stood up and walked to the door. She wondered what would happen if she just started making things up. If she took out all the cups, and started talking about the joys of solitude.

There was clanking going on in the kitchen. Ramona had come by for dinner and was bustling around, slicing cantaloupe and toasting bread she would eat without butter. She'd lost thirty-five more pounds since Savannah had been gone. She'd dyed her hair jet black and taken to wearing Cleopatra-style eyeliner.

"As I see it, you can let this woman rule your life," Savannah said. "Or you can be brash. You can be daring. You can be a whole new person, if you choose to."

The man looked up. His eyes were dark brown and round. He was like a puppy she wanted to take into her arms to stop its pitiful whining. "Are you sure?" he asked.

"Of course. And this." She pointed to a card in the events beyond his control, the Ace of Cups. "That's ecstasy."

He just sat there, staring at the card. "Well, I can't imagine where that's coming from."

"It can come from anywhere. It comes from everywhere, Ned. Let the novelist go and see where life takes you. Think about what it is you really want to do and do it. Whether you want it or not, you've got a good fortune."

"I just don't think . . ."

Savannah didn't hear the rest. She was making money like crazy, and every dollar felt dirty. It turned out she couldn't say anything; the only fortunes that got through were the ones a person wanted to hear. It turned out she wasn't happy here, either.

She and Ramona sat up late drinking the latest Sonoma Merlot. Sometime after midnight, Ramona tucked her newly sleek legs beneath her.

"So are you going to tell me about him or not?"

Savannah was not surprised. Ramona had always known everything. She was the real fortune-teller. "Not."

"You know what I think?" Ramona asked.

"I really don't care."

Ramona laughed and went on, regardless. "I think it's easy to be happy when you have no life. It's love and marriage and jobs and babies that screw everything up."

Savannah got up and walked to the small window. Even from there, she could smell Ramona's scent of caramel. Whenever Savannah kissed her cheek, she swore the rouge that came off was made of powdered sugar.

Ramona came up beside her and took her hand. "You loved him that much, huh?"

"He's got a bad heart. His father died at forty-one."

"Ah-ha."

"He killed a man. The police could be picking him up right this minute."

"Well, sure."

Savannah yanked her hand away. "You could act a little shocked."

"Oh, honey, come *on*. A bad ticker, homicide,

whoop-de-do. This is Ramona you're talking to. This is San Francisco, for crying out loud. When I first moved here, I lived in the Tenderloin. We had three murders in two weeks, I kid you not."

Savannah just stared at her.

"It's true. Don't be taken in by those sunny days in October, Savannah. It's as vicious here as anywhere else. You know Monty Wells, the healer over in Berkeley? You know those scars on his arms he said were from a car accident? Ha! That was no accident. That was a knife blade from his ex-wife. When he fought back, he pushed her beneath a moving van."

"You're not serious."

"The hell I'm not. Shit happens everywhere, that's all I'm saying, and it skyrockets when love's involved. Just wait. Johnny Pells might be giving his lover roses now, but I've seen him checking out women. He's thinking of switching sides, and he's crazy enough to do it too. Next door, Sarah Alder is into freebasing, so it's really just a matter of time before something explodes around here. If you're not careful, it could very well be you."

"Don't be so dramatic."

"Why not? Life's dramatic, and if it's not, let's all just shoot ourselves now and be done with it."

Savannah hugged her friend fiercely. When the phone rang, Savannah squeezed tighter, because it was late, and the ring sounded fierce and impatient, just like her mother.

"Sweetheart?" Ramona said.

Finally, Savannah pulled away and went to the kitchen phone. She didn't need tarot cards or shadows to explain the panic that went straight down to her gut. She only needed her mother to say honey.

"Honey, it's Mom," Maggie said. "Your dad's in the hospital. You need to come home."

# SEVENTEEN

## THE STAR ❧ HOPE

The mountains had been playing tricks on them. Savannah should have known thin air would cause hallucinations, in their case conjuring what they wanted least and most, a mean-spirited ghost and all the signs of remission. When Doug had collapsed in Jake's garden, Maggie and Jake had rushed him to Yavapai Regional Medical Center in the flatlands, where people were thinking straight and not mistaking suntans for cures. Now, when Savannah stepped into her father's hospital room, she found Doug lying flat and still, his arms sticking out of the blanket like half-buried bones. He finally looked like what he was—a man who did not have the energy to open his eyes.

Savannah's gaze whizzed past the gadgets and IVs and ominous monitors to her mother, who sat on the edge of the bed holding Doug's hand.

"Begonias," Maggie was saying. "Rhododendrons. Azaleas. Bougainvillea."

Savannah leaned against the wall. She banged her head against it once, just hard enough to see stars, but not a single one of them was red.

"Purple coneflower," Maggie went on. "Black-eyed Susans. Lilies of the valley."

Savannah squeezed her eyes shut. She remembered a few years back when a good friend, Carol Deidrich, had come to her after her mother died of heart failure. Savannah had held her and told her that death was a release, a beginning. She was surprised now that Carol hadn't hit her, that she'd had the grace to simply walk away and never speak to her again.

Savannah walked to her mother's side and put a hand on Maggie's shoulder. Maggie stiffened, then sagged. She was wearing cotton pajama bottoms and a raincoat. There were tears in her eyes.

Savannah sat down next to her. She leaned over her father and kissed his cool, moist forehead. What she should have told Carol was that death was indeed a beginning, of learning how to live with less, often without the very sustenance of your life.

"Chamomile," Savannah said. "Winter honeysuckle, golden trumpet trees, magnolia grandiflora."

Maggie nodded and leaned against her. She took a sip of water. For all Savannah knew, she'd been naming plants all day.

"Jacaranda," Savannah went on, choosing only the flowering trees now, the ones her father had always grown best. She called on whatever magic a daughter had, and maybe it was all in her imagination, but she swore the air around them swelled with the scent of orange blossoms, and her father's breathing evened out, the way it always had when the plants in his garden had bloomed.

\* \* \*

Doug saw colors. Exotic variations on green. Lime, jade, emerald, green so green it blinded him. His entire field of vision was a landscape of grass and well-tended perennials. Begonias. Rhododendrons. Azaleas. Bougainvillea. Then suddenly a grove of navel oranges just coming into flower. Plants shot up and bloomed in seconds. It was the most amazing thing.

Somewhere beyond the garden, though, he heard his wife and daughter crying. He wished he had the strength to open his eyes and tell them it was all right. All the pain was gone. Every thought in his head was a poem.

> *Maggie Sweet*
> *Sugar treat*
> *Around the bend*
> *We will meet.*

He was going to die with dirt beneath his fingernails, and that was a good thing. That way God would know what kind of man he'd been. He wondered if he'd planted enough flowers. He wondered if any of those gladiolus he'd sneaked into the soil around his neighbors' yards had come up yet. He wondered if he'd done enough.

After a while, he heard the slapping of cards in the corner. He could smell his daughter's sweat and Juicy Fruit gum. He swam through the green grass, laughing when it tickled his stomach. He forced himself up through the top of it, and was suddenly gasping for air.

Maggie was above him, trying to get him to drink, but he pushed the cup away. Savannah leapt off the floor and came to his side. They both moved so fast they were blurs to him. He wished they would slow down so he could see them clearly. They spoke in some language he could not understand.

He shook his head and said:

*"The air is clear,*
*the end is near."*

Or that was what he thought he said. Maggie and Savannah only looked at each other. He concentrated hard, until he could make out a little of what they said.

"—doesn't know . . . for the . . . pointless now."

"How can . . . please."

Doug took a deep breath. "Green," he said, and they both looked at him.

"Green?" Maggie said.

He smiled. With all his strength, he squeezed her hand, but she must not have felt it, because she pulled away to stroke his head.

"Rest now, love," she said. "You don't look green. You look fine. Everything's going to be fine."

The green was misting over his eyes, but he managed to keep them open for a few seconds more. He looked straight into his wife's eyes. He spoke the truest thing he knew.

*"Heaven is right here.*
*Heaven is the one you hold dear."*

He thought he'd reached her, and he closed his eyes in relief. But just before the grass closed over his head, he heard Maggie crying. "What's he saying?" she said. "I can't understand a word he's saying."

Maggie had insisted on sleeping at the hospital, so the next morning Jake packed her clothes and brought them to Doug's room. The blinds were closed, the room dark, and Maggie was not there. According to the machinery, Doug was still alive, but Jake could see no sign of the man's chest rising and falling. His eyes were closed, his skin blue. A tube went into his nose, another into the bruised vein on his wrist, feeding him the things he needed to survive, but there was no doubt in Jake's mind that Doug Dawson was already somewhere else. If he wasn't, Jake pitied him. Though there were fresh bouquets of roses and carnations in his room, there was no scent of soil here.

He heard cards slapping, then finally noticed a black-dyed Panama hat bobbing in the corner. Savannah didn't even look up when he said her name. She sat on the floor, laying out her cards again and again. Once, she began to flip over a card, then placed it instead on the bottom of the deck and picked another.

He had known he would deteriorate without her, but he hadn't realized to what extent. First, he'd lost his concentration and sawed through the headboard of a two-thousand-dollar bed. A few days later, he'd thrown away a bottle of Digoxin, so now his heart was skipping beats regularly, and he was always gasping for air. Yesterday, he'd forgotten to feed his dogs. When they jumped up on the table to snatch his steak, he felt so light-headed and awful, he just let them have it.

Rufus and Gabe were no better. The dogs had gone into mourning, pacing the floor where Savannah had lain at night, howling from dawn until dusk. Even Roy had not been able to stand it; since Savannah had left, Jake hadn't seen him once.

He stepped forward, but couldn't think of anything to say, except that he'd been stupid enough to hope she would come back for *him*.

Maggie arrived a few minutes later. Jake heard her barreling down the hall, arguing with a security guard.

She carried an armload of Doug's plants, their roots hanging clear to her knees, spilling fishy soil. It was obvious the guard would have to tackle her to get her to stop, and finally he simply stepped back and let her through with her contraband.

She brushed past Jake and dropped the flowers on the chair beside the bed. She picked up a cutting with small leaves and red tubular flowers. She laid it on Doug's chest.

"Beard tongue," she said, and Jake watched the man's eyes. Not a flicker. She grabbed the next three. " Bitterroot. Honeysuckle. One of the fans from the ensete."

She piled the plants on Doug's chest. When he gave no response, she twined a strand of fragrant blueberry climber around his ear. She crushed the chamomile leaves in the palm of her hand and held them beneath his nose.

Jake saw it from clear across the room. Doug's nostrils flared for a moment, then went still. Maggie dropped the leaves on his chest and leaned forward to kiss him.

"Now go," she said. "Stop dawdling. You're driving me crazy."

Jake walked across the room and put his hand on her shoulder. She was trembling, but her eyes were dry. She leaned against him a moment, until Savannah slapped down another round of cards.

"For God's sake, stop that," Maggie said. "What's it going to prove?"

Savannah said nothing. Where she'd parted her hair, Jake could make out the pink line of her scalp, and his chest tightened. The problem with devotion was that it was bad for the heart. It clogged major arteries, took years off his life, but the alternative was a long, healthy life without ever getting worked up at the sight of someone's tender skin. The alternative was a life with dogs.

He crouched down beside her. "Any luck?"

She slammed down the cards in answer. Then she picked them up and shuffled again. "I don't accept this."

"Savannah." He took the deck from her hand. She tried to snatch it back, but he held on tight and waited until she looked him in the eye. "There's no good fortune here."

"You don't know anything."

"I know it's no challenge to lay out cards and come up with a good result every time. That's just a circus trick. Anyone could do it."

"You couldn't."

Jake leaned back. She reached out to him, then drew away her hand before even getting close. She was not going to love him; that was clear as day. He was everything she couldn't accept—unhappiness and guilt intensified by years of neglect. He was the Three of Swords.

"Well, I'm another story," he said, standing up. He tucked her cards into his shirt pocket. He was keeping something, even if it was only that. Maggie was sitting at Doug's side, holding his limp white hand. He walked to the door.

"I was wrong about Sasha," Savannah called after him. "There was no reason to thank God."

Jake breathed in deeply. He put his hand on the door. "In a rich and beautiful world, there are still horrors. The real challenge is to find a way to be happy anyway."

Emma had wanted to come to her grandfather's funeral, but now she couldn't figure out why. As far as she was concerned, sitting in a church didn't prove your devotion to anything except ritual and what people thought of you. If anything, once they closed the thick double doors and started the funeral hymn, whatever trace of Doug Dawson had been lingering in the air vanished. No doubt her grandfather's spirit had escaped through a stained-glass window and was out in the church garden right now, trying to figure a way to get solid enough to rip out the rows of junipers and replace them with those outlandish giant allium he'd adored.

At least she wasn't crying. She had promised herself that much. After two weeks of doing nothing but that, she'd finally given it up. Tears and prayers changed nothing. Probably, if it was this easy to lose the love of her life, God wasn't even there.

Harry put an arm around her and pulled her close. On her left, Melinda dabbed at her tears before they damaged her makeup. Emma chanced a look around, but all she saw was a sea of coarse white hair. There wasn't a soul under thirty, not a patch of brown hair and green eyes in the bunch.

"You want to say hello to your mother?" Harry asked, when the service was finally over.

Emma shook her head vigorously. She wanted one thing, and he wasn't here. Harry took her hand and led her instead to Maggie. Maggie shook off one of her neighbors and took Emma in her arms. "Well, thank goodness. Someone I actually want to see."

Emma hugged her tightly. She was not going to cry, then Maggie pulled back to touch her face, and her eyes betrayed her. Worse than that, she started gasping—big, gulpy noises that only got louder when she tried to rein them in. Maggie and Harry each took an arm and led her outside.

Emma was still sobbing when she saw her mother

by the oak tree, hiding beneath a huge black hat festooned with ebony feathers. Savannah had that slightly green tint she always had when there was too much crying going on.

"Honey," Savannah said, coming forward.

Emma had seen her after midnight some nights, parked outside her father's well-lit house. Whenever Savannah called, Emma locked herself in her room and refused to acknowledge Melinda's pleas to come to the phone. When she felt herself weakening, she remembered her mother just standing there while her father and Melinda led her away from everything that mattered.

Savannah reached out and ran a finger over Emma's wet cheek, but Emma slapped her hand away. For a moment no one breathed. Then Savannah tossed her hat on the ground and walked away.

Emma had lost ten pounds over the summer, but it wasn't until that second that she felt too thin. A strong wind could break her. Once she had fallen in love, she'd put herself at the mercy of everything.

"That was cruel, Emma," her grandmother said. "Your mother's walking a very thin line."

Emma's throat burned as Maggie led her to the family limousine. Emma got in beside her grandmother, and her father and stepmother took the seat across from them. She tried to quiet herself down to sniffles, but her grandmother nudged her.

"Don't tone it down for me," Maggie said. "If I were twenty years younger, I'd cry like that too. But I can't do it anymore, Emma, and I don't know why."

The guests pushed up to the limousine, and Maggie rolled down the window. "Don't even think about coming to my house. I don't have any cold cuts. I'm not even in the mood for a party, if you can believe that."

Then she put her arm around Emma's shoulders and told the driver to move.

Back at the house, Cheryl Pillandro had brought in the last of Doug's vivid purple coneflowers and set them in vases on the table. She'd set out wine and cheese and a box of tissues, and when Maggie came in, she touched her cheek softly.

Maggie poured them all a glass of wine. "To Doug," she said, and then she left them all standing there and took her wine outside.

Emma drank her wine and found it dull. In the last two weeks, she'd lost her taste for alcohol and cigarettes and anything criminal. She walked to the front door and watched her grandmother through the porch screen. Maggie touched every plant in Doug's garden. When she reached the ensete, she crouched down.

"You doing all right?" Harry asked. "You want to watch some TV or something?"

Emma stared at him, then walked out after her grandmother. Sometime during their stay at Jake's cabin, the ensete had bloomed. Its tiny bronze flowers were insignificant beside the huge palm leaves, and it was amazing to think something so delicately beautiful could be the very thing that ruined everything.

"Well," Maggie said. "This is where it gets dicey. Go get your grandfather's shears. We've got to cut it all the way back. We'll do the best we can."

Emma walked to the garage apartment, where they had lived amongst garden tools and strange fortunes. She found the shears on the wall, along with two of her mother's hats left behind. She put on a straw one, then walked back to the garden.

Maggie pruned the plant ruthlessly, cutting the blooms and fronds clear back to the plant's crown. It was nothing more than a dead-looking stump when

Maggie was finished with it. She tossed the shears onto the lawn of chamomile, and Emma started to cry again.

"Come on." Maggie put her arm around her. "It's all right. I don't have Doug's touch, but it might grow. You never know."

Emma didn't think so. Her grandfather had had some kind of magic. Fragile plants had grown just to please him. They might grow for her grandmother, too, just to keep her from getting riled, or for her mother, to make her happy again. But they would not grow for Emma; she inspired no devotion. No one was breaking down doors to get to her. The one boy who could fill the hole in her heart hadn't even noticed she was bleeding.

That boy stood down the street, watching Emma and her grandmother bend over the ensete. Twice, he took a step around the boxwood hedge he was hiding behind, but he couldn't cross his own shadow. It hid nothing, not his mangy hair or gangster clothes or the fact that he was so thin and jittery, he'd never be able to hold Emma tight enough to get the point of his love across.

He would never consider himself a hero, but every morning for the last two weeks he had done something no one, especially not Emma, would ever appreciate. He had woken up and not driven to California. Instead, he had returned another stolen stereo. He'd left them on retail doorsteps all over town, and when his cabin was finally cleared out, he slept the night through for the first time in nineteen years.

Turned out falling in love was easy. The hard part was making sure he didn't contaminate what he loved. It was also the only gift he could give Emma.

He closed his eyes and stood behind a boxwood hedge; he left her to her life. When he finally tried to walk away, every step hurt. When he reached the corner, he froze. He breathed deeply, then whirled around again. But by then Emma and Maggie were walking back into the house. By then it was all over.

Melinda would not fly on anything less than a full-size jet, so Savannah drove all the way to Sky Harbor Airport to see Emma off. Once in the terminal, Emma never unhooked her arms from her waist or looked her in the eye. She was still intent on despising her, and there was no telling someone like that she was the love of your life and always would be.

Savannah turned her attention to Melinda, who was making all the conversation anyway, talking about her cousin, a pilot for United.

"So he likes the job," Savannah said, when they reached the boarding gate.

"Oh yes." Melinda glittered in her pale pink traveling ensemble. "You would not believe the process he had to go through to get hired. Phenomenal. These pilots are the best. The safety features on these jets are phenomenal."

"No one thinks it's going to crash," Harry said.

Everyone within earshot looked out at the plane, shimmering beneath the Phoenix sun. When the pilot stared hard at a wing, you could hear people swallowing. A young woman said, "Fuck it," and turned around and left.

They started boarding First Class, and Harry grabbed his carry-on. "That's us."

Savannah turned to Emma. Her daughter's eyes were red-rimmed. Last night, she had stayed with Harry and Melinda at the Holiday Inn, and probably spent every waking moment praying Eli would kidnap her. She had no idea Eli had sat on the curb in front of the garage apartment from midnight till dawn, thinking Emma was inside and might come out to him. She had no idea her entire future could hinge on one night of missed opportunities, and Savannah wasn't about to break that to her. She could hardly bear it herself.

"Try not to worry," she said.

"Right, Mom."

Savannah grabbed her hand. "No, I mean it. The odds of an asteroid falling on you are like a billion to one. The same odds that you'll never fall in love again."

"You still don't get it. I don't want to fall in love again. I only want him."

Harry took her arm. "Come on, honey. Let's go."

Savannah watched them walk into the boarding chute, then she went to the window. Outside, the sky was clear to the horizon, except for three clouds in the west, which they would have to fly right through to get home.

She left the airport and drove back to her mother's house. Maggie had not returned to Jake's cabin after Doug died, and Savannah doubted she ever would. She found her on the porch step with Cheryl Pillandro, both sipping spiked lemonade and circling items from an L. L. Bean catalog.

"Cheryl's thinking about an Alaskan cruise," Maggie said. "We're ordering her Gore-Tex."

"I got a new pre-approved Visa application in the mail last week," Cheryl said.

Savannah had never envied Harry until this moment. He had his daughter at his side, he knew which way was home. She, on the other hand, no longer felt at ease in either bright sun or fog. Up here, sorrow was as abundant as sky. Every widower on Maggie's block would agree to die tomorrow, if today they could be someone's darling again. Back at sea level, no fog was thick enough to conceal the obvious: She read good fortune for everyone but herself.

"So I take it you're leaving?" Maggie said.

"I suppose."

"Running," Maggie said to Cheryl. "That's what she was always good at."

Savannah put her hands on her hips. Without her father here, she didn't feel the need to restrain her anger, and that scared her. She felt capable of saying just about anything, even what she really felt.

She took a step toward her mother, and saw Maggie smiling. "You want me to crack."

Maggie shrugged. "Maybe I do. Maybe I like cracked people. Maybe the only real things are on the inside."

Savannah shook her head. "You were never very good to me."

For a moment, there was pure silence, then Cheryl Pillandro let out her breath. She got up to leave, but Maggie pulled her back down.

"Oh no. I need a witness. They always blame the mothers."

Savannah took a good whiff of her mother's perfume and realized she'd been hating it since the moment she came back. "You are the villain here."

"My husband just died on me. Don't you dare start with me now."

Savannah stepped forward. She took short little breaths, then spit them back out. "I'm starting, all right. If there's anything good in me, it's because of Dad. You never supported me. Never consoled me when I needed you. Never even took me seriously. You were too busy spitting at God."

When Maggie said nothing, Savannah wrapped

her arms around her waist. "You can't stand to see anyone happy, including me," she went on. "You contaminate joy. You sabotaged me at every turn. Well, congratulations, Mom. I'm scared to death now of the basic process of living."

She was shaking, trembling so hard against the clematis-covered trellis she caused a downpour of deep purple petals.

Maggie just waved her off. "That's hogwash. You're mourning your father, Savannah. Don't confuse that with a personality trait."

"Why can't you just be nice?"

Her mother actually seemed to consider the question, then she just shrugged. "I don't know."

"You've hurt me beyond belief."

Maggie sighed. "I'm sure I have. I never said I was a particularly good mother. But the truth is, you're an exceptional person, and if you give me credit for the bad things, then you have to give me credit for that too."

Savannah tilted her head to the sky. She shouldn't try to win. Her father had known the odds of topping Maggie were a million to one, so instead he'd stayed silent and happily married for thirty-six years. The trouble was, lately she'd been feeling less and less like her father.

"I don't give you credit for anything," she said quietly, "except making yourself nearly impossible to love."

She walked to the garage and slammed the door behind her before her mother could hear her crying. She grabbed a pillow and flung it across the room. She hated her mother and worse, she hated the hate. It was traitorous. In less than an hour, she was curled up on the bed sobbing, afraid she had broken her mother's heart.

* * *

Maggie watched her daughter slam the door to the garage, then stood up. Cheryl stood up too, and squeezed her hand.

"You all right?" Cheryl asked.

Maggie smiled. Without Doug to temper her, she was only going to get meaner, and that was all right with her. Meanness got her through a day quite nicely. Meanness covered up the fact that her heart was broken and there was no chance of fixing it. Sometimes, too, it snapped people to their senses.

"She's coming along," she said.

Cheryl looked at her in astonishment, then laughed. Maggie was glad she had asked Cheryl Pillandro to stay on. When Cheryl ruined a casserole, which she did nearly every day, she cussed like nobody's business, and Maggie admired that. And it had been something, knowing someone would be in the house that first night she came back without Doug. It was something just to hear someone in the bathroom, turning on and off the water, brushing her teeth, breathing.

Maggie walked through Doug's garden, yanking off a few yellowed leaves. She had vowed to let the garden go, but so far she had not been able to do it. It was all drip-irrigated, but nevertheless each night she was out watering. She must have picked up Doug's techniques by osmosis, because somehow she knew it was time to fertilize the small patch of lawn and prune back the dying petals of the coneflowers. She knew her chances of saving the ensete were a hundred to one.

Jake showed up while she was watering the sheared stump. He had the bench in the back of his pickup, and she didn't say a word as he unloaded it. He looked at her to see where she wanted it, and again she remained silent. She didn't want it at all, and that was the truth. It was morbid, a dead man's life, and if Doug had thought it would help her get over him, he was stupid as a man could be. She was never going to get over him. She didn't even want to.

Jake set the bench on the cobblestone patio, then walked over to her. "I carved in the sun. There's still room for one more design. I think Doug was leaving the choice up to you."

"Then he was an idiot. I want nothing to do with it. Staple on a picture of a frog for all I care."

Jake stared at her, then took something out of his back pocket. "I found this under the bench. I read it before I realized it was for you."

Maggie didn't take it. Her husband had been too sweet for his own good, and look what it had gotten him. He should have been mean like her. Mean people never died young.

"Take it, Maggie," he said. "It was all he could give."

He put the paper in her hand, then scanned the yard. Maggie put her hand on his arm. "She's in the garage and not coming out. She'll sneak off in the middle of the night again and never come back."

Jake closed his eyes briefly, then lifted her hand and kissed her palm. Maggie hoped Savannah was looking out her window, so she could see what she'd be missing. She ought to fall in love whenever she had the chance. She ought to kiss a man like there was no tomorrow, because very often there wasn't.

Much later, after Jake had gone, and Cheryl was inside botching another casserole, Maggie looked at the poem. At the top, Doug had been doodling. He'd drawn eight stars and a woman. Then she got to the poem.

*They told me the years would dull it,*
*like shiny shells ground and matted by waves.*
*Once we discovered each other's pathways,*
*mastered each other's etiquette,*
*the thrill of navigating uncharted waters*
*would be dead.*
*But they didn't realize*
*novice sailors rarely enjoy the ride.*
*Now, after years of research,*
*I've mapped your constellations*
*and crossed all your salty seas.*
*I'm an expert on your currents,*
*knowing exactly when you peak and fall.*
*I can move you*
*the way you move me,*
*like the wind behind a sail.*
*We are old and expert captains,*
*you and I,*
*masters of sailing each other's seas.*

Cheryl found her sitting on the bench an hour later, the poem clasped tightly in her hands, her face raw from crying. She sat down beside her.

"After Paul died," she said, "I was afraid to tell anyone what I was feeling, because it wasn't exactly sorrow. I was furious that he'd done this to me. Every day he didn't walk through the door, I hated him more."

Maggie said nothing. Her throat was completely closed now. Doug had had the words all along. He'd been quiet because he'd been hoarding them, stuffing them into his poetry, so that when he was gone, she would be mute with love for him. She would be stuck in this garden, breathing him in with every scent.

"But that wasn't the worst," Cheryl went on. "The

worst was when I woke up one morning and didn't think of him first thing. The worst was letting him go."

Maggie leaned her head against Cheryl's shoulder. "I just don't see—"

"Of course you don't. What's to see? You loved him and he left you. There's no great lesson to be learned from that. Right now, all you've got to do is get up every morning. Right now, that's all that can be expected of you."

Maggie ran her hand over the arms of the bench, carved now into wrists and hands, with bracelets and rings on all its fingers.

Maggie patted Cheryl's hand. "Jake will be all right, you know."

Cheryl jerked her head up. They hardly ever talked about Jake, but now Cheryl squeezed her hand tightly. "They scheduled the lineup for Monday. It doesn't seem to matter that Jake's already been in jail for fifteen years."

"No, it doesn't matter," Maggie said. "In God's eyes, what you want most doesn't even count."

The next morning, the last of summer led an awesome assault. It started out hot and turned wicked. The garage apartment was eighty degrees by nine, ninety by noon. Flies who alighted for even a second on the roof found their legs melded to the cedar shingles. By late afternoon, birds were falling right out of the sky.

Savannah packed her one bag, but in that heat could not find the energy to get in her car and drive sixteen hours back to San Francisco. Instead, she walked to the mermaid fountain, where even the algae beneath a foot of water had turned brown and died. She crawled right into the bowl, her red dress fanning out around her. She scooped lukewarm water onto her neck and shoulders, but it dried on impact.

Her mother came out ten minutes later. Savannah scooped another handful of water and splashed it on her face.

"I spit in that bowl every morning," Maggie said.

Savannah hesitated, then went on splashing. Maggie reached into her pocket and handed over a twenty.

"Are you serious?" Savannah asked.

"Don't I look it?"

Savannah looked at the cash, then climbed out of the fountain. "Well, it's thirty now."

Maggie turned and went back in the house. She came back carrying another ten, shoved it at her, then walked into the garage.

Savannah stood there as steam rose up from her dress. She was having trouble reading fortunes. She'd let in a few customers last night, and had predicted new love for a man who'd been happily married for thirty years and revenge for a woman who had everything. She might get the Ten of Cups, the card of peace and contentment, in her mother's recent past. She might get anything.

Blisters were forming on her feet, though, so she went in the garage. Maggie had already sat down at the table and swiped everything that had been on it—books and magazines and Savannah's hats—to the floor.

The fan was oscillating in the corner, but the torpid air refused to budge. Already, the hem and arms of Savannah's dress were dry. Sweat slid down her neck, curling around each shoulder blade. She picked up the vivid Voyager deck, but Maggie scoffed at it.

"Those are too pretty," she said. "Get me the ruthless cards. You think I've got anything to fear now?"

"I threw them all out."

Maggie smiled and walked to the makeshift kitchen. She opened the top drawer and started pulling out Savannah's old decks. "Rider-Waite. The Yeager Tarot. The Thoth. My God, what kind of name is that?"

Savannah stared at her, too hot to ask why her mother had saved what she did not believe in.

"Which has the worst odds?" Maggie asked, swiping at the sweat on her forehead.

"The Rider-Waite."

"All right then." Maggie brought the deck to the table. She sat down, brushed the sweat off her palms, and started to shuffle.

"You don't believe in this," Savannah managed to say.

"Well, maybe I don't have the luxury of not believing anymore. Did you ever think of that?"

"I don't know if I can read this for you. All my fortunes have been coming out strange."

"Stop acting scared. I don't care what you have to do, Savannah, just read my fortune. My husband's dead and I've got one more chance to tell him I love him, so you just sit down and tell me how to do it."

Maggie shuffled the cards ruthlessly, twelve times, then held them out. Savannah hesitated only a second, then sat down and laid them out. The heat strangled clear thinking, because she automatically reverted back to the old Celtic spread.

The first card was the King of Swords, which was no surprise. The King was the card of force, an authoritative, controlling person. The crossing card, though, was the Hierophant, the card of timidity, mercy, and forgiveness.

"I don't know what that means," Savannah said.

Maggie stared her down, and Savannah looked back at the cards. It was getting hard to even breathe now. The flies in the window were languid, lying on their backs on the sill. Savannah pulled her dress away from her chest and fanned it. "Your future and destiny go together. The Tower and Six of Swords. Both are cards of major changes. A trip or journey."

Her mother said nothing, and Savannah noticed she had stopped sweating. She was looking over Savannah's shoulder at the corner. Savannah laid out the last four cards, then massaged her temples.

She could have started crying when she turned over the King of Wands, the card of fathers and honest men. Or later, when the Star, the card of hope, came up as her mother's final result. Then the room turned cool as rain and was drenched with the smell of garden soil, of incense cedar and sweet peas and Breath of Heaven. Squeaky sounds escaped her mother's lips, and she looked up to find Maggie Dawson crying.

Savannah followed her gaze to the corner, but saw nothing. If anything was truly there, it had not come for her. Her father was bred to love her, but loving Maggie had required of him a daredevil leap of faith. For thirty-six years, Doug had risen to the challenge of loving his wife despite everything, and he may never have known that in return, Maggie had become a different person from the one she had intended to be. She had had a happy life despite herself.

Savannah got up from the table and walked outside. She stood in the hottest spot, where the sun reflected off the garage and melted pavement, where even the sun-loving sage had wilted. She stood until she was burning up. It was a sad, sad thing to realize her mother was more prone to romance than she was. It was pitiful that Maggie Dawson was the one seeing her lost lover as a shadow on the wall.

Maggie came out ten minutes later with the Star tucked into her pocket and tears all down her cheeks.

She reached into her other pocket and pulled out a wrinkled piece of paper.

Savannah looked at it, then began to shake. Somewhere along the way, she must have stopped believing in everything, because she even doubted this. It was a poem written in her father's hand, and at the top was a hand-drawn portrait of eight stars and a woman, a perfect copy of the Star.

"I don't know how to break this to you," Maggie said, "but one way or another, if you're lucky, love will break your heart."

Savannah reached out to touch the paper, but recoiled when she felt how cool it was, like a slab of ice. She slid her hands into the pockets of her dress.

"Did you see Dad?" she asked.

Maggie turned away. She slid the poem back into her pocket and looked at the sky. "It's all mumbo jumbo," she said, but she was crying hard.

"That may be, but that doesn't mean it isn't true."

Maggie walked to the mermaid fountain and ran her hand over the copper rim. "The lineup is on Monday. In case you want to stay."

Savannah walked over and laid her cheek against her mother's shoulder. Right now, in San Francisco, it would be cool as a cave. The bay would be dotted with sailboats, the hills smothered in pastel houses that looked like flowers. Tonight, there would be a chill in the air, the better for lovers to kiss and girls to wrap themselves up in red-hot dreams. San Francisco was the city of desire, but only if her heart was in it. Only if there was nowhere else on earth she'd rather be.

# Eighteen

## JUSTICE ❧ JUST REWARD

Whoever opened the front door was light on their feet, nearly silent, but what unnerved Jake more was that the intruder didn't rouse the dogs. Rufus and Gabe were both downstairs, lying by the fire, and they ought to be going crazy. Instead, he heard their toenails clicking on the hardwood floor, Gabe's fat tail thumping against the wall.

He sat up in bed. Since he'd moved back to the loft, he'd been disoriented and achy. Maggie and Doug must have moved the bed a few inches, because whenever he looked through the skylight, all the stars seemed out of place. Orion and Cassiopeia sneaked closer together each night, until she'd coiled herself around his belt. When dawn broke, he swore the sun rose out of the west. Besides that, he'd grown used to the unyielding concrete floor in his workshop. Softness just taunted him.

He got to his feet soundlessly. The gun was still in

the locked gun cabinet downstairs, useless. He looked around for a weapon, then froze when he heard footsteps coming up the stairs.

"You're this close to a bullet between the eyes," he bluffed.

The footsteps stopped, then started up again. Jake grabbed the lamp off the bedside table.

"Don't shoot," the voice said, and then a feathered hat rose up out of the stairwell.

Jake set down the lamp. It was almost certain he was dreaming, and if he was, then he just wouldn't wake up. Someone had come back for him, and he would like to end it right there, with the one happy ending he was entitled to. He prayed she didn't say another word.

Savannah walked toward him and would have kept on coming, if he hadn't stuck out his hand and stopped her a foot away. "Whatever you're doing," he said, "you might want to reconsider. No doubt I'll be picked out of a lineup Monday morning."

She brushed aside his hand and slipped her arms around his waist. He closed his eyes tight. He might not be good enough to love, but that didn't mean he wasn't going to take what was offered. That didn't mean he was a fool.

She tilted back her head to kiss him, and when she was done, she smiled. "We're ditching Roy."

She grabbed a few of his clothes, then pulled him downstairs. The dogs were already in her car, tearing up the leather upholstery. Jake looked back at the house, where he swore he saw Roy Pillandro standing on the roof, meteor dust building up on his shoulders.

"You see that?" he asked.

Savannah followed his gaze, then slipped her arm around his waist. She smelled so good he didn't care if he was crazy or not. She kissed the warm pulse at the corner of his neck.

"He can haunt you all he wants," she said, "he's still dead."

Jake pulled himself up straight. He knew he couldn't outrun the police—they would hunt him down eventually and bring him back. All at once, though, he knew he could do something about a ghost. It was as easy as turning his back on him. All he had to do was walk away.

They got into the car and Savannah turned the key. The roar of the engine drowned out any outrage Roy might be spewing. Her headlights cut right through the heart of his black soul.

"Ready?" she said.

Jake reached out and fingered the green silk feathers on her hat. He marveled at the blue glow of her rings on the steering wheel. "Let's go."

She pulled out of the driveway and he didn't look back. He let out his breath when they reached the road. Sometime life masqueraded as complicated, when really it was as simple as moving on.

She drove for twenty minutes down the treacherous road before even looking at him. "You want to know where we're going?" she asked.

"I don't care."

She stopped the car and turned off the engine. In a painful heartbeat, she crawled onto his lap. She ran her palms down the smooth skin of his cheeks and chin. He had shaved off the beard the day Doug Dawson died, and no hair had grown back since.

"Did I tell you I love you?" she asked, tracing his jaw, the curl of his ear.

"Not that I recall."

"Well, I'm telling you."

He took off her hat and tossed it in the backseat with the dogs. "All right."

He opened the door and carried her to a soft spot by the road. The meteor shower was worse than ever, poking holes through the sky. Up around Flagstaff, four thousand hits had been recorded in a two-hour period, shattering windshields and choking off lakes, but miraculously killing no one. No one knew where the next strike would land, and if it would be deadly. People led braver lives than they imagined just by walking out their front doors.

He slipped his hand under her dress, around the hot, inner curl of her thigh. He could live without her, he'd proven that, but there were degrees of living. You measured its quality by the things you dared to love: a home, a dog, a woman, a child. Each demanded a greater offering and returned a bigger slice of rapture, until it was as fierce a thing as a man could stand.

She tugged at his pants and he pulled them off. When he slipped inside her, he closed his eyes. He didn't even bother to check what was streaking out of the sky. He was just going to take his chances.

"I love you too," he said. Where she kissed him, he could feel her lips curling up in a smile.

Later that night, as Savannah drove them wherever it was she thought they would be safe, Jake slept soundly for the first time in weeks. When he finally opened his eyes, it was morning, and they were in the green, wrinkled hills of northern California. Savannah was drinking coffee, which she must have picked up somewhere along the way.

"We won't go to my house," she said. "We'll stay at Ramona's a couple days. I already called her. She's got some ideas, some friends in out-of-the-way places. We can disappear off the face of the planet, if we want to."

He woke up a little more now that he knew what

she wanted. He reached for her hand and held it tightly. No one had ever tried to save him before.

"Savannah," he said, but she just shook her head.

"Don't even think about saying you'll just wait around for Cal to arrest you. Don't even dare."

He wouldn't, not with the look in her eye. He just reached over and turned on the radio, as if everything might still turn out fine.

Emma registered for eleventh grade at Danville High because she had to, because her stepmother was standing right there, watching her every move. But she wasn't going to show up for a single chemistry class. If it was up to her, she wouldn't come out of her room ever again. She wouldn't even breathe.

Melinda took her home after registration and poured them each a glass of milk. Emma hated milk, but she didn't have the energy to fight Melinda's kindnesses. Her stepmother had already bought her new flannel sheets for the fall and pasted stars on the ceiling of her bedroom. She'd slaved over her previously favorite meals, none of which Emma could eat, because food just stuck in her throat.

Melinda picked up an envelope from the counter and held it out. Emma didn't take it. She recognized her mother's handwriting, and just the sight of those curlicue letters made her stomach roll. She wasn't going to forgive her mother for anything. She was never going to speak to her again.

Melinda opened the envelope for her. She read the letter, then took out the card behind it and set it face down on the table. Though she ought to have been drained dry, Emma still managed to start crying all over again.

She was not going to turn over that card. She

thought about how quickly she could be up and out of that house, throwing herself in front of traffic, but instead Melinda put a hand on her shoulder. Somewhere along the line, this woman Emma had had every intention of hating had thrown out an unexpected lifeline, and it had taken hold. Melinda never gave her enough time alone to kill herself. She spent all her time and energy making up reasons Emma should just hang on.

Melinda slid the letter in front of her. "Mothers just go on adoring you," she said. "I'm sorry, but there's nothing you can do about it."

Despite herself, Emma looked up. She stopped crying for the barest instant. She took the paper out of Melinda's hand and read it.

> *Emma,*
> *Loving you has always hurt going down, and*
> *I'm glad. I surrender.*
>
> *Mom*

Melinda sat down beside her and gathered her in her arms. Emma didn't want to love anyone but Eli, but they were making it so *hard*.

At some point, she reached for the card her mother had enclosed and flipped it over. "Jeez, she is *so* obvious."

Still, after Melinda had gone, she slipped the card in her pocket. The Three of Cups, the card of compromise, the card of mothers and daughters.

They had one good night at Ramona's, and that was something. A few blissful hours of thinking they were free. The night even lingered a while, the sun stayed dim behind the fog, to give them time to say what they needed to say. It was all they could have asked for, under the circumstances.

In the morning, Savannah and Jake and Ramona sat at the kitchen table planning where they should go.

"The Russian River," Ramona said. "Carol and Fred Tarkinton live in a little cabin you'd never know was there. Fred's still hiding out from the draft."

Savannah looked at Jake, but he was staring out the window, watching the fog drift past in clumps.

"All right," she said. "Give me directions. We'll be there by this afternoon."

After Ramona left the room, Jake walked back and took her hand. "What I'm thinking is—"

Savannah rose up and kissed him. "Don't think."

"Savannah—"

"Just don't. For once in your life, you've got to trust another person. Do you think you can do that?"

He stared at her, then finally nodded. They went to the guest room and packed their things.

Savannah kissed Ramona goodbye. She had one moment of thrilling expectation, then she opened the door and walked straight into Cal Bentley.

"It was Dan Merrill," Cal said. "He's been antsy for weeks. Once we got the lineup scheduled, he went on out to Jake's cabin. It wasn't hard to track you down."

Cal took out a cigarette and lit it. In forty years on the force, he'd been solid as a rock, but now his hand was shaking. "He took it on himself to let San Francisco PD know you'd crossed state lines. They took it out of my hands. All I could do was ask to come along when they picked you up."

Savannah looked past him, to where two more cops waited on the curb. "He's not under arrest."

"No. But he's a prime suspect. It all depends on the lineup. The rest, well, it's all circumstantial. A judge would throw it out in a heartbeat. But that woman . . . We're just going to have to see what the witness says."

"This is crazy," Savannah said. "The man's been dead fifteen years. He's a goddamn ghost, Cal. There are some people who plain deserve to die."

Once the words were out, she knew she couldn't take them back. She didn't even want to. They were words that hung in moist California air forever.

"That may be. But it's not up to me anymore."

"It's all right," Jake said. "Really. I want this, Savannah. Can you understand that?"

She started crying, because all she understood was that the people she loved most would not let her save them.

Cal led them to the squad car, and Jake turned to her. "Have faith," he said.

Savannah shook her head. It had taken her thirty-six years to realize that, at times, faith alone was not enough. Sometimes you had to do a little more than hope for the best. Sometimes you had to stack the cards.

Monday morning, Savannah wore a blood-red dress and the most colorful hat she owned—a green velvet bowler, smothered with red silk peonies and purple feather plumes a foot high. She told her mother what she wanted to do, and Maggie squinted at her. Finally, she broke into a slow, satisfied grin. "I knew you'd come around."

They went into Cal Bentley's office and shut the door behind them. Cal had been bent over paperwork, but now he leaned back in his chair. "Ladies?"

"We'd like to talk to the witness," Maggie said. "Just for a few minutes."

Cal stared at the papers in front of him. Half of his photographs had already been packed in boxes, his in-box was nearly cleared out. But more than that, the sheriff didn't grow outraged or order them to leave; in every way that mattered, he'd already retired his badge.

He got up from his desk and walked to the window. He kept his back to them while he spoke. "You wouldn't do anything stupid, would you? Because fool-ishness, at this point, could land Jake in prison with-out parole."

Savannah walked up beside him and put her hand on his arm. "Ten minutes. Isn't he worth that much of a risk?"

The anteroom outside the lineup chamber reeked of stale tobacco and nerves. Three torn black vinyl chairs had been pushed to the walls, the floor was orange and brown linoleum, an old paisley design Sa-vannah was fairly certain her mother had once had in a bathroom. A brown-haired woman and her five-year-old daughter sat fidgeting in the chairs, the woman flipping through a three-year-old copy of *Good House-keeping*. Savannah took a deep breath and sat down beside Bethany Appleton, while her mother stood watch at the door.

"They called me in for a lineup," Savannah said. "Can you believe that?"

The woman stiffened. She was wearing a tight skirt and oversized black sweater. There was a single bead of sweat in the hollow beneath her ear. Her daughter was grabbing cigarette butts out of the ash-tray and popped one in her mouth.

"Good God." The woman expertly inserted a pinkie into her daughter's mouth and swiped out the stub. "Don't be gross."

She turned back to Savannah, but didn't smile.

"For that murder?" she said. "The one fifteen years ago?"

"Well, I don't know if it was a murder. They just want me to look at someone I saw a lifetime ago. Like I can remember. Like anyone can be sure."

The woman hesitated, then shook her head. "I'm Bethany Appleton. I thought I was the only witness."

"Well, I don't know about that, but I'm glad you're here too. I don't want it all on my conscience. I don't want a man's fate riding on my recollection, which believe me, can change according to mood and time of day and what I had for breakfast."

"I remember," Bethany said. "Some things are, like, etched in your brain."

The girl reached out to touch one of the feathers in Savannah's hat, but her mother grabbed her hand.

"Tara, for God's sake."

"That's all right." Savannah took off her hat. "She can have it."

Savannah smiled at the girl, while Bethany beat the arm of the chair with her purple fingernails. "This is fucked. I mean, sorry, no offense, but I thought I was, like, this star witness. The *Enquirer* even called me. Did they talk to you? Have you been getting crank phone calls?"

Savannah reached into her purse and took out her cards. She got down on the scuffed vinyl floor. When the girl came over to look, she turned the cards over briefly, but didn't let her touch them.

"Tarots," she said. "I'm a fortune-teller."

Bethany sat forward. "So did he talk to you? That guy at the *Enquirer*? Because I don't know what fortune-tellers make, but I'm a single mom on welfare. I've got to get a job by November, and you tell me who's gonna hire a thirty-one-year-old with no experience and a kid who gets sick every other day. If someone wants to pay me five grand for the rights to my story, well then, I'm gonna take it. I'm not gonna feel guilty about it. Especially when all I have to do is tell the truth."

Savannah turned the cards back over and didn't shuffle. She could hear movement in the room next door, possibly the sound of a row of black-haired men being aligned. She looked at her mother, then tucked the cards into her lap when she began to shake.

"They didn't offer me anything," Savannah said, and Bethany unclenched her fists. Her daughter was pulling the feathers out of the hat one by one. "I wouldn't have taken it anyway," she went on. "It's been so long. I mean, fifteen years. Even if something did happen all those years ago, would you want to be held responsible for what you did in your teens, when you were just a stupid kid? A man can change a lot."

"Not that much," Bethany said. "Believe me. I know men."

Savannah lifted the cards. "You want a reading? Want to know how this all comes out?"

Bethany touched the cards, then quickly drew back. "A friend of mine went to a psychic and the woman told her she'd be a young widow. Two weeks later, bam, her husband was dead from a drug overdose."

"That was no psychic. That was plain old awful coincidence."

Bethany shook her head. "No thanks."

"Suit yourself."

Savannah began laying out the cards. Bethany picked up her magazine, turned a few pages, then set it back down.

"What is all that?" she asked.

"It's a Celtic spread." Savannah had bought a dozen new bracelets, and they jingled all up one arm.

When she tried to still them, the rest of her body took up the trembling.

"Are you all right?" Bethany asked.

Savannah glanced up, but didn't meet her gaze. "Oh, sure. Just nervous about the lineup. See this?" She pointed to a card with a snarl of different-colored crystals. "That's the Six of Crystals. The card of confusion. Sometimes it's hard to tell what's what."

She laid out a few more, and right after the six came the Nine of Crystals. "Narrowness. That's weird. This is the Voyager. It's really a very positive deck. I'm surprised you could get this many bad cards in a row."

"I told you I didn't want a reading."

Savannah could hear Cal Bentley's voice in the other room, and then the scratching of chairs. "Considering you're about to go in there and maybe sentence a man to life in prison, I'd have to say this is a sign to watch yourself. It would be awfully easy to just pick somebody out and say, 'That's him.' To not even consider the consequences, especially if you're figuring on getting some kind of reward in the end."

"Look, lady—"

"Well, look at that," Savannah went on. "Your final result is the Hanged Man. That's the card of an upside-down world. Some fortune-tellers call it the dark night of the soul."

She started picking up the cards, but Bethany grabbed her arm. "Wait. What does that mean?"

Savannah looked at her now, even though Bethany would see the tears in her eyes. "It means you're running the risk of ruining not only someone else's life, but your own. It means the world's not perfect. Sometimes one quick horror is the kindest thing a man can do."

She gathered up the cards and put them back in her purse. She put her hand on Bethany's shoulder, then got to her feet. Bethany jerked, her mouth formed an O. Where she'd touched her, Savannah knew, the skin burned. Savannah walked past her mother, then kept right on going. She was shaking, but she wasn't about to break now, not when she'd finally mastered the art of the curse.

Savannah was still trembling when she walked out of the station. She lit a cigarette and walked around the block. By the time she got back around, her mother had come out. She and Cheryl Pillandro were standing on the front steps.

Maggie plucked the cigarette out of Savannah's fingers and ground it out. "You don't smoke."

"Please. Like that matters."

"It'll matter once Jake gets out."

Savannah lit another cigarette.

"I think I liked you better happy," Maggie said.

"No, you didn't."

Cheryl was pacing, her high heels clicking on the stone steps. She had done herself up that morning, set her short hair with curlers and put on bright red lipstick, but that lipstick was now dribbling along the creases of her mouth. She kept jerking whenever a police car pulled out of the lot.

"I can't believe you two," Maggie said finally. "I can't possibly be the only one here who believes everything will turn out fine."

"I've got to walk," Savannah said.

She'd gone around the block two and a half times when she saw Bethany Appleton and her daughter being escorted out the back door of the station. Bethany's face was set, unreadable. Then Savannah started to run.

Halfway around she was crying; she was so agoniz-

ingly slow. Love had filled her with the heaviest
things—longing and fear and the dense core of desire.
Even worse, it had upset her equilibrium, so she stumbled over seemingly nothing, over microscopic cracks
in the sidewalk and the words he most needed to hear.

It seemed half a lifetime before she turned the
corner and looked down the street. Then she saw him.
Jake stood alone on the top step, staring at the painfully blue sky. His hands were behind his back, and for
a moment she thought he was in handcuffs, then he
swung his left hand around, palm up.

She looked around for her mother and Cheryl Pillandro, then spotted them down the street. They were
opening the back door of Cheryl's car to let out the
dogs. Rufus and Gabe came barreling down the street,
barking joyously, but this once Savannah moved
faster. She was not going to let anyone beat her to
him. No matter what else happened, she would be the
first one to tell him he was free.


In late September, when the heat finally broke and
autumn rushed in on a cold, startling wind, Maggie
Dawson packed the last of her things. She had piled
boxes near the front door for the movers, then put an
even bigger stack near the back for Jake. He was going
to take her castoffs to the women's shelter, and she
had a stunning amount of gleaming castoffs. Mountains of steamers and sweaters and amazing apple cor-
ers, none of which she'd used even once. She had the
number of Williams-Sonoma in her phone book, and
her eye on a Chasseur Dutch oven, but for now she
was packing light.

All she needed was a winter parka, a couple of
sweat suits, and an evening dress. She and Cheryl
were setting sail tomorrow from Vancouver, on a Royal

Caribbean cruise to Alaska's Inland Passage. After that, she was headed up north to a rented house in northern Idaho. Coeur d'Alene was a place she hadn't even heard of until Cheryl mentioned she'd once vacationed there with her first husband, and that was exactly why Maggie had chosen it. Cheryl might cry when remembering how Paul Grey had admired Idaho's lush forests and alpine lakes, but the state was nothing to Maggie. Memory-free and therefore powerless. Just a place she might be able to stand looking at alone.

She walked downstairs and out into the yard. The For Sale sign had been sunk a foot deep in the rich soil, and in the back, Jake had just finished the bench.

He stepped aside to let her see his work. Maggie brushed her hand across the carving of the Star, then drew back, as if he'd left a sharp edge. She'd felt sparks fly through her fingers, though she wasn't going to admit this to anybody, and the fact that Doug's ghost came to her every night was going to be her secret for as long as she lived.

She looked around the garden, now rich in crimson and gold. The house would sell quickly, she was sure, to a couple who didn't mind putting a little work into the things they loved.

"He was a damn fool," Maggie said, but nevertheless when the movers arrived, she directed them to wrap the bench carefully in blankets, and place it in the van first.

Jake took her elbow and led her to the porch. He was still huge, but without the beard, she just couldn't picture him killing anybody. That was disappointing. She had rather liked the glamour of living with a psycho.

"You never told me what I owe you," he said.

"I don't know what you're talking about."

"Maggie, Cal told me he let you and Savannah in to talk to Bethany Appleton. He was fairly certain he saw money changing hands. Bribing a witness is a felony."

"Only if you get caught." She laughed out loud. She had felt positively marvelous ever since she'd given Bethany Appleton those crisp hundreds. She wasn't about to trust fate to one of Savannah's feeble curses. If she couldn't have her husband, then by God she would commit a few crimes. She would get a little crazy. She would live the rest of her life as if she were eighteen years old and slick as slime.

She looked past Jake to Savannah, who was in the back, deadheading Doug's prize roses. She had no idea what would become of her daughter and this man, and she liked it that way. It left her with something to think about. Savannah could not live far from Emma, and Jake could not breathe anything but mountain air. One of them would have to make a sacrifice, and she wondered if Jake knew it would be him. She wondered if he would fight the way she had, or simply give in and accept that love took as much as it gave. Aim for forever, and you're in for a wild, bumpy ride.

She squeezed Jake's arm, then went into the garden. She would never have another one. There was no way she was going to torture herself any longer with the smell of lilacs and honeysuckle. One garden a lifetime was enough.

She took her daughter by the arm and led her to the Juneberry trees near the curb. The leaves had turned yellow three weeks ago, and were now deepening to crimson. Doug would have been thrilled to see that, beside them, the stalks of his ensete were three feet high and still growing.

Maggie reached into her pockets, where she'd stuffed Doug's poems. She had thought about bringing them with her, but they were all committed to memory anyway, and a woman alone had to travel light. She handed half to Savannah, and kept the rest for herself.

"All those years," she said, "he was ashamed of his poetry. He was worried about syntax and sentimentality. He thought they gave away too much."

Savannah looked down at the poems in her hand. The swirling wind was scented with cider and wood smoke and other people's tender evenings, and Maggie would be relieved to be rid of it. She wanted to smell things she'd never come across before. A surprising mix of spice and someone else's desire, a stranger's cool, exotic dreams.

She waited until the wind aimed skyward, tugged at her fingers, then she lifted one arm in the air. "All right. On three."

Savannah blinked until the tears slid down, but she leaned into her mother and raised her arm.

"One," Maggie said.

It was better this way. The wind would yank the poems up over the Juneberry trees, then scatter them in the tidy backyards of her neighbors. Some might get trapped in juniper hedges or in the slats of committee-approved brown siding, but one might very well land on a tortured widow's front step and change everything.

"Two."

A few, it was certain, would get snagged on the rose-like Juneberry branches, stuck to the juicy purple fruit. Sometimes, no matter what your plans, you just got stuck. Sometimes getting stuck was a good thing.

The wind yanked at the edges of the poems, and one slipped out of Maggie's hand. She opened her palm, and Savannah did the same. Together, they said, "Three!" and let the love letters fly.

## ABOUT THE AUTHOR

CHRISTY YORKE was born and raised in the Los Angeles area, where she married and went to college, graduating magna cum laude with a degree in psychology. Craving quiet and a view of trees, she, her husband, and their two children moved to the moutains of southern Idaho.

# THE VERY BEST IN CONTEMPORARY
## ❧❧❧WOMEN'S FICTION

## SANDRA BROWN

___28951-9 Texas! Lucky $6.99/$9.99 in Canada    ___56768-3 Adam's Fall $6.99/$9.99

___28990-X Texas! Chase $6.99/$9.99    ___56045-X Temperatures Rising $6.99/$9.99

___29500-4 Texas! Sage $6.99/$9.99    ___56274-6 Fanta C $6.99/$9.99

___29085-1 22 Indigo Place $6.99/$9.99    ___56278-9 Long Time Coming $6.99/$9.99

___29783-X A Whole New Light $6.99/$9.99    ___57157-5 Heaven's Price $6.99/$9.99

___57158-3 Breakfast In Bed $6.99/$8 .99___29751-1 Hawk O'Toole's Hostage $6.50/$8.99

___57600-3 Tidings of Great Joy $6.99/$9.99    ___57601-1 Send No flowers $6.99/$9.99

## TAMI HOAG

___29534-9 Lucky's Lady $6.99/$9.99    ___29272-2 Still Waters $6.99/$9.99

___29053-3 Magic $6.99/$9.99    ___56160-X Cry Wolf $7.50/$9.99

___56050-6 Sarah's Sin $6.99/$9.99    ___56161-8 Dark Paradise $7.50/$9.99

___56451-x Night Sins $6.99/$9.99    ___56452-8 Guilty As Sin $7.50/$9.99

___57188-5 A Thin Dark Line $6.99/$9.99    ___10633-3 Ashes to Ashes $24.95/$35.95

## NORA ROBERTS

___29078-9 Genuine Lies $7.50/$9.99    ___27859-2 Sweet Revenge $7.50/$9.99

___28578-5 Public Secrets $7.50/$9.99    ___27283-7 Brazen Virtue $7.50/$9.99

___26461-3 Hot Ice $7.50/$9.99    ___29597-7 Carnal Innocence $7.50/$9.99

___26574-1 Sacred Sins $7.50/$9.99    ___29490-3 Divine Evil $7.50/$9.99

---

**Ask for these books at your local bookstore or use this page to order.**

Please send me the books I have checked above. I am enclosing $_____(add $2.50 to cover postage and handling). Send check or money order, no cash or C.O.D.'s, please.

Name _____

Address _____

City/State/Zip _____

Send order to: Bantam Books, Dept. FN 24, 2451 S. Wolf Rd., Des Plaines, IL 60018
Allow four to six weeks for delivery.
Prices and availability subject to change without notice.      FN 24 4/00